BODIES BUILT FOR GAME

BODIES BUILT FOR GAME

The *Prairie Schooner* Anthology
of Contemporary Sports Writing

EDITED BY NATALIE DIAZ

Hannah Ensor, Associate Editor

UNIVERSITY OF NEBRASKA PRESS / LINCOLN

Library of Congress Cataloging-in-Publication Data
Names: Diaz, Natalie, editor. | Ensor, Hannah, 1986– editor.
Title: Bodies built for game: the prairie schooner anthology of contemporary sports writing / edited by Natalie Diaz; Hannah Ensor, associate editor.
Description: Lincoln: University of Nebraska Press, [2019]
Identifiers: LCCN 2019013807
ISBN 9781496217738 (pbk.: alk. paper)
ISBN 9781496219107 (epub)
ISBN 9781496219114 (mobi)
ISBN 9781496219121 (pdf)
Subjects: LCSH: Sports—Social aspects. | Sports—Physiological aspects. | Nationalism and sports. | Sports stories. | Sports—Poetry.
Classification: LCC GV706.5 .B63 2019 | DDC 796.01/9—dc23 LC record available at https://lccn.loc.gov/2019013807

Set in Vesper by E. Cuddy.

Contents

Introduction: Bodies Built for Game   xv
Natalie Diaz

In Defense of Allen Iverson   1
Hanif Abdurraqib

Bolting into Throat   3
Patricia Smith

last summer of innocence   5
Danez Smith

American Pharoah   7
Ada Limón

Takes Enemy   9
Shann Ray

Professional Wrestling Holds   27
Ashaki Jackson

He takes me   29
Paul Tran

The Hit Man   32
Stacey Waite

Psych Ward Visitation Hour   34
b: william bearhart

The Wars   36
Louise Erdrich

After Simone Manuel's Olympic Victory
in the Women's 100m Freestyle   45
    Lauren Espinoza

In the outfield, daydreaming   47
    francine j. harris

The Meaning of Serena Williams:
On Tennis and Black Excellence   49
    Claudia Rankine

Serena Williams Walks   57
    Kwame Dawes

Boxing Out   59
    Adrian Matejka

Summertime   60
    Joel Salcido

Aaron Hernandez is my brother   62
    Randall J. Tyrone

The Church of Michael Jordan   63
    Jeffrey McDaniel

Built For It   65
    Lisa Olstein

Federer as Irreligious Experience   66
    Porochista Khakpour

prayer when knees give   77
    Nate Marshall

Days of '95 II   78
    Shane Lake

Baseball   80
Izzy Wasserstein

To Prevent Hypothermia   81
Fatimah Asghar

Give and Go   84
Toni Jensen

Perfect Form   95
Kamilah Aisha Moon

Black Boxers: A Brief History   96
Benjamin Krusling

The Cock Fight Place   100
Alberto Ríos

A Note on Process   102
Meghan O'Rourke

How Are You Feeling   120
Ana Božičević

The Wrestler   122
Kazim Ali

War Training: An Athletics   123
Nomi Stone

A Boy & His Mother Play Dead at Dawn   124
Michael Wasson

As If We Were Called   126
Reginald Dwayne Betts

Run   131
Gary Jackson

From Heaven, My Father Sends His Regrets   132
Cornelius Eady

Russian Sport   133
Vera Pavlova
Translated by Ilya Kaminsky and Valzhyna Mort

Feel for the Water   134
Christian Campbell

I reckon, a latitude   141
Asiya Wadud

A Perfect Game   143
Yesenia Montilla

Dennis   146
Kaveh Akbar

At Eighty-Two My Father Is
Learning to Walk Again   148
Esther Lin

Clank   150
Tomás Q. Morin

Liquid   155
Aaron Smith

Losing the 440-Yard Dash   157
Afaa M. Weaver

Sports Analogy   159
David Tomas Martinez

Why to Run Racks   161
Lisa Fay Coutley

El Barril   167
  James Thomas Stevens

Who Got This Far   168
  Marissa Johnson-Valenzuela

Project Artifacts: Through the
Banks of the Red Cedar   169
  Maya Washington

La Llorona Runs Alone   175
  Claudia D. Hernández

Alone in the Schoolyard at Dusk   177
  Dorianne Laux

why i can't play basketball anymore   179
  Richard Vargas

The Condition of Being a Sports Fan   181
  Sue Hyon Bae

Take Me Out   186
  Iliana Rocha

Parking Lot Poem with Fernando Valenzuela   187
  Matthew Lippman

Strike Indicator   189
  Pamela Hart

Minor League Legend   191
  Matthew Olzmann

Losing to the Invisible: An Ars Poetica   192
  Traci Brimhall

High School Yoga   196
  Kat Page

Southpaw Skin the Gloves   198
   Alicia Mountain

Playbook   199
   Hannah Oberman-Breindel

Games   201
   L. Lamar Wilson

Mudita World Peace   202
   Hannah Ensor

At the gym, moments after I failed a
 squat attempt that would have been easy
pre-sitting-induced pinched nerve   217
   Candace Williams

Inside the City Walls   219
   Norman Dubie

Diana Nyad as J. M. W. Turner   220
   BK Fischer

game recognizes game   222
   t'ai freedom ford

Off Sides   223
   Susan Briante

The Chain   232
   Elyse Fenton

Young Woman Wrestler   234
   Tria Blu Wakpa

Self-Portrait with Ghost, Rising   236
   Dean Rader

Infield Contrapuntal 237
Meg Day

Shots Missed 239
Celeste Adame

Sports History 240
Brett Fletcher Lauer

The Yo-Yo Heir's Lament 243
Eugene Gloria

Stadium Mocs 245
Chip Livingston

Bad Love Affair 246
Joseph Millar

Ode to the Dream Shake 247
Ben Purkert

Catch 249
Trevino Brings Plenty

The Sum of Our Doing 251
Holly M. Wendt

Who Holds the Stag's Head Gets to Speak 265
Gabrielle Calvocoressi

Polaroid: Links 266
Stacey Lynn Brown

Of Competition or "And the sheeted dead
did squeak and gibber in the Roman streets" 268
Brendan Constantine

Darkening the Belt 272
Anders Carlson-Wee

From *Farewell to Soccer: Ninety-Minute-Long Stories*   274
    Valerio Magrelli
    Translated from the Italian by Will Schutt

¡Sangre! ¡Sangre! ¡Sangre!   287
    Nandi Comer

This Is Not an Essay about Wrestling, or If David Markson Loved the WWF Like I Did When I Was 12   290
    John Findura

The Curtain   295
    Ryan Black

Ladies' Arm Wrestling Match at the Blue Moon Diner   299
    Jenny Johnson

Scorekeep   300
    Tommy Orange

Ghazal at the End of Hogpen Road   308
    J. Scott Brownlee

Can We Have Our Ball Back?   309
    Matthew Dickman

untitled   310
    Kevin Goodan

Productive Antagonisms   311
    Saretta Morgan interviews Christina Olivares

The Rookie   318
    January Gill O'Neil

Cross Country   320
   Roger Reeves

Another Kind of Faith   322
   Joaquín Zihuatanejo

Why Pam Hates Sprite and Sunflower Seeds   324
   Alison Rollins

The Tribes   326
   Chee Brossy

All the Flesh, Singing   329
   Shivanee Ramlochan

Between Practice   331
   Terrance Hayes

Source Acknowledgments   335
List of Contributors   339

Introduction

Bodies Built for Game

Natalie Diaz

Before each of my basketball games, from rec league to high school, my mother told me, "Knock 'em dead," as I walked out the door. Even after I moved across the country to Virginia to play Division I basketball, she ended our pregame phone calls with the same phrase, "Knock 'em dead." She never said, "Good luck."

*

I didn't learn how to read poetry, how to let poetry into my body in a physical and emotional way, until my basketball career was over. It makes sense if I consider how much basketball needed and took of my body—it is a sensual and intuitive game, a relationship of movement and space, momentum, timing, a defiance of the body's socialized limitations, a corporeal inquiry that shapes the imagination. The game itself exists within and also creates the conditions of futurity. Yes, basketball is a game of the future! On defense you must think two steps ahead of the ball or your opponent, toward what has not yet happened but could. On offense you must envision every opportunity that might occur and then risk entering into that unknown, taking what the game offers you, or demanding it give you something else, conjuring a pass or a move that didn't exist until you arrived there in its perfect moment, prepared and lucky.

Basketball also gave me my future, leaped me from the desert rez I was born on and into my life. At this point in my life, I have played basketball longer than I have not—I played basketball longer than I have done anything else. In the game was where I was always the most possible. In the game was where I had the most future. It was where I learned to imagine what I might be capable of.

*

The intense physicality of both basketball and poetry has at times made me ecstatic. A good shot is called "touch." On a rebound, you locate your player and "put a body on her." A poem too can make you realize your body in a way that doesn't require you to break it or to perform the stories and fears America has always projected onto women and men of color—though every page is white, the language of poetry itself is made of dark figures, inked bodies of sound, building, aching, reaching out, all up and down the page.

*

Though I was early to basketball and late to writing, the two have a long relationship, an entanglement that is my lucky inheritance—

Poet and rapper Tupac Shakur starred in the movies *Above the Rim* and *Poetic Justice*.

In his own gesture of justice—justice for his body and that of other straight, white men—poet Charles Bukowski wrote a letter to the editor of the *New York Quarterly*, complaining, "In our age, the only safe target for the writer is the white heterosexual male." He continued, "Nobody protests. Not even the white heterosexual male. He's used to it. Also, things like 'White men can't dance,' 'White men can't jump,' 'White men have no sense of rhythm,' etc." He wrote that letter in 1992, the same year the movie *White Men Can't Jump* premiered. Prior to the movie and Bukowski's self-proclaimed victimhood, we always knew the statement was true—white men have never needed to dance, or jump, or have rhythm to be afforded the privileges they offer to and accept from other white men.

In the basketball flick *Finding Forrester*, Sean Connery plays Forrester, a writer who mentors or saviors a young black basketball star become writer.

Kareem Abdul-Jabbar spent a season as the assistant varsity basketball coach of the Alchesay Falcons. Alchesay High School is located in Whiteriver, Arizona, on White Mountain Apache or N'dee land, "N'dee" meaning "the people." What originally brought Abdul-Jabbar to N'dee territory was research for a book about a black cavalry regiment nicknamed Buffalo Soldiers who had been stationed at Fort Apache. He later wrote a book about his experience, *A Season on the Reservation: My Soujourn with the White Mountain Apache*.

Poet Jim Carroll was a high school basketball star at Trinity in Manhattan. His experiences there, including his addiction to heroin, led to his writing *The Basketball Diaries*, a book later adapted to film.

Poet Marianne Moore taught the phenomenal multisport Native and Olympic athlete Jim Thorpe at the Carlisle Indian School, officially the United States Indian Industrial School. Thorpe played basketball, as well as football, baseball, and track and field. Moore preferred baseball and was known as an avid fan.

John Edgar Wideman, author of the memoir *Hoop Roots*, was All–Ivy League forward at the University of Pennsylvania. I played against his daughter, Jamila Wideman, in the 1997 Women's NCAA Final Four. She was Stanford's point guard, and I was a 1-2 guard for Old Dominion—we beat them in the semifinals. Though I didn't meet John Edgar Wideman in person until twenty years after that game when we judged a writing prize together, he had been in the stands watching his daughter all those years ago, which meant, in a way, he and I had met before. Before either of those meetings, I met Wideman in a different way and with much more at stake—I met him in the many pages he wrote about brothers, about his brother, and in my mind about my own brother. The way he held his brother on the page, a brother some might call "bad," gave me a place to love and hold my own bad brother. It was a tough lesson—I can sometimes love my brother best on the page, in a poem, better than I can manage to love him in real life.

Spike Lee knows basketball is holy—he created Jesus Shuttlesworth in the movie *He Got Game*, played by real-life baller Ray Allen. It was Jesus Shuttlesworth who said, "Basketball is like poetry in motion, cross the guy to the left, take him back to the right, he's fallin' back, then just 'J' right in his face. Then you look at him and say, 'What?'"

*

My mother had eleven kids. If we'd all survived, we'd have been a soccer team. We are nine now, enough for a baseball team. But in the Southwest fervor of pavement and blacktop, where temperatures can exceed 120 degrees, basketball is currency, is credibility, especially on the rez.

*

Writer and philosopher Albert Camus, no stranger to sports, was on a soccer team—goal keeper for the Racing Universitaire Algerios juniors. He said, "After many years during which I saw many things, what I know most surely about morality and the duty of man I owe to sport and learned it in the RUA."

I lived years on a court, in the driveway, at a park, in a gym, on a bus or plane to or from a game, drilling, sprinting, stretching, watching film, attached to an electrical stim machine, in an ice bath, in a season—preseason, in-season, postseason, off-season, next season. My brain, my muscles, my emotions have been shaped by my life as an athlete, in the way each triggers or smooths, attacks or defends. It's hard to comprehend "sport" as "game" when you've been built by its rules, triumphs, failures, and wagers, as I've been built. I am the game's machine. I am its apparatus as much as it is mine.

*

I frequently dream basketball. In a recurring dream my college coach, Wendy Larry, calls me back to play for her. She and I didn't always get along. She thought I was wild, and I was. I didn't understand her motives or mind games yet respected her authority—feared it sometimes and resisted it other times. I loved basketball too much in those years, and I played through many injuries for her, injuries that might have caused another player to sit out. Part of the wildness in me was an eagerness for a fight, for a challenge, for a reason to put my body up against another body and see what might be at stake, what I might win or lose.

I gave my coach my body to break down and build back up, to push toward ecstasy—in the form of a spin move with a release so high not many could stop it, or the sound of the band's trombones and drums, the applause of a crowd of strangers, with my teammates in a congratulatory huddle, a win—even the ecstasy of failure and losing, which made me feel more alive and whole, a dissatisfaction and ache as close to desire as anything else I've touched.

*

During my NCAA career inner-city student-athletes were discouraged from going home over holiday and semester breaks—to keep us out of trouble. My teammates' inner city and my rez meant "trouble" to our coaches. These undesirable places were our homes and apparently also meant desirable basketball, since we were all on full-ride scholarships. So when my grandfather died, I couldn't go home to my desert for his funeral.

For the record, trouble did happen. Neighbors called the cops to my sister's house the night before the funeral. One of my brothers went to jail; the others attended Mass the next day with gouged or blackened eyes and busted lips. My family mourned together while I ran the point for a new offense in our practice gym three thousand miles away. I was angry—a convenient mask for my grief back then. I let the new play break down again and again, on purpose, until I had to run suicides as punishment.

A few weeks after the funeral I wasn't allowed to attend, I caught an elbow in practice that severed the infraorbital artery beneath my orbital bone and eye. I grabbed my face and fell to my knees. My teammates crowded around. As I lifted my head, one teammate screamed—it was an ugly, painful injury. I had a concussion, and my bloodied black eye lasted the entire season. I didn't cry when it happened, but my tear duct was injured upon impact and wept on its own. That year, basketball was the way I mourned.

I have learned, now that I no longer play competitively, basketball was always my way through grief. A suffering as much as a pleasure. A fine balance of control and the wilderness of my feelings.

*

Athletes learn to read the body, another's body, like a text—and there is a way of learning one's own body as intimately as if you had written it, into your own flesh. It is an art to tell the body's story not with words but with itself, as if movement and touch were the only language. And it is a power to imagine having a story to tell about what is possible with what gift you've been given and then think, "Watch me tell it."

In a 1998 interview in the *Atlantic*, John Edgar Wideman was asked what the bodies in his work revealed. He replied, "All my life I've been very aware of my body. I have always used it as a gauge of things. When I look at a person and I see their body, that's the beginning of knowledge about them. Furthermore, I respect the body."

*

In the 1997 Women's NCAA Championship at the Riverfront Coliseum in Cincinnati, my team, the Old Dominion Lady Monarchs, faced the Tennessee Lady Vols. We had beat Wideman's Stanford in the semifinals two days before, and I'd had a strong game. The championship was a different story. We blew a lead that turned into a 12–2 Lady Vol run, and Tennessee beat us with a final score of 68–59.

Days after the game, newspaper reports came out about Tennessee coach Pat Summitt's husband, R. B. Summitt, having yelled racist remarks to one of our international players. We had heard him during the game—he was sitting behind our bench. Once it was public, the Summitts apologized to our coach, who relayed the information to our team, and it wasn't mentioned again. But it was something that stuck in me, that two white female coaches smoothed over this white male's transgression toward my black African female teammate, my center, my target in the post, my high-post pick-and-roll, my sister.

I tried to research this incident in print many years later, and I finally found one or two articles quoting R. B. yelling, "Go back to Mozambique!" though I remember him screaming, "Go back to Africa!" as do some of my teammates, and screaming it more than once. What was the intent of this edit? Was saying "Mozambique" less violent? As if it simply referred to geography, a city like any other city? A place one might travel from and then return to, as in

"Go back home"? In my memory, he yelled, "Go back to Africa!" and he, Coach Summitt, and my coach explained it by saying he got "caught up" in the heat of the game.

In a 1998 *Sports Illustrated* article about Pat Summitt a year after the above incident, focus momentarily shifted to R. B. and his behavior. The reporter wrote: "Sure, sometimes he goes off the deep end in the heat of action and yells things at opposing teams that she wouldn't, but Pat can live with that. She knows what it is to enter another realm during a game"—"another realm" referring to the place R. B. Summitt went, a place where it is okay to scream at a black woman competing in a sport to go back to Africa or, according to someone else's memory, to go back to Mozambique. And not only Coach Summitt lived with it; we all did.

*

Athletic fandom is one of the most beautiful and horrific human conditions. It can join a group of strangers in a bond of loyalty or love akin to family, all for a team, all for a game. Fandom is also one aspect of sports I trust least. It doesn't take long for fans to revert to Colosseum-like behavior. The only thing worse than a man overcome with anger or inadequacy that he masks and channels toward another body, or a man given an arena-sized mirror in which he seems himself victorious over or superior to another body, is a group of men under those same circumstances.

In 2015 at a hockey game in Rapid City, South Dakota, it was reported that a group of fifteen white men in a VIP area poured beer on the heads of several Lakota children and their chaperones from American Horse Middle School, while yelling, "Go back to the rez!" Only one man was charged. The magistrate judge who acquitted him said this in the verdict: "The Court concludes that Defendant's actions of spraying beer were the result of an excited reaction to a very important score in the Rapid City Rush hockey game."

In 2010 a group of mostly white, mostly un-athletic-looking, male Cleveland Cavaliers fans burned LeBron James's jerseys and T-shirts when he left the team to join the Miami Heat (and win a few championships). "Witness is real!" a man hollered as one after the other white man fed his LeBron shirts and jerseys to the flames. The historical and racial implications of this action didn't seem to cross their white minds—if it did, it didn't matter, because American hunger and hatred, and white men's assumptions of power and property, have never abided by logic and rarely demand introspection. The game, especially one they are not playing in, becomes a place where they can act like gladiators, or, worse, emperors.

In George Orwell's "The Sporting Spirit," published in 1945, while Britain was at war with Hitler and the Axis powers, he asserted, "Serious sport has nothing to do with fair play. It is bound up with hatred, jealousy, boastfulness, disregard of all rules and sadistic pleasure in witnessing violence: in other words, it is war minus the shooting." Sports were a great mobilizer for Hitler, and the young athletes who competed for Germany in the 1936 Berlin Olympics, behind the symbol of the eagle and the swastika, would be called to join the Hitler Youth less than a year after their participation in the Games.

In America, where Native Americans are killed by police at a higher rate per capita than any other race, yet volunteer for the military at a higher rate per capita than any other race, and black and Latino men and women are being killed by law enforcement with seeming impunity, we begin to understand the games we play are part of a larger social structure. A war that began hundreds of years ago.

When I followed both stories—the white men dumping beer on the Native kids' heads at the hockey game and the mostly white men burning LeBron's jerseys—I recalled a passage from Orwell's *Animal Farm*: "The creatures outside looked from pig to man, and from man to pig, and from pig to man again; but already it was impossible to say which was which." Athletics can bring out those animals, though I doubt athletics created them. Instead, I have come to believe that athletics are also structures of racialized and gendered diminishment, and it has caused me great stress to consider this at the same time I consider how athletics made me who I am today, who I am still becoming.

*

In 2015 Thabo Sefolosha played for the Atlanta Hawks and was known to guard LeBron James during matchups with the Cleveland Cavs. There is a video on YouTube of LeBron crossing up Sefolosha in a game from 2014: LeBron dribbles once to the right, then crosses and loses him left. The cross-up was so brutal, Sefolosha tripped and fell. The highlight reels announced LeBron "broke Sefolosha's ankles" with that "nasty" cross.

So before going on to meet the Golden State Warriors in the 2015 Finals, when the Cavs met the Hawks in the Eastern Conference Championship, Sefolosha should have been defending LeBron. Instead, he was on the bench, out with a season-ending injury sustained a month before. On the morning of April 8, 2015, Thabo Sefolosha had his right fibula, or his ankle, broken when a white police officer came up behind him after an altercation at a nightclub and swept his leg out from under him. He required surgery and missed the rest of the postseason and playoffs.

LeBron never got another chance to break Sefolosha's ankles that year—the NYPD did. The Cavs swept the series, or the NYPD swept Sefolosha.

*

In *The Stranger* Camus wrote, "It was as if that great rush of anger had washed me clean, emptied me of hope, and, gazing up at the dark sky spangled with its signs and stars, for the first time, the first, I laid my heart open to the benign indifference of the universe. . . . To feel it so like myself, indeed, so brotherly, made me realize that I'd been happy, and that I was happy still. For all to be accomplished, for me to feel less lonely, all that remained to hope was that on the day of my execution there should be a huge crowd of spectators and that they should greet me with howls of execration."

Isn't Camus describing the game in its purest form? Isn't this what fills your chest when you're at a park after dark shooting elbow jumper after elbow jumper with only the stars and planets keeping score, and more and more stars appear because you can't miss—yes, you are making the stars light up—and nothing exists outside the concrete court, not your shut-off electricity, or the rifle reports in the middle of the night, no brother who thinks spiders are crawling on him, no coyotes crying at the edge of the rez, not your friend's dad stumbling the alleyway with a needle dangling from his arm, or the fact that your cousin will overdose soon—it's just you, you triumphant, and teammates hoisting you on their shoulders, carrying you out to the parking lot, down the high school hill, over the railroad tracks, along the Colorado River, past the stand of mesquite trees and their glowing yellow beans, off into the bright dunefields of your desert, while the fans of the opposing team jeer and curse your jump shot?

Or maybe Camus meant something darker, like in 2017, when Boston fans threw peanuts at Baltimore Orioles center fielder Adam Jones and called him "nigger" multiple times during a game at Fenway Park. Or the way Jeremy Lin was treated, whether he played well or poorly, because fans couldn't get over their projections onto his body and race, or because they thought his body and race didn't belong in the NBA. Or darker still, like the beating two Los Angeles Dodgers fans gave to a San Francisco Giants fan after a game at Dodger Stadium in 2011. Their victim was left brain damaged and now requires twenty-four-hour care. One of the perpetrators was overheard saying, "Fuck the Giants. That's what you get," as he kicked the victim in the head.

*

I met Grace Thorpe at a nuclear protest in my desert town, Needles, California, located in the southwestern sliver of the Inland Empire— reservations are attractive places for white people to dump and hide poisonous things. In the minds of most Americans, Native lands have as little value as the Native body. Grace Thorpe was an activist, and she was at my home rez, Fort Mojave, as part of a coalition to help us fight a nuclear waste dump in our desert. My Elders told Grace I was soon off to college on a basketball scholarship, and she began telling me stories about her father, Jim Thorpe. I had never heard of him. He was a Sac and Fox and attended Carlisle Indian Industrial School like some of my relatives had. He played professional baseball for the New York Giants and the Boston Braves. He helped cofound and played in the NFL. He was the greatest ~~Native~~ American athlete.

Carlisle was run by Captain Richard H. Pratt, later a brigadier general. In describing General Pratt and his wife, poet Marianne Moore—a canonical American poet I have been expected to study and acknowledge as a master—said this about them: "They were romantic figures, always dashing up with their horse and carriage, and they were intelligent and cultural. But General Pratt was so monumental no one could dare approach him to tell him one approved of the work he was doing."

An oft-quoted excerpt from a speech Pratt gave at George Mason University in 1892 tells about the work he was doing: "A great general has said that the only good Indian is a dead one, and that high sanction of his destruction has been an enormous factor in promoting Indian massacres. In a sense, I agree with the sentiment, but only in this: that all the Indian there is in the race should be dead. Kill the Indian in him, and save the man."

*

In the 2016 season the NCAA reported 0.3 percent of its male athletes and 0.5 percent of its female athletes were "American Indian/ Alaskan Native." I didn't know any Native collegiate athletes when I began to dream of a place other than my reservation, didn't even know any Natives in college. When I was a kid I saw Dawn Staley and the Burge twins play for the University of Virginia once, in an NCAA Tournament game on television, and suddenly, I knew I could make it there, even though I wasn't yet sure where that place was.

*

Robert Griffin III, or RGIII, played for the Washington Redskins. He had an awesome first year and then was hampered by numerous knee injuries, including a torn anterior cruciate ligament or ACL. It was a disastrous equation from the start—a black body wearing a representation of a fragmented Native body in the form of a Redskins helmet. It's a historical problem, or a long-division problem. Both bodies divided/broken by X, where X = wealthy white men = American sport.

*

The brown body, nonwhite body, poor body, female body, queer body, disabled body has always been measured by what it can bear, what it can endure of pain and ecstasy. But whose pain? Whose ecstasy?

The spectacular brown body. How it swings from a rope. How it breaks when swung at. How long it can hold its breath or a bullet. How it handles a virus, a blanket, sterilization. The fearful and fascinating brown body. How close it can be to animal in its spectacle and glory, in its grief and mourning.

Sports are the intersection and the collision. The performance of the brown body on a court, a field, around a track, for the entertainment, financial gain, projection, and validation of the white body. Sports are often the appetite of the rich white men who own them, who sit in the box in suits and ties while the brown and black bodies fly and break and sweat and glow. Yet how many young brown and black girls and boys are out in the streets, beneath the streetlamps, enacting what they view as heroic, supernatural, destiny, and possibility—sticking their tongues out like Jordan while they jump from the free throw line, tossing imaginary chalk up into the air like LeBron, or pulling up for a Steph Curry three from too far out? I was once one of them.

*

Sports also feed and pique the appetite of the average person, the not agile, the not able, the not *gifted*. In the Colosseum of Rome, people crammed in to see the *bestiarii*—mostly slaves or criminals— fight to the death against bears, elephants, jaguars, cheetahs, and boars. Audiences craved this, and emperors gave them more and more spectacle. It is believed certain species were wiped out because of mass slaughter performed in the Colosseum, not to mention the slaughter of the *bestiarii* themselves—even if a *bestiarius* managed to win against one animal, another animal was sent out to fight, on and on, until the *bestiarius* was finally felled.

*

In a game where RGIII suffered a concussion, the Redskins reported instead that he was "shaken up." Redskins head coach Mike Shanahan stated he didn't know about the concussion diagnosis until after the game, which is why RGIII returned to the field, whereas the Redskins' head trainer said the concussion was confirmed "two to three minutes" after it occurred. In fact, the Redskins were fined $20,000 for violating the safety protocol. After a week off, RGIII returned to play. Many thought it was too soon.

Shanahan formerly coached the Denver Broncos. At Denver he once sent running back Terrell Davis back onto the field after Davis had been kneed in the helmet, suffered a migraine, and lost his vision. Shanahan sent him back onto the field even after Davis told him, "I can't see."

Mike Shanahan knows what all white coaches know—there is value in a brown or black body, the way it takes and takes and takes what it is given.

RGIII broke. And they loved it. They loved calling him weak.

*

I've existed in a separate space of gender—not masculine or feminine, not even queer. I was all athlete—a 1-2 guard, a wing, a scorer, a defender, back of the 1-3-1, ball handler on the break, cutter in the triangle, expected to be strong, to take up space, to lean forward, *una guerrera*. Today I get called "Sir" all the time, especially in airports. At a gas station in Searchlight, Nevada, on the way from my rez to Las Vegas McCarran Airport en route to a poetry reading, a man grabbed my arm as I walked into the women's bathroom and said, "Dude, you almost went into the ladies' toilet. Ours is over there."

My mother was waiting outside in the car, and when I told her, she replied, "It's just the way you hold yourself."

"And how exactly do I hold myself?" I asked, a little defensively.

"Like you belong there," she answered. "Like you know how to take care of yourself in a way that will let you stay there."

"Yeah," I replied, "but you don't have to be a man to do that."

*

Taking and holding space has always been natural to me—boxing out, setting screens, showing big on the baseline, knocking down cutters, flashing the lane, finishing a layup through a foul, even the way I walk into a gym or a room. I suppose I learned spacing the way most Native, brown, and black people do, the way most queer people do, by being defensive. In college I was known for my defense, regularly guarding the other teams' best guards. And I first learned defense on the rez.

When we played Smear-the-Queer, our cousins and friends intentionally threw the football to my little brother John or me. We were mixed, and lighter complexioned than they were, and this was our penance. This was also one of the ways we learned to be fast.

When John's legs slowed, when I heard him sucking air, when the pack began to catch him, I raced to the front and let him pitch me the ball; the pack chased me instead. They didn't catch me often— their pudgy boy bodies hadn't hardened yet, and I was more agile, even stronger, at that age. Times I wasn't fast enough or tired before they did, their knees, elbows, feet, and fists crashed down on me, and I found myself at the bottom of the heap of our bodies. They pressed my face into the yellowed grass and dirt, the way I would learn to press their faces into the grass and dirt when they had the ball, hollering out, "Smear-the-Fucking-Queer!" This was also one of the ways I learned not to cry.

Here is the second half of the earlier-referenced quote from John Edgar Wideman's 1998 *Atlantic* interview: "It's one thing to be smart and quick-witted, but can you back it up? In the world that I grew up in, if you said something, if you acted in a certain way, you had to back it up—and that meant being physical. It didn't mean you had to win all your fights, but it meant you had to be willing, with your body, to back up what you were saying. I trust the body. I trust pleasure, I trust pain." What Wideman is expressing is a constellation of my relationship to my body and sports—how one often leads to the other, how in some ways my body has depended on sports to become itself, to know what it fears and desires.

*

In the summer of 2016 the National Book Foundation held a fundraiser called "The Other NBA: The Most Storied Basketball Game in Literary History." The matchup was billed as "award-winning writers against publishing powerhouses." I agreed to play, even though I hadn't run a full-court in years. I ran half-court pickup games with some scrubs at the Princeton YMCA a few weeks before the game, in half-assed preparation.

I had planned on taking it easy, jogging a little, maybe being a passer—however, at a certain point I found myself hurtling toward a loose ball I'd deflected. A white woman from the other team moved toward the ball too. Something in me snapped, not in a disruptive way, more of a falling-into-place way, like a memory rushing through me. A memory of myself. It happened quickly: I was back. I was the body I'd been built to be. Next thing I knew I stood over where she lay on the ground, where I had knocked her, the ball in my hands, looking down court, where I hit my wing on the fly with a bullet of an outlet pass.

I saw it in the others that afternoon, too, those who had the game in their blood. We all unraveled and became those locked-away parts of ourselves. Mitchell Jackson, author of *The Residue Years* and *Survival Math*, missed a handful of three-pointers until he found himself, deep behind the arc, where he lifted again and again, unleashing and draining triple after triple. The air was something else for him—gravity couldn't hold him because he was gravity. Dwayne Betts, poet, lawyer, activist, was half locomotive and half butter as he throttled and slicked through the lane for easy buckets. We were all out on the hardwood, returned to the cities of our bodies, doing what we were built to do on the busted courts of our childhoods, among our friends and enemies. And, of course, we won. This was our inheritance—these bodies, these games.

*

What often draws me to people is often the way they move, especially if they move with the game in them—a series of long lines, neck to shoulder, torso, arms and legs, a certain lean, a glide, a grace. It is a movement I recognize and gravitate toward when I encounter other athletes in a crowd, in a room, at an awkward post–poetry party or writerly gathering—a smooth swagger and muscularity that immediately put me at ease.

*

Borrowing James Baldwin's term, my body was my "gimmick"—it is what got me off my rez. My brother's body was also *his* gimmick: it is what he burned down trying to escape. I sometimes wonder why it was me and not my brother who got "the gift." How easily it could have been me with pipe-burn blisters on my fingers and my big brother snapping his wrist to rattle a jumper through the rim to a crowd's applause. The most shameful thing to ever cross my mind in these contemplations is that I don't know if I would change this if I could—if I would trade his life for mine, my winnings for his losings.

As it was in Baldwin's days, in many nonwhite and poor environments today there are two dreamlike and spectacular paths toward mobility: entertainment and sports. Only very few of those who buy into this dream will ever reach elite levels in either entertainment or sport, though the glimmer and opportunity of it seem to be enough. If you can see your life reflected in someone who has "made it," the notion of a way out, even if it is one that never arrives, is enough to keep your body moving toward a future. To move toward a future is to move away from a lot of choices that might end you early.

My strong body, my obedient body, my body that found its gimmick early—run and run and jump and jump. Maybe my gimmick on the page is the same—isn't the brown body the body I come back to and offer you, my own body, my brother's body, my lovers' bodies? Or maybe I'm trying to trade in this gimmick for love. Maybe I can, maybe I can't.

*

I've pushed my body beyond what I thought were its limits, and I've had my body pushed beyond where most bodies can go. Isn't one game or another—from memory or from some future—always calling? In my dreams when Coach Larry asks me to take the floor for her, I always say yes. The body's demise happens in many ways. The dreams usually end the way my real-life basketball career ended—tearing my left anterior cruciate ligament, medial collateral ligament, and my meniscus.

*

I have a crafted and earned intimacy with my body. I know and trust it differently than a nonathlete can. It's the way I make sense of the world, a lover, a book, the earth—put my hands on/in them, see how I can open them or be opened. I touch them, looking for whatever energy I might become in that touching. There is nothing I am more confident or vulnerable in than my own body. You know the body differently when you break it, whether the breaking is your own or someone else's.

*

Even though most sports commentaries are politically numb and historically ignorant, it is true, in a sense, when announcers say, "The Natives are restless." They say this more frequently when talking about the Kansas City Chiefs, the Cleveland Indians, and the Washington Redskins. It is no secret—the Natives haven't been able to rest for hundreds of years.

After reinjuring his knee in a game between the Redskins and the Ravens, RGIII went back onto the field without the team doctor checking him. Shanahan okayed his reentry to the game. Only a real body needs a doctor, and RGIII's was not a real body. He was a dark machine. A body of dusk and sinew must go and go until it cannot.

*

The patellar tendon functioning as my current ACL is called an "autograft" because it came from my own body. *Harvest* is the word the doctors use—my patellar tendon was *harvested* from my body. Harvesting is associated with Natives, maybe because of corn and cornucopias, or Thanksgiving and Indian summers. My tribe's casino has a Native Harvest Buffet. Most of my brothers worked there during high school.

*

Some missing or deceased persons' bodies or body parts are in such bad shape, they can only be identified by the serial numbers of the surgical hardware implanted in their bodies from reconstructions and replacements.

*

Coach Larry taught us, "Defense is the best offense." If memory is passed down in DNA, I learned defense centuries ago, from my ancestors, from all they defended themselves and our people and land against.

From a CNN article with the headline "Who's More Likely to Be Killed by Police": "In fact, despite the available statistical evidence, most people don't know that Native Americans are most likely to be killed by police compared to other racial groups. Native Americans make up about 0.8% of the population, yet account for 1.9% of police killings."

Natives between the ages of eighteen and twenty-four have a higher rate of suicide than any other ethnicity, and Native women have the highest suicide rate of other female ethnicities in the United States. Is suicide considered defensive or offensive?

What will my DNA give to my children? Poetry? My long arms and relentless defense? My sadness? My anxieties? Will their bodies know to sweat when they are pulled over, to be still, to relax and not resist as they are bent into an impossible position?

*

In *Hoosiers* Coach Norman Dale, played by Gene Hackman, tells his team, "I've seen you guys can shoot, but there's more to the game than shooting. There's fundamentals and defense." I agree—defense is the best offense, unless offense is the best offense. I am tired of defending. This page is a kind of offense.

*

Jaylen Brown, the Boston Celtics' number-three pick in the 2016 NBA Draft, was called "too smart for his own good" by a conveniently (and typically) anonymous NBA executive. Brown is an intelligent man, plays chess, plays piano, learns languages, all the things that make him dangerous to a system that requires a brown body to perform its physicality but not its mentality or emotionality.

In a 2018 interview with the *Guardian*, Brown said he knew the NFL wouldn't let Colin Kaepernick back in after his peaceful protests before NFL games, explaining, "That's the reality because sports is a mechanism of control. If people didn't have sports, they would be a lot more disappointed with their role in society. There would be a lot more anger or stress about the injustice of poverty and hunger. Sports is a way to channel our energy into something positive. Without sports who knows what half of these kids would be doing?"

It was sports, however, that gave Colin Kaepernick the platform that has slowly begun to chip away at the well-known facade of the NFL and other professional sports leagues. He chose the lives of black men and women and children in America over his space on an NFL roster. He took a knee, to protest a country—a country that takes more than a knee, a country that takes entire lives, here and in other countries across the world, in order to maintain its system of white power and control.

Before Kaepernick, Mahmoud Abdul-Rauf of the Denver Nuggets made the same wager. Remember him? It was 1996, the year I graduated River Valley High School in Mohave Valley, Arizona. He had converted to Islam a few years before and decided to stretch or stay in the locker room for the national anthem because, as he once said, the flag was "a symbol of oppression, of tyranny."

This was the same year sportscaster Billy Packer referred to Georgetown Bulldog Allen Iverson as "one tough little monkey." In defense of Packer's comment, people mentioned how Packer had supported the Black Coaches Association. Mike Patrick of ESPN added, "We need to get past the words and look at the intent, and I know Billy Packer has no racist intent."

Today, just like in 1996, nobody is "racist." Not in academia, not on a police force, not in the White House, and certainly not in sports. There is no real "racism" anymore; there is only the "offense" brown and black people take at innocent gestures and words used by white people. We might as well quit using the antiquated word *racist*, retire it from our lexicon, since it no longer applies to anybody. Instead, we prefer to use words like *misunderstanding* and *miscommunication*, or, as Packer did back in 1996, we "apologize profusely."

Jaylen Brown pointed out that it is common for reporters and fans to expect athletes to remain quiet about political events, often saying things along the lines of "You should be happy you're making X amount of money playing sports. You should be saluting America instead of critiquing it."

James Baldwin, whom many Americans quote lately—though I wonder if they are actually reading him—once said, "I love America more than any other country in this world, and, exactly for this reason, I insist on the right to criticize her perpetually."

*

In 2017:

> Approximately 70 percent of the players in the NFL were black.
> Approximately 75 percent of the players in the NBA were black.
> Approximately 68 percent of the players in the WNBA were
> black.

How many black head coaches or owners are there?

*

In reference to protests by professional athletes during the national anthem, in particular those in the NFL, Trump addressed a rally in Alabama: "That's a total disrespect of our heritage. That's total disrespect of everything we stand for."

I have often had these same sentiments when I consider American Empire. Much of what *American* stands for, and arguably all of its "heritage," is disrespectable. My father, who built me a four-foot-high hoop so I could reach the basket when I was a child, is from a family of Mexican and Spanish immigrants. He fought in the Vietnam War and almost died when a missile hit his bunker. He continues to suffer that war in many ways. My little brother John, who was always my first pick, my on-the-ball screener, my in-bounder in hundreds of two-on-two games on indoor and outdoor courts all over our rez and small desert town, is still haunted by his participation in the Afghanistan war. Neither my father nor my brother is seen as fully human, and both are denied basic dignities in many ways. No mythology of a flag, of a colony, of an empire will change that. America will sacrifice my brothers' and sisters' bodies on a battlefield in the same way they will sacrifice them in an agricultural field or on a field of play, or on any street of any city or town in this country.

Captain Pratt, founder of the Carlisle Indian Industrial School, the man Marianne Moore so admired, in that same speech he gave at George Mason University way back when, also said, "We make our greatest mistake in feeding our civilization to the Indians instead of feeding the Indians to our civilization."

America is certainly that for many of us—a feeding, a consuming, a hunting ground, an appetite for and a lessening of our bodies.

*

At Denver, before RGIII was even in college, Shanahan coached John Elway, a white quarterback, who played his entire career without an ACL. Possibly, Shanahan equally disrespects black and white bodies—but I don't buy it. That season I watched Shanahan try to break RGIII. Finally, I watched him succeed. I watched the black body fall.

*

At the 1912 Stockholm Olympics, Jim Thorpe's shoes were stolen. He won one of his two gold medals competing in a borrowed shoe and a shoe he found in the trash. In the photo taken after the race, the two mismatched shoes are noticeable—one is too big, so he has extra socks on that foot.

My siblings and I shared shoes as kids. Five of us are within a six-year range of ages—John, Desirae, Gabrielle, Belarmino, me. We played in different divisions for the city rec league, took turns with a single pair of shoes. It was embarrassing.

Is this why we played so hard? To forget everyone saw us poor, in our bare socks, waiting for our turn to wear the shoes? I distrusted kids with fancy shoes, so I worked hard against them, ran faster, stole the ball every chance I got, until eventually I was better—I was the best.

*

There is a terrible structure of goodness in America that is designed to be unattainable for most nonwhite Americans, most poor Americans, most immigrants, most queer, most differently abled bodies. We are taught early to be good, to behave, to be quiet, to not take up space, to be invisible. Maybe this is why we gravitate toward sports—a place where we can be good. Not an equal playing field as we have seen, but as close to one as we get. It's the gimmick Baldwin was talking about—sport/game—our way up and out from under the thumb or boot of American power structures.

    *

The attributes that make us lauded on the courts, on fields, in rings are the same attributes that make us hunted and killed off the courts, off fields, out of the rings—quickness, fight, aggressiveness, unwillingness or inability to quit, pride and shame, strength, quick thinking, fearlessness, the way we know and own and carry our bodies, the grace, the muscle of us, the beauty and shock of our brown and black and exotic bodies gleaming in motion.

Like bulls we are. When yoked, we are beautiful. When refusing to be yoked, we are wild and whippable, butcherable.

    *

As we've seen throughout time, the combination of athletic prowess, intellectual complexity and autonomy, as well as human sensuality is threatening to white America—Tommie Smith and John Carlos standing shoeless and raising their gloved fists in protest on the podium at the 1968 Mexico Olympics, Kareem Abdul-Jabbar boycotting those same Olympics, Jackie Robinson not singing the national anthem, NBA and WNBA players protesting with T-shirts they wore in warm-ups even before Colin Kaepernick's peaceful protest rippled, then exploded, across the NFL. The brown or black athletic body coupled with intellect is dangerous, defiant even, to empire. It challenges the idea of the master and the beast, of the fan and their spectacle.

    *

Thabo Sefolosha testified that the NYPD officer who came up behind him that night and swept his leg out from beneath him said, "With or without a badge, I can fuck you up."

    *

To repair my torn ACL, the middle third of my patellar tendon was used along with bone fragments from each end. A surgeon drilled tunnels in my bone to thread the tendon through, then screwed the bone fragments and tendon into my tibia and femur, where my ACL used to be.

If I'd had an allograft, it would have come from a cadaver.

In Mojave we burn our dead—transplanting tissue from a dead body into mine wasn't an option for me or was an option I considered troublesome. In fact, if I'd done the entire procedure in Mojave way, I'd have had a small funeral pyre for my ACL, sent it off to the other side so it would be waiting for me when I passed on and over. Now, it's possible I'll arrive to the afterlife without an ACL. I'll have to have this surgery all over again after I die.

*

Because I am a Native woman born on the reservation, I am more likely to be assaulted, raped, or disappeared and to die as a result. According to the Department of Justice, in 2009, when Attorney General Eric Holder, was briefed by the FBI that one in three Native women are physically assaulted in their lifetime and on some reservations the murder rate for women is ten times higher than the national average, he couldn't believe the statistics were correct. He asked his team to fact-check the numbers.

According to the U.S. Office of Juvenile Justice and Delinquency Prevention, "Native girls are 40 percent more likely than white girls to be referred to a juvenile court for delinquency; 50 percent more likely to be detained; and 20 percent more likely to be adjudicated." Another disturbing report by the National Women's Law Center concludes, "Girls who spend time in juvenile detention facilities are nearly five times more likely to die before age 29."

A United Nations document titled "Sport and Gender: Empowering Girls and Women" reports that female athletes showed "increased self-esteem, self-confidence, and a sense of control over their bodies." According to the UN findings, sports also foster "positive changes in gender norms, giving girls and women greater safety and control over their lives." There are myriad articles and studies that claim I am less likely to be in an abusive relationship because I am an athlete.

If the statistics of me being assaulted, raped, and disappeared as a Native woman meet head-to-head with statistics that say I am less likely to be abused and will have greater safety because I am a female athlete, which statistics will win?

And if I lose that matchup, if my body is found the way most murdered Native women's bodies are found throughout the Americas—discarded, decomposed, on a rarely traveled tract of land, at the bottom of a canyon or riverbed, in pieces, and by accident because police aren't looking—it is quite possible that my body will be difficult to identify.

If my body is difficult to identify, then the titanium screws in my knee will become significant. The authorities will interview my family, look through my and other missing Native women's medical records. They will see that I once had surgery on my left knee. They'll check the left knee of the body for signs of a fractured tibial condyle, for titanium screws and their serial numbers. If it is me, if it is my Native, female, queer, athletic body that they find, basketball will not have saved my life—but it will have saved me from being added to the thousands of missing Native women in the Americas.

*

The king of Sweden called Jim Thorpe the world's greatest athlete the week he won those two golds for the U.S. track and field team. The next week Thorpe had to return his medals according to Rule 26 of the Eligibility Rules of the International Olympic Committee. It was discovered he'd received a small amount of pay from two semipro baseball teams.

It was about rules, they said, not about his Nativeness. Rule 26.

Twenty-six is a bad number for Natives. A deck of cards has twenty-six red cards and twenty-six black cards, but really all the cards are white. On the twenty-sixth day of December 1862, Honest Abe Lincoln, the Great Emancipator, ordered the hanging of thirty-eight Dakotas. He *ordered* them to be hanged. The periodic table is an *ordering* of elements. Twenty-six is the atomic number for the element iron. The word for iron or metal in the Mojave language is also the word for bullet. Because this is how iron or metal first came to us, like bullets still come to us, through our bodies. In twenty-six years I will still have played basketball for longer than I have not played it.

*

I had a lateral X-ray taken of my left knee, and it looked like there were two .22 caliber rounds lodged in me, except for the deep threads of the titanium screws.

*

Even though the International Olympic Committee presented Jim Thorpe with replica gold medals, they snuck in some fine print that allowed them to not enter his actual records back into the Olympic books. It's as if he never participated. They have erased him, as has always been their way with Natives.

*

I would buy a ticket to watch the 6′2″ Sefolosha take that 5′7″ officer, *with or without a badge*, out onto the court and work him, school him, take him to the rim, break his ankles, *fuck him up*.

*

A few years before leaving the Redskins, when asked to describe his relationship with Coach Shanahan, RGIII replied, "Heartbreaking."

*

Writing is an extension of my body. I am seeking the body on the page, even the broken body, even the ecstatic body—even the broken *and* ecstatic body. I am looking for a new field for the body to run in. I am looking for a field where the body might be struck down. I am looking for a field where the body might rest or hide or flee or reap or build a house or set a fire. The body doesn't want solace— the body wants to be possible.

The page has never solved my troubles, but the page has let me know them better, let me know the body of myself better through those troubles. Maybe.

*

I never thought much about what my mother meant all those times, before all those games, when she told me, *Knock 'em dead*. Now, I think she meant, *This isn't just a game for you. Don't let them hurt you, even if it means hurting them first*. I think she meant, *Live*. It's funny how a game can teach you that.

In Defense of Allen Iverson

Hanif Abdurraqib

bless the men who grasp at the air
where there was once another man dancing before them.
his hips and the bright sun he cradled in his palm, already a
    forgotten
memory. forgive me for ever believing myself fragile.
forgive those who make the work look easy.
if it must be about performance, I prefer sweat to
blood, but have given enough of each to earn a
night
without a tie stretched along
my neck while I answer
questions from a
man who has never walked from a shovel
with calloused fingers, dirt covering someone newly
departed. if gold is the only metal that has never
tried to end your life,
I imagine you would also let it anchor you. pull you closer
to the earth. a chain big enough to see from home. I say
home and mean
wherever the people count the hours
they've been alive and say a new
prayer for each one.
or *where the people clap a hand*
to each other's backs during a
hug that came after a good dap
that came after a how yo' mama been lobbed
across a parking lot. how much money would
you give to keep your hood close when they
hand you a suit? when a man asks you to dress
yourself as you would for a funeral?

it costs a lot to get out of the ghetto.
it costs even more to carry the ghetto with you after you
have left it. lay the coins at their feet and let the world see
the names of everyone you have survived in black ink on
your black skin. let the Virginia slang
spill mighty from the corners of your half-open mouth.
let the words grow fall to the carpet and resurrect as one
    hundred black
children who dribble in front of walls trying to shake their own
shadows,
the waltz that will retire a mother while she can still be held in
the wind while she can still drink from cicada's songs being
carried from the fields where they sound most like what poured
from parked cars in the projects.
their windows down, their tires unmoving, their rims still
    spinning toward an impossible
future.

        *

Allen, I wish you a T-shirt down to
your knees in any season. I wish it to
fall from you the way the holy robe
falls from any messiah. I wish you hair
that spills out of whatever thinks
itself bold enough to contain it. the rows
of corn in Ohio did not make
themselves ready for harvest again this
fall. families will have
to find another way to make
themselves full, but you have
endured another year. at some point,
every sin must envy the one that came
before it. and so on, until the mirror swallows

Bolting into Throat

Patricia Smith

First, somebody's got to run. There's no sport
in it otherwise. Everybody needs to be drunk
on sun first, then just straight drunk, and there
will be rotted-tooth cackling, dog-tired horses
spewing snot, whips slashing gashes in dead
air. But somebody has to run like he needs
a place he can't see, like Jesus blew a whistle.
The hunt needs a man who finally believes
the murmured come-ons of that blaring star,
who lingers a second too long in the inflamed
twist of a gospel lyric, and thinks that being free
just may be that muted flash at the other end
of his pointed finger. *Over there, out there, over
yonder, north, always north,* he chants, his whole
body primed, fixed on a fleeting and luminous
orchestra. But first he's got to run. Every word
he utters will suddenly drip with a stupid, sugary
faith, his first few halting steps click into rhythm,
and the night will lunge forward to scar him.
Sometimes he is minutes gone, maybe hours,
sometimes a day—but he will come to realize
that all land is throat, that it swallows and swallows
then dribbles a dust that lies and calls itself light.
The fear that he's begun a journey that has already
ended sparks the stench, the sweet blade-edged
salt that just barely changes his skin. And the dog
doesn't know why it hates or what it hates, just
that Negro blur and the damn repeated stink of it.
The old hound's heart is everything, a giddy blue
muscle that thumps as backbeat for its flailing rage.

It fevers against the leash, snorting the deep bowl
of the gone man's hat, his one stiffened gray sock,
an old work shirt. The dog's whole body aches with
what it was born to do. There's just no sport in it
otherwise. The hunters whoop and strain forward
on their steeds, addicts for the thrill of the chase.
Even the stars are crazed, blasting the length of
the quest with northern light, leading the hunters
and the game to their different versions of free.

last summer of innocence

Danez Smith

there was Noella who knew I was sweet
but cared enough to bother with me

that summer when nobody died
except for boys from other schools

but not us, for which our mothers
lifted his holy name & even let us skip

some Sundays to go to the park
or be where we had no business being

talking to girls who had no interest
in us, who flocked to their new hips

dumb birds that we were, nectar high
& singing all around them, preening

waves all day, white beater & our best
basketball shorts, the flyest shoes

our mamas could buy hot, line-up fresh
from someone's porch, someone's uncle

cutting heads round the corner cutting
eyes at the mothers of girls I pretended

to praise. I showed off for girls
but stared at my stupid, boney crew.

I knew the word for what I was
but couldn't think it. I played football

& believed that meant something.
when Noella n 'nem didn't come out

& instead we turned our attention
to our wild legs, narrow arms & pig skin

I spent all day in my brothers' arms
& wanted that to be forever—

boy after boy after boy after boy
pulling me down into the dirt.

American Pharoah

Ada Limón

Despite the morning's gray static of rain,
we drive to Churchill Downs at 6 a.m.,
eyes still swollen shut with sleep. I say,
Remember when I used to think everything
was getting better and better? Now, I think
it's just getting worse and worse. I know it's not
what I'm supposed to say as we machine our
way through the silent seventy minutes on 64
over pavement still fractured from the winter's
wreckage. I'm tired. I've had vertigo for five
months and on my first day home, he's shaken
me awake to see this horse, not even race, but
work. He gives me his jacket as we face
the deluge from car to the twin spire turnstiles,
and once deep in the fern-green grandstands, I see
the crowd. A few hundred maybe, black umbrellas,
cameras, and notepads, wet-winged eager early birds
come to see this Kentucky-bred bay colt with his
chewed-off tail train to end the almost 40-year
American Triple Crown drought. A man next to us,
some horseracing heavy, ticks off a list of reasons
why this horse—his speed-laden pedigree, muscle
and bone recovery, et cetera, et cetera—could never
win the grueling mile-and-a-half Belmont Stakes.
Then, the horse with his misspelled name comes out,
first just casually cantering with his lead horse,
and next, a brief break in the storm, and he's racing
against no one but himself and the official clocker,
monstrously fast and head down so we can see

that faded star flash on his forehead like this
is real gladness. As the horse eases up and we
close our mouths to swallow, the heavy next to us
folds his arms, says what I want to say too: *I take it all back.*

Takes Enemy

Shann Ray

> Let me enfold thee, and hold thee to my heart.
> —Shakespeare, from *Macbeth*

1.

In the dark I still line up the seams of the ball to the form of my fingers. I see the rim, the follow-through, the arm lifted and extended, a pure jumpshot with a clean release and good form. I see the long-range trajectory and the ball on a slow backspin arcing toward the hoop, the net waiting for the swish. A sweet jumper finds the mark, a feeling of completion and the chance to be face to face not with the mundane, but with the holy.

2.

In Montana, high school basketball is a thing as strong as family or work and when I grew up Jonathan Takes Enemy, a member of the Apsaalooké (Crow) Nation, was the best basketball player in the State. He led Hardin High, a school with years of losing tradition, into the state spotlight, carrying the team and the community on his shoulders all the way to the state tournament where he averaged 41 points per game. He created legendary moments that decades later are still mentioned in state basketball circles, and he did so with a force that made me both fear and respect him. On the court, nothing was outside the realm of his skill: the jumpshot, the drive, the sweeping left-handed finger roll, the deep fade-away jumper. He could deliver what we all dreamed of, and with a venom that said *don't get in my way.*

I was a year younger than Jonathan, playing for an all-white school in Livingston when our teams met in the divisional tournament and he and the Hardin Bulldogs delivered us a crushing 17-

point defeat. At the close of the third quarter with the clock winding down and his team with a comfortable lead, Takes Enemy pulled up from one step in front of half-court and shot a straight, clean jumpshot. Though the range of it was more than 20 feet beyond the three-point line, his form remained pure. The audacity and raw beauty of the shot hushed the crowd. A common knowledge came to everyone: few people can even throw a basketball that far with any accuracy, let alone take a real shot with good form. Takes Enemy landed and as the ball was in the air he turned, no longer watching the flight of the ball, and began to walk back toward his team bench. The buzzer sounded, he put his fist high, the shot swished into the net. The crowd erupted.

In his will even to take such a shot, let alone make it, I was reminded of the surety and brilliance of so many Native American heroes in Montana who had painted the basketball landscape of my boyhood: Jarvis Yellow Robe, Georgie Scalpcane, Joe Pretty Paint, Elias Pretty Horse, the Pretty On Top family. And Cleveland Highwalker, my father's closest friend back then. Many of these young men died due to the violence that surrounded the alcohol and drug traffic on the reservations, but their natural flow on the court inspired me toward the kind of boldness that gives artistry and freedom to any endeavor. Such boldness is akin to passion. For these young men, and for myself at that time, our passion was basketball.

But rather than creating in me my own intrepid response, seeing Takes Enemy only emphasized how little I knew of courage, not just on the basketball court, but in life. Takes Enemy breathed a confidence I lacked, a leadership potential that lived and moved. Robert Greenleaf said, "A mark of leaders, an attribute that puts them in a position to show the way for others, is that they are better than most at pointing the direction." Takes Enemy was better than most. He and his team worked as one as they played with fluidity and abandon. I began to look for this way of life as an athlete and as a person. The search brought me to people who lived life not through dominance but through freedom of movement.

In the half dark of the house, a light burning over my shoulder, I find myself asking who commandeers the vessels of our dreams? I see Jonathan Takes Enemy like a war horse running, fierce and filled with immense power. The question gives me pause to remember him and his artistry, and how he played for something more.

3.

Our family was distant. Basketball held us together. As a boy I felt we existed in a nearly rootless way, me and my brother Kral like pale windblown trees in a barren land. Our father's land to be precise, the land of a high school basketball coach.

We were raised in trailers and trailer parks.

My father was a bar fighter.

Getting ready to fight he'd say, "I'm taking my lunch and I'm not closing my eyes."

He meant he wasn't going anywhere. He meant hit hard until it's done.

In college he'd fought his way into the starting line-up, his first two years at Miles City Community College, his final two at Rocky Mountain College. He was a shooter, runner, rebounder, a 6'3" wiry swing man with a great outside touch who loved to mix it up on the boards.

After college, he led the family to Alaska and back, then crisscrossed Montana, moving seven times before I was fourteen—all in pursuit of the basketball dynasty, the team that would reach the top with him at the helm and make something happen that would be remembered forever. He'd been trying to accomplish that since before I was born and it got flint hard at times, the rigidity of how he handled things.

4.

By the time Kral and I reached high school, we both had the dream, Kral already on his way to the top, me two years younger and trying to learn everything I could. We'd received the dream equally from our father and from the rez, the Crow rez at Plenty Coups, and the Northern Cheyenne rez in the southeast corner of Montana. In Montana tribal basketball is a game of speed and precision passing, a form of controlled wildness that is hard to come by in non-reservation basketball circles. Fast and quick-handed, the rez ballers rise like something elemental, finding each other with sleight of hand stylings and no-look passes, pressing and cutting in streamlike movements that converge to rivers, taking down passing lanes with no will but to create chaos and action and fury, the kind of kindle that smolders and leaps up to set whole forests aflame.

Kral and I lost the dream late, both having made it to the D-1 level, both with opportunity to play overseas, but neither of us making the league.

Along the way, I helped fulfill our father's tenacious hopes: two state championships at Park High in Livingston, one first as a sophomore with Kral, a massive win in which the final score was 104 to 64, with Kral totaling 46 points, 20 rebounds, and three dunks. And one two years later when I was a senior with a band of runners that averaged nearly ninety points a game. We took the title in what sportswriters still refer to as the greatest game in Montana high school basketball history, a 99–97 double-overtime thriller in '85 at Montana State, the Brick Breeden Fieldhouse, the Max Worthington Arena, before a crowd of 10,000.

Afterward on the bus ride through the mountains I remember my chest pressed to the back of the seat as I stared behind us. The post-game show blared over the speakers, everyone still whooping and hollering. "We're comin' home!" the radio man yelled, "We're coming home!" and from the wide back window I saw a line of cars miles long and lit up, snaking from the flat before Livingston all the way up the pass to Bozeman. The dream of a dream, the Niitsítapi and the Apsáalooke, the Blackfeet and the Crow, the Nēhilawē and the Tsitsistas, the Cree and the Northern Cheyenne, the white boys, the enemies and the friends, and the clean line of basketball walking us out toward skeletal hoops in the dead of winter, the hollow in our eyes lonely but lovely in its way.

5.

At Montana State, I played shooting guard on the last team in the league my freshman year. Our team: seven African Americans from all across America and five white kids mostly from Montana. We had a marvelous, magical point guard from Portland named Tony Hampton. He was lightning fast with wonderful ball-handling skills and exceptional court vision. He brought us together with seven games left in the season. Our record at the time was 7 wins, 16 losses. Last place in the conference. "We are getting shoved down by this coaching staff," he said, and I remember how the criticism and malice were thick from the coaches. Their jobs were on the line. They'd lost touch with their players. Tony said, "We need to band together right now. No one is going to do it for us. Whenever you see a teammate dogged by a coach, go up and give that teammate love. Tell him good job. Keep it up. We're in this together."

A team talk like that doesn't typically change a season.

This one did.

Tony spoke the words. We followed him and did what he asked, and we went on a seven-game win streak, starting that very night when we beat the 17th ranked team in the country, on the road. The streak didn't end until the NCAA tournament eight games later. In that stretch, Tony averaged 19 points and 11 assists per game. He led the way and we were unfazed by outside degradation. We had our own inner strength. Playing as one, we won the final three games of the regular season. We entered the Big Sky Conference tournament in last place and beat the number fourth, second, and first place teams in the league to advance to March Madness. When we came home from the Conference tournament as champions, it felt like the entire town of Bozeman was at the airport to greet us. We waded through a river of people giving high fives and held a fiery pep rally with speeches and roars of applause. We went on to the NCAA tournament as the last ranked team, the 64th team in a tournament of 64 teams. We were slated to play St. Johns, the number one team in the nation. We faced off in the first game of the southwest regional at Long Beach, and far into the second half we were up by four. St. John's featured future NBA players Mark Jackson (future NBA All-Star), Walter Berry (collegiate player of the year), and Shelton Jones (future winner of the NBA dunk contest). We featured no one with national recognition. We played well and had the lead in the second half, but in the end we lost by nine.

When my brother graduated from Montana State I transferred and played my final two seasons of college basketball for Pepperdine University. Our main rival was Loyola Marymount University, featuring consensus All-American Hank Gathers and the multi-talented scorer Bo Kimble. My senior year at Pepperdine we beat Loyola Marymount 127–114 in a true barn-burner! Also a fine grudge match, considering they beat us earlier in the season at their place. We were set to play each other in the championship game of the West Coast Conference tournament but before we could meet at the top of the bracket, Hank died and the tournament was immediately canceled. The tragedy of Hank's death stuns me. He had just completed a thunderous alley-oop dunk, and was running back on defense when he collapsed near mid-court and fell, dead of a heart attack. The funeral was in Los Angeles, a ceremony of gut-wrenching grief and bereavement in which we gathered to honor one of the nation's young warriors. We prayed for him and for his family and for all who would come after him bearing his legacy of love for the game, elite athleticism, and the gift of living life to the full. His team went on to the NCAA tournament and made it all the way to the final eight teams, the Elite 8. Bo Kimble shot his first free-throw of the NCAA tournament left-handed in honor of Hank. The shot went in. The nation mourned. The athletes who knew Hank were never the same.

As a freshman in high school, I was tiny, barely five feet tall, and my goal was to play Division 1 basketball. I'd had this goal since I was a child and because of my height and weight it seemed impossible, and actually felt impossible. I was small, but I made a deal with myself to do whatever it might take from my end to try to get to the D-1 level, so if I did not accomplish the goal, I knew at least I had given my all. I grew eight inches the summer before my sophomore year in high school, thanked heaven, and began to think perhaps the goal was not totally out of reach.

Hour after hour. Every day. The dream was now fully formed, bright shining, and excruciating. I played 17 hours in one day. The days of solitude and physical exhaustion were plentiful. I gave my life to the discipline of being a point guard and a shooting guard. I worked on moves, passing, shooting, defending, ball handling. The regimen involved getting up at 7 a.m. at the trailer we lived in, on my bike by 7:40, traveling downtown in Livingston, yellow transistor radio (borrowed from my mom) in the front pocket of my windbreaker, the ball tucked up under the coat, and me riding to Eastside, the court bordered by a grade school to the east, the Sheriff's station and the firehall to the north, and small residential houses to the west. A few blocks south, the Yellowstone River moved and churned and flowed east. Above the river a wall of mountains reached half way up the sky.

Mostly I was by myself, but because the town had a love for basketball, there were many hours with friends too. In those hours with others, or isolated hours trying to hone my individual basketball skills, I faced many, many frustrations, but finally the body broke into the delight of hard work and found a rhythm, a pattern in which there was the slow advance toward something greater than oneself. Often the threshold of life is a descent into darkness, a powerful and intimate and abiding darkness in which the light finally emerges.

"Beauty will save the world," Dostoevsky said.

Because of basketball I know there exists the reality of being encumbered or full of grace, beset with darkness and or in convergence with light. This interplay echoes the wholly realized vision of exceptional point guards and the daring of pure shooting guards, met with fortitude even under immense pressure.

6.

I'm missing the rez, Northern Cheyenne, and I wish I could bring it back, here, now, bring back Lafe Haugen, Russell Tall White Man,

Stanford Rides Horse, or Blake Walks Nice with his little side push shot that hits the net in a fast pop because it flies on a straight line, lacking any arc.

After I left the rez, Blake married a Wooden Thigh girl, and they had kids.

Then I heard he was found dead behind Jimtown Bar, stabbed five times in the chest.

7.

At Eastside, both low end and high end have square metal backboards marked by quarter-sized holes to keep the wind from knocking the baskets down. Livingston is the fifth windiest city in the world. The playground has a slant to it that makes one basket lower than the other. The low end is nine feet, ten inches high, and we all come here to throw down in the summer. Too small, they say, but we don't listen. Inside-outside, between-the-legs, behind-the-back, cross it up, skip-to-my-lou, fake and go, doesn't matter, any of these lose the defender. Then we rise up and throw down. We rig up a break-away on the rim and because of the way we hang on it in the summer, our hands get thick and tough. We can all dunk now, so the break-away is a necessity, a spring loaded rim made to handle the power of power-dunks. The break-away rim came into being after Darrel Dawkins, nicknamed Chocolate Thunder, broke two of the big glass backboards in the NBA. On the first one Dawkins' force was so immense the glass caved in and fell out the back of the frame. On the second, the window exploded and everyone ducked their heads and ran to avoid the fractured glass that flew from one end of the court to the other. Within two years every high school in the nation had break-aways, and my friends and I convinced our assistant coach to give us one so we could put it up on the low end at Eastside.

The high end is the shooter's end, made for the pure shooter, a silver ring ten feet, two inches high with a long white net. At night the car lights bring it alive, rim and backboard like an industrial art work, everything mounted on a steel-gray pole that stems down into the concrete, down deep into the hard soil.

A senior in high school, I'm 17. I leave the car lights on, cut the engine and grab my basketball from the heat in the passenger foot space. I step out. The air is crisp. The wind carries the cold, dry smell of autumn, and further down, more faint, the smell of roots, the smell of earth. Out over the city, strands of cloud turn gray, then black. When the sun goes down there is a depth of night seemingly unfathomable, and yet the darkness is rent by a flurry of stars.

This is where it begins, the movements and the whisperings that are my dreams. Into the lamplight the shadows strike, separate and sharp, like spirits, like angels. I've practiced here alone so often since Kral left for college I no longer know the hours I've played. I call the ballers by name, the great native basketball legends, some my own contemporaries, some who came before. I learn from them and receive the river, their smoothness, their brazenness, like the Yellowstone River seven blocks south, dark and wide, stronger than the city it surrounds, perfect in form where it moves and speaks, bound by night. If I listen my heroes lift me out away from here, fly me farther than they flew themselves. In Montana, young men are Indian and they are white, loving, hating. At Lodge Grass, at Lame Deer, I was afraid at first. But now I see. The speaking and the listening, the welcoming: Tim Falls Down, Marty Round Face and Max and Luke Spotted Bear from Plenty Coups; Joe Pretty Paint from Lodge Grass; and at St. Labre, Juneau Plenty Hawk, Willie Gardner, and Fred and Paul Deputee. All I loved, all I watched with wonder—and few got free.

Most played ball for my father, a few for rival teams. Some I watched as a child, and I loved the uncontrolled nature of their moves. Some I grew up playing against. And some I merely heard of in basketball circles years later, the rumble of their greatness, the stories of games won or lost on last second shots.

8.

Falls Down walked with ease in his step, his body loose and free. Tall and lanky, he carried himself with the joy of those who are both loved and strong. He wore his hair tall too. As if guided by wind and light he flew from the ground to the sky, snatched the ball in mid-air and rocketed an outlet pass to Dana Goes Ahead. He followed his outlet pass, taking a wide arc to the lane where Dana laid down a no look pass and Falls Down finished with a reckless flare, falling to the hardwood as the ball came through the net. I was seven years old. After the game, he spoke to me with humor in his voice and something electric, like lightning.

He was buried at eighteen in buckskin, beads, and full head-dress, his varsity uniform, turquoise and orange, laid over his chest: dead at high speed when his truck slid from an ice-bound bridge into the river.

People packed the gymnasium for his funeral.

The old women wailing, their voices ripping a hole in the world.

9.

Paul Deputee stood with his chest high, his chin on a level. He looked straight ahead, eyes focused as if on a distant point. His leadership was calm and fast. He took few shots, a selective point guard who always put others before himself. When he chose to shoot, he used a set shot and put a lot of air under the ball. Like water in a cut riverbed his teams followed him without resistance.

Quiet and steady, Paul looked boldly to the future.

He was shot in the head with a high powered rifle at a party near Crow Agency.

10.

Pretty Paint died before he was twenty-five, another alcohol-laced car wreck.

Half-Cheyenne Bobbie Jones, dead. A suicide, I believe.

By knife or rope or gun, I can't recall.

There are these and many more. "Too many," say the middle-aged warriors, the old Indians, "too young." They motion with their hands as if they pull from a bottle. With their lips they gesture and place their index finger and thumb to their lips in a mock image of dope. They spit on the ground. Some of those who died held me in their hands when I was a boy, when they were young men. I remember their faces, their hair like a black wing, eyes the push of mountains, silvery laughter ever-present in their smile.

Of the living and the dead, two above the rest: Elvis Old Bull and Jonathan Takes Enemy. Stars I played with and against. Both Crow. Elvis was three-time MVP of the state tournament: ambidextrous, master passer, prolific point maker. And Takes Enemy scored like none other. He shot the leather off the ball.

The Crow reservation runs the Montana-Wyoming border in a place of plateau flatlands. The carved canyon of the Bighorn River like a vein on the land. A haze of mountains at the edge of the eye. Top a grassy rise and make a slight descent to the Little Bighorn battle site where Lakota, Cheyenne, and Arapaho forces took Yellow Hair Custer and kissed the earth with his blood. Crow Agency is the centerpiece, the town like a tangled chessboard made of sticks and gravel, frayed to open fields. Out there horses stand in twos and threes, windblown and slope-backed. Lodge Grass, a smaller outpost further south.

Old Bull, long-legged with a slender barrel-chest, like a fluted wine glass. When he was a few years out of high school and I'd finished college we played a money tournament together in northeast Montana. Three grand in prize money for the champions. To raise money for the local high school, on Friday night the small white town gathered and auctioned off the shooters for Saturday's three-point contest. Elvis Old Bull's jumper went for a couple thousand dollars to an old rancher, and Elvis made good on the investment. In the championship game on Sunday against a group comprised of wingmen slashers and a few guards from the Canadian National Team, we rode to victory on the back of Old Bull's beautiful passing. He threw assist after assist, dime after dime, opening wide the dunk lanes to the delight of a crowd made up of mostly farmers and ranchers, their wives, and children. In the second half the crowd raised the roof after a shot Old Bull made that still stands like a torch in my memory. He crossed half-court hounded by defenders, a spin move once at the hash mark, another at the top of the key where he went directly into his jumpshot. But when he spun, the defender was draped on his shooting hand. In midair, nonchalant, Elvis switched the ball position and shot left-handed, holding his follow-through with gorgeous form even with his off hand.

All net.

Applause and shouts of praise from the crowd.

Elvis smiling on an easy backpedal down court.

Year by year, I saw less of him.

He grew large, heavy-headed with alcohol.

Much later I met his son at a tournament in Billings. I didn't see Elvis, and haven't seen him since.

11.

27 feet. 30. The NBA line is 23 feet, nine inches. The message is an echo in my mind, only one shot at the game-winner. In the 99–97 double-overtime title game my senior year in high school our team rallied, my friend John Moran hit two game-sealing free throws and we won in the closing seconds, the gym-noise like an inferno. My brother met me and we stayed up the whole night and laughed together and talked hoops.

12.

The body in unison, the step, the gather, the arc of the ball in the air like a crescent moon—the follow-through a small well-lit cathedral, the correct push and the floppy wrist, the proper backspin, the arm held high, the night, the ball, the basket, everything illumined.

We are given moments like these, to rise with Highwalker and Falls Down and Spotted Bear, with Round Face and Old Bull and Takes Enemy: to shoot the jumpshot and feel the follow-through that lifts and finds a path in the air, the sound, the sweetness of the ball on a solitary arc in darkness as the ball falls into the net.

All is complete. The maze lies open, an imprint that reminds me of the Highline, the Blackfeet and Charlie Calf Robe, the Crow and Joe Pretty Paint, a form of forms that is a memory trace and the weaving of a line begun by Indian men, by white men, by my father and Calf Robe's and Pretty Paint's fathers, by our fathers' fathers, and by all the fathers that have gone before, some of them distant and many gone, all of them beautiful in their way.

13.

The moon is hidden, the sky off-white, a far ceiling of cloud lit by the lights of the city. Snow falls steady and smooth like white flowers. I put the ball down and blow in my hands to warm them. My body is limber, my joints loose. I have a good sweat going. It's just my hands that need warming so I eye the rim while I blow heat into them. The motion comes to me, the readying, the line of the ball, the line of the sky. I remove my sweat top and throw it out in the snow toward the car. I'm in a gray T-shirt. Steam lifts from my forearms.

Oceans and continents away from home, pro ball in Germany, in an old small gym in Düsseldorf, four seconds on the clock and the team down 1, I missed the free-throw we needed to get to the playoffs.

Growing up I missed my father. We missed each other.

The Blackfeet reservation is in the far northwest corner of the State, tucked against two borders. Glacier National Park to the west, to the north Canada. Bearhat and Gunsight and Rising Wolf Mountains. The Great Garden Wall. The Marias and Two Medicine Rivers. The backbone of the continent. Browning is a lean spread of buildings on the windswept steppe below the great rocks. Thin rail line near black in the dark. Amtrak's Empire Builder like a shout on the outskirts of town.

Fresh from professional ball in Germany I went with my dad to the Charlie Calf Robe Memorial Tournament on the Blackfeet rez. The tribe devoted an entire halftime to my father and he didn't even coach on that reservation. They presented him with a beaded belt buckle and a blanket for the coaching he'd done on other reservations—to show their respect for him as an elder who was a friend to the Native American tribes of Montana. During the ceremony they wrapped the blanket around his shoulders, signifying he would always be welcome in the tribe.

On that weekend with him, I received an unforeseen and wholly unique gift. Dedicated as a memorial to the high school athlete Charlie Calf Robe, a young Blackfeet artist, long distance runner, and basketball player who died too early, the tournament was a form of community grieving over the loss of a beloved son. The Most Valuable Player (MVP) award was made by Charlie's wife, Honey Davis, who spent nine months crafting an entirely beaded basketball for the event. When the tribe and Honey herself presented the ball to me, and I walked through the gym with my father, an old Blackfeet man approached us. He touched my arm, and smiled a wide-smile.

"You can't dribble that one, sonny," he said.

14.

Marty Round Face was smooth and fast. He ran strong and flew high. When he cut to the middle and parted the defenders he rose like something celestial and let the ball fall off his fingers into the net, echoing the Iceman, George Gervin, of the San Antonio Spurs. As a boy, when I watched him my heart filled with expectation.

"How does he jump so high?" I asked my father.

"He works at it," my father said. "He cut a lodge pole and stuck it in the field behind his house. He placed small pieces of yarn up high on the pole, each one six inches above the other. That's how he leaps, son. Practices day after day until he reaches the next piece of yarn."

Marty Round Face leapt to touch the sun.

The entire town flocked to see him.

Not long after high school he committed suicide.

15.

Young, I spent much of my life lost in loneliness and fear. My father, as I grew to know and love him, may have been lonelier still.

I saw my father's father only a handful of times.

He lived in little more than a one room shack in Circle, Montana. In the shack next door was my grandfather's brother, a trapper who dried animal hides on boards and leaned them against walls and tables. I remember rattlesnake rattles in a small pile on the surface of a wooden three-legged stool. A hunting knife with a horn handle. On the floor, small and medium-sized closed steel traps. An old rifle in the corner near the door.

My father and I drive the two-lane highway as we enter town. We pick up my grandfather stumbling drunk down the middle of the road and take him home.

Years later my grandpa sits in the same worn linoleum kitchen in an old metal chair with vinyl backing. Dim light from the window. His legs crossed, a rolled cigarette lit in his left hand, he runs his right hand through a shock of silver hair atop his head, bangs yellowed by nicotine. Bent or upright or sideways, empty beer cans litter the floor.

"Who is it?" he says, squinting into the dark.

"Tommy," my dad says, "your son."

"Who?" the old man says.

When we leave, my grandpa still doesn't recognize him.

On the way home through the dark, I watch my father's eyes.

My grandfather was largely isolated late in life. No family members were near him when he died. He once loved to walk the hills after the spring runoff in search of arrowheads with his family. But in my grandpa's condition before death his desire for life was eclipsed. He became morose and very depressed. In the end, alcohol killed him.

16.

One shot. The ball is perfect, round and smooth. The leather conforms to my hands. I square my feet and shoulders to the rim and let the gathering run its course. At the height of the release my elbow straightens. I land, and my hand as it follows through is loose and free, the ball the radiant circle I've envisioned from the moment I looked out the trailer window, even now in sheer darkness a small sphere in orbit to the sun that is my follow-through, a new world risen with its own glory here among the other worlds, the playground, the schoolhouse, the Sheriff's station, the firehall.

The Cheyenne rez abuts the Crow rez but moves further east. The Powder and Tongue Rivers run through a dry land of flats and coulees, sandstone ridges and scrub pine. The main town, Lame Deer, is set at the juncture of a crossroads among low hills. Dirt side streets and makeshift cul-de-sacs, clusters of pastel colored HUD houses. Jimtown Bar is just past the north rez line, a neon flash on the highway before the big industrial smokestacks of the Montana Power Company in Colstrip.

When young, my father drove the backroads of that rez with Cleveland Highwalker. The two were inseparable. Town ball and tournaments, laughter and brotherhood. I remember my dad's hand on my jaw, gently. Him telling me how he went with Cleveland into the far hills in winter to make a trade with Cleveland's grandmother for two sets of beaded moccasins. Him punching through snow to bring two deer, a gopher, and a magpie to the old Highwalker woman who spoke only Cheyenne and traced his footprints on leather she later chewed to soften. The picture of it makes me wonder now if there is still blood for forgiveness. Dead things for the new day.

"Cleveland was flat-out an athlete," my dad said. "And he could sky. Leap straight out of the gym."

My father shakes his head. Water in his eyes. "Wouldn't find a better player anywhere, and no better friend."

Not long after high school, married and on the way to fatherhood, Cleveland took his own life.

At the funeral, the small box church overflowed.

People lined up outside and looked in through the open windows.

17.

My cousin Jacine, a beautiful young woman, fell headlong into drug culture.

She died of multiple bullet wounds in a drug shootout on the south end of Billings near Montana Avenue. I think of my aunt in Montana. Our family, still mourning.

I think of Takes Enemy, and Walks Nice. Joe Pretty Paint's father, his generations, his country overcome by violent men. I think of his mother loss, and father loss. And my father and mother, their sisters and brothers . . . the losses that reside in our blood like shards of glass.

18.

In present-day Montana, with its cold winters and far distant towns, the love of high school basketball is a time-honored tradition. Native American teams have most often dominated the basketball landscape, winning multiple state titles on the shoulders of modern day warriors who are both highly skilled and intrepid.

Tribal basketball comes like a fresh wind to change the climate of the reservation from downtrodden to celebrational. Plenty Coups with Luke Spotted Bear and Dana Goes Ahead won two state championships in the early eighties. After that, Lodge Grass, under Elvis Old Bull, won three straight. Jonathan Takes Enemy remains perhaps the most revered. Deep finger rolls with either hand, his jumpshot a thing of beauty, with his quick vertical leap he threw down 360s, and with power. We played against each other numerous times in high school, his teams still spoken of by the old guard, a competition fiery and glorious, and then we went our separate ways.

For a few months he attended Sheridan Community College in Wyoming then dropped out.

He played city league, his name appearing in the Billings papers with him scoring over 60 on occasion, and once 73.

Later I heard he'd done some drinking, gained weight and become mostly immobile.

But soon after that he cleaned up, lost weight, earned a scholarship at Rocky Mountain College and formed a nice career averaging a bundle of assists and over 20 points a game.

A few years ago we sat down again at a tournament called the Big Sky Games. We didn't talk much about the past. He'd been off the Crow reservation for awhile, living on the Yakima reservation in Washington now. He said he felt he had to leave in order to stay sober. He'd found a good job. His vision was on his family. The way his eyes lit up when he spoke of his daughter was a clear reflection of his life, a man willing to sacrifice to enrich others. His face was full of promise, and thinking of her he smiled. "She'll graduate from high school this year," he said, and it became apparent to me that the happiness he felt was greater than all the fame that came of the personal honors he had attained.

Jonathan Takes Enemy navigated the personal terrain necessary to be present for his daughter. I hope to follow him and be present for my daughters. By walking into and through the night he eventually left the dark behind and found light rising to greet him.

19.

Inside me are the memories of players I knew as a boy, the stories of basketball legends. The geography of such stories still shapes the way I speak or grow quiet, and shapes my understanding of things that begin in fine lines and continue until all the lines are gathered and woven to a greater image. That image, circular, airborne, is the outline and the body of my hope.

Even now, at 46 years old, in the evening the drive is not far and before long I take the ball from the space in the backseat of my car and walk out onto the court. I approach the top of the key where I bounce the ball twice before I gather and release a high-arcing jumpshot.

Beside me, Blake Walks Nice sends his jumper into the air and Joe Pretty Paint's follow-through stands like the neck of a swan.

The ball falls from the sky toward the open rim. The sound is a welcome sound.

I breathe and stare at the net, at the ball that comes to rest in the key.

Behind us and to the side only darkness.

An arm of steel extends from the high corner of the building in the schoolyard.

A light burns there.

Professional Wrestling Holds

Ashaki Jackson

"We didn't know anything about a chokehold or hands to the
neck until the video came out," said a former senior police
official with direct knowledge of the investigation. . . . "We
found out when everyone else did."
—*New York Times*, June 13, 2015

An Arm-hook Sleeper an Anaconda
Vise or an Arm Triangle Choke

A *Bay Street Swing* and a *Black
Out* or a Corner Foot Choke
Maybe a *Danny Dance*

Double Choke Dragon sleeper
Figure-Four Necklock We saw
a *Garner Mount* and immediately knew
that move

The Gogoplata sounds ancient like a Guillotine
Choke

Half Nelson Choke or a Hangman's Choke
and Koji Clutch or Leg Choke
Call it a *Last Loosie a New York noose (a Nigger
noose)* and a *Pantaleo Press*

A Pentagram Choke or a Rear Naked Choke
or a Single Arm Choke and a Sleeper
hold

The *Staten Island Squeeze*
and the Straight Jacket or a Three-quarter Nelson

A Thumb Choke Hold a Tongan Death Grip
for assorted Blacks or a Triangle Choke
or a Two-handed Chokelift and
an arena of bystanders

He takes me

Paul Tran

to Colina Del Sol
on Orange Avenue.

We play tennis
on courts
of azure seawater,

a border
between us.

Wind passes through
the net
like a memory.

He serves me.

I pretend
the ball
is a fish

I catch only
to release
back

to the world.
That's why my father
calls me a Sissy Boy,

chugs a six-pack
of Heineken,
Bud Light,

and later,
with his racket,
smashes

my fish tank:
a world inside
the visible world

spills onto the living
room carpet,
the kitchen tile.

Using his racket
as a net, I separate
goldfish from glass,

living from dead.
I try to save them,
each tiny corpse

exposed to the wind,
too much memory
and not enough

water in their lungs:
that's how you die

in the desert.
There's no escaping
Death's cunning

precision.
So I surrender
his implement.

I flush the fish
down the toilet.

I don't wonder
what happens next.
I accept

his sickening definition
of manhood,
his love.

I stand on the other side
of the court, a mirror
image—a child

no longer a child.

I wait
until it's my turn.

The Hit Man

Stacey Waite

I'm a nine-year-old girl. All I can think about is Don Mattingly.
Mattingly was a no frills hitter, something endlessly compelling
about how relaxed he was—his hands loose around the grip
of the bat, his eyes clear and meditative. He never stood still

after hitting a homerun to admire it; he never strutted.
But people still called him "Donnie Baseball"
or sometimes "The Hit Man." I'd watch Yankee games
holding my pee wee Louisville Slugger. I'd mirror him

in the living room—my mother yelling from the kitchen,
"If you swing that bat in the house, I swear to Holy Lord."
I was careful. I'd wait until my mother was a safe distance,
make sure there was no chance of getting caught. Then swing.

I held up the new camcorder to the television to tape
Mattingly's at bats—study them later in slow motion.
But I was not Don Mattingly. At least not until Little League
when Brian's dad says to my dad—loud enough for me to hear,

after I hit a single to right center, rounded first base,
put my hands together for one single Mattingly clap—
he says *she hits like Donnie*. My body lights up in recognition.
I tell Mrs. Sullivan, the school librarian, about my batting average.

"That's pretty impressive, Sir," she says on a day I stayed
to laminate book covers in the back room—a job given
to only the most careful and efficient library aid.
Mrs. Sullivan only called me "sir" in private.

She'd come to the back room and say,
"How many books covered, Sir?"
Or sometimes walk me out to the late bus and say,
"See you tomorrow, Sir."

Sometimes, even now, I dream I marry Mrs. Sullivan.
And I am wearing a tie: the sharpest, simplest tie.
In the dream, I am Donnie, the Hit Man, the kind of man
for whom being a man is nothing special, nothing whole.

Psych Ward Visitation Hour

b: william bearhart

For 7 days and 7 nights, I've been shooting free throws
    The doctor said I needed focus

There is no net because some guy tried hanging himself from it
    But the moonlight betrayed him

In the courtyard where we sit, a dandelion grows
    I see you're uncomfortable. Ignore these

blood-brick walls, cemented ground, nurse station window
    There's forgiveness here. And I need to apologize

You're seeing me in these weed-green scrubs, bone-cloth robe
    I unscrewed the roof from our home
        swallowed all the memories

Did I tell you the cops wrote "superficial cuts" in their report?
    They didn't understand when I said

I needed something red. They didn't understand when I said
    I needed to paint my chest vermillion

I'm scared to go home. Have I told you that?
    I've always been

I keep having a nightmare where my hands grow into copper antlers
    I keep having this nightmare where I hold
        a dandelion in one hand, a robin in the other

I made you something during craft hour. A paint-by-numbers thing
    Two deer in a winter forest full of birch trees
        Look, a tiny spot of orange. Hunter orange

Blaze orange. See the buck? His antlers are still velvet
    See how strong he's standing? No, wait
        his right front leg is soft on the ground. No

He's not standing, he's kneeling. Only,
    He's not kneeling
        He's fallen. Notice

There's only one deer now and he's still
    His tongue juts from the corner of his mouth
        His eyes are focused on me
Wait, his head is missing. The antlers are gone. Everything
    Is gone. There's a bright streak
        of red screaming across the snow

There are only shadows now and boot prints. There's only snow
    I made you something during craft hour
        A cheap paint-by-numbers rip-off of O'Keeffe

A forest of birch trees but the math of it all didn't make sense
    So I painted the numbers blank, then left
        I couldn't focus so I went and shot free throws

I thought about the man who tried hanging himself
    How afraid he must have been about going home
        That dandelion is his ghost. His head

A thousand yellow florets, burning. The sun
    Never felt so good. I'm glad you're here.

The Wars

excerpt from *LaRose*

Louise Erdrich

The Pluto boys were already the Planets, so the Pluto girls had to be the Lady Planets.

Their colors were purple and white. Their mascot was a round planet with legs, arms, a perky face. The reservation team was the Warriors, but the girls weren't the Lady Warriors, they were just the Warriors, also. Their colors were blue and gold. They didn't want to have themselves as a mascot, so they had an old-time shield with two eagle feathers. This was printed on their uniform. The volleyball shirts were close-fitting nylon, long sleeved so that hitting balls on their forearms wouldn't leave them bruised up, though they were covered with bruises anyway. They wore tight shorts and knee pads. Coach Duke made them wear headbands and ponytails because no matter how disciplined they were, girls still got distracted and touched their hair. The girls had come to idolize Coach Duke and his mingy ponytail. The Warriors won every game of the season except their first game with the Pluto Planets. The nights turned colder, colder, and suddenly they were 8-1, with a grudge. Tonight they were playing the Pluto team again and ready to win.

I don't like that they call scores kills, said Nola. Nothing should die.

Peter took her hand. They were crushed into the stands, parent knees in their backs, parent backs against their knees. Nola had packed a small padded cooler with sandwiches. An ice pack slipped into the side kept the sodas stuffed around it cold. She'd even bought green grapes, so expensive this time of year. Peter helped her take her coat off, or lower it anyway. There was no place to put it so she wrapped the puffy sleeves around her waist. The gym was stuffy and there was only one stand, so the parents of the opposing teams had to sit together. They tried to group themselves according to the team they'd come to support, but inadvertently mixed.

The teams warmed up, doing stretches first, then a pepper drill— pass, set, spike, pass, set, spike. Next each player jumped and spiked the ball off the coach's toss. At last, both teams got court time to practice serves. The Warriors' strategy was to look weak to the Pluto team. They would even pretend to argue.

Ravich, hissed Josette. *You awake?*

Invisible wink. Elaborate pout by Maggie. Lots of ball smacking. No smiles at each other. Then the girls lined up.

She's so small, Nola whispered, always struck by the contrast between Maggie and her teammates.

And the Planets are . . . but Peter caught himself.

He was going to say massive or planetary. They were big, solid, formidable girls. Maggie had told them to watch for Braelyn.

I see her, said Nola loudly. The harsh eyeliner!

Peter put his arm around her and spoke, low, in her ear. Remember? The other parents?

Oh! Nola pulled an imaginary zipper across her lips.

Landreaux and Emmaline came in, found a place to sit, wedged in with a group of Warrior parents. The Warriors saluted first the parents, then their coaches, then passed the opposing team fake-touching hands through the net and saying good luck to every Planet. Good luck, good luck, good luck, good fuck, said Braelyn to Maggie with a smile pasted on her face. She passed swiftly, looking straight ahead.

Did you hear it? Did she say it to you too?

Snow had been directly behind Maggie.

Hear what?

Okay, thought Maggie, that was for me. Braelyn knows. Shake it off. Maggie had a little thing she did, a shimmy to get rid of a bad play. It was an almost invisible instantaneous all-over shake. Josette knew about it, though. They made a circle, put their arms around each other. They didn't do the 1-2-3 hands up cheer. They were too tough for that. Diamond was team captain. She looked at each one of them in turn.

We are the one, she said.

They silently rose and put their fingers in the air. Everyone thought they were pointing to Jesus, but it was their special bonding move. Then they roared, jumped, smacked hands.

Josette was first up to serve. She loved the moment when the team slung off its false girly vagueness and became a machine.

Rock that serve, baby! Emmaline's voice was then consumed by the other parent voices.

Josette flew up and bashed it. But a brutal redheaded Planet caught it on one forearm. A mishit, but a setter managed to play it and Braelyn boomed it down the seam. Snow nonchalantly popped it, Diamond set with a precise fingertip pass to Regina, and that was that. Regina could drop the ball on a dime. An actual dime. For fun they had set up shots for her, 20 dimes on the floor. She kept every one she hit, and made two dollars.

A medium blond, pretty, twisted to return Josette's next serve and shanked. So it went. Josette got six serves in before the Planets called time out.

They'll roar back now, said Coach Duke. Maggie you're our secret weapon right now. They haven't tested you. So be ready. Josette, they will try to get your next serve if it kills them, so give 'em heck. Regina, if you get a chance . . .

Don't say it, Coach.

Take a dump, said Diamond.

Let's call it a surprise left hand attack, ok? And everyone, remember, an assist is as good as a kill.

Maggie didn't think so. After each game she totaled her kills on a piece of paper taped to the wall. The scorekeepers added them up too, and if a girl reached 1,000 she got a foot-high golden trophy. Maggie wanted one. She had developed her jump and a delicately accurate sliding tip. The merest tap, never push, a deflection of trajectory that sometimes happened so quickly that it was uncanny. She could score without remembering how the ball came at her.

Sometimes she'd even feel its shadow and think the shadow off her hand onto the floor of the opposing court. When she was occasionally rotated into the hitter's position up front, the other team always wanted to show the tiny girl what. With her slippery, eccentric, high-leap tips, Maggie got to show them what.

Josette's serving surf was upset by the interruption, as the Planets' coach intended, and Maggie felt the energy on the court shift. The Warriors crouched, pep-talking each other, passing around *call it call it call it* so they'd remember to use their voices. Braelyn was at serve. Square-shouldered, chubb-jawed, goth-eyed, she didn't look at Maggie or seem to aim at her, but Maggie was ready anyway. Braelyn got an ace off her. The ball had hesitated, Maggie could swear, and changed direction. Her face burned. But once she knew Braelyn's trick she could handle it. She watched the ball come off the heel of Braelyn's hand this time and saw where it would break. Maggie was there, but the ball wasn't. That was two points. Back to back aces. The Planet parents were shouting. Her parents were tense and silent. Maggie shimmied all over and stepped back into the game.

She kept her eyes on the serve and pried a weak rescue off the floor, something Josette, on her knees, could put into play for Diamond. But the Planets returned the shot and there began a long, bitter, hard-fought, manic volley with miracle saves and unlikely wild hits tamed into dinky wattle-rolling blurps off the top of the net that drove the parents nuts. They leaped up gasping, yelling, but it was friendly pandemonium. By the time Regina finally won a joust with the shorter Planet redhead, everyone was in a good mood. Except the redhead who hissed at Regina, a startling freckled cat. Regina turned away and said, *freaky*. The players bounced into formation and although the Warriors continued their 5–6 point lead they fought hard for it. Luck was with them in close calls, causing a few Planet parents to grumble. The Warriors took the first game. Then the Planets bore down, the luck went their way. So did the second game. The tiebreaker third game was now on.

Most volleyball games were competitive but affable, everyone straining toward good sportsmanship. Coach Duke had even sent home a code of conduct that the player and her parents had to sign. But during the second game there had been hard hits, harder looks, a few jeering yells, smug high fives on points. By the third game, an ugly electricity had infected the gym. Nola knew which parent was for which team. There was no placatory murmur, *nice hit*, when the opposing team scored a point, no friendly banter. Nola had yelled hard but held back her glee, as the Coach's flyer counseled, when the other team faulted. She had tried not to contest line hits. Tried not to call *out* when she thought she knew better than the player where the ball would strike. She had tried, as Coach begged, not to dishonor the game of volleyball.

Nola surreptitiously ate a grape. It was disappointing, with a tough tasteless skin, a watery chemical pulp. She tried another. Maggie didn't always serve, but the coach did not remove her from the line up. There she was, up. The Warriors had lost the first two points. This serve had to stop the Planets' momentum. The pressure! Why Maggie? Peter shouted encouragement, but Nola was silent. She stared hard at her daughter, trying to put her soul and magic that she didn't own into her.

Maggie served into the net. Desolate, her mother threw her hands into her lap like empty gloves.

The Planet parents with the knobby knees in the Ravichs' backs cackled in pleasure. Peter caught Nola as she turned, put his arm around her.

Don't go there, honey, he said into her hair.

The Warriors were relaxed and intent on the next serve. Coach had directed them to breathe from the gut, focus, and high five every play even if it ended in a lost point. His philosophy was based on developing what he called "team mind meld" where each player visualized exactly where her team mates were on the floor and where each player had the power of the whole team inside of her. But Nola only saw that Maggie was now stuck, playing left back. Right in the line of fire. A sob of anxiety caught in Nola's chest. But a buttery warmth now spread across Maggie's shoulders. The coach had signaled them not to worry if they had to sacrifice a point to get Maggie into a position that the Planets didn't know she could play.

Maggie looked so small and vulnerable, with her sylph frame and spindles. She could have been standing on the court alone. She crouched, arms out. The pretty blonde-y Planet served straight to her and Maggie set for Regina's surprise left dump. Point. Next serve, from Snow, the Redhead burned the ball down Maggie's left but Maggie flipped underneath and socked it high. Josette assisted Diamond, who landed a swift spike. Another point. Another. Tie. Braelyn stepped up and this time burned her vixen fury eyes at the center. Maggie's stomach boiled. Braelyn slammed the ball twice on the floor, impassive and stony mad. With a flick of power she sent Maggie her booby trap special. It was supposed to break just over Maggie's head and land behind her, but Maggie knew Braelyn's arm now and with a surge of exuberance lifted off her feet. She swerve-spiked the ball into the donut. Kill.

Nola had been standing the whole time. A parent nudged Peter and he tried to pull her down.

Kill! She screamed into a spot of silence. Kill! Kill! Kill!

Maggie heard it and the butter swirled down around her heart. Peter tightened his arm around Nola's shoulder, whispered in her ear, but she was someplace else. And this, oddly, filled him with relief. Because this was not fake or unreal, there was no hidden meaning. This was the Nola he knew, not the super smiley one. This was the family dynamic, not the manufactured happy family with no aggravation, no anger, no loud voice, no pain allowed. So that when he did feel these things, he, Peter, was alone.

Except that now he was not alone because Nola was going batshit.

Hey shrimp mom, said the woman behind her, sit the hell down.

Nola heard that command with a grape in her cheek. She turned, opened her mouth to give a dignified piece of her mind, and out it flew, exactly like a glob of green snot-spit, landing on the mother's broad pink nose. A shocked pause. The father lifted himself, a squar-ish, bearlike man with sloping shoulders, a walrus mustache, a trucker hat that said, Dakota Sand and Gravel. He put his arms out to shove Nola down, but having perfected her move on Father Travis she leaned forward and popped her breast into his grip. Trucker Hat yelped.

Get your paws off me, shrieked Nola.

Peter saw only the hands. Mrs. Trucker Hat was still wiping grape off her face when Peter let his fist fly. It felt so good to let the rage out, then instant remorse as Trucker Hat bent over, face in hands. Nola, however, went numb with pleasure. The game was stopped and a thin, apprehensive teacher was forced to extract the four parents from the stands. Nola dreamily slid out, clinging tight to Peter's arm. Both failed to see that their daughter had blazed a ball straight at Braelyn as the whistle sounded to stop play. Distracted, Braelyn let down her guard and sustained a facial. Now her nose was bleeding all over the floor.

The coach subbed Maggie out. The Planets, hearts blistering, played with vengeant energy but lost control, faulted, missed easy returns, tried for nasty cut shots without the set up and lost by eight points. The Warriors high fived it and made a subdued exit. It didn't feel exactly good, like a win, it felt like something bigger and darker had just played out.

They didn't know the half of it, thought Maggie, still quiet with joy at the sight of Braelyn's blood on the floor.

When Peter and Nola were escorted out, Landreaux and Emmaline followed. The bearlike father with the sore nose and his wife, built the same and with a sensible Prince Valiant haircut, walked over to their pick up. There was no one in the lot to make sure the parents didn't start another brawl, but the fight was out of Braelyn's parents. And Maggie's parents were embarrassed that the one to escort them out was Maggie's science teacher. Mr. Hossel turned his soul-wounded gaze upon them, gestured helplessly with his red hands, and turned away. Nola was hyperventilating.

What if he takes back her A because of us?

We can bring Maggie back, said Emmaline, if you want to bring Nola home.

No, no, leave me alone, Nola gasped out. But Emmaline didn't step away or change expression. Nola wouldn't get in the car. Mist had frozen in the air and sparkling auras hung from each halogen light, cloaking the cars and frosted windshields and gleaming asphalt with the peace of another world.

Emmaline nodded at the idling pickup. That's the Wildstrands, Braelyn's parents. Mrs. isn't even supposed to go to games. Last year she got suspended. She called Snow a stork.

A stork? Nola blinked.

And Regina. Giraffe, she called her. The girls just laugh now.

She called Maggie a shrimp.

Maggie's got the biggest heart of anyone, said Emmaline.

Before Nola could stop her, Emmaline put her arms around her and then released her so suddenly that the hug was over before Nola could even react.

We should stay here until the girls get to both cars, said Peter. I don't like the way that Braelyn looked when Maggie punched the ball at her.

It wasn't Maggie's fault, said Landreaux. The ref blew the whistle while her hand was in the air.

The four of them stamped and beat their hands together against the cold.

Come on, said Peter, we'll watch from in the cars. He coaxed Nola to him, cajoled her along.

Nola gave Emmaline a long look as she turned away. It was something, the way Emmaline had hugged her. It hadn't felt bad. It hadn't felt good. She didn't know how it had felt. Maybe normal was the way it felt.

Snow and Josette walked Maggie out the gym door. Braelyn passed but they stink-eyed her and she strode to her parents' pickup.

How come she's got it out for you?

She's from my old school. Remember that pencil stab? Her brother's best friend stabbed LaRose and I gave him, you know, the ball kick. Guess they're still mad.

No shit. She was gunning for you.

They watched the pickup, with Braelyn in it, roar from the parking lot.

Oh my God! Holee!

Diamond caught up with them.

You know your dad punched out Braelyn's dad? Your mom spit on Mrs?

You got a badass family, Diamond said.

Maggie jumped into her car's back seat.

Mom? Dad?

Maggie?

Nice game, said Peter.

After Simone Manuel's Olympic Victory in the Women's 100m Freestyle

Lauren Espinoza

At swim practice today my coach calls Simone Manuel's swim
    last night "beast."
I imagine LeBron James's 2008 Vogue cover—"LeBron Kong"—
how easy it is to forget that black men and women have been
    called beasts
for years. But now, when the first African American swimmer
    wins gold for the USA those words echo

again. NBC doesn't air the medal ceremony, thinking instead
    gymnastics is better suited for the audience.
The announcer doesn't understand the implications of this win
    past a tie, a tie for gold
in a country of clear winners or losers, the collective memory of
    water. My grandfather was a lifeguard
at the Mexican pools in South Texas; years later, I became a
    lifeguard at the McAllen Municipal Pool,

but I don't know the history of the water. I don't know how
    many people have shed their skin in the pool,
epithelia left after a close race, a fast swim, a boy pushed down
    too far, too long
by white classmates who later kicked the submerged body as
    they played.
So many drowned brown and black bodies lift Simone Manuel
    to the win—

she drips them on the podium, holding her gold for everyone to see.
My swim coach doesn't remember that African American
      women and men
have had acid thrown on them to force them out of the pool. He
      doesn't remember that our swim group is called a Master's
      team. What it is again to think of beasts.

In the outfield, daydreaming

francine j. harris

The slugs we called caterpillars, some of them larvae, a lot
of them worm, but stuck with good hairs, and stinging at
    things
like the ball I dropped, their pretty heads urticating, their fat
    color
diamond, which settled among critters, parting too, like the
    caterpillar,

the green sea of ants which mounded the outfield and made it
    horizon. I
forget which pitch, which player at bat, whose team I was on,
    the boy
with three braids—running and running for it, and how the
    soft fur
of a body means it's a caterpillar you could hold, and the boy

running from the ball. no, to the ball. because I guess I was
covering my mitt with my shoe, or my knee, or the hairs of my
stomach watching, so the dew was wrapped around my skin,
    and the grass

incredible and wet as a spring green blade, kind of like

a cat's weedy tongue, the way the bumps on the tongue move
things into his belly without my
        help I lean, on both
            feet then, both

ball and sky roll prickly to the grass, it is
        rarely about them. Even

the pitcher is a girl with glasses, who might grow up to send

                thank you cards. Her name
                    a season.

The Meaning of Serena Williams

On Tennis and Black Excellence

Claudia Rankine

There is no more exuberant winner than Serena Williams. She leaps
into the air, she laughs, she grins, she pumps her fist, she points
her index finger to the sky, signaling she's No. 1. Her joy is palpa-
ble. It brings me to my feet, and I grin right back at her, as if I've
won something, too. Perhaps I have.

There is a belief among some African-Americans that to defeat
racism, they have to work harder, be smarter, be better. Only after
they give 150 percent will white Americans recognize black excellence for what it is. But of course, once recognized, black excellence
is then supposed to perform with good manners and forgiveness in
the face of any racist slights or attacks. Black excellence is not supposed to be emotional as it pulls itself together to win after question-
able calls. And in winning, it's not supposed to swagger, to leap and
pump its fist, to state boldly, in the words of Kanye West, "That's
what it is, black excellence, baby."

Imagine you have won 21 Grand Slam singles titles, with only
four losses in your 25 appearances in the finals. Imagine that you've
achieved two "Serena Slams" (four consecutive Slams in a row),
the first more than 10 years ago and the second this year. A win at
this year's U.S. Open would be your fifth and your first calendar-
year Grand Slam—a feat last achieved by Steffi Graf in 1988, when
you were just 6 years old. This win would also break your tie for
the most U.S. Open titles in the Open era, surpassing the legendary Chris Evert, who herself has called you "a phenomenon that
once every hundred years comes around." Imagine that you're the
player John McEnroe recently described as "the greatest player, I
think, that ever lived." Imagine that, despite all this, there were
so many bad calls against you, you were given as one reason video

replay needed to be used on the courts. Imagine that you have to contend with critiques of your body that perpetuate racist notions that black women are hypermasculine and unattractive. Imagine being asked to comment at a news conference before a tournament because the president of the Russian Tennis Federation, Shamil Tarpischev, has described you and your sister as "brothers" who are "scary" to look at. Imagine.

The word "win" finds its roots in both joy and grace. Serena's grace comes because she won't be forced into stillness; she won't accept those racist projections onto her body without speaking back; she won't go gently into the white light of victory. Her excellence doesn't mask the struggle it takes to achieve each win. For black people, there is an unspoken script that demands the humble absorption of racist assaults, no matter the scale, because whites need to believe that it's no big deal. But Serena refuses to keep to that script. Somehow, along the way, she made a decision to be excellent while still being Serena. She would feel what she feels in front of everyone, in response to anyone. At Wimbledon this year, for example, in a match against the home favorite Heather Watson, Serena, interrupted during play by the deafening support of Watson, wagged her index finger at the crowd and said, "Don't try me." She will tell an audience or an official that they are disrespectful or unjust, whether she says, simply, "No, no, no" or something much more forceful, as happened at the U.S. Open in 2009, when she told the lineswoman, "I swear to God I am [expletive] going to take this [expletive] ball and shove it down your [expletive] throat." And in doing so, we actually see her. She shows us her joy, her humor and, yes, her rage. She gives us the whole range of what it is to be human, and there are those who can't bear it, who can't tolerate the humanity of an ordinary extraordinary person.

In the essay "Everybody's Protest Novel," James Baldwin wrote, "our humanity is our burden, our life; we need not battle for it; we need only to do what is infinitely more difficult—that is, accept it." To accept the self, its humanity, is to discard the white racist gaze. Serena has freed herself from it. But that doesn't mean she won't be emotional or hurt by challenges to her humanity. It doesn't mean she won't battle for the right to be excellent. There is nothing wrong with Serena, but surely there is something wrong with the expectation that she be "good" while she is achieving greatness. Why should Serena not respond to racism? In whose world should it be answered with good manners? The notable difference between black excellence and white excellence is white excellence is achieved without having to battle racism. Imagine.

Two years ago, recovering from cancer and to celebrate my 50th birthday, I flew from LAX to JFK during Serena's semifinal match at the U.S. Open with the hope of seeing her play in the final. I had just passed through a year when so much was out of my control, and Serena epitomized not so much winning as the pure drive to win. I couldn't quite shake the feeling (I still can't quite shake it) that my body's frailty, not the cancer but the depth of my exhaustion, had been brought on in part by the constant onslaught of racism, whether something as terrible as the killing of Trayvon Martin or something as mundane as the guy who let the door slam in my face. The daily grind of being rendered invisible, or being attacked, whether physically or verbally, for being visible, wears a body down. Serena's strength and focus in the face of the realities we shared oddly consoled me.

That Sunday in Arthur Ashe Stadium at the women's final, though the crowd generally seemed pro-Serena, the man seated next to me was cheering for the formidable tall blonde Victoria Azarenka. I asked him if he was American. "Yes," he said.

"We're at the U.S. Open. Why are you cheering for the player from Belarus?" I asked.

"Oh, I just want the match to be competitive," he said.

After Serena lost the second set, at the opening of the third, I turned to him again, and asked him, no doubt in my own frustration, why he was still cheering for Azarenka. He didn't answer, as was his prerogative. By the time it was clear that Serena was likely to win, his seat had been vacated. I had to admit to myself that in those moments I needed her to win, not just in the pure sense of a fan supporting her player, but to prove something that could never be proven, because if black excellence could cure us of anything, black people—or rather this black person—would be free from needing Serena to win.

"You don't understand me," Serena Williams said with a hint of impatience in her voice. "I'm just about winning." She and I were facing each other on a sofa in her West Palm Beach home this July. She looked at me with wariness as if to say, Not you, too. I wanted to talk about the tennis records that she is presently positioned either to tie or to break and had tried more than once to steer the conversation toward them. But she was clear: "It's not about getting 22 Grand Slams," she insisted. Before winning a calendar-year Grand Slam and matching Steffi Graf's record of 22 Slams, Serena would have to win seven matches and defend her U.S. Open title; those were the victories that she was thinking about.

She was wearing an enviable pink jumpsuit with palm trees stamped all over it as if to reflect the trees surrounding her estate. It was a badass outfit, one only someone of her height and figure could rock. She explained to me that she learned not to look ahead too much by looking ahead. As she approached 18 Grand Slam wins in 2014, she said, "I went too crazy. I felt I had to even up with Chris Evert and Martina Navratilova." Instead, she didn't make it past the fourth round at the Australian Open, the second at the French Open or the third at Wimbledon. She tried to change her tactics and focused on getting only to the quarterfinals of the U.S. Open. Make it to the second week and see what happens, she thought. "I started thinking like that, and then I got to 19. Actually I got to 21 just like that, so I'm not thinking about 22." She raised her water bottle to her lips, looking at me over its edge, as if to give me time to think of a different line of questioning.

Three years ago she partnered with the French tennis coach Patrick Mouratoglou, and I've wondered if his coaching has been an antidote to negotiating American racism, a dynamic that informed the coaching of her father, Richard Williams. He didn't want its presence to prevent her and Venus from winning. In his autobiography,

"Black and White: The Way I See It," he describes toughening the girls' "skin" by bringing "busloads of kids from the local schools into Compton to surround the courts while Venus and Serena practiced. I had the kids call them every curse word in the English language, including 'Nigger,'" he writes. "I paid them to do it and told them to 'do their worst.'" His focus on racism meant that the sisters were engaged in two battles on and off the court. That level of vigilance, I know from my own life, can drain you. It's easier to shut up and pretend it's not happening, as the bitterness and stress build up.

Mouratoglou shifted Serena's focus to records (even if, as she prepares for a Slam, she says she can't allow herself to think about them). Perhaps it's not surprising that she broke her boycott against Indian Wells, where the audience notoriously booed her with racial epithets in 2001, during their partnership. Serena's decisions now seem directed toward building her legacy. Mouratoglou has insisted that she can get to 24 Grand Slams, which is the most won by a single player—Margaret Court—to date. Serena laughed as she recalled one of her earliest conversations with Mouratoglou. She told him: "I'm cool. I want to play tennis. I hate to lose. I want to win. But I don't have numbers in my head." He wouldn't allow that. "Now we are getting numbers in your head," he told her.

I asked how winning felt for her. I was imagining winning as a free space, one where the unconscious racist shenanigans of umpires, or the narratives about her body, her "unnatural" power, her perceived crassness no longer mattered. Unless racism destroyed the moment of winning so completely, as it did at Indian Wells, I thought it had to be the rare space free of all the stresses of black life. But Serena made it clear that she doesn't desire to dissociate from her history and her culture. She understands that even when she's focused only on winning, she is still representing. "I play for me," Serena told me, "but I also play and represent something much greater than me. I embrace that. I love that. I want that. So ultimately, when I am out there on the court, I am playing for me."

Her next possible victory is at the U.S. Open, the major where she has been involved in the most drama—everything from outrageous line calls to probations and fines. Serena admitted to losing her cool in the face of some of what has gone down there. In 2011, for example, a chair umpire, Eva Asderaki, ruled against Serena for yelling "Come on" before a point was completed, and as Serena described it to me, she "clutched her pearls" and told Asderaki not to look at her. But she said in recent years she finally felt embraced by the crowd. "No more incidents?" I asked. Before she could answer, we both laughed, because of course it's not wholly in her control. Then suddenly Serena stopped. "I don't want any incidents there," she said. "But I'm always going to be myself. If anything happens, I'm always going to be myself, true to myself."

I'm counting on it, I thought. Because just as important to me as her victories is her willingness to be an emotionally complete person while also being black. She wins, yes, but she also loses it. She jokes around, gets angry, is frustrated or joyous, and on and on. She is fearlessly on the side of Serena, in a culture that has responded to living while black with death.

This July, the London School of Marketing (LSM) released its list of the most marketable sports stars, which included only two women in its Top 20: Maria Sharapova and Serena Williams. They were ranked 12th and 20th. Despite decisively trailing Serena on the tennis court (Serena leads in their head-to-head matchups 18–2, and has 21 majors and 247 weeks at No. 1 to Sharapova's five majors and 21 weeks at number 1), Sharapova has a financial advantage off the court. This month *Forbes* listed her as the highest-paid female athlete, worth more than $29 million to Serena's $24 million.

When I asked Chris Evert about the LSM list, she said, "I think the corporate world still loves the good-looking blond girls." It's a preference Evert benefited from in her own illustrious career. I suggested that this had to do with race. Serena, on occasion, has herself been a blonde. But of course, for millions of consumers, possibly not the right kind of blonde. "Maria was very aware of business and becoming a businesswoman at a much younger stage," Evert told me, adding, "She works hard." She also suggested that any demonstration of corporate preference is about a certain "type" of look or image, not whiteness in general. When I asked Evert what she made of Eugenie Bouchard, the tall, blond Canadian who has yet to really distinguish herself in the sport, being named the world's most marketable athlete by the British magazine *SportsPro* this spring, she said, with a laugh, "Well, there you have it." I took her statement to be perhaps a moment of agreement that Serena probably could not work her way to Sharapova's spot on *Forbes*'s list.

"If they want to market someone who is white and blond, that's their choice," Serena told me when I asked her about her ranking. Her impatience had returned, but I wasn't sure if it was with me, the list or both. "I have a lot of partners who are very happy to work with me." JPMorgan Chase, Wilson Sporting Goods, Pepsi and Nike are among the partners she was referring to. "I can't sit here and say I should be higher on the list because I have won more." As for Sharapova, her nonrival rival, Serena was diplomatic: "I'm happy for her, because she worked hard, too. There is enough at the table for everyone."

There is another, perhaps more important, discussion to be had about what it means to be chosen by global corporations. It has to do with who is worthy, who is desirable, who is associated with the good life. As long as the white imagination markets itself by equating whiteness and blondness with aspirational living, stereotypes will remain fixed in place. Even though Serena is the best, even though she wins more Slams than anyone else, she is only superficially allowed to embody that in our culture, at least the marketable one.

But Serena was less interested in the ramifications involved in being chosen, since she had no power in this arena, and more interested in understanding her role in relation to those who came before her: "We have to be thankful, and we also have to be positive about it so the next black person can be No. 1 on that list," she told me. "Maybe it was not meant to be me. Maybe it's meant to be the next person to be amazing, and I'm just opening the door. Zina Garrison, Althea Gibson, Arthur Ashe and Venus opened so many doors for me. I'm just opening the next door for the next person."

I was moved by Serena's positioning herself in relation to other African-Americans. A crucial component of white privilege is the idea that your accomplishments can be, have been, achieved on your own. The private clubs that housed the tennis courts remained closed to minorities well into the second half of the 20th century. Serena reminded me that in addition to being a phenomenon, she has come out of a long line of African-Americans who battled for the right to be excellent in a such a space that attached its value to its whiteness and worked overtime to keep it segregated.

Serena's excellence comes with the ability to imagine herself achieving a new kind of history for all of us. As long as she remains healthy, she will most likely tie and eventually pass Graf's 22 majors, regardless of what happens at the U.S. Open this year. I want Serena to win, but I know better than to think her winning can end something she didn't start. But Serena is providing a new script, one in which winning doesn't carry the burden of curing racism, in which we win just to win—knowing that it is simply her excellence, baby.

Serena Williams Walks

Kwame Dawes

The crip walk, the quick shuffle of feet,
the pure, homegrown joy of it, a last release,
after the weight of your presence, the force

of each breath rushing into your body,
a sling-shot of power, efficient, precise,
alert to the ticking brain, calculating,

testing, timing, then commanding the arm
to obey, the legs to obey, the thighs
to obey, the ball to obey—a yellow

minion darting over grass and clay,
leaving that hapless body on the other side,
inert, ordinary, as if she too has come

to witness this, and has waited for this,
like she had to wait for you to do your business
since you calculated that seventy minutes

would be too long to hold it, though enough
to turn a game into a rout, to remind us
of the quiet, stare reserved for the few

who can stare with disdain at all who deign
to enter a room where you reign—no smile,
no scowl, just the cool conviction of power.

This is not poetry—for poetry is a fickle art,
and no poet will command a world with the
incontrovertible claim of dominance

like a racket wielded, a score counted,
a foe defeated so thoroughly, so irrevocably—
this is poetry in a world where the poem

speaks a language of prophetic grace
and only fools will question the weight
of truth in the calculus of muscle and bone;

but that dance, that gleeful dance, kicking
up the Wimbledon dust, that Compton,
step, that hip-hop bravado, now there is the poem,

the sweet laughter of a child arriving
at the place she has dreamt of for years—
and all we can do is shake a leg and dance.

Boxing Out

Adrian Matejka

I never had hops, so I got on at Bertha Ross Park the same way
I kept my spot on the middle school squad: immaculately
free-throwing with follow through, flicked wrist left hanging

for the imaginary game winner when *winner* meant *fly girlfriend*
instead of sulking solo in the gym corner like I was back
at the Spring Formal as one slow jam after another played

for the couples-only dance. At Bertha Ross, we bunched into
our pickup corners, right in front of a white construction worker
who said, *Gerry Cooney will put that big nigger in his place*

to no one while chewing a ham sandwich down to the red rinds.
We all heard him say it between warm-up behind-the-back
dribbles & almost-raindropped jumpers, but acted like we didn't.

& we almost won the game anyway until somebody's drunk
uncle in a Peaches & Herb shirt called one of those old-man fouls.
But Cooney didn't beat Holmes. He didn't even come close.

Summertime

Joel Salcido

Whereas many were told go home before the streetlights came
    to life—and listened,
you didn't. You perfected your footwork, shot jumpers in the
    dark, the park's quiet
fogged by the buzz of cicadas heckling your steps, a crowd
    cheering you to miss.

You miss how those summers never slept or yawned, but
    stretched through dusk. Dawn
heat rolling deeper than gangs. Heat you can't cool with what's
    tucked in your waist,
heat hovering like ghetto birds, on corners peddling itself,
    staring down cop cars.

In those sweating evenings walking home on Roosevelt you
    learned how to cope—
discovered a compass to navigate sidewalks, sidestep shadows,
    dance in fading light.
You learned dark was cover for black Regals with illegal tint
    cruising local dope

kings to collect tribute from vibrant villagers. Where the flash
    of banners meant fire
might brighten up the dim like torches. You took cover too—
    shawled walls, slapped
concrete, slid on D. You were grown enough to pull those short
    nights

like a blanket, to wrap yourself in the promise that sunrise
would bring you home,
greet you with warmth, no matter what you did while it
slept—alone on the avenue.

Aaron Hernandez is my brother

Randall J. Tyrone

Dear Mom, i've lied here since 2:30 a.m. Wednesday. i need to
    continue. i don't need to see
the Super Bowl anymore
now. i am the last child you have.
          i don't know when it will be time to go outside again

between those 100 yards wrapped in air
that's a lighter fluid weighted blanket
In the Sun you can hit the temperature
where souls burn Coach is waiting to see
whom are flares & whom are stars Like my brother
on our MLK corner for the neighborhood
where blood washes clean Through the in-zone
i see our church i'm trying to rep
for the neighborhood Coach side line speaks to me
"Did you fumble or were you down? It's a turnover
no matter what." how much blame do i want?
i want all that is mine

The Church of Michael Jordan

Jeffrey McDaniel

The hoop is not metal, but a pair of outstretched arms,
God's arms, joined at the fingers. And God is saying

throw it to me. It's not a ball anymore. It's an orange prayer
I'm offering with all four chambers. And the other players—

the Pollack of limbs, flashing hands and teeth—
are just temptations, obstacles between me and salvation.

Once during an interview I slipped, *I didn't pray well tonight*,
and the reporter looked at me, the same one who'd called me

a player of destiny, and said *you mean play, right?* Of course,
I nodded. Don't misunderstand—I'm no reverend

of the body. Priests embarrass me. A real priest
wouldn't put on that robe, wouldn't need the public

affirmation. A real priest works in disguise, leads
by example, preaches with his feet. Yes, Jesus walked on water,

but how about a staircase of air? And when the clock
is down to its final ticks, a real priest rises up and over the palms

of a nonbeliever—the whole world watching, thinking
it can't be done—I let the faith roll off my fingertips, the ball

drunk with backspin, a whole stadium of people holding
the same breath, the net flying up like a curtain,

the lord's truth visible for an instant, converting nonbelievers
by the bushel, who will swear for years they witnessed a miracle.

Built For It

Lisa Olstein

Maybe age or some other slow cooling
of the limbs one day will will me
from the water, from this desire to
plunge my body in. I tried hot yoga once,
once, winks the fireman on the park bench
overlooking the sea. To be honest, he says,
it felt like wearing full gear in a house fire.
You should try Bikram, says the mother
in workout clothes taking a sticker for her kid.
Whose motives are ever pure? Let's face it,
tennis is mostly about the outfits even if
it is what taught me how to go for the other
girl's jugular, that I should, even with her
daddy watching. Want rings out in the house
of the self and in the self the self must live.
It's Friday morning and I know what I'm doing
here, but what's everyone else's excuse?
There's everything and nothing to want
from the sea, the sea who does not answer.
Complete refusal transforms itself
into a kind of total acceptance, at least
so it seems because one way or another
our voices travel away from us and this is
a relief. Code Red, the children scream
every time they spy a crab. Dozens of men
are killed, says the paper and their wives
are kept for single soldiers of the day's conquering.
Killed, we say, if a war zone. Kept, we say,
if a woman. Love-love we say when the score is
zero. Irrelevant, says the sea into which
everything we throw away ends up, words.

Federer as Irreligious Experience

Porochista Khakpour

In 2006 David Foster Wallace opened his much celebrated *New York Times Magazine* essay "Federer as Religious Experience" with "Almost anyone who loves tennis and follows the men's tour on television has, over the last few years, had what might be termed Federer Moments. These are times, as you watch the young Swiss play, when the jaw drops and eyes protrude and sounds are made that bring spouses in from other rooms to see if you're O.K." In 2015 we still have the Moments but there is now a different type of Moment to reflect on, one that Wallace never lived to see—namely Roger Federer in decline, a sort of half-decline, an uncommitted decline, the sort of decline that makes you question what a decline is really anyway, perhaps a decline that is inevitable for all greats, unless of course, like Wallace, they cut their own game short. Wallace lived only two years past that essay—just over a half year after the August 2006 piece came out, Wallace would get sick after a meal at local Claremont, California, Persian restaurant Darvish, and decide to discontinue the antidepressant Nardil that he'd been on for most his adult life, a decision that would spur his terminal battle with the depression—and so it is hard to imagine the same author of the canonical sports piece being just months away from his own downfall, at a time when Federer's fall was also inconceivable. By the time Wallace actually hung himself on his patio, Federer was no longer at the top of his game, but as time has proven, not quite at the bottom either. I didn't read the piece until a year after it was out—in the summer of 2006, I was in a terrible struggle with depression and was planning on killing myself by the autumn, while just months before, somehow spared from this very abrupt turn of mental health, I often schemed to stalk my favorite writer Wallace at Pomona College, where he taught and where my father also taught. I had eaten at that exact Persian restaurant months before, but by the end of the summer, I was far from thinking Wallace, Pomona, *New York Times*, Federer, tennis, Moments.

In 2006 Wallace wrote that Federer was "at 25, the best tennis player currently alive." We could still say this: seventeen grand slam singles, 302 total weeks on top of world rankings (No. 1 in the world from 2004 into 2008, and again in parts of 2009, 2010, and 2012) are hard to be casual about. It's been mostly uphill since Wimbledon in 1998 when he went pro at seventeen—he had already had his first sponsorship at sixteen—and then in 2001, a still-teenage Federer knocked out reigning singles champion Pete Sampras in the fourth round, prompting the *Sport Illustrated* headline coronation: "Changing of Guard." And since then indeed he has been a giant to pretty much everyone; James Blake: "If you poll the top 500 tennis guys in the world, about 499 are going to say Roger. The only one who won't is Roger himself because he's too nice about it"; Tracy Austin: "Roger can produce tennis shots that should be declared illegal"; Andy Roddick: "Yeah basically nobody stands a chance against him"; Nick Boll: "He moves like a whisper and executes like a wrecking ball. It is simply impossible to explain how he does what he does"; Serena Williams: "The guy is the greatest male athlete of all time"; Sampras: "Roger is the best player in the world"; Boris Becker: "We have a guy from Switzerland who is just playing the game in a way I haven't seen anyone—and I mean anyone—play before"; Andy Murray: "I can cry like Roger, it's just a shame I can't play like him"; even his greatest rival Novak Djokovic: "I don't think that you can always—you can ever—get your game to perfection, you know. Only if you're Federer." Just last week, July 2015, John McEnroe clarified a previous statement, in which he claimed Nadal was the best tennis player of all time: "If I had to pick one person, I'd pick Roger. Generally, I put Nadal as the greatest clay court player, I put Roger all-around, I put Pete Sampras the greatest grass court player, and Rod Laver was my idol. Those would be the top four. But I think Roger is the best all-around. He's the most beautiful player I've ever seen. While he has a losing record against [Nadal], he's been so consistent, has DiMaggio-like records, incredible streaks like 22 semis in a row. . . . Roger, he can do everything, and makes it look easy. That's always the first step of a great player." Wallace himself had followed up his first sentence declaring he's the best alive with "maybe the best ever," and it's a sentiment so common now that it's nearly mundane to profess it.

Even I have said this, and you could barely call me the greatest sports enthusiast, as I'm just someone with an eight-year history of interest in one sport: tennis. This whole interest came in 2007 because of the very essay I'm focusing on here; once I had crawled out of that debilitating depression, I had somehow stumbled upon Wallace's Federer ode and become not just any sports enthusiast but a specific one: a tennis fan. And not just any fan, but a Federer obsessive, all thanks to Wallace, who had already been my favorite writer for many years. His seduction by Federer was contagious, and I read and reread the more than 6,500-word essay over and over.

But it wasn't completely accidental: the truth was I'd taken tennis fifteen years before that, in my teens, at a local organization, hoping to join the school's tennis team. I wanted to be good at tennis for some reason. For two summers at a local park I struggled along with my backhands and volleys with my Prince racket, all to quit by my own free will at age fifteen, never to play again. The reason was the teacher, whose name I can no longer remember, but whose name was, back then, etched in my heart; I had developed such an intense crush on him that I could no longer continue the classes, I had decided. I pretended to my parents that I had heard taking tennis could cause deformities in the arms and that some-how worked on them, though they were no doubt happy to save the money on the expensive lessons. And all I was left with—I had little skill in the game—was the memory of that teacher, proba-bly only in his late twenties, his shock of bleached blond hair and overly tan physique—a sort of Midwestern Agassi. From then on I casually watched the game on the television, here and there, as I did with swimming and ice skating and gymnastics and ballet—all sports that I had taken up at some point in my adolescence and abandoned for various reasons, probably none of them very good.

But it wasn't until the summer of 2007 when I'd encountered the year-old Wallace piece, that I became obsessed with not just following men's tennis but Federer specifically, so grateful to that favorite writer of mine, who unbeknownst to me, at that very moment, was disintegrating rapidly just twenty-seven miles away in my hometown of Pasadena.

*

Wallace wrote in the middle of his essay: "This present article is more about a spectator's experience of Federer, and its context. The specific thesis here is that if you've never seen the young man play live, and then do, in person, on the sacred grass of Wimbledon, through the literally withering heat and then wind and rain of the '06 fortnight, then you are apt to have what one of the tournament's press bus drivers describes as a 'bloody near-religious experience.'" Two greats at the end of their best runs merging at a paper at the end of its best run too, it can be argued. Wallace after all wrote the piece in what could be called to this day Federer's best year, in which he had twelve singles titles and a 92-5 match record, in which he got into sixteen out of seventeen tournaments that season.

Over the past few years I've constantly contemplated writing this very essay, the essay of Federer in descent against Wallace's Federer in ascent, the essay in a world without Wallace. At one point in the middle of the essay Wallace attempts to summarize the personal life highlights of Federer's bio, but today there seems so much missing. Wallace never lived to see Federer the Husband or Federer the Father, which happened—one would have to and in fact need to assume coincidentally only—to correspond with Federer's Fall. Less than a year after Wallace's death in September of 2008, Federer married the former tennis player Mirka Vavrinec, and just three months later she gave birth to twins. It would be his first but not last set of twins, as in 2014 they'd welcome another duo. Even these seem to be Federer miracles: two twin girls Myla Rose and Charlene Riva, followed just five years later with two twin boys Leo and Lennart. It's also unclear how much Wallace could have known that 2008 was Federer's most physically precarious year—just as it was Wallace's—with Federer's bout with mono tainting the first half of 2008, followed by what plagued the end of that same year, a back injury that would never quite go away.

In Wallace's piece his "kinetic beauty" is emphasized, which, he writes, has "nothing to do with sex or cultural norms. What it seems to have to do with, really, is human beings' reconciliation with the fact of having a body." Wallace dissects a Federer-Nadal match for his example, but when I think of beauty and my own Federer Moment, it's not quite on the court but just barely off it, and it also involves Nadal, the original thorn in his side before Djokovic. By the time Wallace had died Nadal had already crushed Federer more than once, but he never lived to see what I'd classify as the most beautiful moment of the Federer decline, "Federer as sacrilegious experience," maybe one could say.

*

It's the 2009 Australian Open, where Federer lost to Nadal in the final. Federer needed just one victory to match Pete Sampras's career record of 14 Grand Slam singles titles but as well as he played, ultimately Rafael "Rafa" Nadal, the Spanish sensation five years his junior, destroyed him. In the postmatch ceremony, Federer got his runner-up plate from one of his idols, Rod Laver, and was positioned at the microphone to speak to the fans, who were lost in overwhelming cheers.

In his blue shirt with the signature white Nike swoosh—Nike had signed a 130-million-dollar ten-year endorsement deal with him just months before—he looks for a moment like he can do this, a man who has been here before. One male voice bellows "I love you, Federer!" and Federer nods and half-waves in acknowledgment, looking a bit embarrassed as if undeserving. He breathes hard and audibly, the half-whistle/blow/near-moan of someone who has been through an unthinkable physical ordeal, the sound of frustration and disappointment, with just a tinge of relief. He shakes his head, looks up and down away from fans and the prize.

"Maybe I'll try again later, I don't know," he begins, with his usual cool smile. But then he breaks character and blurts, "God it's killing me," with a loose fist to his head, eyes closed, and as he looks down, still at the microphone, one can see heaving. The camera pans to Mirka who, like everyone, looks on in total disbelief, an icy horror maybe even, and you get the feeling even she has rarely seen him break like this—her hand is at her face, her eyes on him, as all around people cheer. This is a Moment for sure, for everyone there, a god of our time revealing himself as flesh. The camera goes to Nadal, who is clapping slowly but firmly, and looking embarrassed, almost regretful, like a small boy suddenly, not the ruthless competitor just moments ago pushing Federer around on the court. The Moment feels like forever as Federer raises his hand to his eyes and eventually looks up revealing a red and wet face, his body still in heaves. Eventually, only eventually, he is helped to back away. Nadal, clapping onward. Federer, crying still, looking up once in a while at his audience, not hiding behind his grief, as if the Moment itself has taught him that is what courage is, to break character in front of the whole world, to let his most private self come out, the only way to overshadow the victory of the game without even trying. Mirka, still with hand on face; Nadal, still clapping, a bit red now; Federer, crying and crying.

Suddenly the four hours and twenty-three minutes that was the match seem to disappear in the nearly five minutes when Roger Federer broke down before the world.

The tournament director eventually steps up the microphone, shaken himself, and says, "Let's give Roger a moment to settle down."

Federer is turning twenty-eight. The average tennis pro peaks at twenty-three.

In the end Federer still won this one, his display of emotion mythic, what I would classify as one of his most beautiful Moments, in its rareness, in its lack of control—that control that has defined him his whole career—in its intimacy, in its honesty and vulnerability. We love the boastful, unflappable, brash Federer who never seems to blink, but his final words that day, like his sobbing, also felt special in their overwhelming humanity: "I don't want to have the last word; this guy deserves it. So, Rafa, congratulations. You played incredible. You deserve it, man."

*

In an interview with Charlie Rose, David Foster Wallace talks about his own tennis days—saying that he was "good, [but] not even very good." At age fourteen, he was ranked seventeenth in the US Tennis Association's Western Section (Illinois, Indiana, Ohio, Michigan, most of Wisconsin, and West Virginia). He also appears to have been ranked second in his USTA district in central Illinois. But by eighteen, he was no longer ranked in his section. We have only Wallace's 1996 magnum opus—his 577,608-word word debut novel *Infinite Jest*, centered on the junior tennis academy, Enfield Tennis Academy—as evidence of his past life.

And of course, the 2006 essay. Apparently Wallace had taken a lot of pains for what would become a number-one-forwarded sports story of 2006, a cover in *PLAY* magazine—the short-lived sports supplement to the *New York Times Magazine*. On a notebook page with the heading "R. Federer Interview Qs" he had a subhead: "Non-Journalist Questions" against the final "Qs the Editors want me to ask [w/Apologies]." He had even mapped out his trademark self-deprecating preface: "I'm not a journalist—I'm more like a novelist with a tennis background." Initially, ESPN's David Higdon reported that Federer found the "questions were inane, the dude weird, and the whole exercise a complete waste of his time," but several years later Federer said "I had a funny feeling walking out of the interview. I wasn't sure what was going to come out of it because I didn't know exactly what direction he was going to go. The piece was obviously fantastic." Federer was again asked about it in 2013, during an Ask Me Anything (AMA) session on the social media platform Reddit, and he wrote "The thing that struck me is that I only spent 20 min with him in the ATP office at Wimbledon, and he was able to produce such a comprehensive piece."

Online you can find many who are obsessed with the Wallace story—and his intersection with Federer—which tells me its influence on my interest in tennis might not be exceptional at all. Some go quite far—I find one bizarrely titled "Roger Federer Killed David Foster Wallace" by "anaesthetica" posted on Saturday, August 22, 2009, at 02:16:46 AM EST. "What did DFW choose to see, to consciously give meaning, to worship? Tennis. More specifically, it was *Federer as Religious Experience*. And it was Rog who ate him alive," it says and goes on to wilder leaps: "DFW imagines Federer as a gnostic Christ, the avatar of God on earth, a *Neo*-like savior with the ability to transcend the constraints of the material world, to return living flesh to the dead." The final section of the episodic post is titled "When God Died" and concludes, "DFW committed *suicide by hanging* himself in September 2008. It is no coincidence that *2008 was a disastrous year for Federer*. . . . Federer would win the US Open on September 13th, but it was likely too late for redemption. God's immanence on Earth had been retracted, the age of miracles was over. DFW was found hung the next day."

*

In 2006 when I was in the throes of the darkest depression of my life—my first stint with agitated depression, still many years from the diagnosis of late-stage Lyme, which was at the root of all my mental health difficulties—there was one thing I could not get myself to do: cry. It was nearly impossible for me. Occasionally I would be close—I'd almost get to an edge and then something would make me withdraw. It was almost as if I'd forgotten how. Only months later when I was mostly recovered did I go back to crying, and almost as if to make up for those many months without tears, I cried and cried and cried, not so much for myself in the present but for that near past that I'd suffered under silently.

Years later stints of depression came and went, and I could never quite find its triggers except that it had to do with fear and unreasonable expectations and perfectionism. And those issues always made crying a sort of stranger—does one let it in or keep it at a distance?

I often think of Federer's moment of release in front of the whole world. Not how hard it must have been for him but how easy. It seemed remarkably natural. Like his game, it went on and on, felt like an eternity, like he'd found his element: a grieving man, an inconsolable man, a broken man. As if for once, he was able to shed that perfectionism and just be a human, a man.

Not someone perfect. Not a god.

Not a religious experience.

Federer as *irreligious* experience, one could say, at his best.

Perfectionism has always been one of my oldest and most lethal struggles—a competition not with anyone else but with myself. I see this with Federer, of course, and I see it with David Foster Wallace.

Who knew better. Wallace: "The perfectionism is very dangerous, because of course if your fidelity to perfectionism is too high, you never do anything." So many have said of his death that his final book was more a catalyst that the antidepressant-cessation—the possibility that his best writing years were behind him.

Which is the very reality that Roger Federer, still in 2015 on the court, lives with every day. And so this is what kills—when you read that essay, the very thing he valorizes, canonizes, casts Federer in pure gold for, is a fallacy: the perfect, what can be most optimally classified as a religious experience. It wouldn't kill Federer but himself, and sooner than he'd know.

*

In our time, Federer the best and Federer the unbeatable has been anything but: second and third even, and beatable by Djokovic, Murray, and Nadal, as well as lesser players like del Potro, Berdych, Tsonga, and Nalbandian.

Brian Phillips, who has tracked Federer's rise and fall, in Grantland wrote in 2011, "Now, in 2011, in his endless middle-sunset as a player, Federer has become something mysterious, an all-time great whose career feels increasingly fragile," but in 2014 he countered his own claim. He wrote the "best athletes usually have a 'still' phase. First they're fast. Then they're slow. In between, there's a moment when they're 'still' fast—when you can see the end coming but can't deny that, for now, they remain close to their best. Federer, I wrote, had spent longer in that 'still' phase than any great tennis player I could think of. Again: *That was in 2011.* Four years later, he's still there. In fact, he's ranked *higher*. His period of epoch-conquering dominance is years in the past, but he's still a reliable top-five player, one who can compete for majors if the circumstances are right."

In 2015, after a loss at Indian Wells, it almost felt as if the rough years might still be here, but Federer's attitude had changed. He was never near tears. He could no longer take defeats seriously it seemed. He had weathered even the Vulnerable Moments—or Moment—and now he was in a phase of pragmatism, acceptance with aging and his past, present, and future, and his place in professional tennis. As whispers of retirement come in and out of the game—his 2014 racket-change decision seemed to indicate he was realizing he had to change something to stay in the game—Federer still played like someone who'd never heard anything of it. This is not the Federer crying before an audience, when he says of his loss to Djokovic at Indian Wells, "I'm not going to look back on that match, on that moment very long. That will be forgotten probably in 25 minutes or so." In its own way, even as it opposes the fragility of his Crying Moment completely, it is startlingly beautiful. Time is not just passing him, he nearly hints, but all of us. What use is it to think in terms of forever? Everything will be forgotten, even the apparently unforgettable.

Andy Roddick once said he would continue to play as long as he felt he could play "relevant tennis." Two months later, at the age of thirty, in 2012, he retired. At his announcement he denied his age had anything to do with it: "I think wear and tear and miles is something that's not really an age thing. If you look at my contemporaries that started with me, Roger is the only one that's still going and still going strong."

And here we are, this Moment: Federer inspires other tennis players and then by turn another tennis player, a lesser one, who becomes a writer, and writes an homage that inspires another once-tennis-player (just two summers), another writer (definitely a lesser one), who writes an homage to the homage.

And if I warn that within this is a cautionary tale about perfection—not ultimately Federer's whose greatest brilliance might be in his survival without the thing we all defined him as: *perfect*—one can't deny the value in the momentary seduction of a sort of celestiality from Federer's racket to Wallace's pen: "Genius is not replicable. Inspiration, though, is contagious, and multiform—and even just to see, close up, power and aggression made vulnerable to beauty is to feel inspired and (in a fleeting, mortal way) reconciled."

prayer when knees give

Nate Marshall

for Derrick Rose

if i should ever have made it
to fame as a basketball player
jumping reckless toward an orange sky
then i would have hoped to explode
on to the scene like a shell casing,
or like a newly minted hit record,
or like an ACL buckling
under the pressure of everyone.

if the good Lord had made me
the one to put the city on
my back like intersecting
beams of oak i would have run
like it was for every life
including my own small, selfish one.

if they ever named me Rose, or thing
that grows from the dying forest, or boy
who shouldn't be, or statistical outlier
then i would praise the brevity of a star's
life in the scheme, knowing that it exists
even if nobody names it and only encounters
it as a black hole.

Days of '95 II

Shane Lake

I know I'm supposed to love Larry Bird,
    Laettner and Stockton and Mullin and Price,
        but when I played ball with the neighborhood kids

we never pretended to be the white guy
    because we already were the white guys
        wearing replica jerseys our frames couldn't fill,

chucking up shots in the Jones's driveway
    with Bone Thugs-N-Harmony radio edits
        blasting from a boombox clean as our sneakers.

We would have given anything
    for a CD with the Parental Advisory sticker,
        six more inches on our vertical, or a wicked

jump shot that lit nets blazing like NBA JAM,
    because we did not know what it was to give,
        had no concept of going without

aside from what we heard in songs.
    Too scared to say what we really wanted,
        too dumb to see what we already had,

we drained summer afternoons playing
    pickup games of 3-on-3, imagined
        ourselves in other bodies, used their names

like rappers adopting new personas,
    the superhero monikers they claim.
        Instead of Ghostface Killah

taking Tony Starks, we had Tommy
        as Latrell Sprewell, Luke as MJ,
            and me as Penny Hardaway,

an all-star squad of counterfeit cool
        who all talked shit like Gary Payton
            and lowered the hoop to dunk like Kemp

until short Eric broke his pinky on the rim,
        short Eric who yelled "Ball don't lie!" on every miss
            not having ever stepped on any playground

where those words first burst like chilly water
        from a busted city fire hydrant
            on a June day. We all said it,

as if blackness was something you could borrow
        like sugar from a neighbor's kitchen,
            as if blackness could be held in a single cup.

We played through Tommy's mom's voice calling and
        pulling him home, played through our dinners,
            played until the sun went down and threw its light

like a no-look pass to the spot-up moon,
        that same moon shining over city parks alive
            beneath its marquee glow, the moon we knew as much about

as all we stole, and closer to it too.

Baseball

Izzy Wasserstein

A love carved across my face,
a scar above my left eye
where the bat split skin from bone.
A clean blow, nothing like the jagged map
the nurse's needle made in closing it.
I was the only kid at the Topeka Public Library
asking for books about the Black Sox Scandal,
begging the other kids to grab bats
when they preferred football.
Like the oversize glasses I wore,
I'd been lifted from another era.
My family didn't own a television,
so I'd lay awake at night listening
to Fred and Denny call the games
on the radio. In the dark, I could smell
the wet grass, chalk, and dust,
see the pitcher framed by floodlights.
I loved baseball as I rarely loved anything else,
loved baseball even when it did not love me back.

After the impact, my friends stood over me,
their summer-dark faces blanched.
That night I dreamed I was stepping to the plate.

To Prevent Hypothermia

Fatimah Asghar

after the race my teammates
kicked the boys off the bus
& into the downpour

blocked the windows
with their sweatshirts
peeled the wet clothes

from my skin, each inch
matted-down
disobedient, hair plastered

to my brown legs.
it took two hungry girls

to remove the spandex

from my paling thighs
their blonde hair a cascade
from heaven, water droplets falling

from their roots, stinging
my body. the ports tore

off my shirt & sports bra

my nipples lighthouses
in a swollen ocean, a trail

of dark hair running up

my belly. my whole boat
witness to my small naked frame

a gulf of shiver in the bus.

& their own hairless
legs disappearing into their shorts
skin ripe as peaches, reaching

for my brown body. these girls
whom I had stolen glances at
while we changed & wished

I could look like, my locker
room crew. my 5a.m. practice
girls. my lean over the starboard

side so she could pee off the rigor
girls, my two mile run after
eating Annie's mac-n-cheese girls.

they took turns rubbing the life
back into my bones

offered clothes off their own

backs to keep me from shaking.
my girls, sandwiching me

in their heat until my joints

flowered, until the warmth
budded through my blood.

what more could I ask

than a team willing to undress
their captain, too cold

& rain-glittered to do it alone?

Give and Go

Toni Jensen

I.

In this basement gym, the Annex of our local YMCA, two men perform
the act known as a chest curl. Each holds a considerable dumbbell and
lifts it sideways across his body. The motion looks like the pledging of
allegiance, the solemn swear, the crossing of a faithful heart.

On my bench, on my back, I work my own chest muscles in a
move called the lying fly. Outside, snow swirls the air but does not
decorate the sidewalk. Though it's early afternoon, the sky holds
no sun. It's one of central Pennsylvania's many secrets, one of this
Happy Valley's many secrets, how little sunshine in the winter, how
little snow actually makes it to ground.

I'm on my second set when the men begin their pattern: curl and
speak, speak and curl.

"That guy got his knob polished," says the one, "and free tickets."

"Sideline, maybe," says the other. "That boy should be grateful."

"A free blow job, and he didn't have to do anything," says the
other. "He didn't even have to pay."

The lying fly, like all other weight-bearing exercise, needs a third
round of repetition to be complete. It's one of my secrets, how much
I need these repetitive motions, especially here in this place, this
valley. The combination of the physical weight paired with the routine of the motion resets my mind like little else. I'm like a dog who
circles once, twice, three times before curling up to sleep. Interrupt
me, and I'll begin again.

But this Sunday afternoon, I stop. I know these men are speaking of the man known as Victim Number One. He has testified
that as a boy, at 13 or 14, Jerry Sandusky performed oral sex on
him about 20 times.

I rise mid-rep and move toward the lifting men, shaking my head. The smaller one locks the eye contact and steps to me, and we meet in the middle, by the weight rack, before the larger man intervenes. He puts a hand out to hold back his friend. We stand like that, an awkward trinity, a long while before I turn away.

It's winter 2011, and in our small town courthouse, a few blocks away, a Centre County grand jury has decided to charge former Penn State assistant football coach Jerry Sandusky with 40 counts of molesting eight boys from 1994–2009. I have been listening to softer versions of this curl and speak for weeks—on my campus, at the coffee shop, at the grocery store. This day, I'm overfull. This day, I'm so angry I'm incapable of return speech, of forming the right sentence, of forming anything like sentence.

I re-rack my weights because nothing but routine is required. The larger man still holds the arm of the smaller. I grab my jacket and head into the flurried gray without another look back.

This town, Bellefonte, sits atop rolling hills, eleven miles from the Penn State campus. This town will hold the Jerry Sandusky trial in spring of the following year. The media will swarm our Victorian village, and I will explain to my daughter, just turned five years old, how a bad man did bad things, how now the world is watching.

"Is he in prison or jail?" she says.

She knows already to parse the difference because she has two best girlfriends, one whose mother is just out of jail, the other whose father is in prison. She knows at five that one is a temporary place, the other, more lasting.

"He'll go to prison," I say before turning up the radio.

Sandusky will be found guilty, and in fall of 2012, sentenced to 30–60 years in prison. The verdict offers the proximity of completion.

But that day, I leave the Annex, incomplete, all lack. Merriam-Webster first defines this word, "annex" as a transitive verb meaning "to attach as a quality, consequence, or condition."

I jog up Allegheny Street past the storefronts and houses of this, our Victorian village, up the steep hill leading to my house.

Inside, my daughter and her father are absent. On the living room television, a football game's been paused, players in mid-crash, a still life of helmet and muscle. I drink down the first beer, scrolling channels.

My husband and I have agreed to stop watching football. I have returned home early.

Later, I will see this moment as a dot on the timeline, the lineage of leaving my marriage. It sits mid-timeline, after the early days: my husband's hand on my daughter's car seat handle, his tight grip, his body over mine, when I say, I'm leaving and he says, Fine, but you're not taking her.

Later, I will think of my of childhood, my family, Métis in Iowa, displaced, brought together each Sunday in front of the television for football or sometimes basketball, collective, cheering together, not for those few hours tearing each other apart.

Later, I will think of my best childhood girlfriend, so fast on the basketball court, so fast playing flag football in the crisp, night air. I'll think of how in the eighth grade, she tried out for the football team, was faster and stronger than the boys, was not allowed to play.

This day, I find the right channel, an NBA game, and settle in with my second beer. It's still the first half, and Oklahoma City is down but not by much.

I lean forward on the couch, knowing if the coach, Scotty Brooks, leaves Russell Westbrook in, there will be a show. If the Thunder are behind, the end of a half, even a first half, brings out in Westbrook the spectacular.

This day, James Harden steals the ball, dribbles twice before passing to Westbrook, who passes the ball to Kevin Durant. Durant lopes the court and pulls up, performing his signature shoulder shimmy and shake as if he's about to shoot. But he doesn't.

The camera has been following Durant. The camera is always following Durant; all American eyes are always following Durant, are always falling for Durant—for his long limbs, his elegant frame, his skin brown but not that hue deemed too dark, in this, our America.

But I have been following Westbrook. He is all compact rage, all wide-shouldered motion. His body, in this, our America, is deemed less acceptable—the rage, the power, the sneer—the complete absence of apology. Westbrook's body flies into frame, catches Durant's look away pass, and he performs a one-armed, windmill dunk, complete with signature sneer and roar.

Webster's defines this move, the give and go, as "a play in which a player passes to a teammate and immediately cuts toward the net or goal to receive a return pass." What I have just witnessed varies only if Harden's steal is counted in the equation. I count it. For me, that fall, all winter, the three of them perform together as trinity. Without Harden's steal, there is no give and go. Without Durant's spider limbs, there is no sleight of hand to allow for Westbrook's explosion. These three young men are attached, are annexed, if only for this remaining season.

This day, the back door swings open while I'm cheering for Westbrook, and my daughter runs in to greet me. Her father follows, shaking the snow from his dark hair, and the look he gives me stops my celebrating, and the look I give him back does not waver, and the tension hangs like that, nobody speaking, until our girl shakes all the way loose from her jacket. She begins stomping her boots onto the hardwood and bringing down each shoulder, left, right, left, right in time with her feet. Her dark blond hair swings wild, and the look on her face is all fierce concentration.

"What," I say, "are you doing?"

She points to the screen. "Westbrook," she says, "bring it."

And then we are three again, collective in our laughter, if only for this brief moment. Soon her father shakes his head at our commotion and takes his leave, and the pattern already begins its forming, its contraction from three to two, and I pull my girl to me, and we settle in for the second half.

II.

The winter I turn ten, men come to my childhood home and lift it. One moment, the front door rests, hinged and ordinary. The next, it levitates, a portal for birds only. That cold, bright morning, I dribble the sidewalk, and the sparrows screech in rhythm with the metal cranes, the whir and grind, the shouts of the men, directing flight.

I have taken from the house the necessary things: my high tops and teddy bear, my basketball. I dribble the sidewalk, shaking my bowl haircut side to side in disbelief until my mother threatens the ball and sends me to the street. My mother cut my pretty hair because I would not stop sneaking gum from her purse. I'd fall asleep with it tucked in the pouch of my cheek like a common squirrel. My mouth needed the gum, of course, the way hers needed her cigarettes, to work and worry, to keep the words in.

She'd been Catholic before my father. She might have had worry beads, a rosary like her sister. But the priest saw my father, my five dark uncles, and declared the whole lot unfit to attend the wedding unless they converted en masse. The point or points scored after a touchdown are Webster's fourth definition for the word "conversion," but in our family, this definition is primary.

I dribble the street, blow improbable bubbles, try to keep the popping mess off my glasses, my hands, my short hair, the ball.

The house is mostly white, a four-square made of two stories. Its foundation has begun a tilt back to earth my mother hopes these men can right. If all inside our house is going to fail and fall, the outside, at least, can be made level.

From the sidewalk before me, my mother shakes her pack, Virginia Slim Menthols, and together but apart, we watch the levitation of our house through her smoke. There rises the living room television, altar to Sunday football. There the brown shag where the children sit, the plaid couch for the parents. There, the site of our everyday violence turned each Sunday toward another target, unified, collective.

Beyond, the bathroom, where my father tries every so often to drown my mother. Beyond, the dining room table from which my father will throw me one future day. He is trying for the window that evening, as in, "throw her out the window." But my back meets the sharp edge of the casing, and I grab hold. The sharp edge meets my ribcage, causing a separation never to be made right.

My father is Métis, my father is all motion, my father teaches me about football, about the trap line, about violence and destruction and despair, and I grow up to teach my daughter some but not all, not all.

We are levitating the house, so we can sell it, so we can move a few miles up the highway to the bigger town. Instead of a hundred people, this town holds a thousand. It holds my best girlfriend and practice; it holds the library and school playground where the basketball hoop has a net. The park in this tiny town holds threads but no net. This levitation is step one of the salvation miracle. And this morning, I want so very much to be saved.

A few miles down Highway 71, kitty corner from our non-Catholic church, sits the elementary school gym, where practice soon will be underway. When I arrive, my best girlfriend, in my absence, shoots free throws too hard, slamming the ball off the backboard and rim, missing on purpose so she can chase down the ball and lay it up. In other words, without me, she's performing a sort of singular give and go. Her dark blond hair is cut short. She will have, then and always, wide shoulders and sharp cheekbones and such explosive stop-and-go power.

Before we lose her, she will run track in the Junior Olympics. Her times will be close to qualifying her for the regular Olympics. Before we lose her, she will start with drinking and graduate to pills and return to drinking. Before we lose her, she will travel the world playing for the American Basketball Team. Before we lose her, she will be the one I tell about my father, about what goes on inside our house. Before we lose her, she will be part and parcel of how I leave this place, and I will be complicit in how she does not. Before we lose her, I will be one of the first to take her to a party, to hand her a glass.

What does it mean to be unified, collective? What does it mean to remove yourself from a trinity, a family, a friendship?

Khelcey Barrs is Westbrook's childhood best friend, and Barrs dies suddenly at 16 of an enlarged heart. They are at practice, they are at practice, they are at practice. They have spent every day together, walking to school, to practice, back. Of the two, Westbrook then held the smaller frame and thus the smaller prospects. He grows five inches between junior and senior year. He transforms; he levitates. On Westbrook's levitating feet, on his shoes, each night, each game, he memorializes his friend with his initials.

What does it mean to memorialize the dead? What does it mean to be present for the living?

When my best girlfriend and I are young, I ride my bicycle beside her on her training runs. I run and compete, too, sometimes in the same races, but this is how fast she is: I need the bicycle. We talk as we move, and the jokes she likes best are wordplay jokes. We trade them and laugh and keep pace up the hills and fly down. My whole life this will be what I want from friendship, from love: movement in sync with language, language in synch with movement and laughter. My whole life I will want these pieces unified, together, a trinity most holy in its ordinary magic.

III.

We're in a church, not our own, in the back pew, solid oak, and I'm hanging onto it with both hands to correct my vertigo. I've driven 800 miles to be here, to sit next to my mother, to memorialize my best girlfriend who has overdosed this winter on pills washed down with wine.

My high school classmates are at the bar on Main Street having a pre-funeral drink. "Can you imagine?" my mother says, and "This is not a class reunion," and "What are they thinking?"

I'm thinking I'm grateful the family has chosen this larger, less familiar church. I'm grateful we're not in our childhood church across the street from the elementary school, where the gym once was. Instead of tearing down the school, last year, the town burned it as part of a fire fighting exercise. This is where I'm from: a place that burns down its elementary school, asbestos and all; a place that memorializes an overdosed friend by pre-gaming her funeral.

Our funeral attire instructions include a note about wearing our team colors, our football jerseys, to honor how our friend was a Denver Broncos fan. I'm wearing a black dress at a funeral, am sober yet still dizzy, am home yet so very far out of place.

The return began in the rain at my in-laws' house, at what would be our last family holiday. The return ends, winding Highway 71 past the once-levitated house, which each year sinks and slumps further into its frame.

In between, I stop over for the night at a hotel in Missouri. The night before my best girlfriend's funeral, Westbrook triple-doubles against the Pistons, tying LeBron James's record. I prop myself up with all the room's pillows and watch the highlights—his rebounding like gravity is myth only. I am sorry to have missed the game. I am sorry to be making this drive. I am sorry for how many years have passed since I heard my best girlfriend's voice, her laughter, for how many years there will be now without.

I am sorry our last interaction was so stupid and sad. On social media, she'd posted a comment on an article I shared about violence against Indigenous women. She wrote: "You know, I'm part Kiowa." And I liked it, then unliked it, then liked it again. Of course, I knew she was Kiowa. Of course, I objected to the language, the "part." Which part? The back of the left knee? The curve of the right ankle? The crook of an elbow? How many ways do we carve ourselves up and portion out our parts, our bodies for other people's comfort? How can a body such as hers—once all flight, all power and motion—be reduced to the language of the partial?

Westbrook will go on this season to surpass LeBron and everyone else. He'll take the record from Oscar Robinson with a last-second, three-point shot against the Denver Nuggets. The shot is from 36 feet. The farthest curve of the three-point line is set at just under 24 feet. So Westbrook shoots from over twelve feet past the line. I don't miss this game. His face, as soon as he releases the shot: all sneer and focus that turns to roar and smile. But the sneer comes before the shot hits the net. He knows its trajectory. He knows who he is and what he's done.

Who I am is someone working toward a memorial. Who I am is sorry for how this working includes my shame and my lack, how I let the parsing of language get in the way of friendship. My childhood best girlfriend was Kiowa, and I am Métis, and we grew up together in a mostly white town, and I never came back, and she was the best of us, and she came back this season for good.

In the last pew, my mother is talking about our childhood church, about my best girlfriend and others from our Sunday School class who've died, how many have died and so young, and "You girls," she keeps saying, "you girls are supposed to outlive us," and then she dabs at her eyes with her wrinkled Kleenex.

"You sang at her wedding," my mother says.

"No," I say, laughing a little.

"You did," she says.

"No," I say again, not laughing.

"'Wind Beneath my Wings,'" she says.

"God," I say, "I hate that song."

"Well, you sang it," she says. She sighs like what is wrong with me, why am I so difficult, so I stop talking and start trying to remember.

The teenage years are like this—full of gaps—some of which have developed into chasms. Webster's first defines disassociation as "the process by which a chemical combination breaks up into simpler constituents." It asks if I want to see "dissociant" in medical. I do. When I click it, though, I'm sent to "mutant," so I try again, to be sent to "mutant" again, and a third try does not offer different results. Webster's medical defines "mutant" as "a mutant individual."

This is my first Webster's failure, my first Webster's humiliation. My associative brain, my interest in Webster's, is caused, in part, by dissociation from childhood trauma, which perhaps makes me a dissociant, which perhaps makes me a mutant, or so says Webster's.

In any of these cases, my best girlfriend knew the how and the why of the dissociation. She offered sleepovers and laughter, bike rides up steep hills, and the steady rhythm of the ball against the backboard and into my hands, on repeat. I left those rhythms when the cost of homecoming became too great, when the cost of time in my father's presence became too great. I saved parts of myself that I believed then and now to be necessary parts, and I left behind both necessary parts and necessary people. This leaving, too, is a carving.

I spend my best girlfriend's funeral gripping the solid oak of the pew and remembering her wedding day. I have to focus, to replay that time like movie stills, like Polaroids ready for the sorting. The memory comes as the funeral unfolds.

In our childhood church basement, I help my friend into her white pumps. Her feet are swollen because she's pregnant, and I'm saying, "You could wear your high tops instead." I'm saying, "We can leave right now. My car is parked by the playground." I'm saying, "You don't have to do this."

Upstairs, I sing "Wind Beneath my Wings." I touch my hands to my collarbone like I do when I'm nervous and try to stop doing it and do it again. These are the hands that will hold her baby boy the first time a nurse needs to draw his blood. These are the hands that touch his today, that reach around his shoulders to say "I'm sorry." He's so tall and handsome, with his mother's cheekbones and broad shoulders. These are the hands that put one of the first drinks into his mother's hands.

After the funeral, I stop my remembering and shift into the now. My mother drives home past the lot that once held the elementary school and gym, and I go to the bar with my classmates. I hold a glass in my hands.

I have drunk down half my glass. I have made all the small talk I know how, and I am inching my way toward the door, when I see my best girlfriend's sister waving in my direction. She is having a hard time standing. She is the one who found my best girlfriend, who called for help, who got the call when it came—that my best girlfriend, that her sister, died in the helicopter, in the Life Flight, mid-air, in motion.

When her hands reach for mine, I am wanting only to be anywhere but here. I am wishing for the thud and fall of feet on a trail, the thud and fall of a ball on the hardwood. When she puts her hands atop mine, I am readying myself for my leave taking. She looks into my face, her hands atop mine, and says, "I remember you," and I say, "I'm sorry, I'm so very sorry," and I stand there a little while longer, her weight resting on mine, and I hold her like that, and I don't let go.

Perfect Form

Kamilah Aisha Moon

North Charleston, South Carolina, April 4, 2015

Walter Scott must have been a track athlete
before serving his country, having children:

his knees were high, elbows bent
at 90 degrees as his arms pumped
close to his sides, back straight and head up
as each foot landed in front of the other.
Too much majesty in his last strides.

So much depends on instinct, ingrained
legacies and American pastimes.
Relays where everyone on the team wins
remain a dream. Olympic arrogance,
black men chased for sport—
heat after heat
of longstanding, savage races
that always finish the same way.

My guess is Walter Scott ran distances
and sprinted, whatever his life events
required. Years of training and technique
are not forgotten, even at 50. Even after being
tased out of his right mind. Even in peril
the body remembers what it has been
taught, keeping perfect form
during his final dash.

Black Boxers

A Brief History

Benjamin Krusling

Jack Johnson (1878–1946)

Born to two former slaves,

Johnson triggered race riots after defeating the "Great White Hope" James Jeffries to maintain his title as first black heavyweight champion of the world.

For that fight, he won 1.6 million dollars, adjusted for inflation.

Convicted under the Mann Act aka the White Slave Traffic Act in 1912 for marrying Lucille Clifton, a white woman,

He fled the country until running out of money in 1920 after which he returned and served time in a federal penitentiary.

Johnson died in a car accident at age 68 after speeding away from a North Carolina diner that refused to serve him.

Sam Langford aka the Boston Tar Baby (1883–1956)

A renowned heavyweight who never held the world championship title.

Jack Johnson, the titleholder, refused to fight him.

He was afraid to lose to Langford and forgo the extra money
   he made by fighting white boxers on the other side of the
   color line.

When asked, Johnson said: "I'm the first black champion and
   I'll be the last."

Langford went blind and broke in Harlem, but after a *New York
   Herald Tribune* article raised money for his care, he spent
   his remaining days in a nursing home in Massachusetts.

Asked about his life shortly before his death, he remarked:

"Don't nobody need to feel sorry for old Sam.

I fought maybe 600 fights and every one was a pleasure."

Reggie Gross (1962–)

Raised by a single mother after his father was stabbed to death
   in a West Baltimore street fight when he was three days old.

Learned to fight at 13 after spending time in a juvenile
   detention facility for purse snatching.

After a brief light heavyweight career which culminated in
   a two-and-a-half minute Madison Square Garden loss to
   Mike Tyson in 1986,

Gross is now serving a life sentence for allegedly executing two
   drug dealers near a housing project in Baltimore that no
   longer exists.

Asked about his sentence, the prosecutor responded:

"If it all shakes out, he'll die in prison."

Clifford Etienne aka the Black Rhino (1970–)

Learned to fight while serving a forty-year prison sentence for attempted armed robbery and became a professional boxer upon his parole in 1998.

Etienne had a 28-4-2 record, but is best known for losing in 48 seconds to Mike Tyson in 2003 at the Pyramid in Memphis, Tennessee.

After his career declined, he was incarcerated again in 2006 for robbing a check cashing business, carjacking and kidnapping a family, and attempting to shoot two police officers in Baton Rouge, Louisiana.

In 2013, his sentence was reduced from 160 years to 105 due to a procedural error.

Najai Turpin (1981–2005)
Turpin was a contestant on an NBC reality show, *The Contender*, which followed amateur boxers competing against one another to win a million dollars.

He grew up in a North Philadelphia housing project where he lost his mother at 18, after which, relatives say, he retreated emotionally.

After her death, he supported his younger siblings by working as a line cook before moving briefly to Los Angeles to take part in the show.

At 23, soon after the *Contender* ended, Turpin shot himself in the head while sitting with the mother of his daughter in a car outside the gym in West Philadelphia where he trained.

In a press conference shortly after his death, *Contender* producer Mark Burnett emphasized:

"These were not fish out of water, people placed in an unusually stressful situation.

This is a bunch of . . . highly trained young men doing what they normally do . . .

Fight each other with the goal to feed their families and try to achieve greatness."

The Cock Fight Place

Alberto Ríos

After they had married, Mariquita one night
Looking for Adolfo went out and found him.

She had to step over a dried phlegm-and-dirt floor
In a dark, cock-fighting barn, had to step over

A ground made of decades-old sputum
Gifted carelessly from half-shaved, thick men

Everywhere, and dying or just barely living cocks,
A floor bloodgiven, scuffed

Into an inexpert, misshapen setting of scab tiles.
Her husband was drunk, and here.

Mariquita collected Adolfo and took him away
From what he needed to be taken away from.

They would never speak of this night again—
Though for Mariquita the sounds of the fight would not go,

The sounds of all those men huddled,
The odor of the cloying perfume they made on that hot night

All of them together and shouting, placing bets, spilling beer.
Mariquita remembered, as she made her way past the rooster fight,

How she had seen the one soul-white cock
Spattered with blood like hot kitchen grease.

This cock had an eye pulled fully out
But it continued to fight,

Then lost the other eye to a beak and a hard pull.
Still, it continued to fight, could not stop fighting,

Stretching its head and neck up higher, then higher still,
Trying to see, imagining that something must be blocking
     its view,

Trying to see, never for a moment thinking it was blind,
Confident that the cheering was its new eyes,

That the noise was sudden muscle.
Both owners kept spraying their fighter birds

Watering them from their mouths, through their teeth,
Spitting a mist on the fury of the birds.

Fooling them into momentary coolness, until the winner,
the not-white one, finished, allowed itself

To be corralled and soothed and rewarded,
And the owner, laughing through his half-beard,

In that old way of these fights, took the cock's head
Into his mouth, that fastest way of cooling an animal best.

A Note on Process

Meghan O'Rourke

1.

I began by keeping track of my time. It was February and
the snow had been falling all morning. I rarely saw any
people on the sidewalk outside, though I could detect
the traces of their passage, which the fresh snow quickly
covered. I was reading a book about a gymnast whose body
seemed to contain an important mystery. I read a little and
then I watched archival footage on YouTube, so I could see
"for myself" what the chapter described. I also searched
newspaper archives until I found articles—uploaded
scans of yellowed microfiche—describing the events. I
surrounded myself with their moment.

2.

Watching the gymnast land a dismount from the uneven
bars gave me a gaudy sense of the infinite, as if the routine
were a process still occurring over and over and over.
Time blurred, so I was an infant, as I had been when she
originally "performed," and I was a girl wanting to be a
gymnast, studying her photographs in the small hot gym
where I practiced, and I was thirty-seven, with a body that
didn't work. The clip of this routine never lost its patina
for me. In it I could see the will competing with itself,
submitting to its needs and surpassing them, with reckless
confidence. This was a kind of order of infinity, a process I
couldn't imagine not being part of.

Even as I had begun to reconcile myself to imagining
exactly that.

3.

After I finished her biography I made a list of what I had "done" all day. This was a failure, as a proper list—a true log—would have taken as much time to write as living the day did. But failing was fine with me. I wanted to formulate myself around the spaces that kept filling in, not merely to fall asleep on the couch again, to slip under. The air was "blue." It was hard to do. I went to the kitchen to take a drug the doctors had given me, a little imploring thing.

4.

Maybe I wanted to fail. And maybe it wasn't fine. I wasn't sure.

"I shall soon be quite dead in spite of it all."

5.

The gymnast was very slim. Her hair was always in pigtails or ponytails, tied with that thick bright yarn so popular in the 1970s. When she moved, it appeared almost as if she had forgotten her will, as if her body, her flexibility, had *become* her will rather than being merely an instrument of it.

The goal: to want something so much that the wanting makes your being become that thing.

At practice they told us to *stay tight* and *create a space under your arms* and *to stick it, keep your legs tight.* We were always hollow and tight and light. We were always spotting, choosing a place to look, and looking for it and only it.

6.

What else is like that?

7.

Before getting sick I had been trying to write a novel.

I couldn't get anything to happen: nothing was happening to me. I was out of story, eventless, unpersoned.

8.

I spent half of most days on the Internet. I had little to do. Facebook, Twitter, the news stories I was following almost obsessively, a video of a stalker cat, foxes bouncing on a trampoline, obscure message boards, music videos. But mainly I read comments threads—on blogs, on YouTube, on websites dedicated to the identification of "mysterious ailments." I read comments for hours at a time. The comments were depressing and fascinating and boring and sometimes oddly thrilling.

Comments didn't demand too much of me. They had no end except themselves.

9.

I knew I could never achieve a working knowledge of the full canon of comments or get better at reading them. I was therefore engaged in a process without an end: which was part of the point, to pass the time.

(Of course, comments meant others had a time problem too.)

10.

Keats said to his friend Charles Brown:

I have an habitual feeling of my real life having past, and that I am leading a posthumous existence. God knows how it would have been—but it appears to me—however, I will not speak of that subject.

Charles was going to go with him to Italy but never did.
Death is so ordinary. Suffering is this thing you wonder how
other people do, until you do it.

11.

Actually suffering isn't as terrible as you imagine it to
be. It's just a total reality. Time slows down, the room
reverse-telescopes.

Then suddenly it *is* as terrible. Worse because it drives you out.

12.

There was one upside: mosquitoes no longer bit me.

I was me but in disguise.

13.

In the leotard as a girl doing gymnastics,
I was me and continuous,
continuously defended and exposed.
My skin got molded, my brain got firm.
My will got girled and fierce.
I took the bus home by myself
in my Adidas gym socks and shoes,
continuous and used up,
muscle by muscle,
triceps to adductor, oblique
by oblique, psoas to calf.
Having stuck the landing
my "rips" (in the palms) bleeding.

Everything was measurable and you always improved.

14.

Of course improvement wasn't the only point. We were
no Protestants! We had stickers on our hands and glitter

on our leotards, shiny blue with white zigzags. It was a joy, an addiction, unhurried and luxurious, the opposite of impoverishment, a muscle-sore pilgrimage, meaning, a way out and a way in all at once, a girlness fabricated and internalized and more real than any other, but so shimmery and ribboned. I loved the way time passed, working on the toe point, waiting to vault, always getting the leg a little higher, or pushing farther from the horse. Admiring each other's skills.

It's play, it has a point: the point is itself.

15.

Once a week I take the bus for twenty-three minutes to get my blood drawn at a lab where two technicians I see four times a month put on latex gloves, tap my vein, and plunge in a needle. The first time I met the lab techs they were diffident, rude. The room was claustrophobic and smelled of urine. I sat for two hours watching everyone else get called back to the cubicles when I realized there was a sign-in form I should have put my name on.

Now we have an understanding. The nicer one feels bad for me. She has a two-year-old she doesn't see much. I'm older than she is, but she mothers me, pats me on the shoulder. The second, the tougher case, calls me "Ms. O." She never says hello. Each time, four times a month, it is as if she has never seen me before. This week, though, she let me hear her complain under her breath about the other patients. Then she said, "I use the smaller needle on you, because your veins are small. So you know." The blood work doesn't seem useful, nor is it joyful.

16.

You might reply: my fascination with the gymnast is the nostalgia of a body no longer able to function. Certainly I kept trying to apply the model of the will to the sick body. But the will fails the sick body. Or rather, the sick body turns out to be a discourse resistant to American truisms, and even to contingency. You don't make it happen, it happens to you.

17.

The rituals: the chalking up, the grips, the stretching, the ace bandages, the crushed velvet of the floor mat in competition, the bounce of the fiberglass bars, their give underhand as you're swinging and flipping. The sticking it, the punctuation of the job well done. Then doing it again and again. Little shin burns and shin splints, the blue hip bruises; the being-willing.

18.

I was by now keeping track of time every day, reading comments, on the blue couch, amidst days of snow. Waiting for emails that might amuse.

19.

A poor reading of gymnastics focuses only on abuse

another reading focuses only on empowerment

but like many things gymnastics is both.

I am convinced I put my skin on to perform living in it.

I can find no other reason for this body I am in.

20.

One day I went for a run determined to *just do it*, listening to *whatever doesn't kill you only makes you stronger*. Gray clouds, an ichor air. The pine needles browning. My legs shaking and numb. Vise around my ears. Home, in bed for hours, out cold, but in.

21.

When I woke I thought, I'm so disembodied. Then I thought, *that's ironic.*

22.

"I" a ghost in the machine, a surreptitious fabrication, a robot mind, a white noise, a wishful star, a soul whaled in, a hoard.

23.

Instead of focusing, I check my email. One is a reminder to participate in an annual day of happiness. A financial software program warns me, "We were not expecting to spend any money on Service & Parts till August." The program tells me how much money I get and from whom and how much money I spend and to whom I give it. But it doesn't tell me how I make this money or whether I will need better disability insurance.

This program is a history of physical process as well as an economic one. It often warns me "we're" spending too much on doctors. Like "we" have a choice.

24.

"Process": from the Latin *processus*, meaning "progression, course." Something inside me progressing, taking its course, but what is it? Not the thing I hoped for.

25.

Early on, you learn the back walkover. You learn not to be scared bending backward unable to see where you are going.

Once you get used to that you do back walkovers on the soft mat, until it becomes natural. You do ten without falling.

For weeks you do ten on a line on the basketball court, until you can "stick it" every time.

Then, the low beam. The coach stacks mats next to it so if your hands miss they hit the mat.

Sometimes your hands miss, a red everywhere pain.

But the body is learning where to put the hands and what it is your mind wants to do with them. You learn how to cross one palm over the other.

Once, I miss the beam, my wrist snaps back. For a moment the red extinguishes you. X-ray, splint, the doctor tells me I can't compete for six weeks. I stare. I have a meet tomorrow, I say. Can you just tape it up? My mother shrugs at him as if to say, *I know*, but she let me do it.

Always that blind backward reach—back-handsprings, back flips—trusting that your body knows more than your mind.

It's when you think about it that things go wrong.

26.

Another definition of "process" is "a series of actions or steps taken in order to achieve a particular end." But what if there appear to be no actions to take? I mean, what if there is no end, except an end I didn't want. A full stop.

Thinking is a problem in gymnastics. But you have to think about the blind backward reach of living-toward-death: you can't ignore it.

27.

In leotards we all wanted to be thin and graceful and fully rotated. Before other things that would matter, like college, summer camp, boys, or calculus, before stonewashed denim, before we threw away the Keds, the Benetton shirts, the friendship bracelets. Long before we threw away the leotards with their fine stitching and stained crotches, their shiny arms.

28.

Watching the gymnast I felt joy, some urge to survive. I took this as a hopeful sign: not that perfection was the goal, but that light was, being light in the air.

29.

Of course there was a subplot: I was trying to conceive a child, and I could not. It took a long time before I understood why: my body had fallen out of immunotolerance (the understanding that parts of the self, organs, blood proteins, the like, are not to be cripplingly attacked and destroyed by the body's own immune system). Instead I lived in—well, I wasn't sure it had a name, but we could call it immune-chaos. It was difficult not to think metaphorically about this: *I* was under attack from *myself*, attacked by the very mechanism that was designed to keep me "safe."

Sometimes in bed I looked down at my legs, my stomach, the veins inside my arms: futile.

30.

One doctor kept saying, "Time is not on your side." As if I were committing a moral failure. My acupuncturist told me, "You think too much."

I wasn't sure how to stop thinking. I practiced blankness for a while, gave up, read the newspaper. "No one on the planet will go untouched," a professor at Princeton said, about the Antarctic shelf that keeps sliding into the ocean.

31.

"One is not born, but rather becomes, a woman," wrote de Beauvoir.

32.

At twelve, I wore a blue windbreaker for a year, all day long, even in ninety-degree heat. I didn't want to be seen. Take it off, my mother was always saying. Take off your coat and stay a while. But I didn't want to stay—that was the whole point. I wanted to go back. I didn't want to be in this body that said "woman."

33.

One day I read about the creative habits of others. Beethoven made coffee using exactly sixty beans and then worked for five hours without interruption, after which he had "dinner" with beer, took a long walk, and then handled correspondence; he concluded his day with a light supper, more beer, and a trip to the pub to read the newspaper. In the past, the upper middle class got stuff done because someone cooked them dinner and supper and there was no email or Internet. Meanwhile I graze all day long from bags on which the word "Superfood" is emblazoned.

34.

Because stress exacerbated my illness, I played at being "normal"—cooking, resting, narrowing my life to self-care. The irony is, it was just what my friends who were new mothers were going through.

35.

A diagnosis is an answer, or maybe just another problem. It was because no one had good answers that I watched gymnastics. I didn't want or need a door, I just needed a window, with a little light.

36.

Once, one of my students talked in class about how, at the height of her depression, she wished something terrible would happen to her, so she would have a reason for her pain. It did—her father died. She blamed herself. Of course, his death did not alleviate the depression.

37.

My process was a keeping track of facts: Woke. Walked 7 min. Took x, a, d, f. Flu-like sensation. Watched the gymnast on YouTube. Read 3 pages. Fell asleep. Pain. Worked, sleepy, made notes.

But what the gymnast did was illuminating. She made it possible to understand something larger than yourself, the way one movement of her body flowed into another. It was as if I were at a play written by a conceptual artist who was still writing it as we watched.

38.

Always at the back of my mind: I had tried, but had I tried hard enough?

39.

Sonograms, blood tests. Multiple antigens, genetic anomalies. Slowly this comes to feel real. And yet you do not want to live bounded by those terms; they mean nothing, you know.

40.

There are many scripts for proceeding, but of course you
want only the one that is denied you, a poet friend told me.

41.

What I liked about gymnastics was the illusion of the
perfectibility of the self. It was always clear what to do.
What to do was to *do it* and to conquer fear by doing it. This
wasn't self-punishing. So the skin scrapes off your leg along
the beam when you fall. You get up and do it again.

42.

I mean grace I guess, which is something.

43.

But—at least in competition—you are also an object of
scrutiny, learning to present every aspect of the self in a
careful script. Later, with other things, you need exactly
this, control and surrender. You aren't sure which came
first: the need or gymnastics, which created the need.

Often I think most people fail to grasp something
important, something the body of the gymnast tells us.

44.

You don't really think about processes till you're screwed by
them.

At some point it's kind of funny:

What a useless sack that body! So baggy and borrowed,
so unreturnable. I mean, who has so many problems?

The best was when people told me my illness was a blessing.

Oh yes! I wanted to agree. *Would you like it?*

I'd be happy to give it to you—

45.

Like standing on a balance beam or an uneven bar after all.

Below the beam that you stand on lies a pocket of air waiting.

Or flipping backward over the bar and trusting you will catch it.

You don't always. Does that mean you shouldn't do it?

46.

Due process is built on the idea of "fundamental fairness."

That many lives are caught in a bad net is of course a fact. When I was sick this began to seem unlivable.

47.

On the crushed velvet floor mat, time slowed down and your visual field became distorted, so you could see very little beyond three meters around you. There was a dim impression of people in the distance, shifting in their seats or waiting, in the case of mothers, with anticipation and fear, but they couldn't be seen, exactly.

The room had become a funnel of music and muscle-thoughts (trying to get that back heel up) and hands (the pinkies as extended as possible). As if your brain was in your extremities and that your body had equalized its intelligence, that you had, for once, begun to fully inhabit whatever this thing was that you could call a "self."

48.

The process solved the problem of: who shall I be. What is natural to us must be learned, Hölderlin wrote. You were this want.

49.

There is no way to demarcate suffering. What one "feels" when "suffering" is not like a "date in history" but like a day that cannot be logged. Keep track of it. See how much "you" manage "to get done." When I say "electric shocks" crawled up and down "my skin," I'm speaking metaphorically. God knows what they are. What "mechanism."

At one point, Keats apologized to Fanny Brawne for the delay in his correspondence, explaining that he had been ill for three days and had been "capable" only "of an unhealthy teasing letter."

He was badgering Fanny near the end, agitated by love and by dying.

Instead of writing unhealthy letters, I watched the gymnast. You can escape the worst by studying these perfect routines: this was the mystery.

50.

Living without a sense of an "end"—being sick—was a transformative process. I felt that I was the mouthpiece for the illness, that only I could translate it, yet no one else seemed to think so.

What if I was not feeling what I was feeling

what if I had to learn it all again

what if forever and flustered

what if—and this was the question I could not bear—

the rest of my life was just this:

the process of surviving?

When in fact *I* had not survived.

51.

There is much to be said about the spectacle of the female body. I'll just say this: it is perhaps not coincidental that the gymnast later got breast augmentation or became a spokesperson for Botox.

52.

My handwriting in the log got smaller and smaller, shakier and unmade.

More and more went unrecorded.
But I will not speak of that.

a thing must *run its course*

: but what if the running of the course destroys everything

53.

In the photos of the gymnast I studied, something is captured. The body is moving but also captured. What's there is surface but in the movement of the body—the splay of her fingers. Her hands are thrust upward and fingers splayed. Stripes along her leotard: the 1970s. Her back is arched as if made of soft plastic. She smiles as if to invite us into her soul but really it's a king's *I permit you to worship me*. What is strange is that later she is the same person but not. Whatever had radiated from her body has dissipated. To lose the thing irrevocably: is that what it means to be her?

54.

But what was sequestered in her body is everything. It is tedious to talk about want. Better to talk about value.

55.

When I got sick, I did think, if I die now, I have spent *way* too much time listening to men talk. And I like men. But really.

56.

I find it a little tiresome when other women write about their masochistic tendencies, their fantasy of total submission.

I do understand the temptation to succumb to the world's invitation to imagine yourself mascaraed and destroyed in the perfect girl's bedroom. A dive off the balcony at the party in the white fur hat and slutty lingerie.

My problem is it glamorizes something flat rather than deep, or it flattens the deep, silvers it. It can't help but be a performance, less pure than gymnastics.

Maybe I just like the part of female pain (or bravery) that insists on its privacy. This may be a failing in me.

Keats told Fanny, "If through me illness have touched you (but it must be with a very gentle hand) I must be selfish enough to feel a little glad at it. Will you forgive me this?"

A window always shows both light and night.

57.

So in the end maybe the process was not about keeping
track of time but discontinuing my belief in my own goals.
I posted one comment, then stopped. This was after an
emergency. The process is your mind acting on the world
and being acted upon by it, whatever comes.

58.

There is nothing sustaining about sickness

there is no end

and because there is no end, there can be no "goal"
and because there is no goal there are no steps to take

and no process

: so what is there?

59.

Of course you could say life is exactly like this.
"I shall soon be quite dead at last in spite of it all"

But I think it's more like gymnastics—

60.

After all this time of waiting and watching, I am not sure
how to describe the gymnast's mystery, only to say that—
years later—I did solve it. For a moment under the white
sky and the white sun with the sound of a Boeing jet
overhead, shot toward the horizon, I understood.

61.

Imagine a line like the one at the gym on which you practice
just for the sake of trying,

for the value of it, which is its own becoming, or joy,
and landing. Sticking it.
Not because the judge is waiting in the corner
for your final salute.
But just because. To land it.
It's like a hunt for light in the body.
The body made of its dead stellar glitter,
its diminishing hydrogen.
The line is uncorrupted even if the body might be.
No, I don't like that old-fashioned, purist way of thinking.
How about:
the body is exhausted but the line is not,
and look glitter on the floor
and the leg a little ribbon shine

How Are You Feeling

Ana Božičević

I'd look into people's windows, imagine
myself into their bodies—and then I thought, no, I should
be fully me, me only. I went home. Just that night a burglar
    broke in and
robbed me at gunpoint. The lesson was: don't be too
dogmatic in your practice. You can still
have an imagination.

is what I remembered a master
jogger told me in a dream as my legs crumpled into brown
    paper bags or shreds of
oh something—right after I woke up to check on you
awake in the night: your stomach hurt

really I was afraid that while I slept you were
reaching after some kind of beauty
I couldn't put my hands on. And you are
you're

holding up a blue flashlight
as I write this down.

I could end this with "how are you feeling"
since that actually matters. I could name

it "How to Get Started with Running" and get all
pseudo Zen on you. Like that dream: too neat. Learn from
    it, though:
just tell a story. Yes, but then I wouldn't

be doing what I am: dredging up these objects
and wiping the seaweed off, rigging them up
and praying that they work somehow, start the poem.

I just can't start the damn thing. There's nothing to end.

The Wrestler

Kazim Ali

My flat breath grows flatter. Who am I now, thick in the tricks
the body plays? No matter.

The fact of this day on fire and these arms twisted
in the effort to master another

draws me in time breathless to afternoons as a boy slick
with sweat and laughter,

horizontal in a spin, one of us in control
and the other on his back and bested.

Later I would read in heaven's books
how my body was wrong, though limber and strong.

In the web of our efforts I aim to fix a position
where the other's strength ebbs and mine kicks in.

Strength splintered to pieces,
a shard in the other we each struggle to reach.

We give in turn, strip down and shift.
I reach for one limb with my right hand, grip harder to
    another with my left.

Our bodies flash their thunder and lack.
I strain for what I'm owed. I read heaven its riot act.

War Training

An Athletics

Nomi Stone

"The wound . . . occurred suddenly, invisibly; it
came out of nowhere." Rooms in the woods

help you prepare to hold it together for whatever
comes from off-center.

Mewling of goats, villagers crying in their language for
water. The chest opening

call to pray de-
leafs, snapping

you when missiles
follow. If your body

is an animal, talk to it
your trembling away.

Note: Quotation is from "The Railway Journey" by
Wolfgang Schivelbusch.

A Boy & His Mother Play Dead at Dawn

Michael Wasson

> The presence of mothers and babies in the blue
> rifle smoke that made dawn more dim.
> —C. E. S. Wood, 1884

Tucked beneath
    a bank of brush.
Held between my legs
    are my hands.
Like prayer.
    Like holding in
my morning piss.
    & I do. It's warmer
at the lip's edge
    of pink water. Is it
the dead we're about
    to become?
She dunks me
    beneath. Purpled
ripples erasing
    what lines I forget
across my body.
    Some hunched men
check the grounds
    for skulls. Some
will drag the dead us
    to the open mouth
of the creek. & of
    course they smell
me. & she whispers
    cepée'yehey'ckse

I'll make you
        soft by soaking
my son when she floods
        around me. I pull in
my tongue from any
        taste. We flower
from the inside out.
        Please don't mistake
her for another now.
        I'm still. Dawn
mirrored then crushed
        by another hidden rain
of hollowed gunmetal.
        This slow-motion
massacre crowding
        silenced. Each body
pressing her freed weight
        into me. Mouth
agape. *tequúuse 'iin. O this*
        warmth. Just drown
me I beg no one. Hurry.
        Just empty me out.

As If We Were Called

Reginald Dwayne Betts

My friends and I gathered on any basketball court as if called, and for hours each day we ran, up and down, teaching ourselves civilization. It sounds cliché now, to think that between two hoops we invented a way to understand the world, or at least a way to understand ourselves in the world. But we did. There is something mathematical in the game, not just in the mechanics of launching a ball through a hoop or executing a crossover dribble, but what drew me there was the way our bodies became pure energy, intuitively feeling every movement that happens across the court's 94 feet. This is all a way of saying that in the second grade I fell in love with a sport that broke me again and again, unfailingly. It also made me a believer: everything in my life could change once I said, *Check ball.*

On the asphalt court we gave ourselves allowances that would not exist later, once our age and skill level shifted to mean the hoop could no longer be the center of our existence. But we were youngins. We went to William Beanes Elementary, named after the guy who didn't pen the Star Spangled Banner but was its catalyst. Dr. William Beanes had been a respected physician in Upper Marlboro, a place where my family lives now but had they lived then would have been slaves. History says that during the War of 1812, Dr. Beanes was captured by British soldiers and held on the HMS *Tonnant*. Francis Scott Key, the poet-lawyer who eventually wrote the Star Spangled Banner, went to the British ship on a mission to gain Dr. Beanes' freedom. Had they taught us history in elementary school, they would have told us that our namesake was important enough to have President James Madison approve a mission to get his release. Their plan was simple, take letters from British soldiers describing how well Dr. Beanes treated them while in his custody. The letters worked. Beanes was released, and while making their way back home, the group witnessed the British attack on Baltimore from a ship near Fort McHenry. Key's poem describes the attack and was set to the tune of "To Anacreon in Heaven," a popular drinking song, no doubt because lawyers then as now favored strong drink. As students at William Beanes, history wasn't drilled into our heads, and no teacher taught us what it meant to be rescued and to be a witness. But I'll be damned if the basketball court didn't drill it in us—to be rescued and to be a witness—sometimes at the same time, with the thing summoning always being a hoop and the interlocking chains falling from it.

Back then, we taught ourselves what it meant to be clutch, what it meant to falter and then call, "Next"—because in the parlance of hoops, things are never over. Not from play to play or game to game. We were out there alone, on our own to teach ourselves—and there is, now, barely a memory of how we got the rules. Maybe it came to us whole cloth—the double dribbles, the travel, the idea of a bounce pass and backdoor cut.

It started early, in second grade. My teacher, the only teacher I have ever had whose name I do not remember, forced us to go to the school library once a week. Our school library was bigger than every room in the building, except the gym and the cafeteria. At the front was a pedestal larger than me holding a book larger than me. An unabridged dictionary. I thought that unabridged meant *without bridge*, as in a book lacking a way to bring you back to reality. And the book was so big it made sense—its heft and weight an impossibility suggesting it did contain all the words. I flipped through that book purely to discover what I could not pronounce.

The only other thing in the library with that kind of pull on me was a set of sports encyclopedias, volumes that sorted out athletes by last name and introduced me to the decades of ball before I was born. This was the year that recess belonged to basketball. Our playground had two full courts, chains for nets, and no three-point line. The asphalt was as cracked as the future many of us would confront. But the future was so far off then. And those encyclopedias were gold, and right there in the now, and inside their pages Earl the Pearl was waiting for me.

Earl Monroe had nicknames that augured the unfathomable: the pearl, black magic, Black Jesus. He dropped fifty-six points in a game as a rookie. Some nameless writer, plugging entries into an encyclopedia, for the one brief entry I first read, seemed to take extreme joy in describing Monroe's spins and jerks. One move, a lay up in which the ball was shown to the defender, then brought down to the knee, as if to be kissed, then brought back up only to bounce from backboard to basket was described so well that I walked onto the court the next day with that secret. It became my move. My version of the Pearl meant I got picked first or second for the rest of the year. It didn't matter that most of us couldn't get the ball to the rim consistently. We were becoming something, and I had unwittingly discovered the way books can gift you a physical language to show the world.

Before we could really play, we all learned how to dream, and we reinvented ourselves each day. We worked hard at a single move or skill, until we had it down, and it became the thing we were known for. Caleb, smaller than the rest of us, learned the scoop shot before it had a name. Jamario heaved jump shots from the outer limits of our imagination. And from those encyclopedias, I had learned to move with what I thought was the grace of Earl the Pearl Monroe.

Each one of us added a little to the chaos that was our bodies flying and leaping over ninety-four or so feet of blacktop, and we kept showing up and coming back until what we brought onto the court became order. I remember Boogie, and the kid he played with all the time, the two of them like brothers, brought the pick-and-roll to the blacktop as if it was their invention. And I remember Blue-eyed Clarence, named for how the color of his eyes seemed odd against the blue-black of his skin, a reminder to us all: mystery is a muhfucka. Clarence and I once got into a fight on the court. To tell the truth, I was unafraid when all I had to do was find a way to get to the basket or make a steal, but when I had to drop the ball and throw my fists instead of a bounce pass, I was terrified. I had fouled Blue-eyes too hard, and he swung a punch my memory says I weaved. What I know for certain is we kept playing. We always kept playing. The game, even then, was already too important to be broken up by a fight.

All of this happened before I turned twelve. Before our bodies could create the funk of puberty. We were boys out there, waiting to be declared worthy. That was my first understanding of what it meant to be free—to recklessly throw yourself into the possibility of becoming a person who mattered, even if just for a play. The order we made out of basketball lasted, and soon the hours on the court began to carry more meaning than the rattling of the chains after a made jump shot.

It was Prince George's County, not a Mecca of any sport. But there was asphalt and we were always there. We hooped on courts or on crates suspended from staircases, wherever. It was just us with a basketball and the street and a game of who could cross up who.

To be good, to be *really* good, you had to be able to tell the person guarding you what move you were going to make on them—and then you had to do it, which is to say, on the court is where I learned the virtue of honesty. Whether hardwood or blacktop, there were no lies that could last longer than it took to crossover and take two steps to the waiting basket. The blacktop was a kind of democracy: territory that belonged to us. There were no parents, no teachers, no older boys dictating the lessons we learned. We took refuge in what awed: the beauty of a bounce pass to a cutting teammate, a jump shot making the chains echo a howling harmonica.

For a time, I ran from the truth of it all—most of who I am came from what it meant to successfully bounce a ball between my legs while running full speed on a fast break and then toss a behind the back pass to a teammate streaking to the rim. We were always out there, learning, alone but together, not always perfection but always beauty.

Maybe the whole point of us being out there was to be able to say that we were out there. And to have someone else to say it to: each other. Out there was a place that mattered. From the perspective of back then, if our futures held some awaiting calamity—and they did hold those calamities—someone might have thought to write about those jump shots we rained from our fingertips. Since they didn't write them down, we do the next best thing, we remember for one another, that we rained those jumpers down, and still do.

Run

Gary Jackson

The title is a lie: when I tell my wife I'm going for a run what I mean
is that I'm going to walk under the hot South Carolina sun for only
ten minutes, followed by a minute of actual running, then another
ten minutes of walking, then more running, but mostly walking,
and by now the sweat has formed a Rorschach mark on my chest
and I hate it. Summers, I imagine the better me: the one who runs
every morning, who writes all afternoon, who waits until evening
to have his first drink. When I say I'm going to write, what I mean
is that I'm not going to idle hours browsing blogs, cruising pornog-
raphy while telling myself it's all in service of the poem I'll one day
write on Mia Khalifa and how she was once ranked the #1 pornstar
in the country and received heaps of hate mail and death threats
because she is Lebanese, and I'll call this all research, but I won't
know what, exactly, to do with this, or how to put it in a poem, and
I forgot to take that run. The run! I will kiss my wife and tell her if
I'm not back in forty minutes, come look for me. A joke, when what
I mean to say is that it will all be fine, except when the sun begins
to set, and a car drives by a little too fast and too close, and my legs
tell me my time is up. And now I hate the run, the street, the town,
myself, the whole fucking state, and this country for making me
feel this way every day I run.

From Heaven, My Father Sends His Regrets

Cornelius Eady

Son, you still don't know squat about fishing. I
Couldn't teach you the bait, the hook, how
The line sings, the fuzzy ride to meet the morning.
Explain to me how a boy could turn
Fun away so fast; you so sure you knew stupid
When stupid pulled up at 4 a.m. and your uncle
And me, we became black sparrows, flashlights burning
Our lawn for worms. All you had to throw back at me
Was stubborn, and stubborn worked. It's what
You forgot when your poems resurrected me
And I turned, in your words, into an oaf. I offered
You a place to wade with me. What do you want, Now
That you're grown, now that you're curious?

Russian Sport

Vera Pavlova

Translated by Ilya Kaminsky and Valzhyna Mort

Thirty years now
he lives
underneath the ground,
that class ignoramus, that featherbrain,
a boy who stalked me
after school, on skis,
on Rollerblades, ice skates.

Once even broke his leg!
Yeah well, I thought,
for a show.
But his older,
beefed-up hockey brother
came to carry him like a girl
off that brilliant skating ring.

Feel for the Water

Christian Campbell

Heat 1

How swimming really began was with the Native Americans, who invented the crawl. Then the white man learned it and forgot them. Then the white man called that style "Australian crawl." Then they called it "free."

How swimming really began was with the Indians—Matsya, fish avatar of Vishnu, steadied and guided the ship during the great flood. Who could tell where the water ended and where his blue skin began?

How swimming really began was with the Africans, who raced back from the New World after the Middle Passage, and before. They all swam butterfly, for it is the stroke of dolphins; a butterfly like Mary T. Meagher's where it seems you could hold perfect stroke forever.

How swimming really began was with the Greeks—Leander swimming the Hellespont to Hero, swimming and drowning for love. At the Battle of Salamis, the Greek survivors were swimmers, so says Herodotus.

How swimming really began was with the foetus in the womb floating. It really began with the blood racing from the heart, with all cells drifting and dividing, submarine, when everything is pure undulation.

Heat 2

He strutted out in a red, white and blue robe and matching trunks, shadowboxing, playing to the crowd. In this Apollo Creed get-up, Gary Hall Jr. was trying for a kind of Ali swag. *Float like a butterfly, sting like a bee.* Float, yes, but not butterfly, freestyle—the splash-and-dash.

Eight years back he was half of one of the most fascinating rivalries in competitive swimming: Hall vs. Popov. In one corner you had the All-American skater kid—the blonde, goofy, showboating, weed-smoking boy-next-door. In the other you had the unsmiling "Russian Rocket"—the shadow-haired, aloof, trash-talking hero-villain. People made it into/said it was like the Cold War.

Heat 3

I first heard about Alexander Popov when I was thirteen, the year I dropped six seconds in the 100 fly. He defeated the brilliant Matt Biondi twice at the Barcelona Games and began his sprint reign. Even the infamous American commentators could not help but regard him with awe. He slayed their Great American Hope. They called him "Alexander the Great" and "The Russian Rocket" and "The Tsar."

Heat 4

["Popov deserve all the respect in the swim world, he is a poet with his mouth closed!!!"—Comment on a popular swimming website]

In a video on Popov's technique, the narrator points out that speed through the water is based on the "three R's"—rhythm, range and relaxation. This is part of Popov's enigmatic genius. Born in Sverlovsk in 1971, he trained in Australia with the legendary Gennadi Touretski and their mission was nearly monastic. He was built like most world-class sprinter-swimmers, 6'6", lean, long-limbed, with an albatross wing-span. But I have never seen a sprinter glide the way he did, or race as *long* as he did, full range in each stroke always. It was extraordinary really, to see that center of coolness amidst the manic energy of his rivals.

Sprinting, like poetry, is about the details, so watching Popov swim, one could think about body position (high in the water), catch, head position, rotation, kick (like a motor), acceleration, timing, smoothness, breathing patterns, streamline, geometry, ballet, kingdom animalia. But what we end up with, above all, is beauty.

Heat 5

How to talk about his stroke? Unlike the straight-armed thrashing/windmill style of many European sprinters these days, Popov had a distinctively high elbow recovery and clean hand placement. I would call it perfect stroke except it was more than technique. He somehow combined a mechanical ingenuity with a kind of soulfulness. Is that the word? What does it mean to race with grace? Popov's style was something for dancers and painters to work through.

Heat 6

Once in college, Bob had us look at videos of ourselves to analyze our strokes. Who was that? Is that what I look like? What I visioned in my head and asked my body to do did not look like the stroke I actually had.

Why could I never translate the image?

Heat 7

After my first year in college, I started to get swimmer's shoulder. It felt like I was always toting two bags of bricks. That was the year that Popov was stabbed.

It happened a month after the Atlanta Games, during a fight with watermelon vendors in Moscow. He needed emergency surgery for a pierced lung and kidney.

Heat 8

What do we do with the contraption of the body? If muscle memory is the body's ability to recall its previous work, then muscle dreaming is the body's reach for the surreal, its aspiration—to be a fish or the greatest sprinter of all time.

When we were small, we would call on certain names like superheroes morphing, and pike into the pool. We raced and became them:

Biondi! POPOV, *boyyyy!*

And then we would command our spindly bodies through the water with the brio of the greats.

Heat 9

After he recovered, he was baptized and the next year defended his titles at the Euros. Somehow I never thought about if his abdomen still ached just a little on the start or turn. Or if his breathing was maybe not quite the same.

I never thought about the hell of lactic acid build-up at the end of a race, which is like an alarm going off in the body but as sensation, not sound.

Or worse, when you die on the last length, when, as they say, the piano is on your back, a particular piano that is always played by Ravel, so it's the feeling of galloping horses, a crescendo stampede that makes you sink, break form, go backwards, flail desperately for the wall.

I was too busy marveling at how his stroke is somehow never rushed. Or how in this particular race, Popov seems to be surfing with his own body, riding a wave of his own creation. Or perhaps what would it mean to be a river. Or to wonder if Popov may have also been a violinist.

Heat 8

I never swam the times I thought I could swim—I never felt like a big-meet performer, a clutch swimmer. But there was one time when I came from behind on the last length to win and break a record. It was as if I stepped aside and watched my body go beyond me.

I didn't plan to quit but I went to grad school and never trained again. This was five years before Popov's last Olympics, the Athens Games. He failed to qualify for the finals of both the 50 and 100 free. Then he retired.

The year I stopped swimming was the year I became a poet.

Heat 9

Beauty deceives. Beauty makes us believe. Popov's form was all cut and line, motion that seemed fugitive to physics.

Witnessing this beauty is always about potential and limit. Serena, Jordan, Federer, Usain, Tiger, Ali, Comaneci, Messi, Phelps,

Popov. It's always a kind of surrogacy—as we watch the virtuosity of their bodies, we are carried with them. As if all our shame about what our bodies are not and cannot do is, for a time, carried off and altered with that force.

Heat 10

Popov, more than most swimmers, had a "feel for the water"— that swimming axiom, at once lucid and elusive, for those who have an aquatic intuition about body, water and space. It's like Dickinson's definition of poetry—you know it when you see it. Those who remember when we were sea creatures have a feel for the water.

Popov was a master technician and a work-horse in practice, but there was something else to his genius—the authority of his instincts. It is to know exactly where you are and exactly how to move in water. For swimming, like poetry (as Bishop suggests), is an unnatural act.

Heat 11

When someone says a swimmer has a feel for the water, they're making a comment about skill, texture, and aesthetics all at once. But how? Does the witness feel what the swimmer feels?

Like Popov, these swimmers often look like they are in cruise control even when they are racing. There is something you want to say about silk and power, when the unnatural looks natural. It's also about illusion. Sometimes I think of Popov when I recall what Toni Morrison says of fiction: *The language must be careful and appear effortless. It must not sweat.*

Heat 12

In front of the blocks, cyborg-like in black Swedish goggles, you notice his fierce coolness. Perhaps severity is Popov's greatest virtue. He once said of Hall, who is a second-generation Olympian, "He comes from a family of losers."

"I am always looking for potential challengers," Popov told the
New York Times on another occasion. "If I see any, I have to swim
faster and make them feel sick. If they have a little potential, you
must get on top of them and kill that enthusiasm right away so they
will lose their interest in swimming."

What must be severed (psychically, emotionally) to achieve such
power, such rigorous, formidable technique?

You have to be scary, you have to be a madman. You need a focus
that is beastly and ridiculous.

Heat 13

When Popov was once asked to speak of his relationship to the
water, he was almost tender:

The water is your friend, you don't have to fight with water, just
share the same spirit as the water, and it will help you move. If
you fight the water it will defeat you. We were born in water—it's
like home to me. This was in Seville in '97. It's as if he was asking
us to return to amphibian consciousness, to sever certain human
restrictions, we who descend from upright man to swim, sleep,
make love and die.

Heat 14

*In the water I am water I am most of me home if you could call it that
to swim is to slip into the water of the mind to move there moving mind
unthinking mind the desire is pure repetition down here everything
looks like a Rothko all things in my body swimming always dream work
of oceans gills are not so frightening then what to say about space one
must have a mind of water*

Heat 15

If a poet is a maker, then Popov teaches me that swimming is a
making and unmaking of the body.

We swim to go through our limits, to best time, a body no longer
but still a body, pure force, foam, water again.

Heat 16

All swimming is a negotiation of borders, boundaries that are never fixed. To swim is to move between one medium and the next—between water and air, to translate oneself, to cross over. You'd think I was talking about dying.

Swimming's beauty is in the animal act of transforming the body you are given, the history you are given.

Heat 17

To swim, then, is to leave a wake, to leave a history that is always new. To swim is to write in water.

I reckon, a latitude

Asiya Wadud

{between Tripoli and Lampedusa, there is nearly the Gulf of Sidra}

you feel pretty perilous. you'd rather perish in the water than languish near Tripoli's sullied edge. you are changed, your lids hang heavy, straight through the sanguine. all through the sinew. the sea beckons and wakes you. a natural death is understated. you cut the tide with exactitude. You cut it with a calm light and you're boundless in the sea, and lifted, too. cut the waves and quell Sidra's doom. The gulf between us elemental and the surest route to Lampedusa is iron salt and oxygen. You name the sea to rise and meet it and put to rest Sidra's obstinance.

Your doom—if anything—would be Sidra, Sidra would ensnare you. Reel you in by life boat only then to anchor you. Your light is rightly steadfast and honed. You insist on a precision, recalling the instructional manual: the breaststroke is a leisurely way to pass through the narrows. You insist and are decisive, count the breaths exactly: 2 for every 1 for the damned and the saved.

but then, too.

the miasma of petrol and saline pocks you. some perish nameless. we search out the remaining phosphorescence. starboard remains keen and searing. near the satisfied edge. your stroke became heavyweight. port is increasingly distant. the dread is manifold it needles, incandescent. a refuge is the voyage the labor is the passage the coming is the collapse the crusade of the Sahara. The desire line snakes irregularly. the steady traffic pauses. we enumerate the loses. we harbour the living and we know all it means to carry their weight.

we begin the task of naming them all. incanting them in a coming fugue. invoking them to ward off Sidra. naming them as a prophylactic. the milieu of the how to canter on, each footfall anew, the archipelago that names the state

others come others onward.
                    [a vessel remains] [the onward,
            itinerant] [the engine, they lift] [i reckon
                we're remnants] [Sierra Leone] [a
                    latitude, we name it]

an equivocation along the illuminated coastline. libya of the bygone—is an insistence. you gesture with exactitude. You cut the waves with a calm light. you're burnished, and lifted, too. an expansive, copious heat stayed near you, all through the passage, all through the mooring.

the gaping sea beckons and breaks you. the impotence the imploring the inured. the inexact. the crisis. the crease. port is increasingly distant. you ache for a semblance of. the vantage of this one. the proliferation. they are out of sight until they are a sightline. black coal as ravens weightless as gold plovers marshal the waters my dear crosslight, feast on your plentiful oxygen. starboard is penetrating. port, sagacious.

you can say you were pretty perilous.

                    you didn't languish near Tripoli's sullied edge.
                    you are changed, all you bears the blackness all
                                you bears the possible goldness.

straight then sanguine.

A Perfect Game

Yesenia Montilla

To this day I still remember sitting
on my abuelo's lap watching   the Yankees hit,
      then run, a soft wind rounding the bases
every foot tap to the white pad gentle as a   kiss.

How I loved those afternoons languidly
      eating jamón sandwiches & drinking root beer.

Later, when I knew something about   the blue collar
man—my father who worked with his hands & tumbled
      into the house exhausted like heat in a rainstorm—
            I became a Mets fan.

Something about   their unclean   faces
            their mustaches   seemed rough
to the touch. They had names like   Wally & Dykstra.
I was certain I would   marry a man just like them

      that is until   Sammy Sosa came along

with his smile a reptile that only knew about lying in the sun.
His arms were cannons and his skin burnt cinnamon
      that glistened in my dreams.

Everyone said he was not   beautiful.

Out in the streets where the men set up shop playing dominoes
I'd hear them say between the yelling of   capicu
      "como juega, pero feo como el diablo."

I knew nothing of my history
    of the infighting on an island on which one side swore
it was only one thing: pallid, pristine.   & I didn't know
    that Sammy carried this history like a   tattoo.

That he wished everyday to be   *white*.

It is a perfect game this race war, it is everywhere,   living
    in the American bayou as much as
    the Dominican dirt roads.
It makes a man do something to his skin that seems unholy.
It makes that same man change   eye color like a soft
    summer dress slipped on slowly.
It makes a grandmother ask her granddaughter

     if she's suffering
    from something feverish
because that could be the only excuse why
    her hair has not been straightened
like a ballerina's back   dyed the color of wild
    daffodils growing in an outfield.

Sammy hit 66 home runs one year
    & that was still   not   enough
    to make him feel handsome

or worthy of that blackness that I believe a gift
even today while black churches burn & black bodies
disappear from one day to the next the same as old
pennies.

I think of him often   barely remember what he looked like

but I can recall his   hunched shoulders in the
dugout   his perfect swing
          & how maybe   he spit out   something black
from his mouth   after every   single   strike—

Dennis

Kaveh Akbar

> Death has always had a prominent place in my mind. . . . I've
> come close at least fifty times.
> —Dennis Rodman

All we want is to never die, but God loves most
the man who offers what he cherishes.

In '93 they found you asleep in your car
with a loaded rifle in your lap.

You said you killed a part of yourself that night,
you could tongue its absence like a missing tooth.

The only cure for sorrow:
more sorrow.

On the court you were all hunger,
filling the spaces no one could fill.

You called yourself *the basketball version
of a gravedigger.*

So often, it seemed:
digging holes, jumping out.

I miss seeing you in action, following
the stars in your hair across the hardwood.

I met you once at a Bulls/Bucks game, called you
Mr. Rodman. You said, *Call me Dennis.*

Dennis, the world of box scores has continued without you
but there are so many kinds of love.

I imagine your evenings are easier now
without all of us tweeping your name.

I hope you've found a happy boring life filled with chamomile,
melatonin, and slow nights laying over themselves

even while the wild moon still hangs loose in the sky
like a ball you could leap for again and again.

At Eighty-Two My Father Is
Learning to Walk Again

Esther Lin

At eighty-two my father is getting steroid shots
in the knees. We tell him he'll be a real menace
on the court now, LeBron better watch out—not

that it was a basketball Olympics, not for us;
this was our summer of Simones—Manuel, Biles,
and our own Simone Lin yelling *the big gals!*

whenever a Simone sprang into her silvers and golds.
During commercials, we visited Rio too,
with Google satellites, spying on our old apartment

on Rua Uruguai. My father cupped his chin and muttered
as he surveyed the losses of the last thirty years:
a market now an office, new crisscrossing street paint,

our pizzeria moved from one corner to another.
And the unchanged—white balconied buildings,
undappled sunlight, our country club's ziggurat-

shaped pool, where my sisters learned to swim
as I buoyed on the stairs. This summer I learned
what my father would not say while my mother lived—

that *we should have stayed.*
Tonight Simone Manuel makes history,
and we wait to the end of the broadcast to see her

jacketed, loose-haired, and weeping. Our tears, too.
How we needed her to win during these months
of *Go home!* and *Do me a favor. Punch 'em!*

We couldn't know how much we needed her
even after the Olympics ended;
Brazil left to a white swimmer's bantam perjuries;

the American refusal of refugees—
how badly we continued to need Manuel's greatness.
Simone sleeps in starfish-pose now, cheeks

flushed, fingers curled. She will sleep just the same
through the speeches of the woman not to be president
through the jeers of *Grab them by the—*

Bob Costas says good night.
We begin our bedtime shuffle; my father still nodding
and saying of Manuel, *Hao, hao! She's too excellent,*

perhaps meaning, *Do we deserve her?*
But he stops midspeech when rising from the couch.
The steroids do their work; he tries once, twice,

then makes it to his walker. Head up, chest out,
don't lean forward. By now he's got it figured out.

Clank

Tomás Q. Morin

You couldn't miss the jersey if you needed glasses. Gold with maroon trim. A giant 23 under the word CAVS. Last year the kid wore a Heat jersey to the courts. This year his favorite player, LeBron James, is back in Ohio. Cleveland is 1,243 miles north of Miami. If the Rust Belt were a real belt, Cleveland would be the cracked red spot in the center of its buckle. One city has sand, the other grit. One Celia Cruz, the other Dwight Yoakum. Both have had their hearts broken by number 23. Except for this kid who is from neither place, who doesn't follow teams but the man. So deep is the kid's devotion that I saw him hit a three-pointer, walk to the other end of the court, and raise one knee, then the other, all while pushing the invisible earth he had just razed back down with his hands. The celebration of his shooting prowess ended with him pounding his chest just like the love of his young life. Sometimes I think "what a sad bastard," and then other times I'm envious that he can still experience a love so naive and pure as to make him impervious to the ridicule of all the guys on the sideline. And at twenty years of age, no less! Usually that kind of idolatry, especially male on male, is stomped on, jeered at, and shamed out of a young boy much sooner.

During the nineties, I was infatuated with Michael Jordan (may the Celtic gods forgive me) when Boston languished and spent the playoffs sitting at home. My tongue wagging every time I drove to the basket, I was trying to fulfill the wet dream of some Gatorade executive and "be like Mike." But jokes behind my back, to my face, all the usual tactics of intimidation and shame that boys are masters at, cured me of this fixation and I relented and began just being me on the court. That and almost biting my tongue in half while trying to do a reverse layup did the trick. But this kid with the thin moustache and floppy hair (he should've picked Pistol Pete) is still at it.

What a piece of luck for him to be already a young man in college and not yet broken on the rack of male shame.

That I call him a kid reveals a sad fact. I'm old. Or at least old enough to be this kid's father. I call him a kid, for Christ's sake! Living in a college town used to make me feel young, but now that I'm the age of their parents, a polite "Sir" or "Mister" waits around every corner for me. One day I woke up and became one of the old guys I played ball with growing up, only without the cool nickname like Joe Dog (animal control officer) or Gator (ladies' man), the Mexican Magic Johnson of Mathis, Texas. Secretly I dream one day I'll play a game with a former student, and after he calls me "Professor," the other kids will pick up on it so that before I know it, I'll be able to step on any court in San Marcos and be known as The Professor. But who am I kidding, what could I possibly teach that they couldn't learn from playing one-on-one with one of their parents? Old equals slow. Surely they can learn that anywhere.

It's been at least six or seven years since I gave up defending guards. No longer can I lock down the opposing team's shooting guards and make them reluctant passers. Where my defense used to be smothering, now it's like a stick of butter on a sidewalk in summer. I'm like the plastic chair the coaches used during practice for us to shoot over and dribble around. Because I'm also just as slow on offense, now I play inside with the bigs, with the guys who at twenty have all the quickness of a thirty-nine-year-old. Sad bastards. Their existence reminds me that things could always have been worse. I need to find some guys my own age to run with, men time has slowed down just as much, so maybe I can move back out to the wing. I never saw my dad or grandfather play basketball. Any sport, really. Maybe they were too old. I once heard my dad had been a good runner, the fastest in his school. Then he moved to another school, and when he realized the black kids were as fast or faster than he was, he started chasing girls and beer instead.

Whenever my eyebrows dip and perch like a bird with black wings in the center of my face, and my mind feels thick with fog, and everything from a yellow light turning red too fast to a drop of rain makes me sad, I grab my ball and find the nearest court. One game of Around the World and Back is enough to set my spirit straight. For years now, seeing the ball go through that metal circle has made my spinning world slow, and in slowing, peaceful and harmless again. And if on an outdoor court, so much the better. The kind Jackie and I played on once when I was thirteen, or maybe fourteen, and we were on the same team. He was winded because it was full court, he smoked, and was thirty-five and never exercised. It seemed as if his every shot found the bottom of the net, though. Bank, fall away, layup, corner three, all as perfect as when we won and he put his tired arm around me. I wanted people to mistake me for his son the way they did when we were out of town, to forget he was black and I was Mexican and looked nothing alike. But this was Mathis and it was home where everyone knew his real son and my real father.

But the kid, I'm forgetting about the kid. He's a couple inches taller than me but chubby. By all rights he should play down low but at some point in his life he probably watched a seven-footer like Dirk Nowitzki sink a three-point shot and found his calling on the court. And boy can he shoot. Before my team took the court to play his winning team, I watched him sink three after three. His defenders would get closer and he'd push his set shot farther and farther behind the arc, accepting the challenge of their dares as he swished one after another. When it was my team's turn to play, I drew the assignment to guard him. Determined not to let him destroy our chances of winning with his outside shooting, not to mention give him an opportunity to emulate LeBron's celebration, I held him scoreless with a simple defensive strategy that played to my speed: I stood next to him. The whole game. The few times he had the ball, he passed it away on account of his not liking to dribble and his inability to shoot while I was standing there. A few minutes in, and I could tell my defense made him mad. Every time I put my hand on his face and denied him a shot, he glared. When I followed him around closely, not letting anyone pass him the ball, he huffed. He even tried to rough me up with a forearm to my chest. I probably shouldn't admit to playing rough with kids, but I couldn't pass up his invitation, so I gave him a hard shove and that's when it happened. Finger jammed. Turned out his chubby body wasn't quite as soft as it appeared. I might as well have jabbed my index finger at a bag of cement. That was three weeks ago and while my finger is getting better, I still can't shoot without pain. So I've done the only thing left to do: learn to shoot with my left.

For a long time now my favorite spot has been the city park. Situated between a spring-fed river and railroad tracks, I don't need headphones to pipe in music because the sound of a train rumbling in the distance and kids on tubes laughing and drinking beer who don't yet know how much the world will mistreat them are a good and proper soundtrack to my life. Not to mention the male grackles who are in heat and puffed up to twice their size and doing their little circle dance and piping their sharp squeaks into the air in the hope of getting laid. Sometimes this is all I need for a day to feel like a win.

On the green court with its white lines I put up shot after shot, badly missing, not even getting the benefit of a gentle roll that my right hand always brought me. And then one goes in. But now I'm farther away as I'm circling the world. And for another to go in I have to be perfect. Perfect spin, perfect angle, perfect height, so it doesn't touch the rim. And I'm in my backyard again when I was nine shooting all day and night at a red milk crate whose bottom I knocked out and nailed to a tree, rotten plywood for a backboard. How that rim wouldn't suffer anything but perfection in order for a shot to go in. Back then I was like the kid and too dumb to know what bravery was and so I threw my round ball, arcing high like Larry Bird's shot, up and at a square hole and wrestled with the laws of geometry.

An hour later (twice as long as it usually takes me), my globetrotting done, I go to the corner and take Jackie's favorite shot and won't leave until it goes in. I square my shoulders, bend my knees, and cock back my arm and flick my left wrist as I rise and leave the ground for a second. *Clank.* That sound over and over. *Clank* for yellow lights. *Clank* for shame. *Clank* for betrayal. *Clank* for pride. *Clank* for the body's sadness. *Clank clank clank* and then, swish. No rim, just a leather globe passing through and snapping the net so that from this spot in the corner, unlike any other spot on the court, when it goes clean through instead of *swish*, the net says *Jack*. When my right hand is well, I snap that net again and again until the world goes calm and mute and all I can hear is *Jack Jack Jack* because everything is right and has stopped burning except for the fire deep in my shoulder.

Liquid

Aaron Smith

The men of Cambridge jog
shirtless this morning

like it's normal to be beautiful
and looked at. Un-secreted

from coats but not-yet-tan,
their meaty chests weave

among overdressed pedestrians.
I'm suddenly shy

when the young guy
with plum nipples, liquid

shoulders taps my shoulder:
You dropped this—a Post-it

I wrote on between his finger
and thumb. Coffee in my one hand

and a bag in the other, he pushes
the note deep in my shirt pocket—

his knuckles to my nipple like they
were always supposed to be there.

So it doesn't fall out again,
he grins. He winks, palms

my shoulder like a father
or boyfriend—he knows that

he knows how to dissolve me—
I better catch up with my girlfriend.

The gesture raw, exposed
as the hair on his flat, damp belly,

as the phone shoved in his shorts
against his hipbone.

Losing the 440-Yard Dash

Afaa M. Weaver

If he hits the curve before you do, all is lost
is all I remember when the coach yelled out
to start, to kick it down the short straightaway

into the curve, the curve a devil's handiwork,
with Worsenski ahead of me, two hundred sixty
pounds, one hundred pounds more than me,

and all I could see were the Converse soles
of a boy I dusted in my dreams on the bus
out here to make the track team, letters

for my sweater, girls going goo-goo over me,
coaches from big-league schools with papers
to say I was headed for glory, my unkempt

disappointment in me now sealed by winged
feet beating me in the curve, Worsenski as big
as the USS *Enterprise* sliding through Pacific

waters, parting the air in front of him that
sucked back behind just to hold me in my grip
of deep shame until I wished I were not there.

I wanted more than being human, a warrior
of field and track would be bursting out now
ripping open my chest with masculinity

to make Jesse Owens proud or jealous,
or inspired or something other than me
the pulling-up caboose slower than mud

running like an old man really walking,
all the most valuable parts of me inside
my brain in wishes, in dreams, in things

not yet born into the world, in calculations
of beauty, in yearning for love, for the word
of love, for some adoration from Wanda,

the most beautiful girl in the whole block,
black like me and wondering just what
life had to give those of us who can fly.

Sports Analogy

David Tomas Martinez

Even if there is no
I in team,
  there is
  damn sure a
  me
  that never fails

   to get
  lost in a
  relationship,

a me, that sees love, as Willie Stargell saw baseball,
  a game where they give you a round bat
and throw you a round ball
   and tell you to hit it square.

Which means love Lawrence Taylor's
me, breaking me like Theisman's leg,
playing
  chin music with each kiss,
  submitting me with a
  guillotine
  she calls hugs, and each conversation
is a red flag the booth is reviewing. *Shit.*
  When I drop back into a relationship,
Anderson Silva cringes.

Allen Iverson once scoffed, *practice?*
   in an interview that convinced fans

he was selfish, but I only saw a frustrated
husband, exasperated from driving around
with his wife,

trying, no begging,
    to decide on where to eat.
        If you have a little capital

I suggest you open a restaurant called
        "No Babe, You Decide."

And I would be grateful for a relationship
full of great pro tips, some good coaching, and decent
        execution, even if there were no *Playoffs* or
        payoffs,

        that pointed me at a
wall, yelled for me to run through it,
        and actually meant it.

        That's why we join teams.

Why to Run Racks

Lisa Fay Coutley

Maybe I shouldn't begin by saying once we die, we can make it rain. Or that I wasn't afraid when a storm knocked the power out and the cat dropped a live mouse at my bare feet while I was peeing before bed the night my sister called and woke me at 4:53 a.m. to tell me that Dad, like Mom, had died in a bathroom. Seven-year-old me might always be sitting upright in a sudsless tub sucking a Fudgsicle and waiting for our sharp rotary phone to set in motion Mom's knees booming to the floor as she pleads, *Oh Jesus, Jesus No,* because Grandpa Rueben had gone too soon to make it rain. The essay always wants to start with her—the girl who knew she'd never again see the mom who'd lose herself to loss—yet the woman looking now so lost through so much loss can only know that every seemingly uncertain beginning is groping toward the same quiet end.

* * * * *

When I bend over the felt, my chin nearly touching my cue, there's never any question where to start or where to go. Catch the edge of the corner ball so it hits the rail and comes back directly to the pocket beneath me. Don't scratch. Knock one other ball loose. Maintain the integrity of the rack knowing the challenge is to consider the next shot while not letting that thought ruin the present moment(um). Of course, I'm thinking none of this as I shoot. I move around the table the same way I walk and talk—fast, exact. I feel my next shot without studying the constellation of balls. I feel where to hit the cue ball to draw it, stop it, or smack the rack. I rarely miss a side-pocket shot. None of this means I know shit about real billiards or have ever learned its principles and techniques. I shoot straight pool by myself to silence every noisy room I'm dragging with me.

* * * * *

This morning—two shopping days left before my first Christmas without parents or sons or blood or love within 1,500 miles—rain from a sky too gray to be sky. By noon, snow-covered mountains as backdrop to birds pecking the mangled tree with bark whipping in long strips like ragged flags in the center of my new yard. I've come to love the duality of weather at elevation—walking the dog in drizzle while snow blankets the crags, hemmed in by mountains impassable yet fragile, within sight of winter but beyond its reach. It's the best way to endure a harsh season, I remember telling my dad. How could I say it was little different than the way I'd learned to prefer distance and solitude to the drama and trauma of family gatherings? The miles made it possible for me to appreciate home, yet each year away meant moving further from my sense of origin and of myself as his familiar little girl.

* * * * *

Running racks is, for me, the meditative act of sinking ball after ball without interruption to my rhythm while challenging no one but myself, which is something that seems to confound most men. Without fail, every time I shoot (often mid-shot), some guy strolls over to comment on my shooting or to ask if I'd *like a game*, as if I couldn't have found someone to tag along if a partner were what I had truly desired most of all. *You're good, but I'm better—wanna play? I sure do like watching you shoot. Hey, you're a good little player. Shark!* I've heard it all, been invited to hustle with men who can calculate every angle but have no heart, and while I'm never surprised to be the only woman in the hall I'm forever flabbergasted that so few shooters can grasp why I'd never play for money or why I prefer to shoot alone or why I couldn't care less about winning or losing to anyone but myself.

* * * * *

After fifty years of three packs (and a six-pack-plus of Pabst) per day, Dad was hypnotized and never smoked again during the six months before lung cancer killed him. Mom had sat vigil over her bottle of vodka so long her leg muscles atrophied till she couldn't walk. She aspirated (breathed her own bile) next to a toilet at age fifty-two. I can't remember how, being right-handed, I became a southpaw shot before I was tall enough to play without a stool in my parents' basement. I can't remember Dad showing me how to hold a cue, but I know the first time I guzzled a can of Budweiser I picked it up from the side rail of said table. I was nine. After six beers I puked six times and passed out in my bed tent surrounded by Pound Puppies. I was nine the first time I smoked a cigarette, ten when I stole and smoked some of Mom's dope, and fifteen the first time I got stoned with Dad. This has nothing and everything to do with the essay.

* * * * *

I suppose every serious shooter wants a true cue and a table as close to flawless as possible, though I'd argue, as it is with learning the body of a new lover, part of the pleasure of playing a favorite table is identifying its weak spots and learning to shoot around, in spite of, or (better yet) into them. My favorite eight feet of slate stands at Fat's in Salt Lake City between a table with a slight roll that I don't want to learn and another that's too close to the bathroom. Mine is in the middle, and although the pockets need repairing, so that every time I make a side shot my ball falls to the floor and hitches my rhythm, I get anxious every time I pull into the parking lot and consider that some other schmuck might be on *my* table, which is little different from someone strumming another musician's guitar or another writer sitting down to plunk away at my laptop at my desk.

* * * * *

Mom once told me that while she was pregnant with me my dad tried to drown her in our bathtub. Us, she said—*he tried to kill* us. *It never happened*, Dad told me when I asked years later. *Make no mistake*, he said, *I wanted to kill her, but not like that.* He went on to tell me about a plan he and his brother had hatched to kill their wives where they'd often drink in Mom's car parked at the yacht club across from the Pulliam Plant that spread its arcade of smokestack lights across the Fox River. I imagine Mom and Aunt Kathy parked there, sharing a joint and bitching about being housewives to Vietnam vets who beat them—two uneducated women without a better outlet for their desires, who went from their fathers' houses to their husbands', and who never could distance themselves from the storm and instead just continued changing the weather inside their only commodities, their bodies.

* * * * *

Dad thought it was *neat* that I love to shoot pool. I suppose in some ways, as a Midwestern, blue-collar journeyman, he was pleased to picture his tiny, female daughter playing men who never expected to have their asses handed to them. He loved an underdog story, and winning was crucial, especially for his girl playing a man's sport. He also understood my need to play alone in the same way he knew my love of lakes and poetry, having instilled in me a need for music since I was a small girl in charge of resting the needle without a scratch and later when called upon to analyze the lyrics of every sad or political song he'd play ad nauseam. Such is the confounding, paradoxical nature of a man who would cry retelling his case of typhoid fever with its endless shots in the ass and months of quarantine and then knock down the biggest guy in the bar in front of his five-year-old daughter.

* * * * *

My parents stopped hating each other under the same roof the same year I slammed my first beer and smoked my first cig. For years I struggled with some form of habit—smoking, drinking, falling for bad men—and it's taken years to be able to say it out loud. In many ways, having distance from the storm is more troubling than the rush of standing in the eye and watching chaos whirl all around me. To be outside of the family squall means quiet (no fighting, no crying), but in truth, the lullaby's a muted wish. Staring myself square in the face and not liking all that I see—yet not smoking or drinking or feigning love or otherwise drowning me out—is fucking terrifying. It took me twenty-seven years to quit smoking—once I realized I was just lonely, and a cigarette was the one friend that never let me down. A year later, I'm still on the prowl for any upset, any reason to fail myself and start again.

* * * * *

I know there is nothing special about my story—nothing extraordinary about a girl who was raised in a volatile home and spent most of her time at the shore's edge behind her house because only in the water's push and pull did she find stillness inside herself; who was eight when she bound her first book and told her mother she would be an author and then promptly forgot herself until she was a young, troubled mother of two, writing by dim light while everyone slept in an attempt to save her own life; who would eventually return to school—much to the amusement of her father who had watched her squander four years of high school—where she would fall in love with words and herself and a man who'd remind her of her need for pool; who would eventually relinquish the man but revel in the game that moves in her and saves her as does water and language and love.

* * * * *

The morning Dad died was really the night (gauged by the darkness). I can't say whether I made my mocha by artificial light, changed out of my robe, or heard what my friend was saying when I turned the corner on the deck to find the sun jackknifing over the mountains. I'm neither superstitious nor religious. I am happy to be stardust, and I've always known in my gut that death is nothing to fear. Watching others go before me and not getting mired in loss—that's the hard part. Losing the last human who knew me in every moment of myself—that felt significant. I was just another sad woman turning another sad corner, and I hit a wall of rain. Everywhere, tinsel. Halfway to the deck's end, the straightest rain fell silent and steady and slow between me and the mountains drenched in sun—silver so still in its movement for one, long moment—never shifting, falling only in half of the yard. Then, it was gone.

* * * * *

Maybe I'm wrong about distance. Maybe (thankfully) the essay can never know its own start or end. Yet I refuse to wait until I'm dead to make it rain. I refuse to need to control the weather inside me. I refuse to pretend that I can embrace the mountains' heft all harsh season long, the heart in the grip of some force I can neither stop nor love enough, but I have found my ways to dance no matter what this valley delivers. Some people do yoga. Others meditate. Many medicate. I've tried them all. Even on a bad sciatica day, I prefer to bend myself level with the felt and aim without thinking *aim*, without gripping the cue too tight, without jabbing at the ball as if I'm as angry as my fear thinks it has a right to be. To follow through smooth means to trust my hands and my eyes and to forget that I exist. It means quiet, despite the storm that I'm in or the storm that I am.

El Barril

James Thomas Stevens

In the one-time mecca of the hard-up honeymoon,
we were both born.

Yours, a life above the waterfall. Mine, below.

And Annie Taylor? We were all schooled in her story. How Miss
Michigan schoolteacher took on the cataract at sixty-three.
In her petticoats and lace-up boots, clutching her good-luck-
heart-shaped-satin pillow, she stepped into the barrel where,
two days earlier, she had placed her cat to test pilot the way.
Air pressured in by a bicycle pump, bung in the hole, mattress
wrapped. And the fall, fall, fall, emerging twenty minutes later.
Only head gashed and rib bruised to proclaim:
I would sooner walk up to the mouth of a cannon, knowing it was
going to blow me to pieces than make another trip over the Fall.

And in our two year, two year, two year fall. What was bruised if
not broken?

Your C-3 vertebra, out of whack.
Slack, from practice. Your tendons overwrought,
too taut from the bow, taught by the bow.

And my base pain, in the neck.
Now I know the days you play,
curse Bach and his concerto
for a doubled violin.

Who Got This Far

Marissa Johnson-Valenzuela

On Beauty. On Boxing. On Seeing. On being.
Being. On laying in bed beside you and not wanting to move.
On rambling and unfinished. On dangers only little a can see.
On poetry that lives and poetry that kills because who knew it could
but maybe it did. That's part of what happened, I believe,
when words failed to replace. When disintegration.

And lines were always just lines even when they sounded new.

On aging. On forgetting. On distillation then drinking.
On avoiding what's in front of you, beside you, brought with you
from Florida to Philadelphia where there are classless
rooms of people reading poetry, life and death drinking on
with complicated pleasure. Greedy residual believers. Who insist
they have evidence. Laughter. Involuntary smiles. Better sex.

And so, the fucker of potential next to the fucker who got this far.

On poem as response. As futile and essential as celebrations
on the inside; shadowboxing. On air hustling to hear secret, honest
    breath
and blood: what ribs protect. Do not forget this feeling, Marissa. It's
    beautiful
to be seen. Brightly colored. And it's okay they don't want
    everything, you
have everything, and you have had luck. So stop forgetting. Play in
    the dead
leaves. And sing. Or swim.

Swim in the cold early morning gray that is this eastern shore.

Project Artifacts

Through the Banks of the Red Cedar

Maya Washington

A documentary film

ABC *World News Tonight. August 3, 2011*

Diane Sawyer: We have a passing to note tonight. A star of sports and later the movies: Bubba Smith, born Charles Aaron Smith in Beaumont, Texas. The 6'7" defensive standout for the Raiders, Oilers, and Colts. He went on to act in the Police Academy movies. Bubba Smith was 66.

Los Angeles, CA—August 2011

You ever thought about how your body fits in the world
How big fits with small and vice versa
How I'm a giant but I can't go in that store
How I left the Golden Triangle with change in my pocket
How I returned in a white Riviera
How I affixed five gold decals on the door to spell my name like
    an address

I've got all the riches, baby, one man can claim

You ever thought about how a body fits in the world
How every article starts out saying I'm 6'7" and 290 pounds
What I hear when a stadium full of white folks chants "Kill,
    Bubba, Kill"
How being this big this black and this fast feels on game day
What it's like to fall for a Lansing girl and take her to a movie
How easily I settle into darkness when her arm rests against mine

How cramped it all feels when the lights come on
What it's like not to hold her hand as we walk home

I've got all the riches, baby, one man can claim

Think about how a body fits in a world
How a heart breaks like a record or a bone
What it's like to be the number one pick
How people only remember a white Riviera
What I weighed
How tall I stood

I've got all the riches, baby, one man can claim

Washington, DC—August 1963

Nineteen sixty-three is not an end, but a beginning. And
those who hope that the Negro needed to blow off steam
and will now be content will have a rude awakening if the
nation returns to business as usual.

—Martin Luther King Jr.

Baldwin Hills, CA—August 2011

I don't know how many times I've cut through Baldwin Hills
to get to 'SC from Inglewood or Culver City over the years.
I could have been walking through the Target parking lot
on La Cienega as he passed in his car on the way home from
the gym. It's been a week since he died—the news teams
and their live shots are no longer on the front lawn. There's
a quaint little potluck spread of fruit, crackers, cheese, and
meats on the dining room table. My dad and his teammates
tell stories. The den reminds me of my dad's trophy room
and the '80s. I sit on Bubba's enormous sofa as if I'm Lily
Tomlin. As if I'm the little girl standing next to him while
he signs autographs at MSU homecoming back when he

was *Police Academy* famous and I heard *On the Banks of
the Red Cedar* for the first time. He was my first real-life
movie star. The only man I've ever met that was bigger
than my dad. Who I realize, in this moment, was once 19,
had friends, and a life, long before I was born. He's been
fielding calls from reporters on his flip phone the whole
trip. Details about how they played against each other as
teenagers in an all-black league. I wonder what would have
happened if Bubba and his dad hadn't spoken up when
Duffy asked if there were any other black boys they should
take a look at. I wonder how many heavily recruited kids
today would go out of their way to tell a Division I school
about an opponent 80 miles away. Most of my life, I
believed magical white men came down to Texas, plucked
my dad out of Jim Crow, and gave him a scholarship to
MSU. He played for the Vikings, got injured, was traded
to the Broncos, retired, and eventually had me. Those
were pretty much all the details I knew. It never occurred
to either of us that I was missing pieces. What good are
details in a *Negro makes good* narrative, anyway? All people
ever want to know is if he still goes to all the games and
if I can get them an autograph. Simply knowing that a
scholarship changed his life was enough for me until we
take pictures outside on the patio. It's perfect LA weather.
With the pool catching moonlight and the occasional fly,
it feels more like a barbecue than a wake. Bubba's friend
Eli, who was with him when he died, tells me how he was
trying some new treatments as he recovered from back
surgery. They were getting ready to go to the gym and
Eli noticed he'd been in the bathroom a little longer than
usual. He discovered Bubba had collapsed on the floor.
The idea that he hadn't planned to die that day—the fact
that it just happened while he was in there reading his
Bible guts me. As the night wears on, nature calls me to

the bathroom. I have a private cry. I dry my hands on the monogrammed hand towel. I whisper *thank you*.

Baytown, TX—May 2013

> The ghosts of segregation
> hang in the air like cicadas
> hissing in the grass. Not far
> from the train tracks, scraggly
> stray heifers graze amid rusty
> junk cars along the narrow road.
> The dirty blonde lifts her head, makes
> eye contact. She turns back toward
> the others as if to say, *As you were.*

La Porte, TX—May 1963

> *They would have taken Gene on a Tiddlywinks*
> *scholarship. All the Big Ten schools wanted Bubba Smith.*
> *Because of that recommendation, Gene made it to*
> *Michigan State.*
>
> —ML Phillips, *Community Elder*

Coach Willie Ray Smith, Sr., was Bubba's father. He was known in Beaumont at Charlton Pollard High School. I played against Bubba in our segregated league when I was bused to George Washington Carver in Baytown. We didn't have a black high school in La Porte. Bubba said he would put in a good word to Duffy Daugherty for me. Duffy would get to know black coaches—bring them up to Michigan State because the clinics in the South were closed to blacks. None of us could go to the major schools in the South. Not even the University of Texas. By the time I was a senior in high school, he was still the only white coach in America getting black players from the South. There were other black players here or there, but Duffy had more

black starters than anybody by the time we made varsity. I
remember when I was being recruited, Danny Boisture was
the backfield coach for us. He came down just to represent
the university, to offer me a scholarship. This was after
Duffy had agreed to bring me on board because of Bubba's
recommendation. Everyone wanted Bubba so they almost
took me sight unseen. Danny came to our home. We had
never had a white person in our home. He came in and we
were sitting at the table and Danny proceeded to talk about
Michigan State, how great the university was, the tradition
of football and East Lansing, all of that. And so my dad
was looking puzzled and said, "What is a scholarship, what
does that mean?" Danny explained to him that everything
was free and everything would be taken care of. Then my
mother asked . . . mom said, "Well, how will he get up to East
Lansing, Michigan?" He says, "We'll pay for all that too."

Washington, DC—August 2013

I'm wearing my cousin's oversized raincoat. We sit on the
ground under a tree near the end of the reflection pool.
Scaffolding is set up in front of us for the fancy people.
In the distance, Oprah and Clinton are specs beyond the
security barricade. I think about freedom.

Dallas, TX—November 1963

In the State of Texas, you can be murdered. Even if you are
the President.

East Lansing, MI—November 1963

On November 23, 1963, Gene Washington turns 19
years old. He stays on campus and shares crackers and
sausage from a care package sent from the mother
of halfback Clinton Jones. Over the Thanksgiving
holiday, the cafeteria is closed. They have nowhere to
go. They eat crackers. When school resumes, Duffy

Daugherty motivates the players with his Three Bones Philosophy: Players must possess a funny bone—to enjoy playing the game and have fun every day of their lives. They need a wish bone—to think big so their deeds will grow and they will dream of winning the Big Ten Championship and dream of going to the Rose Bowl. That they will want to be the greatest to ever play for Michigan State or the best player to ever represent their hometown. The third and most important bone is a backbone—to have a backbone means they have the gumption to get up. The fortitude, the stick-to-it-ness to make all these dreams and wonderful ambitions come true. A wishbone. A funny bone. And a backbone.

La Llorona Runs Alone

Claudia D. Hernández

When I was born, mother said I spun out of her like a torpedo ready to destroy things. Ready to run. I didn't crawl like most babies do at that age. Instead, I dragged my body across the dirt floor as if I were a tiny soldier ready for war. I have always been ready for war. Ready to fight my little battles. When I took my first steps, mother said I ran across the living room trying to hold on to something, someone. She said I fell many times, but I also got up ready to run. Ready to fight.

I fought my first battle when I was seven. It was 1985, the year Mother immigrated to the United States. She left my two older sisters and I under the care of grandma, during the civil war in Guatemala. This was my first war: fighting for space in a crowded home, fighting for food, fighting for love. I was out on the streets every day running until dawn, listening to the Chuchumatan mountains screech, burning with the Ixil people's souls.

Mother returned to Guatemala for my sisters and I when I was ten. She promised us a trip that would pacify our hunger. The plan was to cross the border illegally to the U.S. This was another battle I won—we won—turquoise victory. We walked long distances through the night, beneath the paleness of the moon. Mud up to our knees—shedding broken shards. And all I wanted to do was run to get there, to get here faster. Now I'm home, faraway from home.

When I was in middle school, still struggling to learn English, Ms. Maddy, my PE teacher, noticed my ability to run. "Why don't you join track and field, Claudia?" she asked. With my limited English I explained that I was a Jehovah's Witness. "I can't, it's against my religion." She shook her head in disappointment and never asked me again. During my senior year, I got expelled from the cult for falling in love.

Mother says I'm a warrior. I face my battles head on. I ran my first San Francisco full marathon without training—a raw soldier in the making. I finished it despite the hills. My ups and downs, like the San Francisco hills, became more pronounced as I aged. I tore my right meniscus after running six marathons. And I was still hungry for more. I had surgery and stopped running for two years. When I came back, I joined Team Runners High.

Mother says running comes natural to me like the way lighting pierces the sky on a tempestuous night. But at the age of thirty-six, I had a mental breakdown. Some think Guatemalan women are tougher than an old-fashioned wrought head nail. We don't get mental illnesses. We simply go crazy. We turn into mythical Lloronas. But even the toughest nail crumbles by erosion. Running became my therapy—my only medicine at the time.

Mother doesn't believe in cyclothymic disorder. "Focus and try to control your emotions, especially your suicidal and racing thoughts," she says. I tell her my mental illness doesn't paint my story. Now I contemplate my highs and lows. Zyprexa, my biggest foe, has slowed me down, but I believe Mother when she tells me, "You're a warrior, an unstoppable torpedo. Keep going. Keep running." I laugh. I can only *embrace* myself. I am my Mother's daughter. I am La Llorona who runs alone.

Alone in the Schoolyard at Dusk

Dorianne Laux

I socked the tetherball
and watched it travel high
on its rope around the pole,
the hollow metal pinging,
the rope twisting tighter
and tighter, the ball
traveling faster
as the rope shortened,
finally bouncing off
the pole and back
in the opposite direction
for a while, the rope
slithering down the pole,
loosening its grip,
unraveling, letting go.
Then I lifted it up
with my five curved
fingers and balanced
it there like a smooth
moon, then I socked it
out of my own hand
and each time it arced
and swung close
socked it again like a face
I hated, but featureless,
a few scores down
its sallow cheeks, nothing
remarkable, nothing
that could identify it
in a lineup, though

my fingerprints
were all over it, some
smudged, but surely
at least one that was
perfect, liftable,
traceable, that could be
used against me in a court
of law, that could prove
that the violence inside me
was there all along, hidden
inside my closed fists.

why i can't play basketball anymore

Richard Vargas

i was shooting baskets in the driveway
faking and slicing between the team i hated the most
the Celtics never had a chance on my home court

i knew every crack in the cement
where the surface went from rough to smooth
and how tennis shoes would skid an extra
two inches when stopping on a dime

from which angle i had to attack the basket without
slamming into the garage door like a pancake
my hoop was crooked too, giving me another edge
since only i knew where the rebounds would be

i always won, and while calling the game on the radio
Chick Hearn would praise my ability to put
my opponent "in the popcorn machine"
as the crowd gave me a standing ovation

on this day my stepfather interrupted the game
had to be somewhere in a hurry
i stepped aside while he backed the car out of the garage
it was always a tight squeeze, but if i sucked in my
stomach and pressed my backside into the fence
he could glide by me with a couple of inches to spare

but this time he braked when i was beside the driver's window
and as i stood there, unable to move in any direction
feeling truly trapped by a tenacious full court press

he started talking yard work, something about mowing the lawn
it was on my agenda, and as i tried to explain
he reached out the window and grabbed my crotch

it took everything i had to suppress the whimper trying to escape
through my clenched jaw
then, he let go
didn't say a word
vanished into the street

i stood there, puzzled
waited for the ref to call a foul
but when the whistle didn't blow
i looked up through blurred tears

knew i was alone
under a cloudless sky

The Condition of Being a Sports Fan

Sue Hyon Bae

Not only have I been unathletic my entire life, to the extremes of not knowing how to ride a bicycle without training wheels at age twenty-six and rushing across a room rather than trying to catch anything thrown at me, I always thought love of team sports idiotic. I could understand why the athletes and the athletes' families and friends might care, but I didn't see why anybody else would. What is a team? What does it mean to be a fan of a team? What if you haven't lived in the same city your whole life, or your team up and moves, or literally every player who was on the team when you started being a fan is no longer on the team? What makes some players fan-able, and what happens when your favorite is traded? To the rival team? Why do people remain loyal to teams rather than to players? Why are some teams your mortal rivals when all teams are technically your team's rivals? Why do people whose only participation in the sport is to watch it at home refer to the team as *we*? What does the performance of a group of strangers have to do with civic or national pride?

I was in South Korea during the World Cups of 2002 and 2008. When South Korea scored, I could hear not only my grandmother shouting in one room and my grandfather shouting in another room, but an eerie noise outside, every other person in the country screaming simultaneously, sounding as though every Korean in history had briefly come back as ghosts, and I did not understand it. My biology partner in high school was exhausted every day because of football practice, and I did not understand why American students spent so much time on something as trivial as sports. I went with my boyfriend's family to an Indians game—why would any team still have a logo called Chief Wahoo?—and I did not understand why they paid money to be made to stand up during the seventh inning.

I was proud of my ignorance of sports. I stood aloof above all these irrational people. And then, out of nowhere, ice hockey descended on me like an autoimmune disease: with neither cause nor cure, it simply showed up and settled in and against my body. This is my first season as a sports fan, and these are the changes that have happened to my unathletic body:

Unreliable Memory

I do not know how to skate. I have never been to Pennsylvania. I do not know any other hockey fans. My team is the Pittsburgh Penguins, and my favorite player is Sidney Crosby. I literally can't remember how this happened to me. It must have been during the summer of 2016, because I don't remember paying attention to the 2016 playoffs, and I watched some of the preseason games at the start of the 2016–2017 season. I spent most of the summer in South Korea, so I can't have seen any hockey in person or on TV. My best guess is that I saw a clip or gif of the Penguins online, probably one in which their movements look bizarre to somebody not used to watching skaters, like when players suddenly appear sliding sideways for a celebratory hug, and I looked them up and fell in.

On the other hand, even though this is my first season, I have emotions associated with previous seasons, such as my lingering favoritism for Fleury, how relieved I was on March 1st, the trade deadline this year, when he wasn't traded. We can't trade Flower, he's one of the 2009 Stanley Cup Champions!—which I never watched. I also track former Penguins who were traded years ago, which causes a domino effect: Jordan Staal and James Neal were traded to Nashville in 2012 and 2014 respectively, so I sort of care about the Preds, so I was agitated when the Preds traded Weber to the Habs, etc.

Attention to Detail

Sid's Emmy award says *Sidney Crosby, Talent*, which is the funniest Sidney Crosby fact. I love him more than any other stranger in the world even though he's a human black box. Does he have a personality or personal opinions? Probably, but we'll never know. I think he memorized a few sheets of sports clichés back in Juniors and he just repeats them as though every interview is Mad Libs. I still watch his post-practice, pre-game, and post-game interviews and get a kick out of his gross sweat-salty cap every time, that superstitious fucker.

Identity Confusion

The 2018 Winter Olympics are being held in Pyeongchang, South Korea. It would make sense to root for my birth country, South Korea, or my current country of citizenship, the United States, but I will be rooting for Canada, a country I visited once, ten years ago, to renew my American visa. Sid scored the golden goal in Vancouver, and he captained the gold-winning team in Sochi; I need him to do both simultaneously. Kunitz, my third favorite Penguin, was on the roster for Sochi, along with other Canadians I have somehow come to like: Weber, Luongo, Price, Bergeron, Subban, and I'm guessing McDavid will qualify for Pyeongchang. As for the American team, Phil Kessel's cool, but that's about it. As for the South Korean team, I had no idea hockey existed in South Korea. As for the NHL's insistence that NHL players will not participate in the 2018 Olympics, whatever, Gary Bettman, nobody likes you.

Negative Emotions

I hate the Blackhawks so much I actually don't want to talk about them. I hate the Blue Jackets, especially Dubinsky. I even hated the Yotes and the Avs for a few weeks, even though they're lovable in their terribleness, because the Pens had back to back losses against them in February. The players themselves probably don't hate each other this much. Hockey players have more in common with each other than they do with us deranged fans. Last summer Sid trained with Brad Marchand, so they're probably friends, but when Sid was in a very brief scoring slump and Marchand had more goals than Sid for a few days in mid-March, Marchand's face transmogrified into a Joker sneer every time I checked the stats on my NHL app.

Sid knocked him back down to second place with a hat trick against the Sabres, and that fixed Marchand's face halfway.

Color Perception

The Penguins' colors used to be blue and white, but they changed to black and gold in 1980 to match the Pirates and Steelers. They sometimes wear throwback blue and white jerseys, which are bad colors, because Sid had his worst injuries in them, but their jerseys this season are black and yellow or white and black, which are great colors that go well with the Stanley Cup. The Bruins jerseys look similar with more stripes, but the colors just don't work right on the Bruins. And obvioussly orange is the ugliest color because the Philadelphia Flyers wear orange and are captained by a ginger and I hate all Flyers on principle, except Wayne Simmonds, because ice hockey is really white and I support POC players on principle.

Knowledge of Geography

I now know the locations of seven Canadian cities because there are seven Canadian teams. I know that Philadelphia and Pittsburgh are five hours apart by car, and that Philadelphia is terrible. If I had had the chance to visit Pennsylvania before hockey happened to me, I would have chosen Philadelphia because of its place in American history, but that's all ruined now.

Cognitive Dissonance

Sometimes Sid does something that even I have to admit is bad, like slashing Methot hard enough to damage his finger so severely I don't want to watch the video again to confirm whether the finger was actually cut off or just dangling in an unsettling way, or that crotch shot, or that time he pushed Voracek's glove down the ice like a sulking child. Sometimes the sport itself bothers me, like how the referees don't intervene immediately in fights, or the use of feminizing language as insults by fans, or the struggles of female hockey players to make a living. And then I watch a clip from Sportsnet of Sid netting a one-handed backhand goal, and I am fooled into thinking all is well in the world.

Voluntary Muscle Control

As I was falling asleep one Saturday night in March, at least six hours after the end of the Penguins' last game of the season against the Flyers, my body left my control: my mouth said *I can't believe we lost to the fucking Flyers*, my shoulders twitched as though they were trying to shrug off a burden, my legs shoved the cat off the bed, my hands grabbed fistfuls of Luke's shirt as my mouth continued, *It's okay, we're clinched for playoffs*. It's all okay. This is the year the Penguins are going to win back to back Cups again.

Take Me Out

Iliana Rocha

On our way to the Astros game, my brother photographs
the Southwest Inn on Highway 59, its charred

exoskeleton exposed to hungry rubberneckers. The photo
lasts only seven seconds, mocks memory's ephemerality,

how trouble finds itself combustible in the tiniest of spaces.
Clouds, today, have posed too, a crowd of bleached blondes.

His smile is of the street grates downtown, commuters walking
toward home, workdays marked by Houston's oil-slicked

sun, the orange of a suffering fingernail. Somewhere,
happiness has traveled in front of us as we pass the billboards

of dead firefighters stately portraited. American flags
humbled at half-mast. The outfield deck is what we can afford,

our spare change, ice bobbing in sugary-sweet margaritas.
A woman has the rival team's logo haphazard on her cheek.

We threaten each foul ball as if it's the back of our father's hand.
I buy him one more drink than I should, as if to say,

Tell me how to reach you. Tell me how to lasso lightning.

Parking Lot Poem with Fernando Valenzuela

Matthew Lippman

His screwball is magnificent.
That's what the kid said.
He said it right there on the stoop.
To the TV woman.
Some woman who had gone down to Etchohuaquila, in Mexico,
in the state of Sonora,
to find out what there was to find out
about a screwball.
She cried all the way there.
She cried all the way back.
The whole force of a million Chicanos in her tears.
Her eyes corked up inside her head.
Remember his eyes,
how he looked up before they found the plate?
Some said he was talking to God.
There is romance in everything.
You just have to hold the ball soft enough,
let it go at just the right moment,
the arm contorted,
the seams magnificent neon radiators of heat.
In 1981
if you were not in LA
you were in LA.
In 1981
if you were not Mexican
you were Mexican.
And then, after it was all over,
Fernando quiet in Fernando,
the winter a pocket of snow in a baseball mitt,
what was Mexican in you

never left you
no matter how white, black, Puerto Rican, Japanese, mango
     tree Tahitian, you were.
You were magnífico.
You were the screwball of magnificence,
moving away from the left hand hitter in the box,
you were breaking down and in—
in Diego Rivera purple,
in Siquieros gold.
in Frida Kahlo monkey.
And all of us
were that little kid on the stoop,
one step from humility
and all you had to do was ask,
all you had to do was grab it by the seams,
raise your eyes to the clouds
and hurl.

Strike Indicator

Pamela Hart

Like a small brain tethered to the world
    by tippet and line

it loops, landing with plunk
    or sometimes grace

Explosive as in a dream
    the orange orb

spreads its swirling spine
    into a sideways drift

which isn't about bald eagles carving
    the course of the Yellowstone

While a pattern of water
    folds its dissolve into

river / pool
    desire / seam

you detach from the ticking of a day
    become rod and fly and rock

Always this ongoing story of torrent
    as the indicator bobs, signaling a strike

and the restless globe is pulled into bubbling foam
   line and mind tugged under the fiery riffle

The beautiful cutthroat rising
   to meet you or not

Minor League Legend

Matthew Olzmann

Maybe you're the second baseman for the Montgomery Biscuits. Or the backup shortstop for the Albuquerque Isotopes. Entire civilizations might not know these teams even exist, but the ghosts of Michigan assembly lines still gather in the stands to watch you snag fly balls as centerfielder for the Lansing Lugnuts. Pig iron gets melted down to make steel, and memories of the industrial revolution smolder beneath your city. And look at you: starting catcher for the Leigh Valley IronPigs. Designated hitter for the Ogden Raptors. Middle reliever for the Toledo Mud Hens. Most of history gets forgotten, a foul ball sailing into the dark. Out there, in the crowd, a spectator makes the catch and takes home a souvenir. That could be my grandfather sixty years ago. Or maybe his brother. Whichever one it was, they're both long dead. Perhaps they too dreamed of championships. Instead, tool and die makers. Instead, bleacher seats and a long walk home. Not even a fraction of the eight billion people on the planet can do this better than you. This means you're elite. Third baseman for the Vermont Lake Monsters. Setup man for the Hartford Yard Goats. And somehow, so far from where you hope to finish. The big league. The illuminated field. Your hands lifting a trophy. But for now: utility infielder for the New Orleans Baby Cakes. Pinch runner for the Altoona Curve. Left-handed specialist for the Akron RubberDucks. It's the ninth inning. Someone keeps shouting from the cheap seats. In another life, he's cheering you on. In this one, he's ordering a beer.

Losing to the Invisible

An Ars Poetica

Traci Brimhall

He hands me his wire-framed glasses before turning, bowing, and stepping onto the mats. Today's tournament is one of the days my husband fights his visible enemies. Earlier I packed his *gi*, mouth guard, one-pound gloves, groin cup, bananas, bottled water, and gummy bears, the duffle crinkling with old granola bar wrappers. We spend our Saturdays in old gymnasiums and church basements that smell like weak chili and wet socks. My husband fights new strangers. A curious but easily bored spectator, I watch and read Ovid's *Amores*. The day full of pleasured and damaged bodies. There are no weight classes, and today the man who bows to my husband has twenty pounds on him and is four inches taller. Later I find out he plays football, loves his girlfriend, and wishes his grades in college were better. *Hajime!* the judge shouts, and they begin.

Brown belts are the worst fighters for me to watch. The green and yellow belts jab tentatively, making light contact to the body— *chudan*. The young fighters' heads are wrapped in giant foam to protect against any ambitious attempt to strike *jodan*. Purple belts grow more aggressive, and the rounds of their fights stretch from adorable to brave to tedious. Brown belts have the force and skill to hurt each other without the restraint and practice of a black belt. The man who bows to my husband feints too quickly, charges, and attempts to throw a right cross before landing heavily and crushing my husband's foot. *Good enough for lesser verse—laughed Cupid / so they say, and stole the foot away.* I find out later the fractures to my husband's first metatarsal and medial cuneiform will never heal correctly, and he'll ache when the weather turns.

Yame! the judge calls. Zero points. They go to their sides of the mat.

My husband's gi is stiff as sailcloth folded over the softness of his body. He turns around to the crowd and adjusts his belt and gi, closing the gap that opens over the dark and downy hairs of his chest. It shows respect for his opponent not to step onto the mat in disarray. I admire the gestures of respect, but what I love is the vulnerability of it. *Still all this I can see, but what the cloth may well hide / that's the cause of my secret fears,* Ovid wrote. *I'll make it clear I'm your lover, / and say "they're mine!," and take possession.* My husband shields his body from one set of eyes to show dozens that he's starting to come undone. When I used to model at an art school, I never felt exposed when I was naked. It was only the moment I reached for a robe that made me uncomfortable. The act of switching states from undressed to dressed felt private, more unguarded than the still, reclining nude pose. Even with others watching him, he still feels entirely mine, smoothing his gi, shaking the sting out of his cheeks.

Above the door to his *dojo* a sign reads: "The ultimate aim of karate lies not in victory or defeat, but in the perfection of the character of the participant." The impossible goals are always the most appealing. Like writing a great poem, a goal worthy of my failure. Chudan, *judan,* knowing you'll lose but trying to score those hits on the head and body before time runs out.

My husband winces and limps back onto his line. He's fond of saying it's important to get hit in the face because it makes anything else seem less scary by comparison. This face punch, the *judan-tzuke,* works only if the ball of his rear foot stays in contact with the mat, but it always happens too fast for me to watch where someone's foot is placed. I'm too busy looking at my husband's face going soft, boyish, almost confused. My husband attempts the impossible but loses twice—to his opponent and his anger.

Finished with his fight with the visible in *kumite,* my husband waits for his round of *kata,* his bout with the invisible. Each kata is full of rapid turns and jumps, strikes against the air and sometimes his own body, his instincts training for when the fight is real. His *kiai* is louder than anyone else's. His intention knifes through the air, his focus singular on something I can't see. He often practices around the house, breaking invisible holds in the kitchen, his kiai softer in the apartment, like an arrow in flight that never finds the target. He is better at this than kumite, though I don't tell him that.

I wonder if it's because he can see the invisible more clearly. Even with his glasses off, he can feel in his body where the invisible enemy is waiting in a way he can't when his enemy is two feet away and more power than mastery. His body is all line and swiftness and control. *But, I think, if love were attacking me I'd feel it,* Ovid claims. *Surely he's crept in and hurt me with secret art.* In public my husband always positions himself toward the doors of restaurants or stands between me and strangers. He sees the potential in those moments that I don't see, but in these moments when he stands over the invisible enemies whom he's defeated I love him in the way I love God—foreign, inscrutable, and full of the power to harm but holding back.

I love to watch kata at any skill level. It makes the body more clear to me than the violence. That practice with intent. I understand both ways of fighting but appreciate the technical aspects without the fear in kata. I know this practice. I rehearse line breaks, playing with sound, working on endings as if they are the *ikken hisatsu*— the killing blow. But in that practice, I'm more fearless because the stakes seem low. All the judan and chudan hypothetical.

My husband and I watch our friend dance through her round of kata. She is precise, even delicate. *She is excellent but incomplete,* he says. I want to know how he knows, what he sees that my eyes haven't been trained for. *Because you always know, watching her, that she doesn't feel threatened,* he says. *She isn't losing to anything.* That's what I learn to see, the enemy that isn't there but could be. The threat of air. The fear necessary to really practice for a fight. Before she leaves the mat, she turns and bows to the enemy she never saw.

Though he lost to his visible enemy, my husband wins his round of kata. His sensei talks to him afterward about his performance, and they quietly rush through a hundred details I may or may not have seen. How comforting to have a master in the room. I've always preferred to fail privately. I keep those lessons discreet, my short-comings not much of a spectacle. His losses live in home videos and people's minds, though they live in his own thoughts longest. He is weeks away from his black belt test, so he goes over each missed step, each imperfect strike, each missed opportunity. His sensei has told him that the black belt is not a symbol of mastery. It is the beginning of the practice, not its culmination. Once he has fought his way through the visible and the invisible, he is not a master but a prepared beginner.

We spoon our watery chili out of Styrofoam bowls and pack up to leave. He is quiet, still living in the fight and trying to understand it. When we get home, he unpacks his bag, throws his gi in the washing machine, and puts his medals in a drawer. The first time I went over to his apartment and made out with him on his broken blue couch, the only form of decoration were those medals. Gold, silver, muted bronzes dangling from the undusted bookcase. He told me later he'd been hoping they would impress me, his own pride becoming mine. *Shall I give in: to go down fighting might bank the fires? / I give in!* Ovid cries, surrendering, sublimed. I kiss him and go to my office to write. *What are you doing?* he asks, and I say, *Losing to something.*

High School Yoga

Kat Page

Miss, can you play this song today in yoga class?
    I've been thinking about the story you told us last week
and the question you asked . . . *If we are Krishna, Arjuna and*
    everything what does it matter?

I couldn't go to Five Points for the quinceañera   not that
    she was a close friend
      or family,
she only wanted me there because I fit the height of the rest of
    her *court*.
    A good match to one of her cousins.

My boyfriend is a foot shorter than me and would'a been all
    mad if I went.
    It would turn into him yelling at me *Go with him then if*
      you want someone taller than me.
I didn't want to deal with it.   I didn't want to go anyway.
    She lied to the priest about being a virgin.
She should'a just told the priest, *yes, I've done it*   then
    maybe I would'a gone.

But we lie, we lie, Miss. I lie. She lied. Mentirosa. Everyone lies.
    But it would feel good just to say it. Say things you're not
      supposed to say.

I'd tell my sister *I HATE THE BEATLES because you listen to them*
    too much.

I would say, *I've had sex and had a guy go down on me, but I've never given a blow job.*
But why?

Today's lie is tomorrow's truth. Tomorrow, maybe, I like
    the Beatles
and give a guy a blow job.

I get the Gita, the everything is everything stuff. I'm Krishna
    and Arjuna and the people
        he's gonna kill even though he feels bad for them—he has
            to do it.

It is his to do, and if he doesn't do it, he messes up history and
    shit like *Back to the Future.*

Does that answer your question, Miss? Do we start in
    mountain today, Miss?

Can I pretend to be the Sandias?

Southpaw Skin the Gloves

Alicia Mountain

The coroner's children are fat
in a happy way.

Not in a Kwik Mart way,
where my entourage is a bench
in the sun and more than one man
tells me the bus doesn't run
here anymore.

But the one who stops and squints with me says,

I watched Boom Boom Mancini
kill a man in the ring
watched it live, on TV, TV-live.

Saw the punch that laid him into the ropes,
put him in a coma,
put him in the ground.

I was a kid and it ruined me,
I still see it.

Even the ref
killed himself after
he didn't stop the fight.

Playbook

Hannah Oberman-Breindel

Every day we play football,
me and the woman I love.

We call it *football* because that's the kind
of ball we use, but otherwise,
there's no name for what we're doing.
We don't get four tries, and there's no
line of scrimmage, just an open stretch of beach
between her body and mine,
two lines in the sand, and this ball,

this ball we've carried in the back
of the car, from New York
to Massachusetts to Iowa to Washington,
which is where we're playing now,
on a yellow spit of land nearly lost
to the Pacific.

I know it's love because
of what she does to me at night,
how I would never need a helmet or pads.
There's never enough moon to harness,

and I think I could live forever like this,
me and this woman, these nights,
pressed together so tight
you couldn't fit a ball between us.

Once in a while, a late morning
will strike us in a way:
too bright and too slow,

and suddenly the light hangs like a question
waiting to be answered. The one knife
in our kitchen drawer is too big
and too sharp to slice an apple,
and our phones that tell us
about the world outside don't get service,
which is just as well anyway,

since there are wars happening,
and we want to forget, to be convinced
that rules still exist
which govern all of us.

That's why we call it *football*,
because we want to pretend
we're playing that kind of game. A hit might be
too high or too low. We'd know how hard
was too hard, or if one of us
had won. We'd know if it was
time to stop.

Games

L. Lamar Wilson

I've never been keen on clandestine pickups,
men hungering for honeyed holes to shoot into,
their bleating eyes & lips moaning a message
made plain by beards who ache to feel
ambient heat threading through ingrown hairs
yet know bigger hands palm flushed cheeks
in dark gym locker rooms' darkest corners.
When I refuse behind-the-back passes
& demand face-to-face, man-to-man D,
they cower & tell all their boys I'm no good
at keeping secrets, their collective lullaby. Lie.
Play horse. Keep the balls close to the chest.
Bedtime stories can be soothing that way.
I hear a fifth with some Henny helps, too.
                I don't know. I've never swallowed such heat.

Mudita World Peace

Hannah Ensor

> *a reckoning with the basketball player born Ronald William Artest,*
> *also known as Ron Artest, also known as Metta World Peace, also*
> *known as The Panda's Friend*

For some time I continued to call him Ron Artest. I now see that this was unfair, or at least an impulse I should have taken less pride in. I recognize my willful and stubborn misnaming as a mistake, though not necessarily because he would have minded, and not because he ever could have known.

If you're familiar with the name(s) Ron Artest, Metta World Peace, or The Panda's Friend, it's likely you're familiar with an event known as The Malice at The Palace that took place at The Palace of Auburn Hills on November 19, 2004. If you're not familiar with The Malice at The Palace, you can continue not knowing for another few minutes.

My first witnessing, in real time / on television, of a Metta World Peace outburst, a MWP act of violence, was when he elbowed then–Sixth Man of the Year, James Harden, in 2012. It was late in the regular season, and both teams—the Lakers and the Thunder—had mostly wrapped up their playoffs seeding. Harden came bobbing down the court to get back on offense after an emphatic MWP dunk at the other end, his goofy beard bobbing along with him over his powder blue uniform. MWP's elbow flew—was thrown, theoretically by accident, and theoretically in celebration, joy—into Harden's head, his temple.

This moment was jarring in real time, and continues to be so in replay, from the violence right down to the illegibility of MWP's face as his arms move into Harden's head: is that an expression of rage? of ecstasy?

There's real wind-up, and Harden goes down hard. MWP was ejected immediately (a "flagrant 2") and suspended seven games.

Harden suffered a concussion and was out for the remainder of the regular season. MWP returned to join the Lakers for the second round of the playoffs, having at that point served his third NBA career ban.

MWP currently goes by the name The Panda's Friend, a name he chose, in his words, *to honor China*, where he began playing after having his contract waived by the Knicks in 2014. In game situations, he often wears sneakers with white stuffed pandas affixed to the tongues. He plays for Pallacanestro Cantù in the northern Italian province of Como; the back of his jersey contains not merely "Friend" nor "Panda" but the full name: THE PANDA'S FRIEND.[1]

MWP legally changed his name from Ron Artest in 2011. First name Metta, last name World Peace. Whereas his colleagues' jerseys said FISHER 2, BRYANT 24, BARNES 9, MORRIS 1, the player formerly known as Ron Artest had a jersey that read WORLD PEACE 15.

Many people thought that Ron failed to correctly spell "meta-," as in the prefix, from the Greek, "with, across, after," used to describe something that refers to itself. One more reason this name, Metta World Peace, might sound ridiculous or ironic, even self-ironizing.

Metta, though, is a Pali word, meaning lovingkindness, universal love, benevolence. A boundless warm-hearted feeling. Friendliness. Empathy. Metta, in the Buddhist tradition, is *an attitude of recognizing that all sentient beings (that is, all beings that are capable of feeling), can feel good or feel bad, and that all, given the choice, will choose the former over the latter; a recognition of the most basic solidarity that we have with others, this sharing of a common aspiration to find fulfillment and escape suffering.*[2] Metta can also be adjectival, used to refer to the meditation on these qualities: a meditation focused on the development of boundless, unconditional love.

World peace, according to Wikipedia, is *an ideal of freedom, peace, and happiness among and within all nations and/or people. World peace is an idea of planetary non-violence by which nations willingly cooperate, either voluntarily or by virtue of a system of governance that prevents warfare. The term is sometimes used to refer to a cessation of all hostility amongst all humanity.*

"Planetary non-violence" is, to me, a new but alluring phrase; in fact, I find this passage really beautiful overall, especially for something I read on Wikipedia. Just above that passage, the page reads, "For the basketball player, see *Metta World Peace*."

Metta meditation is fairly structurally rigid. Every teacher I've come across has instructed that it's important to start by sending lovingkindness to oneself (usually with a script of precomposed statements, along the lines of "may I be happy; may I be free from suffering; may I live with ease"), then to a benefactor (say, a parent or a friend or someone else toward whom you already have generally positive feelings), then to a neutral party (someone, perhaps, who you occasionally see at the grocery store), then, finally, and not before the prior steps have been followed, to whom some might call an enemy or an antagonist.

Of the handful of truly powerful meditation experiences I've had, metta meditation has been the most consistently overwhelming. I'm most likely to weep when I consider offering unconditional boundless love to myself. I'm second most likely to weep when I offer unconditional boundless love to the enemy.

The name ARTEST (91) was on the back of MWP's jersey at the Palace of Auburn Hills in the last game he played in the NBA in 2004. The Palace of Auburn Hills is in Auburn Hills, Michigan, which is a suburb of Pontiac, which is itself a suburb of Detroit. It is thirty-three miles north of Detroit's city center. Auburn Hills is home to only about twenty-two thousand residents, but has five colleges, three private high schools, the Palace of Auburn Hills, and "one of the state's largest destination shopping centers," Great Lakes Crossing. As of the 2010 census, Auburn Hills was 66.3% white, compared with 77.7% nationally, 78.9% in the state of Michigan more broadly, and 10.6% in the city of Detroit.

Here's what Ron said, three years after The Malice, in 2007: *Detroit is a gangsta arena. Detroit is gangsta. Like, I don't think any other arena woulda did that. . . . If I'm him, I had to be drunk, to throw a beer at somebody like me. . . . It's definitely not right. I shoulda got a pass on that one: you know, going up into the stands. It wasn't okay, there are different ways to react. Nobody really thought about that beer coming into my eyes or whatever it was. But fortunately beer doesn't harm your eyes, you can just wipe it out, fortunately. It coulda did more damage than it did; I coulda probably got a little cut in my eye, the tip of the cup coulda hit my eye, a little blood clot, you know, that was a possibility. I don't think any severe injuries coulda happened out of that beer being thrown at me, but it was very very disrespectful. . . . Detroit's a crazy arena. The owner of Detroit, he's a . . . he's a trip. He said, "If Ron Artest wouldn't have been laying on the table, the guy would've never thrown the beer." That don't make sense, 'cause I lay on tables a lot. You know, I lay on a bench in my neighborhood and no one throws cups at me, or rocks at me. It just doesn't make sense. It was a horrible situation.*

The gist of The Malice at The Palace is as follows: an increasingly physical and contentious game on the court between the Indiana Pacers and the Detroit Pistons escalates with a hard foul committed by Pacer Ron Artest against Piston Ben Wallace, who takes offense and charges at Artest. Players and coaches come off the bench to get involved. Artest is pulled away and goes to lie down on the scorers' table to calm down. This is an odd place to lie down, but we do what we have to do, and there aren't that many places where a professional athlete can go to decompress in the middle of a game. While on the table, reclining, a cup of beer soars from the crowd toward, and eventually onto Ron Artest. Ron is suddenly up and in the stands, swinging at fans, both at the ones who did not throw beers and at the one who did. Two words that have been used, accurately, to describe what happened next (in addition to "malice") are "melee" and "bedlam." It wasn't just Ron; several other NBA players, coaches, and assistants were in the stands. A few were trying to break up the fighting. Many were fighting. There was a lot of violence, some arrests. All in all, it lasted five minutes, which—depending on your perspective—was either a very short or a very long time.

I didn't see The Malice at The Palace in real time, or even at any point in 2004. I'm not even really sure how much of it was televised, or on what channels, or shown on replay on what kind of cycle. I do know that when Ron Artest became Metta World Peace, I was annoyed. I refused to call him that; I said, "I refuse to call him that," and "you can't just call yourself whatever you want"; I probably said something about having to earn a name like World Peace. I, along with some sportscasters, players, coaches, refused and continued to call him Ron Artest. Nobody noticed that I was doing this, obviously, as I mostly talked about sports to myself and with my sister, being at a great distance from a position of relevance in sports discourse.

In 2013, I went on a meditation retreat. The topic was mudita, which means boundless joy, joy for all beings, free of self-interest (antonyms include schadenfreude, jealousy, spite). In the fourth or fifth hour of sitting, moving, talking, lying down, sitting more, I thought: *Mudita World Peace*. I thought: *happy for Ron?*

Depending on the periodical, different style guides are followed by the press for referring to a person. The Associated Press (AP) provides guidelines across media outlets with the aims of "consistency, clarity, accuracy, and brevity," as well as to "avoid stereotypes and unintentionally offensive language." The AP instructs, *Always use a person's first and last name the first time they are mentioned in a story. Only use last names on second reference.* Some style guides also discuss pronoun usage. The *New York Times*, for one, refuses to use third-person plural pronouns (e.g., "they") for gender-nonconforming individuals, even those who identify clearly and directly in that way. One way to follow this rule while also not choosing a single-gendered pronoun (i.e., "he" or "she") is to make up one's mind not to use pronouns at all: a true feat, given that pronouns are quite useful.[3] Another choice one could make to navigate the *New York Times*'s stylistic refusal, if you are a writer for said periodical, is to consistently use the wrong pronoun(s), by which I mean the pronoun(s) that the person in question does not use.

My first friend to transition from one legible-and-given gender to something other than that one gender needed a new name, and I was asked to choose it. We were all in the woods, taking a seven-week pause from the wider world and our loved ones at home, and there were only about fifty of us there. We used male pronouns for my friend; we were happy. Upon returning, a couple of mutual friends complained to me that it was too hard for them to remember to change pronouns, to call our friend what he was now asking to be called. I thought this was just the most disappointing thing and kept pointing out, self-righteously and incredulously, how much harder it must be to be called the wrong name, to be referred to by the wrong pronoun, to be known as the wrong self. All day, so tiring. All day, hard. I was pleading for empathy, or at the very least, sympathy, for our friend who was struggling.

When it comes to achieving world peace, our old friend the Dalai Lama suggests that compassion is key. He uses the metaphor of a pillar, as in *compassion is the pillar of world peace.*

When it comes to spectacle, our old friend Guy Debord says, *The tautological character of the spectacle stems from the fact that its means and ends are identical. It is the sun that never sets over the empire of modern passivity. It covers the entire surface of the globe, endlessly basking in its own glory.*

Marcus Smart played NCAA Division I basketball for Oklahoma State University for two years, from 2012 to 2014. Between his two seasons in college, he decided to play another year at Oklahoma State rather than entering the NBA Draft, where he was projected to be picked at least in the top five, if not, by some projections, first. He came back after Oklahoma State, which had been 24-8 in the regular season, exited the NCAA tournament earlier than expected. He stayed in part (we assume) to help the team do better the next year, and in part (we assume) to strengthen his game, his draft resume. His second year, though, was frustrating all around. Defenses had figured out that he was the star to watch tape on, defend. They did so intently and suffocatingly; his midrange game (which was one of his areas for improvement) did not improve; he suffered some tough non-calls and shooting slumps; he lost his cool a few times in games: he kicked a chair once, and at another point he gave himself a little timeout by leaving the court for a breather. As Jalen Rose, former NCAA and NBA player and current media analyst said, *As a nineteen-year-old kid, how do you deal with that frustration?*

In February 2014, at an away game at Texas Tech, Smart was defending a player who—with seconds left in the game—broke away down the court for an easy layup to break a late-game tie. Smart, though, never gave up on that play and defended it well (in that he went flying up to contest the shot without fouling the offensive player) but not effectively (in that the ball went into the basket, almost certainly putting the game away). Smart's momentum sent him tumbling into the stands behind the basket, where he found himself surrounded on all sides by press photographers and fans. Watching the replay, you can see what happens next: from his position on the ground, his head whips up and back, quickly locking onto one specific fan. The camera moves with him as he stands up; we miss the moment he's reacting to, but we see what's next. I'm no lip-reader, but I see the fan say something like, *Sorry 'bout that*, once he's face to face with Smart. Smart shoves him; his fingers touch the fan's chest for roughly three tenths of a second, and then with almost nothing in between, Smart swiftly turns, takes himself back onto the court, only to be guided by refs, teammates, staff, once he's there.

Seconds later, he pleads, *Coach, he called me a n*——. This is what major media outlets will go on to call "a racial epithet." The fan, later identified as Jeff Orr, claims that he called Smart *a piece of crap*.

Around this same time, President Barack Obama appeared on a podcast and discussed this selfsame "racial epithet," though he used the word itself, not the euphemism. The part of the podcast wherein he refers to usages of the n-word, when he himself utters it, is intricate and layered, challenging; of course, given our media infrastructure as it stands, this moment and conversation went on to be deeply flattened. CNN had anchor Don Lemon hold up a sign that said the word, with the question, *Does this offend you?* Fox News called Obama *the rapper in chief*. Writer/actor/comedian Natasha Rothwell offered this perspective on Twitter: *Barack Obama isn't the first American president to say it, but he's certainly the first one who's been called it*. And, as a Salon.com headline adds: *past use has been anything but academic*.

Around this same time, representative John Lewis talked with Krista Tippett on the radio show *On Being* about the overlap of nonviolence, political activism, and the civil rights movement. He said, of the training he and the rest of the Student Nonviolent Coordinating Committee (SNCC) put themselves through in the mid-sixties: *We, from time to time, would discuss: if you see someone attacking you, beating you, spitting on you, you have to think of that person, you know, years ago that person was an innocent child, an innocent little baby. And so what happened? Something go wrong? Did the environment? Did someone teach that person to hate, to abuse others? So you try to appeal to the goodness of every human being and you don't give up. You never give up on anyone.*

My absolute least favorite part of the Marcus Smart video is the woman who was with Orr, probably his wife. She's got this look on her face, this horrified look at the notion that Smart's fingers made contact with her husband's chest, that tells me that she was thinking more than "piece of crap," was used to hearing more than "piece of crap." I hate the way her face contorts. I hate the way her arm straightens and points at Smart as he leaves the situation to go back on the court. I hate the way Orr chuckles as he tugs on his shirt a little, straightening himself up. And, actually, when I see the two of them, the debate in the media about whether Smart heard this exact word stops mattering. When I see the two of them, I don't care what he did or didn't say, and if it matched what Smart did or didn't hear. The word, in this three-second interval, is almost irrelevant. If only because it would be so unsurprising if he said it. If only because the woman's face makes the context very clear, word or no word.

The next day, Jeff Orr voluntarily agreed not to attend the rest of the season's home or away games. In a public statement, he said, *I would like to take this opportunity to offer my sincere apologies to Marcus Smart,* and then, *I regret calling Marcus Smart a "piece of crap," but I want to make it known that I did not use a racial slur of any kind.*

I don't want to spend too much time talking about Jeff Orr except to say: he graduated from Texas Tech in 1983. He's white and at the time of the game in question he was in his early fifties. He's a longtime supporter of the Texas Tech basketball program who has been known to offer grandiosely crude gestures and "epithets" to opposing players from his carefully chosen, annual, under-the-basket seats. As analyst David Jacoby points out, *It's an interesting place to sit on a basketball court, because it's not a good seat. When the action's on the other side of the court, you can't even see what's happening.* In other words, this is kind of his thing: showing up to basketball games and yelling at student-athletes. In a 2010 interview, he said, *I don't hunt, fish, golf or any other normal guy activities. I just sort of follow the team around.*

Jalen Rose said, *The security in these arenas have to do a better job of protecting the asset that's performing. If you go to a Kanye West show, if you're harassing them, they'll throw you out. Because you paid to come watch me, but you're harassing me. . . . How can the fan go to them and say "For my punishment, I'm not gonna come to no more games this year." I don't like that. If the Big 12 is gonna suspend Marcus Smart the next day, I want the Big 12 to say "He can't come to the games anymore." . . . That's what I wanna see happen.*

The fact is, though, only one of these two parties is responsible to a governing organization. One of these parties is bound, is capable of having his actions monitored and punished, and the other one bought his tickets, is a paying customer.

A dharma name is a name given as part of a spiritual ritual in the Buddhist tradition. When a teacher knows a student well, the name is tailored to the student's traits. The name is more aspirational than it is descriptive; it reflects an area in which the student struggles. For Marcus Smart between his freshman and sophomore years at Oklahoma State University, for instance, draft analysts may have suggested a dharma name of "effective midrange jump shot," if there was a Pali equivalent to that phrase. *An aspiration to incline toward.*[4] A reminder, maybe, or a possibility—one currently at a distance, hopefully not too far off—to grow into, or with.

I bought one of Phil Jackson's many memoirs in hopes that I could learn, from "The Zen Master" himself, about the transition that MWP made from Ron Artest to Metta World Peace. Was Phil involved? Did MWP have a guide? Did his agent weigh in, was there a PR guy at the Lakers who had thoughts on the matter? What changes did or didn't happen in the offseason of 2011? The single most gratifying gem I came across while reading, though, was what Artest said when he first joined the Lakers in 2009: *I don't know what Zen means, but I'm looking forward to being a Zen man. I hope it makes me float. I always wanted to float.*

The word television is made up of two parts. The prefix "tele-," from the Greek "far off," means *to, or at, a distance; denoting actions or impressions produced at a distance from the exciting cause.* To be a sports fan certainly involves being a "telespectator." To be far off; to know irrefutably that the ball and the players moving it are over there, so way over there that there is no hope, no expectation, that we would ever confront each other's bodies. Fans' bodies are separated by tremendous distances from athletes' bodies, by all conceivable measures of space, but also by most measures of agility, strength, size, intensity and success of training, ability to draw widespread public attention, relevance. This is largely true too (my rough math places the percentage at 99.997%) for fans who are attending a live sporting event.

I haven't taken the precepts to follow Buddhist ethics. I don't often meditate in the evenings or in the mornings when my partner does. I keep forgetting what the Three Jewels are. I've picked up, and I think internalized, a great deal. I've kind of stopped believing in binary truths as well as in stable objectivity (consistent, legible, or shared realities), which is or isn't related.

I'm charmed by how many names MWP can hold at once. It feels in some ways post-identity, though I regret having typed that phrase in this context. Metta World Peace is still his official and legal name, even as he goes by The Panda's Friend. Some folks still call him Ron, some even Ron-Ron, which is fine by him (*I don't really have a preference. . . . I told the guys don't feel bad if you call me Ron*, the *New York Times* quoted him as saying in 2011). While it was a small news story when he started going by The Panda's Friend midway through 2014, it in some ways seemed unremarkable in comparison to everything else.

In many of Emily Dickinson's poems, some words have alternate options indicated by a plus sign accompanied by lists of "variant" words below or beside the poem. It would be easy to think of them as swap-in words, choose-your-own-adventure words, but that's not where literary critics currently land on interpreting this practice. Instead, it's that the poem includes options number one *and* number two, though also neither of these two, at least not either of them as they exist in isolation from each other. Maybe it's also the space between options one and two, maybe it's what options one and two do when they're thrown in a sack together. Is it sparring? a proximity? a confluence? something that flows directly from the overlapping de- and connotations of the two? If you ask me, it's coexistence and it's chemistry, and not a little bit of thwarting, overload, shorting the fuse.

Metta World Peace is so funny; Metta World Peace is so troubled, troubling. My sense is that people bounce between these, or similar, poles: laughing at his antics on the one hand, and fearing, condemning, loathing, judging his rage, his violence, on the other. Holding these two traits at once, and adding a third thing, may enable a portrait of the man himself. It's very possible that the third thing is, in fact, metta.

Though, before we get too far down this road, I get to remind myself: we have zero actual access to the inner lives of celebrities (athletes) (strangers).

In an essay about sports documentaries, Joshua Malitsky notes that many sports documentaries *articulate the position that these sports figures are both very much like us and completely distinct from us. [The films] mark the athletes' experiences as wholly unique and yet make them utterly human in what they care about—friendship, camaraderie, and relating to someone with comparable experiences.*

Sharon Salzburg writes, *What unites us all as human beings is an urge for happiness, which at heart is a yearning for union, for overcoming our feelings of separateness. We want to feel our identity with*

*something larger than our small selves. We long to be one with our
own lives and with each other.*

There exists a theory about social progression and peacekeep-
ing called the contact hypothesis. It suggests that contact between
groups that are experiencing conflict is one of the best ways to
improve relations and general attitudes. One example of a socio-
logical finding that is consistent with the contact hypothesis is that
*heterosexuals who personally know a lesbian or gay man manifest
more positive general attitudes toward gay people as a group.*[5] In Representative Lewis's conversation with Krista Tippett, he discusses
SNCC's practice of making eye contact with aggressors: *We [went]
through the motion, the drama, of saying that if someone kicks you,
spits on you, pulls you off the lunch counter stool, continue to make
eye contact. Continue to give the impression, yes, you may beat me,
but I'm human.*

Fans are trained as telespectators, are used to being telespectators,
even those who share physical space with the action of the sporting event (yes, Jeff Orr and the fan who threw a cup of beer at Ron
Artest as he laid on the scorers' table, but also the other hundreds
of millions of fans who attend sporting events each year). Specta-
torship is, at most times, an impermeable barrier. Sometimes that
barrier is a screen, and the *tele-* refers to a pane of glass, electricity,
hundreds or thousands of miles, slight time delays, and corporate
mediation. Sometimes that barrier is closer and more singular, as
in a sheet of Plexiglas (e.g. hockey). This does not keep spectators
from pressing as hard as they can against that barrier. It feels like
being involved, implicated.

In thinking about my friends' dharma names, I've noticed that
some of them seem more hopeful than others; some feel almost
punitive. The name that translates to "discipline," for example,
is a stern reminder. When a friend mentioned that hers means
"good enough," I cried. I don't have a dharma name, haven't
yet been given one. When I mention that I've been thinking
through this question for myself, my partner suggests "boundaries," which is much closer to *tele-* than I initially think could

be true. Another friend of mine, after witnessing my being called into work on a Sunday—and what it did to the rest of our time together even once I physically returned—made me a flower tincture and called it "healthy boundaries," with a little heart drawn on the dropper.

I find myself wondering about causes and conditions, and what it might look like for a person, for MWP, to aspire toward metta, toward boundless lovingkindness, what it might look like to aspire toward world peace. This is an interesting intellectual exercise that I take part in as if I am peering out a window, drink in hand. I notice that I can barely even wonder what it might look like to aspire toward boundaries. Something inside of me starts buzzing and I wonder why I don't have a massage therapist, a talk therapist, a spiritual guide.

I wonder, briefly, what it might have been like to be MWP's spiritual guide. If the guide considered "restraint," or "pause," or "one long, slow breath after another."

MWP, in his current incarnation as The Panda's Friend, was ejected from a playoff game in Cantù. To watch the YouTube video is an odd experience. First, because I can't find the reason he was ejected (no blatant elbows to his opponents' foreheads, no charging into the stands swinging his fists). Second, because unlike in an American basketball game, the fans at this Italian league game *are* separated from the court, the bench, the action, by a hockey partition. Is this true for all Italian league games? Or is this just for games in which The Panda's Friend, née Metta World Peace, née Ron Artest, is playing?

The fans in the Cantù arena understand what it means to be behind a Plexiglas partition. One man (close to Orr's demographic, it seems, though likely white Italian rather than white U.S. American) is directly behind the Pallacanestro Cantù bench as the team huddles, regroups after a foul is called on The Panda's Friend. This man tosses small objects over the partition, and yells joyously. He seems to be at the game alone, which does not diminish his pleasure. The boundary between him and the players allows him to be a full-on clown, a trickster figure. His slightly younger fellow fans try to calm him. Again, I can't read lips, and I can barely speak Italian. I get the sense that they're telling him to be cool.

In 2012 sports and pop culture blog Grantland posted what the author called *an oral history of the scariest moment in NBA history*. It's reproduced as a fifty-page insert in their print anthology, which is where I read it. It's a fully comprehensive and deeply emotional text, telling the whole story of The Malice with minimal editorial intrusion. The text is made up of testimony from players from both teams; coaches and coaching staffs; media members both on-site and remote; spectators (active and offending spectators as well as farther-away spectators); representatives of The Palace of Auburn Hills, from executives through to security and other venue staff; officials; and representatives of the NBA, including the then-commissioner, David Stern.

I very rarely read novels. I think it comes down to the fact that I'm not all that interested in narrative. But when I read this fifty-page insert on my lunch break, I looked up at the end only to notice that I had been away from my desk for several hours, sitting over an empty bowl. Even once I'd finished reading, I sat there for a while, if not unable to move, then uninterested in doing so.

Let's look at Ron Artest's face as he lies on the scorers' table. We can watch it, read it as a text, because (a) it's all on YouTube, (b) we feel comfortable scrutinizing surface appearances as legible indicators of lived experience, and (c) basketball is not a sport that requires its players to wear any protective headgear. *Helmets, visors, pulled-down caps, and sunglasses, temper, to a point, the possibilities of articulation* (Melitzky again). Ron lies there vulnerable and on fire.

What work am I meant to be doing on this side of the screen? If I was to be careful about that work. If we were.

If we were careful about our work, would The Malice at The Palace have happened? Would Jeff Orr hold season tickets under the basket? I see a floating beer cup above Ron Artest's body. It is, or it isn't, the n-word. It's there, suspended for an eternity; a bubble unpopped in a Chardin painting, or a playing card midflutter, halfway to the ground.

At a gathering of the meditation group I attend, a woman suggested that we engage with media to have emotional reactions without risk. She also said, *What even is a tv anymore?*

Notes

1. This essay was written in April 2015. In September 24, 2015, Metta World Peace signed a one-year nonguaranteed deal with the Los Angeles Lakers, where he continued playing until the end of the 2016–17 season. In the 2018 offseason, he played in the BIG3 league under the name "Ron Artest." He was hired as the player development coach for the South Bay Lakers in the NBA G League in October 2017, where—as of March 2019—he still serves.
2. This definition and its variations appear in many places, but this exact phrasing comes from *wildmind*, a site run by members of the Triratna Buddhist Community.
3. Ariel Lewiton of Guernica describes one instance of the achievement of this avoidance, with a bit of tongue-in-cheek surprise, as "impressive."
4. This particular phrasing about dharma names comes from the Buddhist Peace Fellowship.
5. This quotation is from Gregory M. Herek, "Heterosexuals' Attitudes toward Lesbians and Gay Men: Does Coming Out Make a Difference?," which first appeared in *A Queer World*, ed. Martin Duberman, 331–45. (New York: New York University Press, 1997).

At the gym, moments after I failed a
squat attempt that would have been easy
pre-sitting-induced pinched nerve

Candace Williams

trembling
muscles
admit
atrophy

a reminder the
literal body forgets
itself

My love
handle is
a form

of existential
anxiety a
luxury of
lunchtime
crisis
splurging

on the cheapest fried

delivery when boss
implies I can't afford to
leave

I earn

living
slumped
over typing
content until
boss is
content with
my body

of work:
disremembering
my skin

torso and spine

This courtship is a gesture

of defiance—

the marrow of
ancestral bones
holds stock

and
bonds
so
great
great

great gran could not afford
to read but here I am
lifting
under a sign that says *free weights*

Inside the City Walls

Norman Dubie

A small boy in shock with a blue Popsicle
In the dark hallway of a Montreal hospital—
His mother floats past me
Away from the nurses' station,
Her dead husband's silver glasses in her hand
Exactly as I had learned to hold the javelin:
The first position,
Arm trailing while the wrist turns,
Thumb in rebellion, the whole body
Mindless of its gathering speed, head lolling
Impossibly, the spear
Is pulled from the chest
Where the foot is first firmly planted . . .

Diana Nyad as J. M. W. Turner

BK Fischer

Her age makes her invisible
in the water except to sharks,

a blur composed of brackish
fluid beneath the nimbostratus.

Primetime icons love her line
about striving to "touch the other

shore" but Oprah gets touchy
on wonder and awe, questioning

how there can be awe without awe
in a Creator, and the interview

veers from the occasion of
accolades for being the first

person confirmed—first person
(confirmed)—to reach Florida

from Havana by swimming
continuously in open sea.

Parenthetical, because persons
without CNN cameras on them

may have made it into the reeds
before, by raft and capsize and

desperation, although not as
many people as have not—

made it, that is, that way. When
she touches the other shore she

emerges almost a corpse, but not,
thanks to IV hydration, salts.

game recognizes game

t'ai freedom ford

In honor of my half-brother Calvin's graduation
from high school, I fool myself down to Virginia
half-curious, full of anger, and burdened by silence.
Solely on the strength of my genetic inheritance
I am there to show you this mirror: your nose,
eyebrows, turned down mouth, childish pout.
To show you how fine I have turned out in spite
of your absence.

When you and Calvin show up, me and Tiffany
are in the garage, knocking balls around
on the pool table. Red-eyed and haggard,
you insult me right off talking bout
what I don't know or something like that.
You say, *I don't get no hug?*
and I say, *no,*
offer you my hand.

Folks have gathered: liquored
and feeling festive. Beer in hand,
I summon my project hustle. Balls scatter,
drop like snitches. All five brothers, tight
with defeat, quietly root for you. I am undaunted
remembering me at ten chopping down dudes
twice my size the cocky rise in my voice yelling,
next! But you were gone by then.

Your shots are quick and sure, as they should be
in your house, on your table. But when you miss on the 8,
I bank it in the corner, offer my hand
say, *good game.*

Off Sides

Susan Briante

When we heard the screams of the crowd, my father started running. We had just disembarked from a NJ Transit train, wound through the tiled corridors of New York City's Penn Station, and rushed up stairs into Madison Square Garden. As we got off the escalators and heard the fans roar, my father said "C'mon."

I was probably seven or eight years old. I have no other memory of running next to my father as child.

I remember very little else from that first hockey game except the jolt of energy and amazement I felt when we turned a corner, handed over our tickets, and, finally, stepped into the aisle to see the whole arena open up beneath us: the unimaginably bright glare of lights reflecting off ice and some 18,000 people—mostly white, mostly men—up on their feet, hands thrust into the air, screaming at two players who had dropped their gloves and were using bare fists to pummel one another against the boards.

*

As a child I didn't wear pink or princess dresses. I wore blue suede Pumas with orange laces like my older brothers. With short hair, I was easily and often mistaken for a boy.

I played with Barbie dolls and with fighter jets.

I sometimes believed that there was nothing I could not do or be.

*

Despite my mother's strong grades, my grandfather told her he would not pay for her to attend college. Instead, he offered to send her brother.

After high school my mother worked briefly as a secretary for an insurance company, married at 19, had her first child at 21, her second at 23, and me at 30.

My father went to college on a baseball scholarship and became a linchpin in my family's transition from the working to middle class. A claims adjuster for an insurance company, he traveled often. At some point when I was still in elementary school, my mother's threats and rage revealed his travel was not always for business.

My mother like other mothers in my family often simmered with resentment and anxiety.

*

As a child I followed some baseball and football. I played soccer and softball, not very well, and eventually gave them both up for jazz and ballet classes. I tried ice-skating maybe once or twice and found it humiliating. I borrowed my brother's skateboard, rode a bike.

Despite the fact that I never played the game, I fell for hockey because of the glide and hustle of its players: their quick spins and unimaginable leaps, their strength and speed. I fell for their joy and camaraderie as they hugged on the ice after each goal. The only girl in an Italian American family, who felt alternately put upon and neglected, I fell for the underdog story that was the NY Rangers who when I began to follow them had not won a Stanley Cup since 1940.

With my father at my first game high up in the cheap seats (known as the Blue Seats) of Madison Square Garden, where the (mostly white, mostly) men sitting around us drank beer and smoked and swore I fell for hockey because it was my first glimpse into a world of unabashedly rowdy, bad behavior: a world of freedom, of men.

*

In the 1970s, the National Hockey League introduced the animated character Peter Puck to explain the rules of the game in short segments between periods. "Howdy fans," the spunky character would proclaim, "Peter Puck here to lay some facts on you about hockey: the world's fastest team sport."

For the next few minutes the animated puck would zoom around an animated rink occasionally darting between or off the sticks of enormous players, spouting facts about the game:

"The puck must always precede players across an opponent's blue line."

"I travel around this rink at speeds over 100 miles per hour."

"No fighting is permitted and offenders are removed from play."

*

I watched so many hockey games as a child I still know all the words to the Canadian national anthem.

*

Over Sunday dinner, when tensions in my parents' marriage peaked, my mother asked us which parent we would want to live with if they split up.

My brothers, who were seven- and nine-years older than me, may have understood more about infidelity and unhappiness. Both said they would stay with my mother.

I said my father, which came as a surprise to the rest of my family.

When I said I wanted to go with him, what I meant was I wanted to be like him.

*

In the cheap seats, known as the Blue Seats, where my father and I watched my first hockey game, where the men around us drank beer and smoked and swore, NY Rangers fans invented some of their most lasting chants including "Potvin Sucks," which was "sung" or screamed to the tune of "Let's Go Band."

The chant began when Dennis Potvin, captain of the rival NY Islanders, broke NY Ranger Ulf Nilsson's ankle during an unfortunate (but most observers agree "clean") hit in February 1979. Fans began to chant it every time the Rangers and their cross-division rivals met. Then fans started chanting it when the Rangers played other teams or when the NY Knicks played.

Almost 40 years later, the chant can still be heard.

*

When I was a child, my cousins and I would play improvised games of hockey, soccer or baseball, often inside the house, often in front of a television set while real sports played in the background. In our version of hockey, for example, we'd declare my father's desk was the net, plant one of us in front of it, and let the others try to score against them using a foam ball as a puck and our hands as sticks.

Despite a lack of encouragement or natural athletic ability, sometimes I would imagine myself skating or pitching or kicking a soccer ball past a diving goaltender at what used to be the Meadowlands Stadium. It was the late seventies. Glass ceilings were beginning to crack if not shatter. Anything was possible even the passage of the Equal Rights Amendment.

*

Despite Peter Puck's claim, during much of the 1970s and 1980s, fights broke out at a rate of one or more per game. Fights were so common teams like The Philadelphia Flyers, built a reputation for a "physical game" earning the moniker the Broadstreet Bullies. Teams regularly employed players called "goons" or "enforcers," whose sole purpose was to fight an opponent in retaliation for the treatment of a teammate or as a way to "energize the bench."

The average number of fights per game peaked at 1.17 in the 1983–84 season. Eventually the league implemented rules to discourage brawls in an attempt to expand the sport's appeal. By the 2014–15 season the average number of fights declined to 0.32 per game.

Still, even today Hockeyfights.com lists teams and individuals with the highest fight minutes and includes videos of the season's best fights.

Peter Puck's declaration "No fighting is permitted" may have been my first introduction to the lies and exceptions that undergird the unabashedly rowdy, bad behavior of many men.

*

By the time I was thirteen, I stopped playing sports and stopped watching them.

By the time I was thirteen, I learned that I could not do anything I wanted. I learned, instead, that many men and boys thought they could do anything they wanted to me.

It was a lesson I would learn over and over at any moment, anywhere:

in a taxi, a subway car, at the doctor's office, at a party, in my bedroom

*

A boarding penalty can be called on any player who checks or pushes a defenseless opponent in such a way that causes the opponent to hit or impact the boards violently or dangerously, according to the NHL rulebook. For example, any unnecessary contact with a player playing the puck on an obvious "icing" or "off-side" can be penalized.

But the NHL rulebook concedes that "an enormous amount of judgment" must be "involved in the application of this rule by the Referees." The rulebook continues that the player "applying the check" has the responsibility of "ensuring his opponent is not in a defenseless position." Whether or not a player has his head up to make a play at the time of the check can often be used as evidence that the check could be expected, that the player was not "defenseless."

In hockey, the awareness that a hit might come is a form of consent.

*

When I cried as a child, I was called "an actress," sometimes laughed at, sometimes punished. When I raged as a child, I was told I was not being "a nice girl." When I lashed out, I was punished, called selfish, and left feeling neither protected nor able to defend myself.

*

The unabashedly rowdy men in the cheap seats of Madison Square Garden also started the chant "Beat your wife, Potvin, beat your wife" after accusations of spousal abuse surfaced during Potvin's divorce proceedings in the 1980s. Despite the fact that Potvin denied the claim and no formal charges were ever filed against him, the chant stuck.

As in many professional sports, the violence of the men who play hockey has never been contained to the rink.

For example, in 2015 convicted spousal abuser Slava Voynov, remained on the Los Angeles Kings roster, until he fled home to Russia to avoid deportation. That same year, Mike Ribeiro starred for the Nashville Predators throughout the duration of a now-settled civil suit regarding his alleged sexual assault of his children's teenage nanny. I do not want to imply that hockey produces violence against women or that hockey players are more violent off the ice than other male athletes or other men. But the league's attitude toward such incidents is ambiguous at best.

In 2015, hockey fan Melissa Geschwind started a Change.org petition asking the NHL "to institute a clear, comprehensive policy of zero tolerance for players who commit acts of intimate partner violence or sexual assault" in line with policies of other professional leagues. Geschwind met with Commissioner Gary Bettman at the NHL's New York office in Spring 2015 to discuss the petition and the larger issue of violence against women. No policies were created.

*

I watched the Rangers win the 1994 Stanley Cup in a Mexico City bar filled with Canadians. By that time, I had stopped following hockey with any regularity.

*

Despite challenges, my parents remained married for more than 50 years.

Two years ago, when my mother died, I started calling my father every day. Hockey gave us something to talk about. I found a NY Ranger's app for my phone, then bought an NHL package to watch games on my computer. I fell back in love with the game.

"The thing is," my father might say, "the Rangers have one of the oldest benches."

"Yeah, I watched the game last night," he'd tell me. "Lundqvist looked very ordinary."

When things were going particularly bad for the NY Rangers, he would say: "I don't even want to talk about it."

*

I want to tell you about the beauty of the stretch pass, the break away, the acrobatic save, how a spray of ice flies with a quick stop or turn, the sound of blade on ice, blade of skate and stick, sound of the puck bouncing off the boards or the boards rattling after a clean, hard check, the exquisite or excruciating ring when a puck hits the post.

As a mature fan, I have no use for fighting in hockey. I love the game for the way its best players can weave a puck between a number of defenders, make a pass behind their backs, find a way to shoot the puck at the net while soaring down the ice fending off a defenseman.

But part of what attracted me to the game initially was the rowdy, unabashedly bad behavior of men who played and watched the game, which looked like freedom to a girl whose behavior was in the process of being regulated. As a young woman, part of what I learned was that such rowdy, unabashedly bad behavior could be dangerous to me as well as to men both within and beyond the rink.

*

When our six-year-old daughter hits one of us or slams a door when told to turn off cartoons or pick up her toys, my husband and I try time outs or take away privileges.

A podcast tells me I should let my child cry and tantrum.

When my father comes to visit and witnesses my daughter's rage or defiance, he reminds me that my mother used to say she hoped someday I would "have a daughter just like me," which was meant to be both a blessing and curse.

*

My daughter watches the US Women's Soccer team win the World Cup, watches the US Women's Olympic Gymnastic team dominate the Summer Olympics. For a while, I can convince her to eat fish in order to swim like Katie Ledecky.

Sometimes she watches hockey with me. Sometimes she pretends to skate before our television set.

She has never seen a hockey fight. It's hard to know if she will ever feel like I did when I was with my father at my first NY Rangers game, when I wanted to be one of those men on the ice and in the stands fighting and screaming and seemingly expressing exactly what they felt without consequence.

*

A father and daughter run toward a common destination, but even when running side by side they arrive at different places.

*

After making it to the Stanley Cup finals in 2014 and the semifinals 2015, the NY Rangers were bounced out of the 2016 playoffs in the first round.

As I write this in the middle of the 2017 season, they have a 17-9-1 record and have racked up some decisive wins (with a league best +28 goal differential) credited to the stunning offensive strength of a group of young athletes, some playing their first seasons in the NHL (including Russian star Pavel Buchnevich and college Hovey Baker award winner Jimmy Vesey). But the team has gone 4-5-1 in their last 10 games as opponents have figured out how to clog up the neutral zone and exploit the NY Rangers' defensive weakness.

It's too early to know if this season will end early in the playoffs as last season did or if the team will make adjustments and make another long run toward the championship. Just 27 games into a season of more than 80, I find myself alternately enthralled and bracing for the worst.

But there's a moment at the beginning of each game, as the referee holds the puck just inches above the center ice circle and two centers lean in, sticks poised in the air, for the first face-off that will start play, when all of my attention heaves forward into the absolute present and the promise of what's possible.

The Chain

Elyse Fenton

Maybe inside all our bodies is the fine body
    of an ultramarathoner, a body that needs

to be lubricated against itself, that needs
    to be doggedly watered and hand-fed

and salted periodically with tablets no
    bigger than the sori of a fern, that just

needs the steel-banded calculus of trust
    to take it and take it good, the body, yes,

your own soft body leads by a leash along
    the rocks flanging the dark pines, the body

your body jerks to a stop in the rough
    clearing, hands on shoulders on knees

on unblessed ground, the body your body
    sledges with rusted stakes through the palms,

achilles, nipples, that drives a chain rippling
    through the intestines with the blindness

of water approaching the dam, blindness
    of boys at the edge of the woods cinching

themselves into some dusty unnameable
    shape—threat or surrender with its parallel

lines—toward a voice with a sledge
    in its hands and a chain in its teeth calling

come and get it brother, come and get it.

Young Woman Wrestler

Tria Blu Wakpa

Maybe you wouldn't expect that I'm a fighter
that I found myself one winter at fourteen
in the high school cafeteria, makeshift wrestling room.
The only young woman among fifty young men
slightly sweet stench of bodies and rotten food
panes of glass beaded with moisture tormenting us
who were forbidden to drink.
We could only suck-savor a single cube of ice
if we were lucky.
Dark rimmed eyes and shrunken stomachs
throughout the season, the companionship
of our constant hunger, T-shirts soaked through with sweat.
our own and our teammates, jump ropes turning,
dreams of dominating one another.
Tie up, headlock, shuck, struggle, shoot,
single leg, wrench against thick trunk of thigh,
wiry hair against my cheek and the soft scent of soap,
collapse his will with sharpness of clavicle,
spin behind and ride. Lungs burn for breath
searching for the strength to break a man
down from two feet to all fours to belly to back.
Or the escape: sprint to stand, jut hips,
lean, lean, lean, force him to carry my weight.
Bloody noses: wads of cotton shoved into nostrils.
Stop the blood, but finish the match.
Baths: soaking sore body in scorching water,
inventorying injuries, deep purple bruises striking
against naked flesh fading brown then yellow.
Bets: *She'll last a week, maybe two.*
Doubts: *She'll never win a match.*

Jeers: *You wanna rassle?*
Leers: *She's preoccupied with boys.*
No way did they expect that I would fight six seasons,
make varsity, force young men to forfeit
claiming chivalry, never owning sexism
that I would be the first woman
to train with the men at Oklahoma State University,
make the national women's wrestling team,
win women's nationals twice.
Maybe you wouldn't expect that I'm a fighter:
soft spoken and slender with a feminine face
but sometimes looks are best deceiving
when you're fighting to win.

Self-Portrait with Ghost, Rising

Dean Rader

When Death comes for me it won't be as the
reaper but as my basketball coach he'll
be alone on the sidelines mouthing a
name I pretend is not mine like a bell
I know is meant to wake me from a sleep
I do not want to end I do not want
to end not this game not yet yet I keep
hearing a voice somewhere between a taunt
and a beckon call me to the bench loss
is never a win except when it is
like now as I watch my ghost cut across
the lane set a pick then leap over his
defender and rise into the arched air
like one who needs to pray but says no prayer

Infield Contrapuntal

Meg Day

We have no quarterback to
  throw me

To the grass under the
  bleachers

to pin me like that plastic
  Jesus

in the shade of the
  equipment shed

nailed to his backstop
  crucifix, so

it makes no difference that

it is a girl

who hikes her uniform skirt

who straddles my thigh, who
  rounds

her rage, hurls her weight
  into

third base with ease & rocks
  back

the chain-link dugout with
  my body

against the hot metal to
  show how I am

caught between

She swings aluminum

shaped—for switch-hitting
  & long drives—

along my sidelines; she molds

with her mouth open & eyes
  shut. I field

the flesh of my neck with the
  neck of

her fist; some deep prayer
  releases

the bat. My body might well
  be

a knot in a red cord, opening

the window in Rahab's house:
  empty

or breaking; yes, break
  everything

save the silhouette of Jericho
   as it falls

to crush me. A passerby
   pauses, sees

turns away. Then another
   bat, a foot—

my ribs make a new place for
   the dirt

to black the eye of my
   marrow. Please

Stop—stop. Just let me give
   you my life.

apart. This world does not
   mean

what she wants—& harder
   now, god

good god, deeper into the
   well

to drink. Forget that Jesus
   wants

—don't stop—to give up his
   life.

Good god, let me give you
   my life.

Shots Missed

Celeste Adame

The nets have stopped swaying from all the shots
we missed, all the games we never finished.

It all comes back to me, staring at the backboard
of my childhood court. If the hook shot I taught her

did not shut the crowd up before hitting glass,
dropping in without touching the rim. If I didn't remember

none of us wanted to defend the Pendleton guard.
She had a smile on her face and it made us feel uncomfortable.

I learned coach wasn't lying when she said *it is all in the wrist,*
the feeling when I figured out how

to spin the ball, maneuver it
behind my back while dribbling, between my legs,

dancing with you in the game, on the court,
it was the only time we could touch in public.

Had I never picked up a basketball, didn't learn the curves
of your body were made for my hands,

a poor dribble gets the ball stolen,
and I am taking the last-second jumper.

Sports History

Brett Fletcher Lauer

I understand what
a jump shot is,
certain mechanics

of the body, hand
positions, elbow
alignment, follow

through. Enough
player names to
mention around

the imaginary water-
cooler if I found
myself there. A body

at rest still needs
to hydrate. I cried
watching Bird

and Magic in that
documentary and
own a small collection

of expensive high-top
sneakers in various
colorways—used

exclusively to walk
my pets or to the
coffee shop for

an almond croissant.
Fresh to death. On
my mantle, four second

place trophies from
intramural wrestling
all before fifth grade.

Pitter patter sprawl.
I can't remember
swimming. I mean,

I can't swim. I can't
drive. Sometimes
I miss a high five,

the pat on the ass.
I swung and missed
at tee-ball, golf. Traded

cards for the love
of the potential investment.
George Brett, I'll always

love your name.
I appreciate highlights,
trick plays as much as

the next: The Statue
of Liberty, Flea Flickers,
The Changing Light

at Sandover. I was
born in the suburbs
of the city of brotherly

bullies, poor sports,
famous boo-ers and
stadium court houses.

I was the only boy
cut from my seventh
grade soccer team.

It's in my blood to lose
at all games, even Uno,
especially Monopoly,

and when I do, I spit
into my palm or refuse
to shake hands.

The Yo-Yo Heir's Lament

Eugene Gloria

It was a fever that made the yo-yo—
a brushfire in the homelands.
But a man who calls another a yo-yo
might as well say *tookas* instead of ass.

Now a good yo-yo is hard to find.
And a good man who can master
the craft of string and a pair of joined discs
[I'm talking about the old plastic kind

with a Coca-Cola logo on both sides]
deserves all the honors he is heir to.
So sue me for longing for a place
I never inhabited. Sue me for being

a hobgoblin of a diminished empire
as my Uncle Pedro "The Sleeper" Flores
loves to say at our family gatherings.
Uncle Flo is no match for the young bucks

like the trickmaster chump from Chico
who crushed the Prague competition
with his overtly complex string moves,
or Baby Suzuki from Tokyo

with his menacing stealth and speed:
his yo-yo could literally take out an eye.
I'd give my eyetooth for just one of his tricks.
It's a young man's game like anything else.

So I say *tookas* to my rocking-the-cradle,
tookas for my walking-the-dog,
tookas for Pedro "the Sleeper" Flores
and his yo-yo that set the world on fire.

Stadium Mocs

Chip Livingston

side   to   side
          the moccasins slideshuffle

left then right
       in the round dance

the toe   and heel
         of the chicken dance

these mocs flex
    and stretch   to the   orange rim
of the "don't get me started" on the hoop dance

my sneak-up shoes are the same as my stadium mocs

I don't hear the ref's whistle to stop
         just the emcee's call for another intertribal

Bad Love Affair

Joseph Millar

You walk the night back
circling the park, pollen
stuck to your eyebrows and hair—
oak pollen, jasmine,
clouds of green rust
shedding onto your sleeves.

You are like a man in a film noir
who knows the most important thing
is to keep moving and stay
out of sight. Each step you take
with your collar turned up
the night grows larger inside you,
stars the sparks from a lit cigarette
thrown down onto Dolores Street,
empty Corona bottles, wisps
of blond hair left behind on your pillow.

How long will you be so bereft?
Alone after hours in the dark cantina
watching clips of the great eighties' middleweights:
Hagler and Leonard, Roberto Duran
or Thomas Hearns from Detroit
who would smile in the ring
like he had a secret
every time he was hurt.

Ode to the Dream Shake

Ben Purkert

/
what's it called
when you lose your man
with your shoulders
talking one way,
the eyes another?

//
I remember
how the Dream
stitched together
his fakes, making
his signature move
doing nothing

/
what's it called
when you toy with
your man, when you
promise the world
& turn back?

//
I remember
how everyone
held up their arms
then got caught
in mid-air

/

what's it called
when you tell yourself
no, but your mind
is jumping for
someone else?

Catch

Trevino Brings Plenty

I worked at a residential mental health facility for children. I was part of the Native American unit that mostly managed Indian children.

Resident Adam, 16, was from the Klamath/Modoc tribe. His father was in prison, mother was an active substance abuser. Meth. Adam lived with his grandparents until he started alcohol and marijuana and not going to school. The grandparents could no longer manage him. Adam was on parole and referred to behavioral health therapy.

He was for the most part mature for his age. Other youth residents looked up to him. When other clients were triggered and had to be managed through the disruption, put in safety holds, Adam would not tie in with them. He stayed where staff told him to stay. He eased the other residents by staying calm, distracted them by playing board games.

Adam said he never played baseball. The unit had a few baseball gloves. On scheduled free time I played catch with him. I showed him where the ball was to be caught in the mitt. We researched different throws and tried them. He got the feel of throwing and catching quickly. He was happy when we had one-on-one time, throwing the ball back and forth. He liked playing catch with me more than other staff because I could throw the ball fast and hard, and I could catch his fast throws.

"I never played 'catch' with my father," he said one day, as free time finished.

After he and the residents played scheduled video game time, Adam refused to leave the room when the time came to an end. We shuffled the other clients out and secured the room. Adam stayed. He yelled at staff and threatened violence. We called the county police. The police entered the property. Adam had a pencil in his hand. The police told him to drop it. He refused and yelled at the police with closed fists. The police tased Adam. He was on the ground in fetal position until the EMTs assisted him. Adam was removed from the property and placed in subacute. He broke parole and was discharged to the Oregon Youth Authority.

Afterward, the residents refused to use Adam's favorite baseball glove.

The Sum of Our Doing

Holly M. Wendt

We are walking away from Palas de Rei and a bicycle bell chimes behind us, the thin ringing already overlaid with the humming wheels, and so we step to the side. Three men on sleek, dark bikes zip past, leave us watching them grow smaller, their breathless *Buen Camino!* more an echo than a lived sound. We step back onto the path, and we are so much slower. I try to remind myself that speed is not the point, that pilgrimage is not a race. Even the cyclists hang scallop shells on their panniers. We're all going together, no matter when we arrive.

*

The Camino de Santiago is a medieval pilgrimage route leading to the shrine of Saint James the Greater—called Santiago in Spain—in Santiago de Compostela, in the autonomous region of Galicia. The many arms of the Camino stretch across the country: the Via de la Plata marches up from the south, the Camino del Norte carries pilgrims along Spain's northern coast, and the English Camino, a little north–south spur, invites pilgrims who made the bulk of the journey by sea. Another traverses the length of Portugal. The Camino Frances, though, sees the most traffic and is so named because it is the artery that connects Santiago to France and largely to the rest of Europe, to the rest of medieval Christendom. In walking from the French side of the Pyrenees— Saint Jean Pied de Port is a popular starting point—the pilgrim commits to a journey of more than seven hundred kilometers. Though the distance is surely more impressive by a medieval reckoning, more fraught with uncertainty and danger then than now, the primary apparatus of most pilgrims' peregrination— the legs and feet, parts of great strength and great frailty—have not changed much.

In the eyes of the Church and thus, in the medieval Christian worldview, in the eyes of God, it is the final one hundred kilometers that matter. Pilgrims who complete that much on foot or on horseback, or the final two hundred kilometers on a bicycle, are eligible to receive the *compostela*, a plenary indulgence, formalized in a certificate, granting complete remission of sins. Pilgrims prove their path by showing a paper passport, stamped at the churches and *albergues* (and also cafes and shops and miscellaneous kiosks) they visit along the way, and by filling out a form that requires the pilgrim to declare their motivation for the pilgrimage.

On the Camino Frances, Sarria is the starting point for this final hundred kilometers, and Sarria was where we began our walking. We: six academics and two program coordinators on a ten-day journey through Spain, learning about the Camino de Santiago, and a driver. Of the ten days, we walked the Camino only for three; this the program called the "practical" portion, that language of the classroom or laboratory that signals *doing*. The sum of our doing? Seventy-one kilometers.

*

The trip took place in June, ideally placed to coincide with good weather, smaller crowds, and availability according to an academic calendar. For me, this ten-day span also meant missing the conclusion of the 2016 Stanley Cup Finals. My Pittsburgh Penguins had finally shaken off years of disappointing playoff exits and were facing the San Jose Sharks for the league championship. I watched the Penguins take a two-one series lead and then boarded the plane with a hockey puck tucked into a pocket of my backpack, for luck.

When family members asked if I was disappointed to miss the end of the Penguins' season, whatever end that would be, I joked: I was going on a pilgrimage. Pilgrimage is about sacrifice, right?

*

As soon as I land in Spain, the world is curtained in Spanish soccer kits: the bright primary shades of the national team, cloud white for Real Madrid, striped blue and *rioja* red for Barcelona. I think I should buy one because I'm here, but I don't follow La Liga or cheer particularly for Spain in international play, and I'd rather feel like a tourist who missed an opportunity than a *poseur* or bandwagon fan. Still, the UEFA EuroCup tournament starts on the tenth of June, and to watch some of it here is another way to experience what pilgrims call *communitas*. On your journey, you find your community, your people—in the act of peregrination, the community is created through shared experience, common goals, collective hardship. Walking into a stadium, or a bar, or just down the street wearing team colors, the same thing happens. We announce ourselves to each other; we already have common cause.

I wear a Pittsburgh Penguins polo shirt one day and I'm disappointed that no one says anything about it. In Spain, and in this group of academics, no one knows what it means, or no one cares. That is what tells me I've left home, more than the language, which comes back to me more easily than I thought it would. I don't really try to explain it, either. I know there are so many more important things to say.

Before we start walking, we are issued another kind of uniform: our group leader hands each of us a scallop shell, white and whole and a little larger than my palm. This the symbol of Santiago the Pilgrim; this is how we will be identified as pilgrims, how pilgrims identify each other. But as I tie it to my backpack, happy as I am to have one, something feels wrong. My backpack is very small. It holds water, sunscreen, a poncho, my journal—what I need for the next six hours. My other clothes are in a suitcase, and our driver will deliver all of the suitcases to the place we stop tonight.

Our driver also delivers the backpack of a woman we meet on the Camino. She has been walking since Saint Jean Pied de Port, and her knee is bothering her. She is doing the pilgrimage in honor of her late mother, she says. She can't stop—not now, not so close— but the pain is bad. So our driver, who has stopped to check on all of us at a place where the Camino meets a proper road, where there is a little café and many pilgrims resting, eating, talking, helps her in the way he can: she does not need to carry her twelve-kilo pack, at least. This is the spirit of the Camino: he volunteers the service; she trusts he will do it. We see her again the next day, and she says the pain is not so bad; the relative rest helped. She carries her pack, keeps going.

*

In our journey across northern Spain, we spend no small amount of time talking about the history of Saint James in Spain, and it's a complicated thing. There are many versions of the legend—how the apostle's bones came to be in Spain at all—but my favorite is the version in which Santiago's martyred body—head severed at the direction of Herod Agrippa—floats alone to Spain in its stone sarcophagus, arriving upon the Galician coast wholly covered and protected by scallop shells. Eventually, a holy man, or a shepherd guided by angels or a pagan queen, is led to build a shrine for the saint beneath a field of stars, the *campus stellae* from which the city of Santiago de Compostela takes its name. The Camino de Santiago lies upon an east-west path, and those who choose to walk at night walk beneath the Milky Way, a swirling sea of light.

By the tenth century, significant numbers of medieval Christians were making pilgrimages to Santiago's resting place. By then, too, Santiago had taken on other notoriety. According to another legend still, at the ninth century Battle of Clavijo, the apparition of Santiago appeared to spur a much-outnumbered Christian force to victory over the Muslim army of the Emir of Córdoba. Despite the fact that historians generally agree that the Battle of Clavijo never happened, it was at this mythological battle—with real ripples through the centuries of the Reconquista, the Crusades, and the Islamaphobic tenor of Western Christianity—that Santiago also became Santiago Matamoros: Saint James, the Moor-Killer.

The modern Camino de Santiago overtly rejects that appellation, and the spirit of the Camino is decidedly interfaith, doggedly inclusive. The Camino belongs to the pilgrim, unarmed, compassionate. But history will not be forgotten.

Within the Cathedral in Santiago itself, in one arm of its long cross, a polychromed wooden statue of Santiago on horseback stands in a field of flowers. His arm is raised and in his fist, a sword. From the edge of the grate that protects it, the spaces between the flowers and shiny green leaves reveal themselves as faces: the Moors fallen beneath the horse's hooves. The flowers and leaves are extraneous to the sculpture, added by the caretakers of the cathedral, but everything is still visible for anyone who cares to look closer. I remind myself that looking closer is why I am here, even when I don't want to.

*

There's a word for what we are: *tourigrino*. It's part of the study and the commerce of the Camino, one more reason for *why are you walking?* Part of the answer is surely true for even the most devout pilgrims: *I wanted to see this.* Walking the Camino is an amazing way to see Spain. Admittedly, it is only a fragment of Spain, no matter which route to Santiago de Compostela one takes, but walkers will know that part intimately—how it feels on the soles of the feet, the different scents of rain. There is a holiness in that, but the question changes, I think, when it is posed on a form in the Pilgrims' Office in Santiago. Pilgrims must indicate the reason for their pilgrimage: religious, spiritual and cultural motivations together, or cultural reasons only—like athletic challenge, like tourism. Only the first two options will grant the walker the *compostela*, and there is no reward for speed. Pilgrims professing only secular motivations may receive a certificate of distance instead. Both are handsome objects, both have meaning, but they are not, of course, the same.

*

The work ethic of Penguins center and franchise star Sidney Crosby is well-known, his legacy well-secured. A short list of his accomplishments reveals an Art Ross Trophy for leading the league in points and a Hart Memorial Trophy for league MVP before he turned twenty; two Stanley Cups and a Conn Smythe for being playoff

MVP; another set of Ross/Hart awards after a concussion that cost him more than a year of recovery time; career totals and averages already in historic ranges and he hasn't yet turned thirty. But it is the mythology, already in progress, that interests me most.

In a small sports museum on a hill in Halifax, Nova Scotia, the Crosby faithful and passing tourists can visit—and do—a clothes dryer shining dully under carefully placed lights. The whole thing is daubed and dented by black rubber, its cycle selector long battered away. The dryer stands with its door closed, protecting its damaged heart, the misshapen drum that need never again spin. This is The Dryer, shrine to one of hockey's greats and his uncommon beginnings, where the young Crosby practiced his shot—beginning when he was three—over and over, to the destruction of a machine and the creation of a career. By one measure, the display is absurd: it's a dryer, its abuse the kind of thing few parents would tolerate.

By another, it's evidence. It's the tangible root of miracle. I asked a friend to take a photo of me beside it, and there are more photos of me with the dryer from that summer than there are of me beside anything else. In Spain, I put my puck atop the iconic concrete waymarkers, steady it there with stones or rest it atop the boots other pilgrims have left there, in homage, as sacrifice. I am only in these pictures insofar as my finger is on the shutter, but we were there, together, which is as close as I could be to the game.

*

In Sahagún, we consider architecture. In this town, the churches are brick, not stone, though they too are old, though they too follow the squat, Romanesque shape of the sandstone churches in Santo Domingo de la Calzada and San Juan de Ortega. The windows, though they are so much smaller, so many fewer than we will see in the Gothic cathedrals in Burgos and León, have boxed arches that come into sloped points, and their brickwork suggests patterns, stripes that hint at other marvels inside: a whole room that had once been covered in blue and red motifs, diamonds and curves, flowers and the echo of stars.

Our guide explains: this is Mudejar art. This is one legacy of power on the Iberian Peninsula shifting between Muslims and Christians—a sign of long coexistence and cooperation despite those shifts, despite what certain versions of history would want us to believe. That it still stands—not only in Sahagún, but all over Spain and especially in the south—feels momentous, and for once, the feeling is not simply about age.

We step closer, and I peer up. None of the photos I take do it justice. I try to imagine the frescoes in the fullness of their colors, everything alive, and that works a little better.

*

On the second day of walking, we discover the Camino is put to other uses: a running group in matching shirts outpaces us on a long hill. We pass their training van, its hatchback open and someone sitting in it, water waiting. It shouldn't be surprising that the many people who live along the Camino use it; the path itself is well-maintained and clearly marked, and it is in places preternaturally beautiful. Mossy rock walls and lush Galician foliage, pines and eucalyptus trees, create sheltered tunnels, passages of deep quiet where even the rain does not reach. Elsewhere, the Way borders the gentle slopes of fields, rimmed with wildflowers and stone fences, and in June, even when the clouds drew low and the air lay thick with mist, of course it calls to walkers and runners not going to Santiago de Compostela but simply out for a while. Still, it startles, seeing the group so obviously intent on *practice* on the pilgrimage route. My Spanish is good enough that I can pick out some discussion of times, of what aches or is healing well, a sense of readiness for something upcoming, though each bit of conversation arrives at my shoulder, draws level, and fades away.

Why should I have been startled? They were simply making overt what I felt and did not say: pace and distance must matter, right? They weren't concerned whether they were real pilgrims. Their journey was a different kind.

While we walk away from our transport and toward another Sahagún church, we pass a woman seated on a bench. She is a pilgrim by the leaning backpack beside her with its scallop shell and the set of walking poles, but most especially she is marked as such by the bare foot she props on one knee, the gauze and ointment waiting beside. Our guide offers her all the help the first aid kit he carries can provide and a decade of experience helping people like us deal with circumstances like hers.

In a week, when I am on my way home from Santiago de Compostela, I will wait to board a plane beside a young couple who have just finished their pilgrimage. They will remain sitting as long as they can, and when we have to move forward, they will lean into each other. One will say, "I don't remember what it felt like, before my feet hurt all the time." The other will reply, "It was always that way and always will be."

While walking out of the room with the blue and red frescoes, we see the woman again. She's wearing both shoes now. We share stories: she is German, a nurse, and she has been walking since Saint Jean Pied de Port, but she only has four weeks—twenty-eight days—in which to complete her journey. As of that day, she is on track: Sahagún is the midpoint, and it has been two weeks since she began, but now she has blisters. She has not yet entered the Cantabrian Mountains that separate León and Galicia.

Later, in the van, we do the math: to stay on track, she will need to walk nearly twenty-seven kilometers a day—about sixteen miles. Later still, one of our group develops a blood blister on the top of her second toe. The whole toe is thick and purple; the nail comes loose. She still walks into the holy city. She is going to spend two more weeks in Spain after our program, and the group leader takes her to the hospital to have it cared for once we are in Santiago de Compostela.

*

They call us the gazelles, the two of us who walk faster than the rest. Our pace is set by lifetimes of walking beside people with far longer legs, a shared love of hiking, and, if we're honest, luck—no blisters. We walk together, but for long stretches, we say nothing. At other times, we talk about our lives with the sweet frankness available to relative strangers: there is no image to dispel, nothing to disappoint. We are who we are in this moment, as much or as little as we care to share. She tells me about playing field hockey still; I tell her about my own years with the sport, in middle school. I focused my attention on softball during high school and in the summers outside of college until I aged out of my fast-pitch league. At twenty-two, one is already too old. I did not say that both field hockey and softball stood as surrogates to the sports I really wanted: ice hockey and baseball. Ice hockey was not for me because there was no way to have it, not where I grew up and not for the amazing expense of the sport as compared to one where I used the same glove for a decade. Baseball was for my brother, and there was nothing to suggest I could challenge that system in those years. It didn't occur to me. And age and circumstances render the point moot, anyway: love for a thing does not necessarily come coupled with a gift for it. I had other talents, and these I pursued through college; it was those things that brought me all the way to the Camino—curiosity recast into research, enthusiasm bent to scholarship. But the body remembers: the adrenaline thrill, the muscles' push. Maybe that's why our pace never slacks. We keep time with each other, neither of us willing to slow first.

We stand in the shade at our Portomarín meeting-place for thirty minutes, waiting for the rest of our party. The cool shadow is cast by a massive stair that was once part of a second century Roman bridge. The stairs used to lead down into the old city, now submerged beneath the dammed waters of the River Miño. In the drier months, we've been told, walkers can see the roofs of houses through the water. From the stone steps, we see no drowned marketplace, but we do see the others upon the bridge, can watch the now-familiar colors of their jackets and hats draw closer. We can hear them a long way out. Our legs stretch before us, and we don't say anything, but we feel we've won something, us gazelles, but everything won comes with a loss of something else.

*

It's while we're in O Pedrouzo that the news comes: a man entered Pulse nightclub in Orlando, Florida, and opened fire. Before he was shot by police, he had killed forty-nine people and wounded fifty-three others. Those are the numbers, but there is no quantifying this targeted brutality. In the little circle of wi-fi signal radiating out from our lodging, we assemble the fragments together. In the bar of the restaurant where we eat dinner, footage from the scene rolls between Spanish election news and Euro-Cup updates. Here Spanish voters seeking hope by ballot; here so many stretchers, emergency lights swirling all the wrong colors; here, plumes of smoke and people running through Marseilles. After one of the matches between England and Russia, fans attacked one another. The night before, English fans had clashed with French police, and days later, sixteen people would be hospitalized and thirty-six arrested in Lille, following another altercation between English and Russian supporters. I think, *at least no one was shot.*

I wonder how long we'll keep thinking that way: at least it wasn't worse. Forty-nine dead, not a hundred, not a thousand. I want to never think that way again. I am desperate to stop thinking about it altogether.

That day was our longest day walking, and the sky had stretched on like a slate roof. We wore our rain ponchos and stewed in the plastic-trapped heat of our own bodies. Someone else's blister broke, peeling open the descent to his heel, so impossibly pink. My feet simply reported tiredness, heaviness, reminding me of my life at a desk, whole but too often seated.

Comparatively, we hadn't gone far, and my particular discomfort was nothing. By dinner, it was clear I had not lost anyone particular to me in this attack on the queer community—not like so many people had to discover. Not the way so many people have to discover every single day under the violence of this world, from which I know myself much sheltered. My loss, my unsettling, my grief, comparatively, are nothing.

*

On the Camino, in the province of León, there is a place called Cruz de Ferro where a small iron cross sits atop a tall post, and at the base of the post, a mound of stones and mementos transform the place. This is where pilgrims unburden themselves. Tradition says pilgrims carry a stone with them from home to leave in this place—a symbolic separation of present and past, letting go of sin's weight on the soul as surely as the stone weighs in the pack. Over hundreds of kilometers, those ounces mean something. Pilgrims who are not walking so far leave their stones on Monte de Gozo—the mount of joy, from which pilgrims can finally see their destination.

Our itinerary does not include Cruz de Ferro, but we stand on Monte de Gozo, look down at the city and the cathedral waiting in its heart. All around the base of the monument, not pebbles as one might expect, but real stones, some washed smooth by rivers near or far. I don't leave anything there, though I wish I could leave behind the heaviness in my chest. That is mine to carry.

The puck in my bag has a regulation weight of roughly six ounces. A rock the size of a fist weighs roughly one pound. My own clenched hand, resting on a scale, weighs the same. While walking, the blood settles in my fingers, makes them thick, stiff, difficult to curl.

*

On the morning we start our final leg of the practical experience—the day we will walk into Santiago de Compostela—I see that the Penguins have won the Stanley Cup. I ask one of my companions to take a picture of me, holding my puck, wearing my

Penguins shirt, but it feels wrong to celebrate it, now, the morning after, out of kilter—and also the morning after the morning in Orlando.

In our small group, far away from home, we do what we can, which is very, very little. I swallow my grief, and I walk. I swallow my joy, and I walk, the two tastes mingling on my tongue. In the days to come, we will get details about the shooter; they still won't make anything I can call sense, except that I will think of that statue, the raised sword, the trampling underfoot, how deep and bloody the trench that fear digs. If someone gives hate Santiago's face, that is not Santiago the pilgrim's doing.

In the days to come, I will hear about the injuries all of the players sustained and played through. Some are visible: famously, in the 2013 playoffs against the Penguins, Boston Bruins center Gregory Campbell blocked an Evgeni Malkin shot that broke his right fibula. Campbell collapsed for a moment, then shoved himself to his feet and finished his shift, skating inelegantly but effectively enough that the Penguins could not score: forty more seconds with a broken leg. Campbell was done for the season then, but the Bruins swept the Penguins out of the playoffs. At the end of the same season, Patrice Bergeron revealed, after the Bruins lost in the Stanley Cup finals, that he had a broken rib, a separated shoulder, and had suffered a punctured lung that saw him spend time in the hospital for observation after the final game.

These are reminders that even when hockey is simply reduced to its physics—mass times acceleration—and when the game is being played independent of cheap shots and the actual act of fighting that is still part of the sport, it carries a legacy of violence. It's not even bad luck; it's inevitability, the way marathon runners must give up their toenails. It is not about rationality; it's about what I heard over and over again on the field: you must sacrifice your body for the ball.

So, too, is the communion of saints and martyrs: sacrifice and inevitability. It is the suffering we valorize. That is why pilgrims are walking to Santiago; that is why pilgrims walk, why some go on their knees or barefoot. I am thinking about Orlando, Pulse, a heartbeat, and I want to stop walking. I want to stand and listen to the music that must have been playing before—*before*—and imagine the lights and the joy and the *communitas* of that place, in wholeness. We have saints and martyrs enough.

*

The first person Sidney Crosby handed the Stanley Cup to on that June night was defenseman Trevor Daley. Daley broke his ankle in game three of the Eastern Conference Final, twenty days before. He hadn't played at all in the final series. But he was on the ice in uniform and skates for the celebration, hoisting the 35-pound Stanley Cup over his head and skating very slowly with it. Crosby later said he gave it first to Daley because Daley's mom was battling cancer, not doing well, and Daley had mentioned, as the team played for the championship, that it would mean something to her to see him with the Cup. She died a little more than a week after that night.

The sport was supposed to be a way to look away. But everywhere we look, we see the same things.

*

Once pilgrims arrive at the Cathedral in Santiago, there are more rituals to observe. One is the Pilgrims' Mass. Another is the visit to the sepulcher and the high altar. The sepulcher, perversely, is the place where Santiago himself seems most distant: visitors pass through a narrow hallway in the cathedral's belly, and at the end of another short hall, the pale stone tomb. Duly solemn, it stands in somber contrast to the journey through the camarín, behind the Baroque extravagance of the high altar.

As pilgrims ascend the stairs, small signs indicate that photography is prohibited in this portion of the cathedral, but it is here that truly begs for it. Even the walls are a marvel: Portuguese jasper, swirling green and ochre, and while the perennial line moves slowly, to simply be encased in such color transports—that is, at least, until the statue of Santiago itself comes into view. Then the pilgrim may approach the statue, lean and embrace the saint's gilded shoulders, touch it with bare hands. At that moment, too, the pilgrim offers up a prayer. So close to Santiago's ear, it must be heard.

When I come to the statue, I don't say anything out loud. No one is allowed to linger long, and in my mind, I can say everything at once, trust it will all arrive.

Who Holds the Stag's Head Gets to Speak

Gabrielle Calvocoressi

Dear God who lives inside the stag's head
even after the stag's shot and lies slumped and abashed
on the forest floor. Protect him.

Even after he's been heaved onto the car's dark roof.
Forest Green. Or Pacific Blue. Nowhere he can see.
His body stiffens like a trellis above the driver.
Help him. Hold him in your sight.

I know the age of prayer is over. I read it on my newsfeed.
Someone said someone said someone said, *Faith is a weapon
of the Man.*

When they take him down in the darkness
he looks like any body. Could you rest the muscle of your breath
against his neck so he won't sag? So the man thinks he's alive
and quakes in the awful company of the risen.

You are the Blue Lord I prayed for when I was hunted.
You came to me through the branches. I could hear you
in the upper room where I had hidden in the cupboard.

The moment the blade goes to gut him please make of his entrails
a phalanx of butterflies. And of his lungs a great bear
charging. My Lord. When I was the cowered beast
you turned me clear as water so the Hunter could not find me.

I beseech you. Abide.

Polaroid

Links

Stacey Lynn Brown

Knock-kneed, bucktoothed,
I stand with a small golf bag slung

over my shoulder, my 96
ROCK hat pulled low, shielding

the bright Florida sun.
I am seven, out with my dad

chasing this small white
ball up and down the fairway

while he hits mulligans, calibrates
his swing. He wants me to be

the next Nancy Lopez. I just want
to spend time with him, would never

actually say I don't like playing,
watching, talking about it

for hours on end. All too soon,
his handicap won't refer

to his game but to the night
my mother found him on the floor,

the aftermath, the constant
tallying of the effort it takes

to get from one hazard to
the next. My father is away,

furthest from the hole, choosing
between iron and wood.

Of Competition or "And the sheeted dead did squeak and gibber in the Roman streets"

Brendan Constantine

The act of throwing a body from a window
is called Defenestration. Saying you know this
is called Showing Off.

           Whether people are born
competitive is still unknown. However, exhaustive
research has made one thing abundantly clear;
every scientist intent upon proving the existence
of a "competition gene"

                wants to be first.

The first time I fell out of a window, I was eight
and had just won a race against my brother. Indoors.
What can I say, I kept going.

           The second time, I was ten
and I was thrown out by a bad loser. Some people get
awfully touchy about being told they're awfully touchy.

I beat David Myers in a bread-eating contest, fair and
square, so he threw me from his bedroom window.
I broke two fingers and a flower pot shaped like
a Wooly Mammoth.

        Natural Selection.

A funny thing about competition is that most
      living things compete without knowing it.
A funny thing about competition is humans
      are the only creatures who keep score.

A funny thing about competition is how some
        folks say, *It's not whether you win or lose,*
        it's where you lay the blame.

My grandmother used to say that. She doesn't anymore.

Now she says, *There are men under my bed. I hear them*
all night long. They want to throw me out the window.
They want to take my books. Let them try. I'm a light sleeper
and I've killed a man before.
                                We've told the nurses
she doesn't mean that last part, but frankly we're not sure.

Just as historians aren't sure who invented the window.
Many now say it was a Roman named Septimus Ortho
who first put a square hole in a wall and then covered it
with a pane of glass, sometime during the 100th century AD.

The first person to be thrown out of it
                                        is said to be
a man named Gaius Publius, who, as he fell to earth,
famously cried, *Ille rapuit formam meam!*
Or, *That guy stole my idea!*
                                And then a thousand violins
began to play. And a thousand golden trumpets did rend
the Roman air.

You know the funny thing about competition?
        In German it's spelled with a K.
A funny thing about competition is it's lonely.
A funny thing about competition is some people
        believe competition gets to have its own room
        in the brain and doesn't have to share with anyone.

But that may not be true. It may have to share
with a twin sibling known as Caution.

Last August, scientists in New Zealand announced
competition and caution not only reside together
in the frontal lobe, they have bunk-beds
in the Anterior Cingulate Cortex.

It's tight in there; they fight all the time. And when
they're not fighting, they're racing,
                                racing through the house. It's a race
to the windows and each time there's no telling
who'll win.
                    In America, jumping from a window is
among the least common forms of suicide, accounting for
just 2%. Remarkably this puts it just 1% above paying
a five-year-old to poke you to death with a cocktail sword.

In Hong Kong, self-defenestration is clear favorite,
accounting for over 52%.
                                I don't mean it's a competition,
but if it were, some might say it's fixed because they have
more skyscrapers and no guns. The funny thing about
competition is even when it's fixed it isn't certain.
For example, Albert Camus,

who said there was only one philosophical question
that needed answering: Should I stay or should I go?

Albert Camus, who wrote half his books while
standing at a lectern. Albert Camus who might've
written more if he hadn't been killed in a car wreck
on his way to Paris. Before leaving Provence that day,
he wrote postcards to his wife and each of his mistresses,
same message four times, "Longing to see you."
A fixed game is still a game.

The next time I fall from a window I hope I mean it.
Perhaps I'll climb up on the sill and look down like Caesar,

any Caesar, clap my hands once and jump. And the air
will draw its one syllable past my ear, and my clothes
will billow, and the street will spool out its ledger for
everything I owe, and I'll hit with a sound like a sack
of coins. God,
                    am I serious? Honestly, I don't know.
But that's not the real question. No, the question—
if you're a player—is this:
                              Will I land ahead of you?

Darkening the Belt

Anders Carlson-Wee

You show me my throat,
how you can jam the adam

back into the windpipe, blacken
the breath. Hit him here.

You show me my cheekbone,
you show me my ribs,

how you can fit a thumb
between, how you can dig,

how you can twist.
Hit him here, you say, faking

a haymaker and loading
my groin with the ghost

of a shin. You show me my ears,
how you can sneak up behind

and clap the silence
from the head. Hit him here.

You show me my fingers.
You show me my mouth,

my eyes, my knees, my chin.
You say the body is full

of weaknesses: what can be
stretched, what can be broken

open. You show me how to buckle
my wrist, how to aim

for my temple. Hit him here,
you say. This is how you win.

From *Farewell to Soccer*

Ninety-Minute-Long Stories

Valerio Magrelli

Translated from the Italian by Will Schutt

Minute 1

My son's a soccer fan! And to think he'd once been scared of the ball . . . Fear: fear. To cure him of that loathsome disease, I'd set him down in front of me, at attention, and start him on chest volleys, lightly tapping the ball against his chest from less than a foot away. It was a series of very gentle thumps, and he—rigid, tense to the tipping point—would try to withstand as many as we'd agreed upon. How about ten? Twenty? He must have been five years old and would come away from that exercise exhausted yet happy. They were medicine drops to prepare him for the sport and took effect slowly, like vitamins or mineral supplements. When it was over, he'd run off, relieved until the next round. In the meantime Ronaldo was roaming our fields, and across Italy a generation of children was switching teams. They were the class of '89, practically all of them were destined to enlist in the interminable ranks of that Pied Piper.

Minute 2

Of course they come in all stripes. The latest was a Division I goalie from Germany. I'd always wondered what would happen if you were forced to stand in front of ninety thousand people for forty-five minutes straight. In the end that goalie satisfied my curiosity: he had to take a piss was all. But how can you hold it in when a whole stadium's watching you, not to mention dozens of TV cameras? Evidently, he couldn't, so as soon as there was an opening, he snuck away from the goal, crouched behind some billboards and there, in front of everyone, relieved himself. Like a dog. The most fascinating thing about it was his expression: focused and at the same time absentminded, as if what he was doing were nothing of note. He aroused my sympathy, my sympathy and pity, yet there was also something heroic in the act, however pathetic, of overcoming the obstacle of your body in the simplest, most resigned way, like a matador sweeping the ground with his cape.

Minute 3

The diva I saw play at the children's tournament was another story altogether! Naturally the parents were the real spectacle: hysterical, cruel, clinging to the fence. God knows that crowd of dynamos, that neurotic engine, can't stop spinning at a thousand rpm. Next came the kids, all well trained and diligent. Until I caught sight of the champion. Alone, haloed, totally aware of his superiority, he trotted out to midfield, absorbed, awaiting reverence. Which is what he was shown, continuously, by everyone: friends, enemies, onlookers. He had a stern, self-important, hieratic, annoyed air about him that didn't suit his age. More than an athlete, he looked like a prophet. How effortlessly he moved! He was a monster—the kind only little imitators can be. He was imitating fate. Who knows what became of his talent?

Minute 4

Meanwhile my son was growing up, and I took him to the park to try out a pair of gloves and cleats he'd been given as a present. The cleats I doubt he'll wear again after that. He felt ridiculous standing there on his tiptoes. Now all I need is a tutu, he told me. That's when I knew he was through with soccer, by which I mean endless soccer, where the fields stretch on forever, where you have to claw your way across the terrain in cleats and guzzle air. Truth is, that game had always filled me with dread too. I'd play to play, but it really was neverending, swarming with the fastest wingmen. What was I doing there, stock-still, adrift in those expanses my opponents darted across?

At least he held on to his gloves. Now look at him: a cartoon figure, his two hands bigger than his body—a caricature of childhood, which wants to squeeze the world and starts with a soccer ball.

Minute 5

Playing alone with your father is devastating, unbearable. Those Sunday afternoons kicking the ball around while the radio crackled the day's scores—I still haven't recovered. Yet despite the knot in my throat every time I think of that hour of give-and-take and fatherly counsel, I'm grateful for what ensued after our tête-à-têtes. The light would fade, the temperature drop, and, shivering and sweaty, we would head into an old-timey café near the Villa Borghese. It was a hangout from another age, with ground glass windows and wood paneling; grizzled waiters served *Gran Gelati*. The place was eventually torn down with bulldozers, TNT, CAT machines. Razed it to the ground, the blown-out worksite looked like Baghdad. That one refuge, cozy and lit in the dark, expecting us every Sunday evening.

Minute 9

There's a well-known expression commonly used to designate lousy players: Banana feet. There are plenty of others, but this one I remember with particular fondness because it was attached to a friend of mine with whom I played for years. He was a good defender, and fast, which was why he often broke away and took a shot at the goal. And yet for years he never managed to convert. Not once. It became an obsession of mine. Even after I'd stopped playing, I'd hang around waiting for him to come on the attack so I could watch him miss, miss, miss. How many times can you miss? In his case, the only answer is every time. With those two clumsy, crooked feet, he'd shank each shot, sending the ball sailing every which way but toward the target, in a shocking flurry of blunders. You, too, have entered my little pantheon, with your yellow, curved, fragrant A-grade Chiquita fruit–shaped shoes.

Minute 10

There exists a code of ethics in soccer, which my son, upon turning eleven, learned to recognize on a trip to Munich. But this calls for a bit of context: it was the first time the two of us found ourselves abroad together, and, anxious father that I was, I made every effort to ensure he was having fun. There were only two setbacks, the first when my wife phoned, terrified and in tears. She'd received a call from the zoo where we'd spent the morning. An excitable zoo-keeper called to inform the boy's mother in his war-movie Italian that he had found her son's passport in front of the lion's den, but the poor woman, misunderstanding, thought the boy had been torn to pieces by animals.

Matter resolved, we stopped in front of a magnificent museum. I wanted at all costs a picture of my biblical Daniel having cheated death in the lion's den, and I told him we just needed to stop the first person to pass by. Done and done. Enter a Bavarian who points and shoots. A week later, when we had them printed (this was before digital film), we discovered that the man had aimed the lens the wrong way and photographed his nose.

Trouble comes in threes: by the time we arrived at the European Finals, misfortune hung in the air. Italy came back in the last minute only to blow it in overtime. It was painful for me, but normal. My son, on the other hand, kept staring at me in the hotel room. Now what, he asked. Now nothing, I said, it's over. Then he burst out crying. In that moment, for the first time in his life, he had come into contact with the irreparable, even if it took the form of something as insignificant as a goal. Remembering his tears, I get a knot in my throat, the kind of knot you find on plants when the stem stops growing and coils around itself before it can go on.

Minute 16

Of course a lot has changed. Time was that from the bleachers you could clearly make out the players' breath, could hear them talk.

Now the pitch has become distant and inaccessible. The first thing to change with respect to the game's golden age was the turf itself. In a poem by Vittorio Sereni, the arena is described as a familiar, friendly presence:

At the end of July,
under the pergola of a bar in San Siro
through railings and arches
you catch a glance of the sun-filled stadium
and the big empty bowl astounds you
mirroring the time you've wasted . . .

All that has changed. As the number of stands have doubled and the stadiums have been covered, the relationship between the public and the players, the stage and the stalls, has changed dramatically. The traditional pitch has been transformed into an LED display, a screen surrounded by other screens, immersed in an optical well, placed under the lens of the camera. And yet somehow, in our ridiculous country, this process has produced a perverse side effect; with the rapid growth of Adriatic flora (weed infestation) the fields have wilted (San Siro worst of all), the grass atrophied.

Pretty soon we'll be playing on carpets, like in the English Cup, a form of indoor soccer to match the ultimate act of simulation, as Borges and Bioy Casares chillingly predicted, where:

There are no scores, no teams, no matches. The stadiums are nothing but demolition sites. Today all that happens happens in television and recording studios. Hasn't the contrived excitement of the commentators led you to suspect it's all a work of fiction? The last soccer match was played on June 24, 1937. Since that date, soccer, like the vast majority of sports, is just a show directed by a man alone in his booth, or performed by actors wearing uniforms in front of the cameraman . . . Rampant advertising is the mark of modern times.

Minute 17

Speaking of indoor soccer, I must have been twelve, give or take a year, when my family moved, and for a couple of weeks we had a completely empty house at our disposal. That's when I discovered the foam ball, big as a soccer ball yet soft and light. I'd play for hours on end, running in and out of the newly gutted rooms. It was the weirdest feeling, like being in an aquarium, in a room with no roof. I dribbled down the hallway pretending I was in a Parisian *passage* or the Galleria in Milan. The experience was all the more intense because confined to a few reckless days never to be repeated. Yet I still remember that hybrid arena, that strange chimera, an unlikely cross between a soccer field and a breakfast nook.

Minute 19

In China's Celestial Empire they played with a leather sphere filled with women's hair—a locket, an emblem of desire. In Ancient Rome, they played *pila paganica* using an animal hide stuffed with feathers, perhaps to memorialize some magical flight. In fourteenth-century Great Britain, those who played hurling (an antecedent of soccer) used a leather shell packed with cork, a practical and rough material. Today there's air inside. As for the outer covering, it usually comes from Pakistan, where hundreds of families spend their lives cutting and stitching soccer balls for the Western world's day of rest. Circumference: 26 to 28 inches. Weight: 396 to 453 grams. Pressure: 0.6 to 1.1 atmospheres (at least up until recently). There you have it, the icon, the contested object, the nucleus around which the solar system of soccer revolves.

Minute 20

Here's a memory instead. A powerful installation piece by an Italian artist at the Venice Biennale. In Belgrade, with the former headquarters of the Serbian army reduced to rubble in the backdrop, a little boy is dribbling a cranium. As I recall, all you see are his shorts and the boy driving forward for a while, brilliant and tireless. But then and there you have no idea what's going on. Me, I didn't realize until the day after that he was kicking a human skull.

Minute 21

The Bosnian War reminds me of Chile: it takes nothing for a stadium to turn into a prison. A somewhat similar logic brings campgrounds and death camps under one umbrella. As in music, a major key modulates to a minor. Even natural catastrophes meet a dignified end in sports arenas. Think of Hurricane Katrina and the huge crowds of evacuees in the New Orleans Superdome as it warped into a circle of hell. Georges Perec saw this connection clearly; in one of his novels, he describes how an Olympic Village slowly, relentlessly transforms into a concentration camp.

For my part, I remember a trip to Russia in the early '70s, during which I decided to attend a Dynamo Moscow match with my father. The stadium held tens of thousands of spectators who displayed the same obedient restraint whether they were cheering or ejecting the occasional huff of disappointment. But the beauty part came at the end. We had an appointment to keep afterward, and time to kill, so we stayed in our seats while everyone else filed out. Fifteen minutes later, something marvelous happened. One by one, hundreds of tiny trapdoors swung open and policemen in riot gear emerged from the ground. They'd been under our feet!

Below us, right beneath the pitch, a second public, shadowing the first, had been sitting, hidden away, secretly monitoring everything. They hadn't seen anything. They couldn't see anything. But they had been watching over the onlookers. Duplicate spectators, they rose up out of the ground as if to show a pair of tourists the extravagant folly of a totalitarian world.

Minute 23

Dark blue out, and my son an Inter fan, I decided to take him to see a night game between his team, playing away, and mine. We wound up sitting in the nosebleeds, amid the crowds and chaos, to witness a tumultuous showdown—from the outset seven goals were scored, turnover after turnover committed. He must have been twelve years old, and it was his first time in a crowd. He sat there, dazed and silent, excited yet estranged from the feelings around him, since he was rooting for Inter. I have often thought about his sense of displacement. Why is it that so many of the intimate moments we share with loved ones are spiked with such discrepancies? Me on one team, he on another—pass. Yet he was in the rivals' den, condemned to keep silent, on the very occasion he had the chance to see his heroes win.

"Cheer under your breath," I felt like telling him, but I kept my mouth shut, knowing how absurd such advice would sound. Besides, what would become of my high-minded life lessons were I to advise him to be a hypocrite and coward on the same day I'd taken him to share our love of the game? It's called a double bind, a situation of simultaneous stasis and anguish. What was I supposed to do? All around me large groups of fans, clouded by smoke and beer, suddenly fell silent. With only a few minutes left, the visiting team had scored. The stadium became a large, mute, hostile bowl.

That's when I heard him shout for joy. His joy, my terror. It only lasted a minute, several thousand stunned people turned to look at us, and then everything went back to the way it was before. What saved us? What guardian angel shielded us with its wing? I think they simply couldn't believe that rival fans stood in their midst. We must have seemed like a mirage to them, a fata morgana not to be believed. So, after a moment, they forgot about us. As we exited the stands, I felt like the father in *The Bicycle Thief* (which ends in just such a place). Saved, yes, but broken. He had won on all counts; I had lost on all counts. You might say that was my gift to him.

Minute 24

. . . I continued to play soccer into my forties. At a certain point it became increasingly hard to get a handful of players together. But that all changed when I met the brother of a friend of mine. I began playing with a team of real simpatico types. Nice guys. Too nice. It lasted a few games, until one day—one evening, actually—

something unforgivable transpired. I'd been moving pretty well on the field, I even led a glorious breakaway to the penalty area, when the teammate running beside me was knocked down and the ref called foul. That was when I knew.

If I had been able to slice through the defense like butter, to breeze by fullbacks as I did in my dreams, it was only because they had given me a wide berth. Literally avoided me. Their kindness was exquisite, if rather humiliating, and everything became clear to me when one of my opponents walked up and handed me the ball. You take the kick, he said, then added, "Sir." "Sir"—on a soccer field! I was devastated and had no one to take it out on. I should have known. That was my last game.

Minute 29

Maradona, after his home was burgled: "They made off with a lot of memories. The important thing now is to forget."
—*La Repubblica*, October 29–30, 1989

Minute 30

Maradona was the prototype for an aggressive, vulgar breed of soccer player. It's not his shady past I'm referring to so much as the way he'd celebrate during his last matches, looking directly into the camera and spitting out some epithet. Prior to him, how many people had identified the game with regression, with the freedom to act impulsively? I remember being enticed to go see a regional tournament with my uncle, a habitué, when I was seven or eight, because a famous local champ was playing. It was a small town and the people were anxiously waiting to catch a glimpse of their hero. Naturally, when he did finally show up, he looked resentful (that's sort of written in the DNA of young talent). It was summertime, and after a kick or two he knotted his shirt up over his belly and proceeded to play like that for the rest of the match. At one point he stopped in the middle of the field and let out a spellbinding burp. Needless to say my boyish admiration for him flowered immediately. Now that's a man, I thought, greeting our pointless formality with total indifference. Captivated by this literal embodiment of arrogance, I nagged my uncle all night to find out more about this utterly charismatic figure. His was a primitive charisma, sure, but in the eyes of a kid, irresistible. You're saying someone can do that—in public—and still be cheered? From that day on, I took up practicing with more drive than ever, in the grip of a new goal.

Minute 33

My son's idea of the game is almost exclusively limited to PlayStation. There was a time you could talk about miniaturization, i.e., the transition from soccer to 8v8, from 8v8 to five-a-side, from five-a-side to table soccer. But even a spree of foosball preserves traces of the original physical exertion, what with its whirl of rods and figurines and tiny metal balls. Not PlayStation. The cable signal has supplanted the athlete so well that now there's even a chorus of prerecorded commentary, so that he plays ghost games against ghost teams with ghost scores. Alone, engrossed for hours in a semi-hallucinatory state. It's literally a mirage, an optical effect produced by refracted light. As on a long trip through the desert, a screen stands for the dunes and the image hangs in the air, perfectly disincarnate.

Minute 36

The game as I practiced it was the exact opposite of that alarming devotion. It was material, movement. One detail among many: the lime. Lime was something we reserved for special occasions. When the summer team I marched with would sign on to host another team of particular distinction, we were obliged to paint the field. So, for half an hour we'd mark out the lines on the turf, usually by trailing white dust from a cardboard box that we hauled behind us. I remember a movie where a group of boys in Mexico performed the same operation using cocaine, white lines a hundred yards long . . . ours looked more like a construction site. By the time the game was over, all the lines had bled out, and the field resembled a mask with runny makeup. Take a windy afternoon or a day of rain and the whole lot was lost.

Minute 37

Lime, yes, but more than lime, mud. I played in this one game in particular, a night game, six inches deep in the muck. It's as if I can still summon those times of excitement, of pure fun. Electrified by the water and dirt caking our shoes, we did nothing but fall, fall, fall, and going after the ball became an excuse to make that infinitely long slide back to some kind of Eden.

Minute 38

What I can't stand is the violence. For example, the kind committed by gangs of fans against the unsuspecting traveler, some harmless individual at sea, lost amid the shouting, organized crowd. Just the idea of sharing a short train ride with that human plurality par excellence, with its aggressive, pathological sense of belonging, makes me nauseated. Not individual ultras but the group. If you ask me, "ultras" deserves to be one of those words that are always plural, nouns that are defective precisely because they lack possibility. In the case of ultras, the possibility of referring to an individual. Nuptials, news and ultras, do not have a singular form (as opposed to the "dark," which has no plural). I'm talking about the fascist thug, ferocious and multiple, ferocious because multiple, or at least two-pronged.

I remember reading an article about a boy in Sicily being murdered just for trying to defend a girl his own age. Thrown from a moving train.

Minute 39

I was thinking of the sea, of the great Atlantic Ocean as it appears, sometimes, in TV documentaries. I was thinking of the sea a few years ago, around nightfall, when I noticed people clearing the streets of Rome. The fateful hour of nine o'clock was approaching, and I was still wandering about, looking around, studying the great tide as it slowly drained away, quietly streamed home in time to catch the World Cup final. The most immediate sensation, as I say, was of a huge tide receding. As if prompted by some invisible voice, or attracted by a strong magnet, half the city emptied out. Gradually yet inexorably, its population went on withdrawing, leaving behind emptiness, silence, as sometimes happens on the beach in Breton.

Me, on the other hand, I lingered on the street till just before the first whistle. While the others turned home, I waited, trying to resist, testing the strength of the aquatic, collective pull of the TV. A deserted city in and of itself doesn't warrant much attention; anything will do: a holiday, a long weekend, summer break. Nevertheless, there was a special reason here, an irresistible draw, a kind of magical, moony Soccerlandia capable of governing the tides of a large part of the world's population.

I pictured an extraordinary funnel, a whirlpool that could sweep away the human species, at least the half that is hooked on technology. I tried to picture it from way up high, in one long zoom in: the Earth, Europe, Italy, Rome, the square I stood in, the stairway home, the living room and, finally, her, right in the center of the planetary whirlpool, the TV, calm eye of the storm.

Minute 44

As for strides, how can I forget the night I pulled a muscle at the start of a game? Having barely begun to run, I lit out with a burning desire. After a week at my desk, I spotted an empty flank in the field and sprinted toward it, furious as a boy. But fury was the only thing boyish about it. My muscles had up and gone, and after a few steps, I felt a pang. I retreated to the bench, wounded and embittered and incurably heartsick. Being there, on the field, and not being able to play, that was part of soccer for me too: the defeat to end all defeats. It wasn't losing that mattered so much as giving up without even the chance to participate.

Minute 45

A boy's day of glory at the beach. Three o'clock on an August after-noon. The sand is hot to touch and the air wavy with it. Next to the beach is a private playing field rounded by a few scrawny palm trees and two strips of grass, yet it boasts a regulation-size goal. The ball wasn't even that heavy, actually, yet it was enough to achieve that miracle: a shot at sudden death and the crossbar splits in two and comes crashing down over the goalie!

Admit it, that's pretty remarkable. I doubt many people have done that. Sure, maybe there was a defect, a knot in the wood. Still, the bar came down. In slow-mo. I'd always sworn hitting the beam was better than scoring a goal, and there was my proof. Search far and wide and you may still find a few witnesses to that feat.

¡Sangre! ¡Sangre! ¡Sangre!

Nandi Comer

No one knows if blood will come,
but once Terríble has a handful

of Místico's golden rimmed eyehole
we are all on our feet, stirred up, chanting.

Center ring, both bulgy-bodied men
lift and fall in heavy, syncopated pants.

Every inch of Místico's body goes slack
from las patadas, los sentones

and the choke-out against the ropes.
Each yank wrenches his masked head upward.

Under the weight of so much body,
threads give. This fight is about blood.

Bleeding a masked man starts
with a tiny rip in his costume, maybe

a bite, always broken skin. Once the head
is opened, it takes little pressure

to make a bloody spout. From countless bleedings,
heads callus. It is said some fighters

have been sliced so many times, the skin
forms a buckled blanket of skin

over their temples. The leathered fortress
can be cut only by a skilled blade.

Terríble breaks a hole in Místico's cloth crown.
The crowd's fists pump upward.

Each set of eyes opens in unison
with the tear. We want it.

We want to catch sight
of a damp hairline, a frowzy eyebrow,

then Místico's open skin.
What's so fascinating about watching

an opened temple? Why cheer
for a fighter pushing another man

to the brink of passing out?
Blood comes because we, the audience,

have asked for it. Before this match
the man in the third row, under howls

from his foreman, hauled emptied corn husks
through a second shift at an oil refinery.

The stench of burnt oil still sticks
to his dull frame. The young man next to him

is a waiter who stretches his payday
between university books and his mother's

dinner table. Across the arena is a tired
sixth grade English teacher whose

semester is almost up. Here when we chant
"chair," Místico will shatter the wooden frame

across Terríble's back. When we yell for a flying
head scissors kick, Terríble is already lifting his boot.

Tonight we want blood.
We want to see arms and legs

fold and submit, to hear
the referee's three count.

If this were a street brawl,
planting ourselves curbside,

begging for the blade
would be beastly, but this

is an arena, and we are ready
to watch Terríble take his teeth

to Místico's skull. We lust
for the shaken arms, the loser's

flailing limbs. If any red beads
are to spot up, engorge

and mix with a fighter's sweat,
we will have to yell for it again and again.

We want the trick, the whole bloody craft.
Místico's wound starts its gorge.

We are on our feet. The slick words
grow fat on our tongues.

This Is Not an Essay about Wrestling, or If David Markson Loved the WWF Like I Did When I Was 12

John Findura

Arguments over whether wresting was "real" led to fistfights
in the lunchroom at school.
You tapped your elbow before delivering it into someone's head.

"Macho Man" Randy Savage died of atherosclerotic heart
disease, in Seminole, Florida, suffering a heart attack
while driving his Jeep Wrangler and crashing it into a tree.
He was 58.

There was a clear line of demarcation between "good" and
"bad"–we still look for this today.

Ms. Elizabeth, a former Miss Kentucky who was married
to "Macho Man" Randy Savage for eight years, died in
Marietta, Georgia, of acute toxicity from a combination of
alcohol and painkillers. She was 42.

We had deep discussions on our 8th grade class field trip to
Dorney Park over who would win in a fight: Michigan
State lineman Tony Mandarich or Mike Tyson. We all
agreed Hulk Hogan could kick both their asses.

Atherosclerotic heart disease: the most common cause of
death in the world.

Marietta, Georgia.

The Junkyard Dog fell asleep at the wheel in Forest,
Mississippi and died in a single-car accident. He was buried
in an unmarked grave in North Carolina. He was 45.

My best friend David jumped off his bed and gave his brother
Brian a flying elbow to the head. Brian lay on the floor for
ten minutes. We thought he was dead.

"Adorable" Adrian Adonis died with fellow wrestlers Pat Kelly
and Dave "Wildman" McKigney when, on the way from
Newfoundland to Labrador, wrestler Mike Kelly swerved to
avoid hitting a moose, was temporarily blinded by the sun,
and rolled the minivan. Mike Kelly was the only survivor.
"Adorable" Adrian Adonis was decapitated. He was 33.

"If Shakespeare were alive today he'd be writing wrestling
shows," said Chris Jericho.

North Carolina.

Davey Boy Smith, "The British Bulldog," died from a heart
attack brought on by anabolic steroid abuse. He was 39.

My brothers and I slept on the floor of my grandmother's
family room to watch Wrestlemania. We promised not to
try it in real life.

Dino Bravo was killed in a mob hit related to his smuggling of
cigarettes in Canada. He was 44.
"How do these guys get so big?!"

Bam Bam Bigelow suffered burns over 40% of his body when
he rescued three children from a burning house. He died of a
mixture of cocaine and anti-anxiety medication. He was 45.

Canada.

Owen Hart was being lowered into the ring from the rafters in Kansas City when the quick release mechanism let go early, dropping him 78 feet. He died from internal bleeding due to blunt force trauma. He was 34.

One Thanksgiving my aunt gave all the kids early Christmas presents: all the boys received Wrestling Superstars figures of Hulk Hogan. We all argued over whose Hulk Hogan was the real one.

Forest, Mississippi.

"Mr. Perfect," Curt Hennig, died from acute cocaine intoxication and was found on the floor of his Florida hotel room. He was 44.

My aunt used to cut Sergeant Slaughter's hair. He gave her an autographed record to give to me and my brothers. On the record he covered Neil Diamond's "America." For years afterward I thought Neil Diamond was singing a Sergeant Slaughter song.

"What are you gonna do when these 24 inch pythons wrap around you?" said Hulk Hogan.

Big John Studd died from liver cancer, Hodgkin's disease, and also possibly suffered from amyotrophic lateral sclerosis. He was 47.

The Big Boss Man died of a heart attack at age 41.

The Cobra Clutch.

"Ravishing" Rick Rude died of heart failure due to a combination of various medications and anabolic steroid use. He was 40.

Sergeant Slaughter actually served in the Marines. As a sergeant.

We often jumped off our couch onto pillows, then picked them up and body slammed them.

Jimmy "Superfly" Snuka called the police after a match in May of 1983 and reported his girlfriend had a suffered an injury in their hotel room. Nancy Argentino was later pronounced dead of apparent traumatic brain injuries. The forensic pathologist who conducted the autopsy reported the death should be investigated as a homicide, to which the deputy coroner agreed. Charges were filed against "Superfly" in 2015 when he was arrested and indicted, but the court found him unfit to stand trial due to dementia in 2016.

The Ultimate Warrior legally changed his name to "Warrior" in 1993. He died, walking to his car, of a heart attack caused by atherosclerotic cardiovascular disease three days after being inducted into the WWE Hall of Fame in 2014.

Superfly.

Koko B. Ware is still alive. The whereabouts of his parrot, Frankie, is currently unknown.

Hulk Hogan's sex tape lawsuit bankrupted Gawker.

My brother got the GI Joe action figure of Sergeant Slaughter for Christmas one year. I became depressed. Sergeant

Slaughter was going to beat up all of my GI Joe's and there was nothing anyone could do about it.

King Kong Bundy currently lives in southern New Jersey.

58.

42.

Marietta, Georgia.

45.

34.

I am almost as old as Davey Boy Smith when he died.

George "The Animal" Steele holds a bachelor's degree from Michigan State and a master's degree from Central Michigan. In 2002 he had part of his colon removed to prevent recurring symptoms of Crohn's disease. He currently lives in Florida and is a member of the Michigan Coaches Hall of Fame.

Piledriver.

The Curtain

Ryan Black

Sometimes whole days slipped past without my noticing . . .
—Larry Levis

My youth? I can't hear it anywhere, Larry.
Not in the whippoorwill's call at Jamaica Bay;
not in a Clinton Hill townhouse, single bedrooms available,

$1850/month. No. For a while I was the only white boy
on the team. Then I wasn't. In Delaware, they thought
Puerto Rican. In Virginia, *Light skinned*. That these men

could mistake a tight fade for Spanish Harlem, mistook
a handle for code, as if context were the only determinant.
Ryan? Shammgod joked. *Motherfucker's grandfather*

still try to own us. When I was fifteen, Spike Lee brought
fifty of the city's top high-school players to Clinton Hill
for a 40 Acres and a Mule clinic: three meals a day,

SAT prep, and a week of guest lectures on black masculinity.
At Pratt Institute. We slept in the dorms. At night
we hopped the fence, bought 40s at the bodega on DeKalb.

The best players, the sure things, slept in in the morning,
then busted my ass in the afternoon. I couldn't check them;
couldn't keep them in front. Steph and Rafer. Kareem Reid.

Too much. And the lectures? I remember Spike's.
About money and black bodies, and what a college makes
off your labor, your talent. You. *A plantation mentality,*

he said, ahead of Walter Byers, executive director
and architect of the NCAA, who'd name it the same,
resurrected and blessed. I sat cross-legged in front

of Spike, in my free jersey and sneakers, and a pair
of Riverside shorts, the golden hawk like a bankroll,
access and all I'd ever want. For years Riverside Church

was AAU basketball, rivaled only by the Gauchos
in the Bronx or the New Jersey Roadrunners.
Before Kenny Anderson lit up Bobby Hurley at Georgia Tech,

he lit him up for the Church at Columbia.
And that image, that icon, the ball clutched in its talons,
meant more to us than the scholarships to come.

DI. DII. It didn't matter. You wear the Church once,
you own it. You signify. We got our first pair
of free sneakers after a Citywide game at Gauchos gym.

Adidas. From Sonny Vaccaro. We were sold;
we played bitch for the extras. Sonny's name rang out
in the Bronx, in Brooklyn and Queens. Uptown. Wherever.

A Calabrese from Western Pennsylvania, he founded
the Dapper Dan Roundball Classic in '65, and the
    invitation-only
ABCD camp where all-Americans built their brand.

Sonny was inexorable, like the men in suits—the *abonnés*—
sequestered to the edges of Degas's frame, patrons
of *a world of pink and white.* The *abonnés* kept to the wings,

to the foyers and rehearsal rooms of the Palais Garnier,
selecting their favorites—the girls who bloomed
in the footlights—with a curator's care,

but in *Le rideau* the *abonnés* stalk the canvas,
obscured by stage flats or in plain sight, their dark suits,
their backs turned, cutouts in the dressing. The dancers

are not the point here, the machines of their bodies
reduced to rose beneath a curtain, save for one
in the corner, beribboned, fleeing the decor.

The dance instills in you something that sets you apart,
Degas would write, himself an *abonné*. *One knows*
that in your world / Queens are made of distance

and greasepaint. Of plumb lines and gutter sylphs.
Of a sponsor's foresight, bodies long and lithe as Steph's
or Kareem's. Shammgod was broad shouldered,

legs like goalposts. A McDonald's All American,
if you kept him in front he went right through you.
He had this crossover like a rope trick. He'd toss the ball

out from his hip as if losing control, then change direction,
pulling it back across his body with his off hand
like opening a curtain. You can google it. I'll wait . . .

Once, in Myrtle Beach, Shammgod broke out for thirty
in the second half against a team from Florida, then broke
into their hotel and stole all their sneakers.

The tournament caught word, but Shammgod already threw
the bag off a bridge on the side of a road. The troopers
had to let us go. Shammgod just smiled, a Band-Aid

under his right eye like a family coat of arms.
Shammgod Wells, broad-shouldered son of God the father.
Not Steph or Skip, Boogie or Kareem. The only handle,

God Shammgod.

Ladies' Arm Wrestling Match
at the Blue Moon Diner

Jenny Johnson

My grandma always told me if life gives you lemons
throw 'em away. And so, we loosen. Shuffle off sore tendons.

Mondays. Insults catcalled out Chevy windows.
Clinking whiskey glasses, we wipe away sweat and old flames.

All I ever found in the gravel was the paper body,
what the garter snake shed. Take off that old suit, tonight.

Even as your good arm shudders to the mat, like the moon
meeting the mouth of the Shenandoah. Take off that old suit.

In new skin, come back again and again. Own this acreage,
this new ground rippling under rolled sleeves.

Scorekeep

Tommy Orange

It must seem perfect—to some one, or thing up there, or out there, or inside, pulling the levers or tapping the buttons that control this whole big thing we are—that I'm a scorekeeper, how I have zero worry or care regarding scores, keeping track of points, about winning, how that's my job and that I even like it despite not caring about points in general or otherwise aside from what the job entails. There has to be something at the very least correct about it—even according to me—otherwise I wouldn't keep doing it almost every night of the week, working at the roller hockey rink I work at in Oakland, keeping score for a living. The rink's over there by the Oakland Airport off Hegenberger on the Easternmost edge of Oakland. I even play in the roller hockey league they have for beginners Sunday nights, but me on skates is like a train off the rails, or better yet like a stocky rolling mass of meat with too big a head—so top-heavy—on eight straight rail-lined wheels my feet stand on top of called rollerblades. Don't feel pity. Please? Pity is for the pitiful, and me, I'm too blunt an object to pity, too wide a face to look all the way at. I'm the guy you see behind thick glass who pushes buttons and never utters a single sound beyond the occasional sneeze or cough. And I do really like to do this thing called roller hockey despite not being very good at it. That nonstop stick-in-hand disc-pushing venture in a round-edged rectangle with aims for nets, fast as you can into goals past goalies. I love to roll, and even though I hardly ever score points I do assist the team by passing to someone who scores. That's a bad joke. But points on the board really do drive most people to keep wanting to win. It's not just that I knew early on I would never be a winner. It's not sour grapes. And I must admit that I too sometimes give myself points. If I can think around something and tie something unalike together to make a connection,

I'll say in my head: *Points*. But I don't keep score to myself, I don't keep track because I'm not playing against anyone. I'll just be like: *Points*. To myself. In my head. Or I'll buzz the big buzzer I buzz when people score goals, I'll buzz the one I can hear in my head. As for the real game everyone plays in real life, all acting like they aren't playing, that one was never for me. Grades and points and trophies and medals and all the shit people love to hear from the higher ups, the grown-ups, teachers, bosses, coaches; words and compliments and exclamations for when they've done a good job, things like *Excellent*, and *Outstanding*, and *Yes!*, and *Wait til the guys upstairs hear about this*; or things like high fives or thumbs ups or back pats, none of that stuff ever did anything for me and if it did I'd be hooked on keeping score too like everyone else. Meanwhile my job is to put points on the board. They pay me minimum wage to do that at the rink. The guys in the league who don't know my name, they call me *Scorekeep*, like if I forget to put points up or forget to start the clock back up after stopped time. "Hey scorekeep, clock!" they'll yell. They think I'm dumb. Which I can understand why they might think that. Everyone thinks I'm mute. And not just mute but dumb, even though the latter means the former and vice versa. They think I don't know what's what. Only my mom's cats know I can talk perfectly fine just like anyone else. Actually they're more mine than my mom's now that she's gone. My cats know I know how to talk. But I decided early on I didn't wanna talk. We all actually have this choice but it's as if we don't. I decided not to talk because from when I could first understand what was being said all I heard was lies. My mom to my dad and back. Nonsense and lies. Then my mom went back to work and left me with her sister Charlene, who left me on the couch in front of the TV most of the time with the cats, and because *they* never said anything, just sat there sleeping or licking or watching me watch TV, and because I loved them so much, respected them even, I figured they probably knew what was best regarding this talking or not talking thing, even though they do meow—it's not the same thing. Sammy, Lyle, and, Freud. That's what she named them, and I keep calling them that because that's the sound they've come to associate with themselves.

My dad works at the Lawrence Livermore Labs. He's an engineer. Works there all the time. I don't know on what. Something nuclear I think. But mom went back to work after being off after having me, and then she met a guy there and he picked her up in his pick-up truck and she never came back. I was in school by then and got along okay on the couch with the cats, with Charlene on the phone in the background—she kept coming to watch me or not watch me really after my mom was long gone. I grew up out in Livermore, where it's hot and starts to smell like farm and cow but not as bad as it gets further down 580 past all the windmills in the Altamont Pass that I thought when I was young they put there to blow the bad cow smells back down where they came from. I still live out here with my dad even though he's never home, or not home when I'm home anyway, or he's sleeping by the time I get home and gone by the time I wake up.

I used to share scorekeeping shifts with teenagers but they all ended up doing some other job or quitting and I was the only one left who wanted to do it. Not that I'm that much older than a teenager, just three years past, but I pretty much raised myself if you don't count the cats, so I feel older than just three years older than being a teen. My mom and dad named me Devon, and I always thought if I had friends who weren't cats they'd call me Dev for short. They call me Scorekeep and they're not my friends and that's okay. It would be sad that I don't have friends who aren't cats if I ever had to tell anyone, or if anyone ever asked, but one good thing about people thinking you can't talk is that they don't even try to talk to you. In that way I'm like an object that moves around and serves a function, but not like a person people can talk to and relate things to and share things with, but just like a thick pole moving independently from the ground. It works out for me, because like I said I never wanted to talk, even after I found out it wasn't all lies, it still all feels like lies and silence feels closer to being true.

*

My mom told me once we're Indian, like as in Native American Indian. Me and her not dad. When I asked her what tribe she said she couldn't tell me and that the family had been hiding as Mexicans for so long and quiet about being Indian because they used to pay people to kill Indians, the US government, paid US Citizens to kill us and bring proof as in scalps or heads, and that we'd been telling people we were Mexican in the family so long that no one would even know if she asked, no one in the family probably even knew anymore and who cares about what kind of Indian, that we're Indian is enough, that we didn't die when they did their best to kill and erase us was enough for me to know and then she told me never to tell anyone but that I should know and just to know that I should know and then she told me never to bring it up again but that I should be grateful because not everyone in our family even knew or ever talked about it. The only proof I could make out was her brown skin, which I didn't get mine is white like my dad's. Oh and how Mexican people always speak Spanish to me before they speak English. Like they see the Indian in me that they don't see in themselves, the Indian I don't see either, or hear, that Indian made quiet so long he went mute, but the question I always find myself asking regarding Mexican people being Indian the way I've thought of it is this: Where does the brown skin come from? Spanish people are white I think. Anyway my dad is most definitely white and maybe French because our last name is Lafaille, which means or translates as fault line. I like that because I am and always have been fascinated by earthquakes. That the earth can move and shake to the point of quaking, just slip and slide and break up down there so deep where there's lava, how it can move and roll like liquid is just such a cool thing and I even got to feel the big one that happened back in '89 because even though the fault line was far away from out here in Livermore we felt it out here too just not as much probably as people who felt it in Candlestick Park during the World Series, or people who watched the Bay Bridge collapse and that one guy went over the edge into the water or maybe just down to that lower deck I can't remember. Sometimes I think being Indian and not being Indian like we are must be like some kind of fault line that will one day give and slip and some big great thing or quaking will happen and people will fall or roll or crack or drop down between a collapsed bridge down into the ocean or just another deck we luckily have there so as to not fall down into the ocean with your car and watching it fill up with water and trying to hit the windows but not being able to break them or get your seatbelt off in time, sometimes I think we are all fault lines waiting to slip and show our liquidity and magma base but then I don't know that could just be me because all we can know about for the most part is what *we* think about the world and what it is.

*

I like keeping score and making the loud buzz when anyone scores a goal. The sound is big and sharp as a buzz saw and fills the whole rink for what time it does—just short of a second. I like to make sound especially because I've chosen not to with my mouth which is the place most people make most of their sounds from or I guess we're always making sounds as we move and creak and our organs even probably make sounds like when you close your eyes in a quiet room and listen to your breathing and hear like a kind of whooshing, I bet our organs and blood must whoosh and rush like rivers and wind if you could hear it up close like putting your ear to a shell or a cup and hearing the ocean even though it's not.

But like I was saying I play Sunday nights—Kat Baker the snack bar attendant covers for me. She plays in the league too, got into it because her ex-boyfriend Robert got her into it then they split and she joined a different team. Against him. I play against Robert too but he takes it easy on all us Sunday beginners. He's an elite player. Not such a bad guy really. But Kat Baker really hates him and she covers my shifts so I pretend to not like him in what quiet ways I can when she's watching me play against him and keeping score for me. Something I like about Kat Baker that probably no one else appreciates or even wants to think about is how she's bald and doesn't wear a wig—she has alopecia. It's a weird disease that makes your hair fall out sometimes everywhere on your body. Kat says most women it happens to are lifelong wig-wearers. She says it like it's a thing and I like that too. Wig-wearers. I'm like a wig-wearer in an inverse way in that people don't think I have the ability to talk when I do. Like wig-wearers are pretending to have hair when they can't. Or something like that. See that was almost points but it wasn't. Anyway I talk to Kat Baker through texting. She was sort of forced to give me her number because we have to communicate because we work together there at the rink, her at the snackbar and me at the scoreboard. Not that I'm trying to be a creep or that I *am* a creep and trying to text her or woo her or sneakily trying to turn our work relationship into something else without telling her. I actually tell her almost everything in texts and only when she initiates them. The only thing she doesn't know about me is that I actually can talk and am not hurting in the areas related to speech such as the esophagus or the tongue or the lungs or the larynx—the voice box. In some ways I'm the voicebox of the rink, with a penalty box on each side of me where the players go to sit out for two minutes when they break rules, I'm there between them playing music during warmups or like I was saying making that big buzzer buzz when people score goals or at the end of every period—of which there are three. I like to play roller hockey because being on skates—and so just rolling out of control or into the boards or up against another player—makes me work as hard as I can and when I do I sweat and I was thinking the other day that sweating is like the whole body crying and I like that because it's hard to cry out of your eyes which maybe come to think of it is just your eyeball sweating?

I prefer to be alone at my home in Livermore with my cats and the TV and my dad being gone, I actually really do prefer to be alone and truly alone as in my dad not being there, because that's what I've gotten used to and one thing I know about myself if I know anything is that I don't like change, I like to find what I like and keep it in a state of equilibrium for as long as I can and will do almost anything to be sure nothing changes it. And Kat Baker has helped me to be able to play hockey on a regular basis which I think is good for me in more ways than just keeping in shape—the shape that I am not being an ideal one in the first place, I'm misshapen, in fact, and would prefer to change shape if I could. But so I appreciate Kat Baker, she's nice and has proved to be a loyal—or consistent anyway and what's better than loyalty is consistency—co-worker who keeps score while I roll around out there like a maniac trying to slap a disc into a net.

*

Something I dream about is that one day I will be living somewhere else and I'll talk like everyone else and be normal and have a normal job and maybe even a wife or a husband I don't even know which I like more men or women because they both have horrible and wonderful things about them. But I don't dream about one day leaving because like I said I can't stand change and the process of changing and leaving routine and habit and the life I've carved out for myself by digging into the same groove over and over to where it's comfortable like the couch and how it's formed now to fit me and maybe even the cats to some extent but I do dream that one day things will be different than they are because I do get sad and pretty lonely on certain days when I'm driving back home at night after scorekeeping, like for some reason after I play roller hockey Sundays and especially one night recently because I finally scored a goal and the way everyone looked at me when I did I almost wanted to shout as loud as I could I wanted to say yes, yes, yes, after all this time saying no no no, I could have screamed as loud as the loud buzzer and for just less than a second and no one would have known I could have timed it by watching Kat's finger and when she hit the buzzer button I could have let out some real loud sound out of my mouth like the crust of earth coming loose from hot lava but I didn't then not on the rink or with the buzzer, but then I was driving home after and was sad and maybe just coming down from that great moment after

I rolled down the rink cradling the puck carefully with the curved blade of my stick I looked up at the goalie and saw where to put the puck and it went there between the goalie's pads the place they call the five-hole, it went through the five-hole and into the net and we won and people patted me on the back and glove-fist bumped me so maybe I was just coming down from that brief moment of glory I'd never felt before and I got real sad because maybe it's really been sour grapes all this time and I've known I can't win or score points, or never enough, I've known I could never be enough, so maybe I did decide at some point and then forgot that I did decide that it's better not to play. In the car on that drive home when I dreamed of it one day being different I got real sad and then had the feeling like I wanted to make a sound again, like I'd felt after scoring a point on the rink, I wanted to make a loud loud sound in the car where no one could hear me. I wanted to scream the pain of being me, my specific scream and sound that no one else but me could ever make even if they tried and I did, with the windows down I dreamed about another life, with the wind blowing everything through me and then out of them; I rolled up all the windows and I screamed as loud as I could and I've never felt so good in my whole life but I don't know how to get out of this prison cell of silence I've made because it took so much just to get there and when I was done making that sound the Livermore night came into the car with me, some kind of nuclear silence, my father's absence filled me and the car and I almost couldn't breathe and I almost panicked but made it out of the car and into the living room with the cats and I was like a man washing up on shore to an island all his own. I couldn't imagine or dream after that of ever leaving that island or the habitat I've made of habits and norms and this life that is mine I have to take care not to lose in the storm of sound I know can come out of me that risks blowing me in the winds of change I just know I'd never survive.

Ghazal at the End of Hogpen Road

J. Scott Brownlee

I remember running till my lungs quit on that road
before football practice. Coach Ray filled the whole road

with his bright red pickup. *Get your asses up & down this street
or else we'll do bear crawls.* Wearing our smelly gray T-shirts
   caked with mold

after not being washed on that road where the fat kids got pushed
& picked on, we'd sprint so we weren't bunched with them. On
   that road

Rudy picked his scabs raw. Other boys, disgusted, sprinted past
   him like furies
screaming, *Loser, hurry it up! We'll have to run another mile,
   Stupid Toad,*

if you don't get in gear! There was a short kid named Justin who sat
on his big back sometimes, navigating the sharp objects stuck in
   the road

to help Rudy miss them. Together they walked the last stretch
of their private gauntlet—halfway down that dirt road—

if they finished at all on those miserable days, which was rare
because mostly they sat on the ground asking, *Why run this road*

*& make Coach Ray happy? Who gives a flip if we finish? J. & Rudy
are right,* we thought, bear crawling then. *It's a shit, dead-end road.*

Can We Have Our Ball Back?

Matthew Dickman

Levi's mother liked vodka so much she stopped feeding him
for a week so he and I ate SpaghettiOs at my house.
She loved beating him more than she loved Jesus
and she would always share if I stayed over. Joshua's father
walked through the house like a gun going off
and actually put one to his head on a camping trip.
My mom made Black Russians that would slap you
upside the head if you weren't careful and none of her friends were.
Ian's mom shot heroin between her toes with the needles
from the needle exchange so later on, after Ian dropped out,
he shot heroin underneath his tongue. God was showing up everywhere
but kept his big fat mouth shut. Motherfucker,
can we, please, have our ball back?
Anton came upstairs with his hand bleeding a little bit
and said his girlfriend wouldn't be going to the mall with us.
I dropped two tabs of acid
and rode through the neighborhood on the back of a polar bear
because I thought they were beautiful and I was fourteen years old
and summer had finally passed out
so we could all put our jackets on and look like we were kids
who couldn't wait to carve pumpkins,
walking house to house with bags of candy, dressed like ghosts.

untitled

Kevin Goodan

I yearn differently now
for youth, those days lived out
in shadow of the water tower above
the trailer park, vibratory dust
from the concrete plant churning,
or rock fights along the ditch walking home
with Garcia, Lulow, and Salois,
blood flowing from everybody's head—
Bucky McCallister shitting himself
in third grade, hiding it
until his aunt, the teacher, lifted his shirt,
or the sound Dale Solomon made
blindsided in Smear the Queer,
a fat kid, a soft sound, we all did it
until Doug Bell drowned, then we stopped—
or the day Garcia's cousin
hung himself in their garage before school—
that was the last day any of us
believed the definition
of such a word as joy.

Productive Antagonisms

Saretta Morgan interviews
Christina Olivares

Describe some of your early boxing moments?

When I first entered Kingsway Gym, a trainer, not mine, looked me up and down and informed me that I (a) weighed 175 pounds, and (b) would likely fight at 145. Then he offered his hand to shake hello before walking me to coach Lee, the man who would become my trainer.

Lee spoke to me differently. He didn't pretend to not assess me, but when he had said something about my body, his assessment was clinical, even friendly. My weight as it stood, my body as it existed, had no essential value to him.

In those first weeks of training, I felt my psyche re-center itself in pursuit of functionality as opposed to that semi-conscious, inarticulate grasping toward attractiveness. I didn't think I would become the best boxer in the world, but increasing my body's functionality was and is an attainable goal. I trained hard to re-learn my body as an ecosystem.

None of that means that I didn't see flaws. My coach instructed me to shadow box in front of floor-to-ceiling mirrors under florescent lighting. It was frustrating to see my own failure reflected back at me. The gym—which no longer exists—was low-ceilinged and badly ventilated. I'm generally inclined to cover myself, but I had to wear minimal clothing that allowed my body to breathe. I hated looking at myself for such extended periods. When there was no progress, I had to witness my lack of progress. But slowly I fashioned my body into a home that could protect itself.

That was important. I know that many of us have trauma rooted in our bodies. Prior to boxing, I avoided my body because I carried a visceral feeling that my body was a weapon that had been used against me. I didn't want it. It is weird to write about the self separate from the body but that is often how I experience myself. Prior to boxing, I existed mostly in my mind. But now, as I sit here in a tiny, hot apartment in Havana—my body stationary, peering down at a screen as I attempt to activate language that might convey what can only be experienced physically—I wonder about the "me" that is divisible from my body.

In boxing I'm reminded I have a body and she is good and strong and mine—a beautiful and welcome disruption.

How did things change as you moved from mirrors to the ring?

The mirrors are useful for correcting form. Beginners start there and even the most experienced professionals use them. Shadow boxing requires a basic level of skill because any micro-adjustments to your form are done by feel rather than by sight. Most importantly, you're imagining your opponent. You are inventing her as you bob and weave and throw your left hooks. You're learning to hold a perceived other as you hold yourself.

When I started sparring, training became radically different. I was training with women who needed to be very good in order to win their competitions. I was training, at least initially, to fight also. We couldn't give each other leeway. We had to push and push. In real life, I'd learned how to dim myself in certain relationships, to take up next to no room, to be gentle in order to avoid conflict. This is unacceptable behavior in sparring. We had to surprise each other. Landing a punch meant one of you had accurately assessed and pointed out the others' weakness. It was an opportunity for each of us to learn and improve. Nobody had to feel bad. We were each other's mirrors. This taught me a new way to be, how I wanted to be with people I loved.

Can you speak more about your need to, (re)orient psychically. What is your process of creating a sense of place unfamiliar terrain?

Part of my need to orient, and my abiding feeling of disorientation, comes, I think, from being parented by a schizophrenic person. Years of anticipating and imagining what reality looked like for him, while holding what reality looked like for me, has affected how I understand reality as fluid and relational.

Part of it also comes from being identified as mixed—and mixed across one brown/Black (by American definition) parent and one white one. And also, eventually becoming bilingual, because I do like thinking of languages as distinct sign systems that bound and prescribe distinct reality-universes. Another part of it comes from being raised in the projects but having attended Amherst and in so crossing, now sharing authentic common ground with people across a range of socio-economic experiences. I am very lucky to find community in many places. But I have learned also that because I find community in many places, I might appear suspicious to anyone who finds themselves uncritically rooted in one thing, who, because they have either not existed or not acknowledged their existence in in-between spaces, may become defensive instead of curious in the presence of other thought systems, other realities. I find this lack of desire to listen and be imaginative and flexible more predictably evident when it comes to those who benefit from institutional forms of violence—racism, sexism, classism, etc. Somehow, privilege seems to disrupt authentic self-interrogation.

Understanding myself as sexually queer was useful, because I could extrapolate: *all* of my existence is queered. Yay. But all this stuff can be unmooring, exhausting and lonely-making. I've always had a fear about going crazy like my father, so I am a little afraid of being unmoored. Maybe that is part of why the boxing is so comforting: there is an absolute other, with whom I can make a *we*, and a shared reality for a prescribed set of time bracketed by the bell we both hear and are trained to respond to in the same way.

I feel grateful for Audre Lorde's statement that "difference is a reason for celebration and growth," and for Anzaldua's language work in *Borderlands*. I value disorientation as opportunity for curiosity and play. This happens often for me in Cuba, in sometimes surprising ways because the evolution of island and diasporic people has been so distinct. Here, in Cuba, I learn how to listen differently. It's a process of locating footholds: *how do you think? How do you play? Here is what I feel. Here is what I am feeling my way through.*

*How does this desire for establishing relation extend beyond
your relationships with other people?*

I have been obsessed lately with a thought, which I understand now,
because of your question, might be about comfort and relation, and
a response to how fragile it can be: that we are intimately of the
earth—we are of its imagination. When we die, if left, we become
earth again. We're little mudpeople who move around and imagine.
In addition to science, there are our other stories: love letters, bedtime
stories, recounting slights, history books and grocery lists. Maybe we
have this capacity for dreaming because the dreaming earth made
us through that same process. This is my own creation myth, which
has a lot to do with how I respond to feeling unmoored—I find earth
and I think, hello, I am your dreaming daughter.

Here in Cuba I have moments of feeling overwhelmed by the
unfamiliar. I have panic attacks in the United States, but I ride
them out. Here, it's something else, it's something deeper, tectonic,
that, when it rises, alerts my interior to the possibility of a mental break. I don't know how to describe what it means. I can try to
describe what it is, though, because it just happened in this room
where I am sitting:

> My head was leaning on an open metal slat (storm windows) and
> I was staring out, thinking through a sentence. The kid next door
> was fixing the engine for his moto. The sound rose and fell and
> then stopped. I was listening to that sound and the weird feeling
> came. A clamp in my belly and in my chest. A terror. Some bit
> of my brain that had coasted unblinkingly over the past three
> weeks woke up and put on the brakes: oh, shit, what the fuck am
> I doing here, why am I so physically far from home. I want to go
> home fucking immediately.

Maybe we all have some of that homing pigeon in us. I close
my eyes and see the sea, I see a little map and on it I am far from
people who protect and love me. Now, I do have family here. But
right now I am not with those people. Today I am in Viñales, in

the middle of a corn/tobacco field in a place owned by a lady who is convinced I am lying about being a journalist, and who at the moment is not even home. So. I put my head on the metal slat. I made the thing inside of me that sees the map go fuzzy until the distance collapses. I listened to the wind in the palm tree and in the corn, which is as tall as me or taller. The sound was familiar. I thought: if I die here, I could become this earth that smells so good. And that was enough, that reminder of my body's proximity to earth was enough to pull me back into myself.

As a Cuban-American woman, how do you place yourself in the context of the sport's significance and history in Cuban culture?

In 2016, when I booked a direct flight to Cuba online with a credit card, the first time I have ever been able to do that—praise Jet-Blue—I cried for near four hours, because it felt like a wall had fallen. The forced distance I had adapted to living around vanished, leaving me somewhere between joy and anger and pain and relief.

When I asked abuela if she wanted to go, she said, "It would kill me," and I would have thought that was hyperbole, except for my own response.

I didn't grow up shuttled to the Caribbean for the summer like friends did because of political restrictions and my family's own refusal to return, which I chalk up to the trauma of relocation. I am the first and only person on the Cuban side of my family who "went back." I come here and certain random things are innately familiar—for example: words for fruits, how women suck their teeth at me when I behave in an inadequate way and a wholly unique cultural system of touch and body language. At the same time, much of how life has evolved on this island is shaped by its governance. We've adapted in order to survive separate structures. Maybe we are separate people now?

Cuba isn't mine, in a different way from America not being mine. I have inherited this nebulous space of the in-between, which I am learning to own and occupy.

I do think, here, often, that Cuba reminds of the Bronx because of the dysfunctional ways you have to invent solutions to problems caused by the decay of or gaps in public infrastructure. Boxing often arises from poverty, from lack or the denial of things. It's an experience of knowing what it is to have a stake in your own survival, not in a romantic way, but in a "failed-by-the-social-contract" sort of way. So boxing is excellent in Cuba, for reasons I think similar to why boxing is excellent in the United States. And when I watch Cuban boxers, I do feel at home.

I want to move backward to the "we" you described earlier as being formed by two people in the ring. I'm interested in how this "we" presents both a solidarity—"we're in here together"—as well as an antagonism—"we're in here to fuck each other up." Can you talk more about this particular "we" within the frame of boxing?

Often, the people I end up watching professional fights in bars with are male, and usually they have little or no boxing experience themselves. It seems, and this always feels surprising, that boxing is a *male* sport. The thing that seems to make it *male* is how egregiously violent and personally antagonistic two professional fighters are expected to be during their match. A simplified version of pre-fight antagonism is orchestrated to sell drama and make PPV its money.

The antagonism actually required in the ring of two great fighters is rich, complicated, and useful. It's a productive antagonism. To be carried by the passion of fury instead of a balance of precision and force while fighting a well-matched opponent can be lethal. In the ring, yes, the fighters are antagonists. But it's not about feelings, which is what I think I'm trying to extricate from the word "antagonism" by adding the qualifier "productive." When I'm in the ring with another woman, we are "a we" insofar as we have chosen to engage with one another for the duration of our time in the ring. Until one of us observably knocks the other to her knee three times, or down for a count of ten, or until the final bell rings and the points are tallied in either of our favors, we're locked together. We have a common aim, even if that aim is to dominate the other.

When I first started watching matches, I was surprised by how often professional boxers, ones who went on to be champions, got hit. They got hit again and again, and sometimes they barely eked out their victories, but they kept going. The winning is not total—it's incremental, as is the failure. Both boxers, unless they're terribly matched, will experience failure in the ring at the hands of the other before the match is over. In a good match, the winner will have tasted losing. There's a shared vulnerability and a tolerance for vulnerability in this process that has something to do with that "we."

How does your concept of mutual ruin and victory inform your understanding of the possibilities and limitations of the communities you exist in?

My friend, the thinker Andrea Warmack, today in a message referred to conflict (in the context of intellectual disagreements) as "a rupture that makes things grow."

Difference is useful—is beautiful—when seen and engaged. I'm realizing that the relationships I can rely on are ones that tolerate and grow with conflict. Not cruelty, but an attention to difference and to the space-between that exists in the *we*. Community can be beautiful and reinvigorating, but as a mixed, queer, female bodied person, I often run up against the limits of tolerance in the communities that do acknowledge me, and in turn, I find myself resisting the prescriptive in favor of the conflict, in favor of asserting myself as a distinct other in a shared space.

The Rookie

January Gill O'Neil

America under the lights
at Harry Ball Field. A fog rolls in
as the flag crinkles and drapes

around a metal pole.
My son reaches into the sky
to pull down a game-ender,

a bomb caught in his leather mitt.
He gives the ball a flat squeeze
then tosses it in from the outfield,

tugs his cap over a tussle of hair
before joining the team—
all high-fives and handshakes

as the Major boys line up
at home plate. They are learning
how to be good sports,

their dugout cheers interrupted only
by sunflower seed shells spat
along the first base line.

The coach prattles on
about the importance of stealing
bases and productive outs

while a teammate cracks a joke
about my son's 'fro, then says,
But you're not really black . . .

to which there's laughter,
to which he smiles but says nothing,
which says something about

what goes unsaid, what starts
with a harmless joke, routine
as a can of corn.

But this is little league.
This is where he learns
how to field a position,

how to play a bloop in the gap—
that impossible space where
he'll always play defense.

Cross Country

Roger Reeves

When I ran, it rained niggers. Early in October—
the first creases of autumn, a flag-weary sky
in which yellow birds, in flight, slip through the breast-
bone of God and tear at the coarse threads
that keep the morning knit tightly around his heart.
What was it that they sang about the light, their tongues,
the thistles they pluck from the bitter bark
of an allthorn then thrust into the breast of whatever god
or good animal requires eating, a good piercing?
These blonde bodies thrashing about above me
were death's idea of the morning passing. Here,
below this golden altar, the making and unmaking
of my body. The kettle-clank and souring sumac
of a man yelling at the light slipping in and out
of my mouth. *What name must I carry above the dust
of this field? Bruised ear, blank body, purple tongue, bloody
God bleeding, do you hear me? Deer piss and poison ivy
made pungent by the dew and morning sun rising, do you hear me?*
When I ran, it rained niggers. In a ditch along the road,
A pair of wild boars, slain and laid tusk to tail, point,
as if required in two directions at once, toward my body
pressing the last bits of a hunter's moon into the tar
of this road and away from the meadow-red light coming
up through the chaff rising above this hectored field
and the man yelling. Nigger in the cicadas tuning up
to tear the morning into tatters. Nigger in the squawk
and clatter of a hen complaining of a hand reaching
below her bottom and removing the warm work
of a cold night. Nigger in the reeds covering
the muck of a beaver's hard birth. Nigger in the blue

hour of a field once wet with the breath of a lone horse
cracking along its flanks. Nigger in the fog lifting
from this field and the still-birth it reveals. Nigger
in the running. In the bog at the end of this road.
In the war and in between the wars. Nigger
in the pink salt and eyelashes of a woman I love.
Her mouth pulling water from behind my knee.
Pulling, pulling, pulling. Think: nigger is the god
of our brief salvation. Nigger in a body falling toward a horizon.
Nigger in the twilight that is no longer a twilight
but a black creek fumbling along the spine of a boy
who is running through a city that is running out of water.
Even the lions have left for the mountains.
This is America speaking in translation, in glitter,
in gold grills and fried chicken. Auto-tune this if you must.
Cher will be singing in the brush of static from the attic
radio, believing in love after love or life after love
despite the impure thoughts of evening, despite
the rain soaking the red head of a red bird
now dead in a puddle that refuses to reflect the moon.

Another Kind of Faith

Joaquín Zihuatanejo

Somehow they heard about us. We, an inner city team from the lower east side that had not be beaten. They, a premier league team from some far-off foreign suburb that could not be beaten. The game was inevitable. It was Manifest Destiny. The Great Western Movement. The Alamo. The Mexican American War.

Were they any more American than us? Their team name, *The Cowboys*. Ours, *Aztecas*. You cannot write this. Sometimes it simply is.

It is simple. Good guys wear white, bad guys wear black. We moved as murmurations during the warm ups. They nervously sized us up. Days earlier, they invited us to their facility. That's what they called it, a "facility." In the barrio we played on a field that was two-thirds dirt, one-third dream.

The night before the game I dreamed of war. We were armed with staffs, spears, bows and arrows. They with muskets and swords. I watched my friend die beside me.

A "friendly," that's the word they used, but there wasn't anything friendly about it.

Jesús Santos, my best friend. Jesús Santos, our best player. Jesús Santos, I watched you die in my dream. How many days before you rise and save us from our rage.

Some of us played with rage in our hearts, but not Jesús. Only someone pure of heart could bend a ball like him. He was our savior. And we his ten disciples.

Ten minutes into the game Jesús scored the first goal. They answered not long after, on a two on one breakaway.

They wanted to break us because we were different. We wanted to break them because they were beautiful.

Jesús was a thing of beauty. Watching him weave through defenders his eye never on the ball always ahead; it was part of him. He slept with a soccer ball, kicked one to school and back home again. Left it outside the church on Sunday morning resting on the steps waiting for him. A small practice goal in his back yard. A different position. A different placement. A different scenario in his mind each time. 100 shots on goal every day of his youth.

100 shots X 365 days = another kind of faith.

This was another kind of cruelty. This was brutal. Five on one. Cowboys vs Indian. This was less slide and more tackle. The wounded knee of the most beautiful soccer player to have ever lived. This was freight train made of legs and arms, fists and cleats. Jesús Santos laid out on the field arms outstretched wailing in agony. Crucifixion.

They had turned us into beasts. Made us more Mexican and less American that day.

The fight that ensued was viscous. Boys were not meant to fight like that, but sometimes war cannot be avoided. Sometimes war is there waiting for you all along.

It is a simple thing to hate the way we did that day.

Days earlier I had dreamt of war, watched my friend die beside me. Jesús Santos are you still out there? Did your heart break that day? Jesús please tell me, does one have to be either different or beautiful? Is it possible that one can be both?

Why Pam Hates Sprite and Sunflower Seeds

Alison Rollins

basketball fully pumped
bumpy leather face fit

with glory by the pressure of air
Pam sits waiting on the stoop

her legs bent over steps like the straws
poking out from styrofoam cups of Sprite

Pam's Grandma said flat soda helps
an upset stomach said these here

hoop dreams better pay Pam's way
through that college out-of-state

     *

ranch sunflower seeds litter
the sidewalk like pick-up

games on Sunday after church
when all the boys still had Pam's name

in their mouth fixing their tongues
to say, *she don't play like no girl*

I don't think anyone every saw Pam's teeth
just her mean mug wedged between two

braids those were the days when cotton
candy clouds got licked like grown ass men

*

Pam sits with her pit-bull Cooper
on the cold living room floor

her Grandma down on the last of her
bad knees she palms Pam's belly

like a basketball says, *I can already tell
it's a boy I know just how to take care of it*

Pam's knees now cradled in her
long-reach arms the sun on its way

back out the baby due in only a month
a date set for a loved one to leave home

The Tribes

Chee Brossy

They play dirty, says the old man from Escalante,
lower lip coming out in a frown, shaking his head.
Did you see them yelling at the refs?
The game is tight, the boys lithe, shoulders glistening,
sweat shining off the contours of biceps,
the Lagunas and Acomas against the white
and Hispanic small-town boys like it has always been
since you can remember. The LA coach, a bald
chihuahua of a man, has drilled into them a tensile
elasticity, so they press, pass and run the break,
the string between their hands come alive, patterns
appearing. In the fourth quarter they break free
of the cowboys, themselves balanced
by a heady point guard and attacking wings,
but the Pueblo boys emerge, see the passes unfold
like wings, sail the ball past the orange jerseys.
And the blue defense is everywhere, sneakers squeaking,
trapping in the corners, their coach a mirror
on the sideline, squatting hands out in defense,
hopping at a steal, fists clenched, palms up.
The boys run smiling to each other, high-fiving,
and the crowd of blue-shirted towns, both Laguna
and Acoma, roaring, shaking plastic clappers
and pom-poms so when the orange and black
across the court stand up—the men in cowboy hats
and camouflage, the mothers holding signs—to begin
their *Go Raiders* cheer, the blue crowd raises
its deafening L-A-Ha-*awks* and drowns them out.
A stirring. Orange and blue. Shouting,
shaking fists, heads thrown back,

tribes again. *I remember. I remember why*
I don't like you. This acid tang in my mouth,
smell of burning, kicked awake, neck
bristling until the full roar. The blue have more
and their yell buries the orange. The tallest
cowboy waves his arm to sweep them away
then sits because he can't hear himself anymore
and the rest of the orange fans take their seats
until there is only one woman, a mother,
standing the roar. She holds *Go Raiders Go*
above her head, waves it and howls, pausing
for breath and howls again, no words.
The boys on the court
are trying to beat that tall boy, short boy,
skinny boy, muscled boy to the ball. Boys who
practice their jump shot in supermarket lines waiting
for their mothers, in diners all along the interstate
going east to west a forever tournament that will
hold them high on its shoulders made of
hardwood, Gatorade, cheering girls and red scoreboard bulbs.
Walking through the snow and mud of the pueblo
with sneakers tied across the backs of their necks.
The pressure is on but we can still get a good shot
and the Escalante man waiting
for the next game when his team will play, red
polo shirt and white crew cut, switching from
English to Spanish, points his chin at the blue
crowd, *Pendejos*, shakes his head, glares,
brow furrowing at his audience and you get angry
and say *That's right, they beat*
those cowboys, killed them in that last
quarter did you see that? Because in the end
you are sitting in the enemy's seats.
A few people turn around to stare; you scowl
back. But the blue roar rises above all, drowning

you out. The last buzzer sounds, the orange boys
cover their faces with towels, slump in their folding
chairs, heads in hands. The other bench empties,
the blue boys jump and hug teammates, yell
to the rafters, raise their wings to blue
family, *Louder*, because tomorrow they play
for the championship, for the title, against
the private school, the always champs, the Christians.

All the Flesh, Singing

Shivanee Ramlochan

When I was eighteen
I licked the blood from my shins,
curled around myself:
brown comma woman
of round breasts and tiffins
steeped in curry.

The white girls of track and field
let me know they could smell me.
I still ran through the sweat
and shame of it.

Joy was the muscle I stretched,
joy on the bitumen
joy
in the spasm
joy in dhal and rice and running.

At thirty, I twice outweigh myself-who-ran.
I fold continental food with diaspora's:
tandoori lamb layered on buss up shut,
mutter paneer over Aji's roti,
swollen like a secret pregnancy.

My father says I swallowed myself whole,
devoured a lifetime of races.

At night, I lace the brightest pink Nikes
and break into the Arima Velodrome.
Naked, I confound the moonlight

with the sight of a fat woman, running.
I mastermind my flesh, in nothing
but brown skin and badmind
nothing but folds rippling and muscling,
all the food and fear in me, glorious
samosas / green dhal / seared cauliflower skulls
I river, I promenade, I orchestrate the track
with a body big enough to hold
these thirty years of desserts and early-onset
diabetes,
these widow wails of soul splitting from frame
with each pound of flesh I have ransomed:
O, how the running
stitches it together,
reunites me at the finish and start,
chafed, hungry,
the oxygen bloodying me,
the whistle of my fresh joy,
relentless.

Between Practice

Terrance Hayes

1. Afternoons in Florida while my favorite jocular jockish cousin suffered summer school, I climbed the tall hot fence of the elementary school behind his house to practice layups and dream of dunks. 2. I was 13, my mother was on a Caribbean cruise ship in a state of longing, her husband was on a German army base in a state of longing; they left me with relatives in a distant state. 3. Sometimes I talked with the posters on my cousin's walls: robed Moses Malone dividing a sea of basketballs, Chocolate Thunder aka Darryl Dawkins, whose name I now recall better than the poster, and George "Iceman" Gervin, sitting with his long legs crossed on an ice throne as he palmed two silver basketball spheres with a cool I tried carrying with me out to the basketball court where the heat softened and pulled my bones. 4. I would like to suggest it was a sexual sweat: cleansing, baptismal, mystical, burning as it ran into my eyes, but instead I will say the sweat was simply the byproduct of labor and temperature. 5. Sometimes my cousin Noonpie would stand at the fence and after a moment or two call me in to the terrible boredom of a house packed with her four other sisters. Once the two oldest girls pinned me to the floor and covered my panic in lipstick. 6. I have said so little about poetry because I knew so little about poetry then. 7. Mute, fluid, confused, determined, sometimes Noonpie and I dry humped in a large walk-in closet. She was my age. Sometimes she leafed through my drawing book. Once my jocular jockish cousin, aka her older brother, found us and yanked me by my ankles into the air, upside down and flailing like a fish pulled from a bucket of water. 8. I may have known by way of intuition the silences that come before poetry, which are like the silences that cover photographs, the silences that accompany imagery: a relative named Henpeck appearing on the doorsteps one night with a knife wound's evidence staining his shirt; a neighbor named Fat Nasty,

confined no matter the heat or drama to the bed Noonpie and I spied through his window; the silence of a black boy covered suddenly permanently by the lake near their home; the mute, fluid, confused, determined practice of silence, the silent practitioners of silence. 9. Noonpie and her siblings knew they were not my blood cousins because their parents told them, but I did not know, and because I was loved with the severity and kindness any cousin receives, I spent some afternoons studying old photos of the man of the house: a tall very black black man. In them he wore a basketball uniform and looked more like one of his daughters than his son. I took him as proof basketball was in my blood because I did not know we were not blood. 10. It was his wife that was my stepfather's aunt. Her quick and scything tongue kept the weeds from her beautiful heart. 11. My mother was afraid of her. 12. Once when my jockish jocular cousin took me to play basketball, we stood first with his friends beneath a few trees and smoked weed. Though I only got one puff, it ruined me for the game. I would have been ruinous even without the dope, to be honest. "Man, if I had that nigga height," laughed my cousin's friends. I was wasted, I was a waste. 13. Because it was a small mostly black beach town at the edge of a big mostly white beach town, the teenaged black boys tried harder to be hard. Some of them jumped tourists, taking their money, beach gear, and sunglasses. Some of them vanished quickly into jails or shotgun houses full of drugs and broken women. My cousin survived on charm and luck. His sisters survived because they remained locked in their father's house. 14. "Do you want to be a basketball player," the man of the house asked me when he found me holding his son's basketball in my lap. "Do you want to be an artist," he asked me when I showed him my notebook drawings. "Do you want to be a man," the man of the house asked me when he found me weeping because my mother had not returned. 15. He's going to be seven foot tall, my jocular jockish cousin bragged when his friends asked my age. I was thirteen and already more than six feet high. 16. I'd look at the man of the house looking at the photos of himself as a young basketball player. I'd listen to the way he talked to his son

at dinner. I was there when his wife smoked cigarettes lacing pro-
fanity through the affections she shared with him. Her death, years
later, would be the reason for his death shortly thereafter. 17. You
must be a foot taller, my mother said when she finally returned,
but to me, it was she who seemed smaller. 18. After my cousin told
me strong calf muscles were the secret to jumping power, I set the
balls of my feet at the edge of the stairs in the house, lowering my
heels as far as I could toward the floor, then pressing my heels up
as high as I could for as many times as I could as often as I could.
19. "My mother's relatives are tall," I told the boys in Florida when
they asked where I'd gotten my height. "My father's relatives are
tall," I told the boys back home when they asked where I'd gotten
my height. 20. I used to think practice was preparation for the game,
but now I believe the game is what happens between practice. 21.
What I remember is the way the man of the house looked over my
drawings. Snoopy's nose needed to be longer, he said. Why did the
people only have three fingers, he asked. Then he'd push the pages
back to me and say he wanted to see improvements tomorrow. 22.
Again and again the ball jammed against the front of the rim, jolting
my whole body backward and back to the tarmac. Or the ball rico-
cheted from the rim, arcing overhead. Sometimes I'd glance toward
the fence, relieved Noonpie was not there watching when I jogged to
retrieve the basketball. Rejected object, rejected subject. 23. I failed
so often I came to accept it was failure I was practicing. In poetry I
have failed so often I have come to accept it is failure I am practicing. 24. My stepfather's mother had him when she was fourteen.
She was barely around those summers. My stepfather knew almost
nothing about his father and did not care to ask. He was raised by
a man named "Stick," but if you ask him he will say he raised himself. 25. I never know when a poem is finished. It is like a series of
wrong and half right endeavors before I discover the unforeseeable
approaching. 26. ~~First the mother died and shortly thereafter the
man of the house died. And later my stepfather's mother died. My
stepfather wept.~~ 26. First the mother died and shortly thereafter
the man of the house died. And later my father's mother died. My

father wept and I was angry to see him weeping. Though Florida was his home, he was rarely there those summers. 27. What moves between us has always moved as metaphor. We have never discussed our fathers or mothers, though the space between our fathers and mothers is what makes us like one another. 28. The first time I dunked that summer, no one was there to see it. Not even I was witness. The ball passed suddenly through the rim, and though I had been trying for weeks, I did not know how it happened when it happened. I tried again and again to do it again.

Source Acknowledgments

The following pieces first appeared in *Prairie Schooner* 89, no. 4 (Winter 2015):

"Bolting into Throat," by Patricia Smith

"last summer of innocence," by Danez Smith

"American Pharoah," by Ada Limón

"Professional Wrestling Holds," by Ashaki Jackson

"He takes me," by Paul Tran

"Psych Ward Visitation Hour," by b: william bearhart

"In the outfield, daydreaming," by francine j. harris

"Boxing Out," by Adrian Matejka

"The Church of Michael Jordan," by Jeffrey McDaniel

"Federer as Irreligious Experience," by Porochista Khakpour

"prayer when knees give," by Nate Marshall

"Baseball," by Izzy Wasserstein

"To Prevent Hypothermia," by Fatimah Asghar

"The Cock Fight Place," by Alberto Ríos

"A Note on Process," by Meghan O'Rourke

"A Boy & His Mother Play Dead at Dawn," by Michael Wasson

"Run," by Gary Jackson

"From Heaven, My Father Sends His Regrets," by Cornelius Eady

"Russian Sport," by Vera Pavlova

"A Perfect Game," by Yesenia Montilla

"Dennis," by Kaveh Akbar

"Clank," by Tomás Q. Morin

"Liquid," by Aaron Smith

"Losing the 440-Yard Dash," by Afaa M. Weaver

"Sports Analogy," by David Tomas Martinez

"Why to Run Racks," by Lisa Fay Coutley

"El Barril," by James Thomas Stevens

"Project Artifacts: Through the Banks of the Red Cedar," by Maya Washington

"Alone in the Schoolyard at Dusk," by Dorianne Laux

"Losing to the Invisible: An Ars Poetica," by Traci Brimhall

"High School Yoga," by Kat Page

"Southpaw Skin the Gloves," by Alicia Mountain

"Games," by L. Lamar Wilson

"Mudita World Peace," by Hannah Ensor

"The Chain," by Elyse Fenton

"Self-Portrait with Ghost, Rising," by Dean Rader

"Infield Contrapuntal," by Meg Day

"Sports History," by Brett Fletcher Lauer

"The Yo-Yo Heir's Lament," by Eugene Gloria

"Stadium Mocs," by Chip Livingston

"Bad Love Affair," by Joseph Millar

"Catch," by Trevino Brings Plenty

"Polaroid: Links," by Stacey Lynn Brown

"Of Competition or 'And the sheeted dead did squeak and gibber in the Roman streets,'" by Brendan Constantine

"¡Sangre! ¡Sangre! ¡Sangre!," by Nandi Comer

"Can We Have Our Ball Back?," by Matthew Dickman

"untitled," by Kevin Goodan

"The Rookie," by January Gill O'Neil

"The Tribes," by Chee Brossy

"Between Practice," by Terrance Hayes

"At the gym, moments after I failed a squat attempt that would have been easy pre-sitting-induced pinched nerve," by Candace Williams, borrows and alters phrases from Brenda Hillman's lecture "Cracks in the Oracle Bone: Teaching Certain Contemporary Poems."

"Professional Wrestling Holds," by Ashaki Jackson, is a largely found poem, pulled from Wikipedia, https://en.wikipedia.org/wiki/Professional_wrestling_holds.

The following were originally published elsewhere:

"Takes Enemy," by Shann Ray, appeared in *Narrative* at narrativemagazine.com (Fall 2014).

"The Wars," by Louise Erdrich, is an excerpt from *LaRose* (HarperCollins, 2016).

"The Meaning of Serena Williams: On tennis and black excellence," by Claudia Rankine, appeared in the *New York Times Magazine* (August 30, 2015): 38–43.

"Boxing Out," by Adrian Matejka, is from *Map to the Stars* (Penguin, 2017).

"Built For It," by Lisa Olstein, is from *Late Empire* (Copper Canyon Press, 2017). It first appeared in *Southern Humanities Review* 50, nos. 3–4 (2016): 105.

"A Note on Process," by Meghan O'Rourke, is from *Sun in Days* (W. W. Norton, 2017).

"War Training: An Athletics," by Nomi Stone, originally appeared in *Anthropoid*.

"Liquid," by Aaron Smith, is from *Primer* (University of Pittsburgh Press, 2016).

"Why to Run Racks," Lisa Fay Coutley, appeared in *Double Kiss: Writers on the Art of Billiards*, edited by Sean Thomas Dougherty (Mammoth Books, 2017).

"Who Got This Far," by Marissa Johnson-Valenzuela, appeared in *American Poetry Review* 46, no. 5 (2017): 20.

"why i can't play basketball anymore," by Richard Vargas, is from *American Jesus* (Tia Chucha, 2007).

"Parking Lot Poem with Fernando Valenzuela," by Matthew Lippman, first appeared in the *Green Mountains Review* 29, no. 2 (Spring 2017).

"Southpaw Skin the Gloves," by Alicia Mountain, is from *High Ground Coward* (University of Iowa Press, 2018) and was awarded the Iowa Poetry Prize.

"Inside the City Walls," by Norman Dubie, appeared in *New England Review* 12 no. 2 (1989): 120.

"game recognizes game," by t'ai freedom ford, is from *how to get over* (Red Hen Press, 2017).

"The Chain," by Elyse Fenton, is from *Sweet Insurgent* (Saturnalia Press, 2017).

Portions of *Farewell to Soccer: Ninety-Minute-Long Stories*, translated from *Addio a calico* by Valerio Magrelli. © Giulio Einaudi Editore. Excerpt translated by Will Schutt. Used by permission of the author.

"The Curtain," by Ryan Black, appeared in the Southern Review (Spring 2019): 223

"Ladies' Arm Wrestling Match at the Blue Moon Diner," by Jenny Johnson, is from *In Full Velvet* (Sarabande, 2017). It first appeared in *Best New Poets, 2008: 50 Poems from EmergingWriters*, edited by Mark Strand (Samovar Press, 2008).

Contributors

Hanif Abdurraqib is a poet, essayist, and cultural critic from Columbus, Ohio. His first collection of poems, *The Crown Ain't Worth Much*, was released in 2016 and was nominated for the Hurston-Wright Legacy Award. His first collection of essays, *They Can't Kill Us until They Kill Us*, was released in the fall of 2017 by Two Dollar Radio.

Celeste Adame, Muckleshoot, holds a master of fine arts in poetry from the Institute of American Indian Arts in Santa Fe, New Mexico. Her thesis, "Lovers Landscape," explores gender identity, sexuality, love, basketball, and the landscapes of both Washington and New Mexico. She has been published in *Yellow Medicine Review*, *Cloudthroat*, *As/Us: A Journal for Women of the World*, *hinchas de poesia*, and *Santa Fe Literary Review*. She was also one of the poetry editors for the first two editions of *Mud City*, IAIA's *Low-Rez programs online journal*.

Kaveh Akbar is the author of *Calling a Wolf a Wolf* (Alice James/Penguin UK) and a chapbook, *Portrait of the Alcoholic*, published by Sibling Rivalry. Born in Tehran, Iran, Kaveh teaches at Purdue University and in the low-residency MFA programs at Randolph College and Warren Wilson.

Kazim Ali was born in the United Kingdom to Muslim parents of Indian, Iranian, and Egyptian descent. He received a BA and MA from the University of Albany-SUNY and an MFA from New York University. His books encompass several volumes of poetry, including *Sky Ward*, winner of the Ohioana Book Award in Poetry; *The Far Mosque*, winner of Alice James Books' New England/New York Award; *The Fortieth Day*; *All One's Blue*; and the cross-genre text *Bright Felon*. His novels include the recently published *The Secret Room: A String Quartet*, and among his books of essays is *Fasting for Ramadan: Notes from a Spiritual Practice*. Ali is an associate professor of creative writing and comparative literature at Oberlin College. His most recent books of poems, *Inquisition*, and a new hybrid memoir, *Silver Road: Essays, Maps & Calligraphies*, were released in 2018.

Fatimah Asghar is a nationally touring poet, performer, educator, and writer. Her work has appeared in *POETry*, *BuzzFeed Reader*, *Academy of American Poets*, and many others. Her work has been featured on news outlets like PBS, NBC, *Teen Vogue*, *Huffington Post*, and others. In 2011 she created REFLEKS, a Spoken Word Poetry group in Bosnia and Herzegovina while on a Fulbright studying theater in postgenocidal countries. She is a member of the Dark Noise collective and a Kundiman Fellow. Her chapbook *After* was released by YesYes Books in the fall of 2015. She is the writer of *Brown Girls*, an Emmy-nominated web series that highlights a friendship between women of color. In 2017 she was the recipient of a Ruth Lilly and Dorothy Sargent Rosenberg Fellowship from the Poetry Foundation and was on the *Forbes* "30 Under 30" list. Her debut collection of poems, *If They Come for Us*, is forthcoming from One World/Random House in August 2018.

b: william bearhart is a direct descendant of the St. Croix Chippewa Indians of Wisconsin, a graduate from the Lo Rez MFA program at the Institute of American Indian Arts, and currently works as a poker dealer in a small Wisconsin casino when not writing or editing. His work can be found in *Boston Review*, *North American Review*, and *Tupelo Quarterly*, among other periodicals.

Reginald Dwayne Betts is a husband and father of two sons. A poet and memoirist, he is the author of three books. The recently published *Bastards of the Reagan Era*; the 2010 NAACP Image Award–winning memoir, *A Question of Freedom*; and the poetry collection *Shahid Reads His Own Palm*. Dwayne is currently enrolled in the PhD in Law Program at the Yale Law School. He has earned a JD from the Yale Law School, an MFA from Warren Wilson College's MFA Program for Writers, and a BA from the University of Maryland.

Ryan Black is the author of *The Tenant of Fire* (University of Pittsburgh Press, 2019), winner of the 2018 Agnes Lynch Starrett Prize, and *Death of a Nativist*, selected by Linda Gregerson for the Poetry Society of America's 2016 Chapbook Fellowship. He is the director of undergraduate creative writing at Queens College/CUNY.

Tria Blu Wakpa is a UC President's Postdoctoral Fellow in the Department of Dance at UC Riverside and became an assistant professor of dance studies in the Department of World Arts and Cultures/Dance at UC Los Angeles in the fall of 2018. She earned her PhD and MA in ethnic studies from UC Berkeley and an MFA in creative writing from San Diego State University. Her research and artistic interests are in Native American education, incarceration, and embodied practice; Indigenous contemporary dance and martial arts; North American Hand Talk (sign language); Native American literature and theory; and creative writing. Blu Wakpa has received major fellowships from the Ford Foundation and Fulbright. She has taught a wide range of interdisciplinary and community-engaged courses at public, private, tribal, and carceral institutions. Blu Wakpa is of Filipina, European, and tribally unenrolled Native American ancestries. She is married to Dr. Makha Blu Wakpa (Cheyenne River Sioux) and the mother of their two children.

Ana Božičević is a poet, translator, teacher, and occasional singer. She is the author of *Joy of Missing Out* (Birds, 2017), the Lambda Award–winning *Rise in the Fall* (Birds, 2013), and *Stars of the Night Commute* (Tarpaulin Sky Press, 2009). Ana grew up in Croatia and now lives in Brooklyn.

Susan Briante is the author of three books of poetry: *Pioneers in the Study of Motion*, *Utopia Minus*, and *The Market Wonders*, all from Ahsahta Press. Recent work has appeared in *Guernica*, *Gulf Coast*, as well as the *Boston Review*'s "Poems for Political Disaster." She is an associate professor of creative writing at the University of Arizona and the faculty liaison for the Southwest Field Studies in Writing Program, bringing students to the U.S.-Mexico border to work with environmental and social justice groups. Briante also hosts the radio program *Speedway and Swan*, an hour of poetry and music on KXCI 91.3 Tucson.

Traci Brimhall is the author of three collections of poetry: *Saudade* (Copper Canyon Press), *Our Lady of the Ruins* (W. W. Norton), and *Rookery* (Southern Illinois University Press), as well as an illustrated children's book, *Sophia & the Boy Who Fell* (Pleiades Press). Her poems have appeared in the *New Yorker*; *Poetry*; *Slate*; the *Believer*; the *New Republic*; *Orion*; *Best American Poetry, 2013*; and *Best American Poetry, 2014*. She's received a National Endowment for the Arts Literature Fellowship and was the 2012 summer poet-in-residence at the University of Mississippi. She's an assistant professor of creative writing at Kansas State University.

Trevino Brings Plenty was born on the Cheyenne River Sioux Reservation, Eagle Butte, South Dakota. A Mnikȟówožu Lakota, Brings Plenty is a filmmaker, musician, and poet. Brings Plenty's books are *Wakpá Wanáǧi Ghost River* (2015) and *Real Indian Junk Jewelry* (2012), both from Backwaters Press.

Chee Brossy is a poet, fiction writer, and journalist. He is Diné of the Water-flows-together clan, originally from Lukachukai, Arizona, and holds an MFA from the Institute of American Indian Arts. A graduate of Dartmouth College, he has worked as a reporter for the *Navajo Times*. He is kind of tall and still loves to play basketball when his various injuries aren't bothering him. He is currently at work on his first book of poetry.

Stacey Lynn Brown is a poet, playwright, and essayist from Atlanta. She received her MFA in poetry from the University of Oregon. She is the author of the book-length poem *Cradle Song* (C&R Press, 2009) and is the coeditor, with Oliver de la Paz, of *A Face to Meet the Faces: An Anthology* *of Contemporary Persona Poetry* (University of Akron Press, 2012). She teaches at Indiana University in Bloomington.

J. Scott Brownlee is a poet-of-place from Llano, Texas. His books include *Highway or Belief* (Button Poetry); *Ascension* (Texas Review Press); *Requiem for Used Ignition Cap* (Orison Books), which won the 2016 Bob Bush Memorial Award for Best First Book of Poetry from the Texas Institute of Letters; and *On the Occasion of the Last Old Camp Meeting in Llano County* (Tree Light Books).

Gabrielle Calvocoressi is the author of *The Last Time I Saw Amelia Earhart*, *Apocalyptic Swing* (a finalist for the *Los Angeles Times* Book Prize), and *Rocket Fantastic*, winner of the Audre Lorde Award for Lesbian Poetry. Calvocoressi's poems have been published or are forthcoming in numerous magazines and journals, including the *Baffler*, the *New York Times*, POETRy, *Boston Review*, the *Kenyon Review*, *Tin House*, and the *New Yorker*. Calvocoressi is an editor at large at the *Los Angeles Review of Books* and poetry editor at *Southern Cultures*. Calvocoressi teaches at the University of North Carolina at Chapel Hill and lives in Carrboro, North Carolina, where joy, compassion, and social justice are at the center of their personal and poetic practice.

Christian Campbell is a writer of Bahamian and Trinidadian heritage and the author of *Running the Dusk*. He studied at Oxford as a Rhodes Scholar and received a PhD at Duke. His work has been published widely in journals and anthologies in the Caribbean, the UK, the United States, and Canada. An assistant professor of English at the University of Toronto, he has received grants and fellowships from Cave Canem, the Arvon Foundation, the Ford Foundation, the Fine Arts Work Center, the University of Birmingham, and elsewhere. Pulitzer Prize–winning poet Yusef Komunyakaa calls *Running the Dusk*, "the gutsy work of a long-distance runner who possesses the wit and endurance, the staying power of authentic genius." *Running the Dusk* was a finalist for the Cave Canem Prize and the Forward Poetry Prize for the Best First Book in the UK and is the winner of the 2010 Aldeburgh First Collection Prize.

Anders Carlson-Wee is the author of *The Low Passions* (W. W. Norton, 2019). He has received fellowships from the National Endowment for the Arts, the McKnight Foundation, Bread Loaf, the Sewanee Writers' Conference, and the Napa Valley Writers' Conference. His work has appeared in the *Nation*, *Ploughshares*, the *New England Review*, *Poetry Daily*, the *Sun*, *Best New Poets*, and the *Best American Nonrequired Reading*. His debut chapbook, *Dynamite*, won the 2015 Frost Place Chapbook Prize. Anders is the winner of *Ninth Letter*'s Poetry Award, *Blue Mesa Review*'s Poetry Prize,

New Delta Review's Editors' Choice Prize, and the 2017 Poetry International Prize. He lives in Minneapolis.

Nandi Comer is the author of *The American Family: A Syndrome* (Finishing Line Press) and *Tapping Out* (forthcoming, Northwestern University Press). She has received fellowships from the Callaloo Creative Writing Workshop, Cave Canem, the Vermont Studio Center, and the Virginia Center for the Arts. Her poems have appeared in *Crab Orchard Review, Green Mountains Review, Pluck!,* and the *Southern Indiana Review.*

Brendan Constantine is the author of four books of poetry. His most recent collection is *Dementia, My Darling* (Red Hen Press, 2016). He has received grants and commissions from the Getty Museum, James Irvine Foundation, and the National Endowment for the Arts. He currently teaches creative writing at the Windward School in West Los Angeles and regularly offers classes to hospitals, foster homes, veterans, and the elderly.

Lisa Fay Coutley is the author of *Errata* (Southern Illinois University Press, 2015), winner of the Crab Orchard Series in Poetry Open Competition Award, and *In the Carnival of Breathing* (BLP, 2011), winner of the Black River Chapbook Competition. Her poetry has been awarded fellowships from the National Endowment for the Arts and the Sewanee Writers' Conference, a scholarship to the Bread Loaf Writers' Conference, and an Academy of American Poets Levis Prize. Recent publications include *32 Poems, Prairie Schooner, Kenyon Review, Gulf Coast,* and *Poets & Writers.* She is an assistant professor of poetry in the Writer's Workshop at the University of Nebraska at Omaha.

Kwame Dawes has authored thirty-five books of poetry, fiction, criticism, and essays, including, most recently, *Bivouac* (Akashic Books, 2019) and *City of Bones: A Testament* (Northwestern, 2017). *Speak from Here to There* (Peepal Tree Press), co-written with Australian poet John Kinsella, appeared in 2016. He is Glenna Luschei Editor of Prairie Schooner and Chancellor's Professor of English at the University of Nebraska. He is also a faculty member in the Pacific MFA Program. He is director of the African Poetry Book Fund and artistic director of the Calabash International Literary Festival. Dawes is a chancellor of the Academy of American Poets.

Meg Day is the 2015–16 recipient of the Amy Lowell Poetry Travelling Scholarship, a 2013 recipient of a National Endowment for the Arts Fellowship in Poetry, and the author of *Last Psalm at Sea Level* (Barrow Street, 2014), winner of the Barrow Street Poetry Prize and the Publishing Triangle's Audre Lorde Award and a finalist for the 2016 Kate Tufts Discovery Award from Claremont Graduate University. Day is an assistant professor of

English and creative writing at Franklin & Marshall College and lives in Lancaster, Pennsylvania. www.megday.com.

Matthew Dickman was born in Portland, Oregon. After studying at the University of Oregon, he earned an MFA from the University of Texas at Austin's Michener Center. Dickman's first full-length collection, *All-American Poem*, won the 2008 American Poetry Review/Honickman First Book Prize in Poetry. He is also the author of two chapbooks: *Amigos* (Q Ave. Press, 2007) and *Something about a Black Scarf* (Azul Press, 2008). His second full-length collection, *Mayakovsky's Revolver* (W. W. Norton), was published in 2012, and *Wonderland* (W. W. Norton) was published in 2018.

Norman Dubie's newest collection of poems, *Robert Schumann Is Mad Again*, will be published by Copper Canyon Press in 2019. His previous collection, *The Quotations of Bone* (Copper Canyon Press, 2015), won the 2016 Griffin International Poetry Prize. His most recent book of aphorisms is *Lumen de Lumine* (Paper Press Books, 2017). He lives and teaches in Tempe, Arizona.

Cornelius Eady's seven poetry collections include *Victims of the Latest Dance Craze*, winner of the 1985 Lamont Prize; *The Gathering of My Name*, nominated for a 1992 Pulitzer Prize; and *Hardheaded Weather* (Putnam, 2008). He is cofounder of the Cave Canem Foundation and a professor of English at SUNY Stony Brook Southampton.

Hannah Ensor is the author of *Love Dream with Television* (Noemi Press, 2018). She has published poems, essays, and reviews, often on topics of pop culture, sports, and mass media. With Laura Wetherington and Jill Darling, she cowrote the collaborative poetry chapbook *at the intersection of 3* (dancing girl press, 2014). She works at the University of Michigan, where she directs the Hopwood Awards Program; until 2017 she served as the literary director at the University of Arizona Poetry Center. Hannah is also an editor of textsound.org and a contributing poetry editor for DIAGRAM. She lives in Ypsilanti, Michigan.

Louise Erdrich is an American author, writer of novels, poetry, and children's books featuring Native American characters and settings. She is an enrolled member of the Turtle Mountain Band of Chippewa Indians, a federally recognized tribe of the Anishinaabe (also known as Ojibwe and Chippewa). She is also the owner of Birchbark Books, a small independent bookstore in Minneapolis that focuses on Native American literature and the Native community in the Twin Cities.

Lauren Espinoza earned her MFA in poetry at Arizona State University and her MAIS in Mexican American studies from the University of Texas–Rio Grande Valley. Her manuscript "Before the Body" received an Honorable Mention in the 2017 Pellicer-Frost Binational Poetry Prize. Her work has appeared in *Time You Let Me In: 25 Poets under 25*, *New Border Voices: An Anthology*, the *Acentos Review*, *As/Us*, *Pilgrimage*, *Sinister Wisdom*, and elsewhere. Raised in the Rio Grande Valley of South Texas, she is an inaugural member of the Letras Latinas Poets Initiative, a CantoMundo Fellow, and currently a Writers' Studio instructor and PhD candidate in justice studies at Arizona State University.

Elyse Fenton is the author of the poetry collections *Clamor* and *Sweet Insurgent*. A climber, erstwhile scrum half, and deteriorating runner, she lives with her family in Oregon.

John Findura is the author of the poetry collection *Submerged* (Five Oaks Press, 2017). He holds an MFA from the New School as well as a degree in psychotherapy. His poetry and criticism appear in numerous journals, including *Verse*, *Fourteen Hills*, *Copper Nickel*, *Pleiades*, *Forklift, Ohio*, *Sixth Finch*, *Prelude*, and *Rain Taxi*. A guest blogger for *The Best American Poetry*, he lives in northern New Jersey with his wife and daughters.

BK Fischer's books of poems are *Radioapocrypha*, *Mutiny Gallery*, *St. Rage's Vault*, and the forthcoming *My Lover's Discourse*, a gurlesque remix of Roland Barthes. Her poems have appeared in the *Paris Review*, *Kenyon Review*, FIELD, WSQ, *Literary Mama*, *Modern Language Studies*, the *Hopkins Review*, *Ninth Letter*, the *Southwest Review*, and other journals. Also the author of a critical study, *Museum Mediations: Reframing Ekphrasis in Contemporary American Poetry* (Routledge, 2006), she was a finalist for the 2014 Balakian Citation in Reviewing from the National Books Critics Circle. She teaches Comma Sutra at Columbia University and is poetry editor at the *Boston Review*.

t'ai freedom ford is a New York City high school English teacher and Cave Canem Fellow. Her poetry has appeared in *Drunken Boat*, *Sinister Wisdom*, the *African American Review*, *Vinyl*, *Muzzle*, *Poetry*, and others. Her work has also been featured in several anthologies, including *The BreakBeat Poets: New American Poetry in the Age of Hip-Hop*. Winner of the 2015 To the Lighthouse Poetry Prize, her first poetry collection, *how to get over*, is available from Red Hen Press. t'ai lives and loves in Brooklyn, but hangs out digitally at howtogetover.com.

Eugene Gloria's fourth collection, *Sightseer in This Killing City*, will be published by Penguin–Random House in June 2019. His previous poetry collections are *My Favorite Warlord* (2012), winner of the Anisfield-Wolf Book Award; *Hoodlum Birds* (2006); and *Drivers at the Short-Time Motel* (2000), a National Poetry Series selection and recipient of the Asian American Literary Award. He lives in Greencastle, Indiana, and teaches at DePauw University.

Kevin Goodan is associate professor of English at Lewis-Clark State College.

francine j. harris is the author of *play dead*, winner of the Lambda Literary and Audre Lorde Awards, and was a finalist for the Hurston/Wright Legacy Award. Her third collection, *Here Is the Sweet Hand*, is forthcoming from Farrar, Straus and Giroux. Originally from Detroit, she has received a fellowship from the National Endowment for the Arts, is a Cave Canem poet, and is the 2018–19 Rona Jaffe Foundation Fellow at the Cullman Center for Scholars and Writers at the New York Public Library.

Pamela Hart is writer in residence at the Katonah Museum of Art, where she teaches an education program called Thinking Through Art. Her book, *Mothers over Nangarhar*, is forthcoming in 2019 from Sarabande Books. She received the Brian Turner Literary Arts poetry prize. She was awarded a National Endowment for the Arts poetry fellowship. Her poems have been published in the *Southern Humanities Review*, *Bellevue Literary Review*, and elsewhere. Toadlily Press published her chapbook, *The End of the Body*. She is poetry editor for the Afghan Women's Writing Project and for *As You Were: Journal for Military Experience and the Arts*.

Terrance Hayes is a teacher and student of poetry. His most recent publications include *American Sonnets for My Past and Future Assassin* (Penguin, 2018) and *To Float in the Space Between: Drawings and Essays in Conversation with Etheridge Knight* (Wave, 2018).

Claudia D. Hernández was born and raised in Guatemala. She's a mother, photographer, poet, translator, and bilingual educator residing in Los Angeles. She writes short stories, children's stories, and poetry in Spanish and English and sometimes weaves in Poqomchi', an indigenous language of her Mayan heritage. Hernández holds an MFA in Creative Writing for Young People, with an emphasis in poetry from Antioch University Los Angeles. Various online literary journals and anthologies throughout the United States, the United Kingdom, Canada, and Mexico have published her work. She is the founder of the ongoing project Today's Revolutionary Women of Color, www.todaysrevolutionarywomenofcolor.com.

Sue Hyon Bae was raised in South Korea, Malaysia, and Texas. She received her MFA from Arizona State University. Her cotranslation of Kim Hyesoon's *A Cup of Red Mirror* will be published by Action Books in 2018. She lives in Sacramento.

Ashaki Jackson, PhD, is a social psychologist, program evaluator, and poet. Her work has appeared in CURA: *A Literary Magazine of Art and Action*, *Pluck! Journal of Affrilachian Arts and Culture*, and *Prairie Schooner* among other journals and anthologies. Writ Large Press published her chapbook *Surveillance* in 2016, and a second chapbook, *Language Lesson*, was published by MIEL in 2016. She serves as an executive editor for the *Offing* and a summer instructor for 826LA. Jackson earned her MFA (poetry) from Antioch University Los Angeles and her doctorate (social psychology) from Claremont Graduate University. She lives in Los Angeles.

Born and raised in Topeka, Kansas, **Gary Jackson** is the author of the poetry collection *Missing You, Metropolis*, which received the 2009 Cave Canem Poetry Prize. His poems have appeared in numerous journals, including *Callaloo*, *Tin House*, *Los Angeles Review of Books*, *Crab Orchard Review*, and elsewhere. He currently teaches in the MFA program at the College of Charleston and is the associate poetry editor at *Crazyhorse*.

Toni Jensen's first story collection is *From the Hilltop*. Her stories and essays have been published in journals such as *Orion*, *Catapult*, and *Ecotone* and have been anthologized in *New Stories from the South*, *Best of the Southwest*, and *Best of the West: Stories from the Wide Side of the Missouri*, among others. She teaches in the Programs in Creative Writing and Translation at the University of Arkansas and in the low-residency MFA Program at the Institute of American Indian Arts. She is Métis.

Jenny Johnson is the author of *In Full Velvet* (Sarabande Books, 2017). Her honors include a 2015 Whiting Award and a 2016–17 Hodder Fellowship at Princeton University. Her poems have appeared in the *New York Times*, *New England Review*, *Troubling the Line: Trans and Genderqueer Poetry and Poetics*, and elsewhere. She teaches at the University of Pittsburgh and at the Rainier Writing Workshop's MFA Program.

Marissa Johnson-Valenzuela is a writer, editor, community college professor, abolitionist, founder of Thread Make Blanket press, and sometimes DJ. Her poetry and prose have been supported by the work of many rad people and projects, including VONA, Lambda Literary, Hedgebrook, the *Baffler*, *American Poetry Review*, *make/shift*, *As Us*, *Acentos Review*, *HOLD*, Solstice, Bedfellows, *APIAry*, *Aster(ix)*, Philadelphia Printworks, and *Organize Your Own: The Politics and Poetics of Self-Determination Movements* (Soberscove, 2016).

Ilya Kaminsky was born in the former Soviet Union and is now an American citizen. He is the author of *Deaf Republic* (Graywolf, 2019), *Dancing in Odessa* (Tupelo Press, 2004), and coeditor of *The Ecco Anthology of International Poetry*. He has received a Whiting Award, a Lannan Literary Fellowship, and a Guggenheim Fellowship and was named a finalist for the Neustadt International Prize for Literature. His work has been translated into more than twenty languages.

Born in Tehran and raised in the Los Angeles area, **Porochista Khakpour** lives in New York City's Harlem. Her debut novel, *Sons and Other Flam-*

mable Objects, was a *New York Times* Editor's Choice, one of the *Chicago Tribune*'s Fall's Best, and the 2007 California Book Award winner in the First Fiction category. Her second novel, *The Last Illusion*, was a 2014 Best Book of the Year according to NPR, *Kirkus, Buzzfeed, Popmatters, Electric Literature*, and many more. Among her many fellowships is a National Endowment for the Arts award. Her nonfiction has appeared in many sections of the *New York Times*, the *Los Angeles Times, Elle, Slate, Salon*, and *Bookforum*, among many others. Currently, she is guest faculty at VCFA and Stonecoast's MFA programs as well as contributing editor at the *Evergreen Review*. Her memoir, SICK, came out in 2018 from Harper Perennial.

Benjamin Krusling is a teaching poet and artist living in Iowa City by way of New York and Cincinnati. Their writing and visual work is concerned with radical narrative, noise, (dis)location, ethics, reflexivity, the churnings of the black subject, etc. They have a chapbook, GRAPES (Projective Industries, 2018).

Shane Lake is the author of *The Bone Trees*, a digital chapbook from BOAAT Press. His work has appeared in *Best New Poets, 2017; Beloit Poetry Journal; New Ohio Review; Indiana Review; Narrative*; and elsewhere. He lives and teaches in Oklahoma City.

Brett Fletcher Lauer is the deputy director of the Poetry Society of America and the poetry editor of *A Public Space*. He is the author of the memoir *Fake Missed Connections: Divorce, Online Dating, and Other Failures* and the poetry collection *A Hotel in Belgium*, which was named a Top 40 Book of 2014 by *Coldfront Magazine*. In addition to coediting several anthologies, including *Please Excuse This Poem: 100 News Poets for the Next Generation* and *Isn't It Romantic: 100 Love Poems by Younger American Poets*, he is the poetry cochair for the Brooklyn Book Festival and lives in Brooklyn.

Dorianne Laux's most recent collections are *The Book of Men*, winner of the Paterson Poetry Prize, and *Facts about the Moon*, winner of the Oregon Book Award. *Only as the Day Is Long: New and Selected*, is forthcoming from W. W. Norton in January 2019.

Ada Limón is the author of four books of poetry, including *Bright Dead Things*, which was named a finalist for the National Book Award in Poetry, a finalist for the National Book Critics Circle Award, and a finalist for the 2017 Kingsley Tufts Award. Her fifth book, *The Carrying*, is forthcoming from Milkweed Editions in 2018.

Esther Lin was born in Rio de Janeiro, Brazil, and lived in the United States as an undocumented immigrant for twenty-one years. She is the author of *The Ghost Wife*, winner of the 2018 Poetry Society of America's Chapbook Fellowship, and was awarded the *Crab Orchard Review*'s 2018 Richard

Peterson Poetry Prize. Her poems have appeared or are forthcoming in the *Indiana Review, Pleiades, Ploughshares, Triquarterly,* and elsewhere. She is 2017–19 Wallace Stegner Fellow at Stanford University and currently organizes for the Undocupoets, which promotes the work of undocumented poets and raises consciousness about the structural barriers they face in the literary community.

Matthew Lippman is the author of four poetry collections—*The New Year of Yellow* (winner of the Kathryn A. Morton Prize, Sarabande Books), *Monkey Bars, Salami Jew,* and *American Chew* (winner of the Burnside Review of Books Poetry Prize). He is the editor and founder of the web-based project Love's Executive Order (www.lovesexecutiveorder.com).

Chip Livingston is the mixed-blood Creek author of the novel *Owls Don't Have to Mean Death* (Tincture, 2017); a collection of essays and short stories, *Naming Ceremony* (Lethe, 2014); and two collections of poetry, *Crow-Blue, Crow-Black* (NYQBooks, 2012) and *Museum of False Starts* (Gival, 2010). His poetry, essays, and short stories have appeared in journals, including *Ploughshares, Crazyhorse, Prairie Schooner,* and the *Mississippi Review,* as well as on the Poetry Foundation and Academy of American Poets websites. Chip teaches in the low-residency MFA programs at Institute of American Indian Arts and Regis University.

Valerio Magrelli was born in Rome, Italy, in 1957. The award-winning author of six volumes of poetry, he has also written several books of prose, including the hybrid novel *Addio a calcio* (Farewell to soccer), excerpted here. His selected poems in English translation, *Vanishing Points,* was published by Farrar, Straus and Giroux in 2010.

Nate Marshall is from the South Side of Chicago. He is the author of *Wild Hundreds* and editor of *The BreakBeat Poets: New American Poetry in the Age of Hip-Hop.* His last album, *Grown,* came out in 2015 with his group Daily Lyrical Product. Nate is a member of the Dark Noise Collective and codirects Crescendo Literary. He has received fellowships from Cave Canem, the Poetry Foundation, and the University of Michigan. He is the director of National Programs for Louder than a Bomb Youth Poetry Festival and has taught at the University of Michigan, Wabash College, and Northwestern University.

David Tomas Martinez is the author of *Hustle* and *Post Traumatic Hood Disorder.* Martinez is a Pushcart winner, CantoMundo fellow, a Breadloaf Stanley P. Young Fellow, and National Endowment for the Arts fellow.

Adrian Matejka is the author of four collections of poems. *The Big Smoke* (Penguin, 2013) was a winner of the Anisfield-Wolf Book Award and finalist for the National Book Award and the Pulitzer Prize. His other books are *Mixology* (Penguin, 2009) and *The Devil's Garden* (Alice James Books, 2003). His new book, *Map to the Stars*, was published by Penguin in 2017. He is the Ruth Lilly Professor/Poet-in-Residence at Indiana University in Bloomington.

Airea D. Matthews's first collection of poems, *Simulacra*, recipient of the 2016 Yale Series of Younger Poets Award, has received praise from outlets such as the *New Yorker* and the *Washington Post*. Her work has appeared in the *Rumpus*, *Best American Poets*, *American Poet*, and elsewhere. She received the 2016 Rona Jaffe Foundation Writers' Award and was awarded the Louis Untermeyer Scholarship in 2016 from Bread Loaf Writers' Conference. Ms. Matthews is working on her second poetry collection, *under/class*, which explores poverty. She is an assistant professor at Bryn Mawr College.

Jeffrey McDaniel is the author of five books of poetry, most recently *Chapel of Inadvertent Joy* (University of Pittsburgh Press). He is at work on his sixth book, "Holiday in the Islands of Grief," just finished a semiautobiographical novel, "4,000 a.m.," and is working on a nonfiction book about the intersection of sports and parenting. He teaches at Sarah Lawrence College and lives in the Hudson Valley with his twelve-year-old daughter, Camilla, and his wife, Christine Caballero.

Joseph Millar's fourth collection, *Kingdom*, was published in 2017 by Carnegie Mellon. His poems have won fellowships from the Guggenheim Foundation (2012), the National Endowment for the Arts (2002), and a Pushcart Prize. He teaches in Pacific University's MFA and spends his time between Raleigh, North Carolina, and Richmond, California.

Yesenia Montilla is an Afro-Latina from New York City, a daughter of immigrants, and a graduate of Drew University's Poetry & Poetry in Translation MFA program and a Canto Mundo Fellow. Her poetry has appeared in the *Wide Shore*, *Prairie Schooner*, *Gulf Coast*, and others. Her first collection of poetry, *The Pink Box*, was published by Willow Books and was long-listed for the PEN America Open Book Award. She lives in Harlem, New York, and works in the wild wild west that is Corporate America.

A Pushcart Prize winner and a 2015 New American Poet who has received fellowships to Vermont Studio Center, Rose O'Neill Literary House, Hedgebrook and Cave Canem, **Kamilah Aisha Moon's** work has been featured widely, including in *Harvard Review*, *Poem-a-Day*, *Prairie Schooner*, *Best of the Net*, and elsewhere. Featured nationally at conferences, festivals, and universities, including the Library of Congress and Princeton University, she holds an MFA from Sarah Lawrence College and has taught at several institutions, including Rutgers University–Newark and Columbia

University. A native of Nashville, she is an assistant professor of poetry and creative writing at Agnes Scott College.

As a text-based artist, **Saretta Morgan**'s work engages relationships between intimacy and organization. Recent writing has appeared or is forthcoming in the *Guardian*, the *Volta*, *Nepantla*, *Apogee*, and *Best American Experimental Writing*. She has designed interactive, text-based experiences for the Whitney Museum of American Art, Dia Beacon, and Tenri Cultural Institute. She received a BA from Columbia University and an MFA from Pratt Institute. She is a 2016–17 Lower Manhattan Cultural Council Workspace resident and author of the chapbook *Room for a Counter Interior* (Portable Press @ Yo-Yo Labs, 2017).

Tomás Q. Morin is the author of *Patient Zero* and *A Larger Country*. He translated Pablo Neruda's *The Heights of Macchu Picchu*, and with Mari L'Esperance coedited *Coming Close: Forty Essays on Philip Levine*. He teaches at Texas State University and in the low-residency MFA program of Vermont College of Fine Arts.

Valzhyna Mort is the author of *Factory of Tears* and *Collected Body* (Copper Canyon Press). She is a recipient of the Lannan Foundation Fellowship, the Bess Hokin Prize from *Poetry*, Amy Clampitt fellowship, and the *Gulf Coast* translation prize. Born in Minsk, Belarus, she teaches at Cornell University and writes in English and Belarusian.

Alicia Mountain's first book, *High Ground Coward* (University of Iowa Press), won the 2017 Iowa Poetry Prize. She is also the author of the chapbook *Thin Fire*, which was released digitally by BOAAT Press. She is a queer poet in the PhD program at the University of Denver. Mountain earned an MFA in poetry at the University of Montana.

Hannah Oberman-Breindel's work has appeared, or is forthcoming, in *Forklift, Ohio*, *Connotation Press*, the *Literary Review*, *Best of the Net*, *Court Green*, *Muzzle*, BOXCAR *Poetry Review*, *Thrush*, and elsewhere. She is a two-time fellowship recipient from the Vermont Studio Center and was a Tennessee Williams Scholar at the Sewanee Writer's Conference. She completed her MFA at the University of Wisconsin–Madison and now lives in New York City, where she teaches high school English.

Christina Olivares is the author of *No Map of the Earth Includes Stars*, winner of the 2014 Marsh Hawk Press Book Prize, and of the chaplet *Interrupt*, published by Belladonna* Collaborative. Her second full-length book is forthcoming from YesYes Books. She is the recipient of a 2018 BRIO Award in Nonfiction, a 2015–16 LMCC Workspace Residency, and two Jerome Foundation Travel and Study Grants (2014, 2010). She is a CantoMundo,

VONA, and Frost Place Fellow. Olivares is a queer Cuban American poet and educator from the Bronx in New York City.

Lisa Olstein is the author of four poetry collections, most recently *Late Empire*. Her first book of prose, *Pain Studies*, will be published in spring 2020. She teaches at the University of Texas at Austin.

Matthew Olzmann is the author of two collections of poems, *Mezzanines*, which was selected for the Kundiman Prize, and *Contradictions in the Design*, both from Alice James Books. He teaches at Dartmouth College and also in the MFA Program for Writers at Warren Wilson College.

January Gill O'Neil is the author of *Rewilding* (2018), *Misery Islands* (2014), and *Underlife* (2009), published by CavanKerry Press. She is an assistant professor of English at Salem State University and boards of trustees member with the Association of Writers and Writing Programs and Montserrat College of Art. From 2012 to 2018, she served as executive director of the Massachusetts Poetry Festival. A Cave Canem fellow, January's poems and articles have appeared in the *New York Times Magazine*, the Academy of American Poets' Poem-a-Day series, *American Poetry Review*, *New England Review*, *Ploughshares*, and *Ecotone*, among others. In 2018 January was awarded a Massachusetts Cultural Council grant and was named the John and Renée Grisham Writer in Residence for 2019–20 at the University of Mississippi, Oxford. She lives with her two children in Beverly, Massachusetts.

Tommy Orange is a graduate of the MFA program at the Institute of American Indian Arts. An enrolled member of the Cheyenne and Arapaho Tribes of Oklahoma, he was born and raised in Oakland, California.

Meghan O'Rourke, a poet and nonfiction writer, is the author of the poetry collections *Sun in Days*, *Once*, and *Halflife*, as well as the best-selling memoir *The Long Goodbye*, about the death of her mother. A former editor at the *New Yorker* and *Slate*, she teaches at Princeton and at the MFA Program at New York University and writes for the *New Yorker*, the *New York Times*, the *Atlantic Monthly*, and others. A graduate of Yale University, O'Rourke is the recipient of a 2014 Guggenheim Fellowship, the May Sarton Poetry Prize, the Whiting Award, the Union League Prize for Poetry from the Poetry Foundation, a Lannan Literary Fellowship, two Pushcart Prizes, and a Front Page Award for her cultural criticism, among other honors.

Kat Page is mestiza born and raised in Albuquerque, New Mexico. Her work has appeared in *Prairie Schooner*, *B O D Y*, *Inch*, *BOXCAR Poetry Review*, *Verse Daily*, *Otis Nebula*, *Tidal Basin*, and *Cutthroat*, among others. She earned her MFA from the University of Maryland. She was a finalist for a Joy Harjo

Poetry Prize and received an honorable mention for a Rita Dove Poetry Prize and Work-Study Scholarships for Bread Loaf writing conferences.

Born in Moscow, **Vera Pavlova** is the author of fourteen collections of poetry, four opera librettos, and lyrics to two cantatas. Her works have been translated into eighteen languages. Her books available in English, *If There Is Something to Desire* and *Album for the Young (and Old)*, are published by Knopf.

Ben Purkert is the author of *For the Love of Endings* (Four Way Books, 2018). His poems and essays appear in the *New Yorker*, *Ploughshares*, *Kenyon Review*, *Guernica*, *Agni*, *Tin House Online*, *Boston Review*, and elsewhere. He teaches creative writing at Rutgers University in New Brunswick, New Jersey.

Dean Rader's debut collection of poems, *Works & Days*, won the 2010 T. S. Eliot Poetry Prize, and *Landscape Portrait Figure Form* (2014) was named by the *Barnes & Noble Review* as a Best Poetry Book. His most recent projects, all published in 2017, include *Suture*, collaborative poems written with Simone Muench (Black Lawrence Press), *Self-Portrait as Wikipedia Entry* (Copper Canyon), and *Bullets into Bells: Poets and Citizens Respond to Gun Violence*, edited with Brian Clements and Alexandra Teague (Beacon Press). He is a professor at the University of San Francisco.

Shivanee Ramlochan is a Trinidadian poet, arts reporter, and book blogger. She is the book reviews editor for *Caribbean Beat* magazine. Shivanee also writes about books for the NGC Bocas Lit Fest, the Anglophone Caribbean's largest literary festival, as well as Paper Based Bookshop, Trinidad and Tobago's oldest independent Caribbean specialty bookseller. She is the deputy editor of the *Caribbean Review of Books*. Shivanee's first book, *Everyone Knows I Am a Haunting*, was published in 2017 by Peepal Tree Press.

Claudia Rankine is the author of five collections of poetry, including *Citizen: An American Lyric* and *Don't Let Me Be Lonely*; two plays, including *Provenance of Beauty: A South Bronx Travelogue*; and numerous video collaborations, and she is the editor of several anthologies, including *The Racial Imaginary: Writers on Race in the Life of the Mind*. Her most recent play, *The White Card*, premiered in February 2018 (ArtsEmerson/American Repertory Theater). Among her numerous awards and honors, Rankine is the recipient of the Bobbitt National Prize for Poetry, the Poets & Writers' Jackson Poetry Prize, and fellowships from the Guggenheim Foundation, the Lannan Foundation, the MacArthur Foundation, United States Artists, and the National Endowment of the Arts. She is a chancellor of the Academy of American Poets and teaches at Yale University as the Frederick Iseman Professor of Poetry. In 2016 she cofounded the Racial Imaginary Institute. She lives in New Haven, Connecticut.

Shann Ray's work has appeared in *Poetry, Northwest Review, Esquire, Narrative, McSweeney's,* and *Salon.* Winner of an American Book Award and the High Plains Book Award, he has served as a National Endowment for the Arts literature fellow and is the author of *American Masculine* (Graywolf), *American Copper* (Unbridled), *Balefire* (Lost Horse), and the forthcoming poetry collection *Dark Horse Bright Field.* Because of his wife and three daughters, he believes in love.

Roger Reeves received an MFA in creative writing and a PhD in English from the University of Texas, Austin. His poems have appeared in *Poetry, Ploughshares, American Poetry Review, Boston Review, Tin House, Best American Poetry,* and the *Indiana Review,* among other publications, and he was included in *Best New Poets 2009.* Reeves's honors include a Ruth Lilly Fellowship from the Poetry Foundation, two Bread Loaf Scholarships, a Cave Canem Fellowship, a National Endowments for the Arts Fellowship, and a Whiting Award in Poetry. He is also the recipient of a Pushcart Prize for his poem "The Field Museum." Reeves is an assistant professor of poetry at the University of Illinois, Chicago, and was a 2014–15 Hodder Fellow at the Lewis Center for the Arts, Princeton University. *King Me* (Copper Canyon Press, 2013) is Reeves's first book.

Alberto Ríos, Arizona's inaugural poet laureate and a chancellor of the Academy of American Poets, is the author of eleven collections of poetry, including *The Smallest Muscle in the Human Body,* a finalist for the National Book Award. His most recent book is *A Small Story about the Sky,* preceded by *The Dangerous Shirt* and *The Theater of Night,* which received the PEN/Beyond Margins Award. He has also written three short story collections and a memoir, *Capirotada,* about growing up on the Mexican border. Ríos is the host of the PBS program *Books & Co.* and in 2017 was named director of the Virginia G. Piper Center for Creative Writing at Arizona State University.

Iliana Rocha earned her PhD in English literature and creative writing from Western Michigan University. Her work has been featured in the *Best New Poets, 2014* anthology, as well as the *Nation, RHINO, Blackbird,* and *West Branch. Karankawa,* her debut collection, won the 2014 AWP Donald Hall Prize for Poetry and is available through the University of Pittsburgh Press. She is currently an assistant professor of creative writing at the University of Central Oklahoma and lives with her three chihuahuas, Nilla, Beans, and Migo.

Alison Rollins, born and raised in St. Louis, currently works as the librarian for Nerinx Hall. She is the second prizewinner of the 2016 James H. Nash Poetry contest and a finalist for the 2016 Jeffrey E. Smith Editors' Prize. Her poems have appeared or are forthcoming in *American Poetry Review, Hayden's Ferry Review, Meridian, Missouri Review,* the *Offing, Poetry,* the *Poetry Review, River Styx, Solstice, TriQuarterly, Tupelo Quarterly, Vinyl,* and elsewhere. A Cave Canem and Callaloo Fellow, she is also a 2016 recipient of the Poetry Foundation's Ruth Lilly and Dorothy Sargent Rosenberg Fellowship.

Joel Salcido was born in the San Fernando Valley and raised in West Phoenix. He is the son of Mexican immigrants, a first-generation college graduate, a husband, and the father of three sons. Joel characterizes his work as hood magical realism—a navigation between the grief and ecstasy of place and experience. His poetry and prose are written not simply *to* or *about* his culture and community—but from it. His work has been featured in *Write On, Downtown, Public Pool,* the *Decolonizer,* and *Four Chambers Press,* among others. He is the recipient of a University Graduate Fellowship from Arizona State University and a Virginia G. Piper Creative Research Fellowship. Joel is the editor in chief of *Hayden's Ferry Review* and an MFA candidate in poetry at Arizona State University.

Will Schutt is the author of *Westerly* (Yale University Press, 2013) and translator of the selected poems of Edoardo Sanguineti (Oberlin College Press, forthcoming) and Fabio Genovesi's novel *Chi Manda Le Onde* (Europa Editions, 2017).

Aaron Smith is the author of three books of poetry: *Primer, Appetite,* and *Blue on Blue Ground,* winner of the Agnes Lynch Starrett Prize. His work has appeared in numerous publications, including *Ploughshares* and *Best American Poetry.* A three-time finalist for the Lambda Literary Award, he is the recipient of fellowships from the New York Foundation for the Arts and the Mass Cultural Council. He is associate professor of creative writing at Lesley University in Cambridge, Massachusetts.

Danez Smith is a black, queer, poz writer and performer from St. Paul, Minnesota. Danez is the author of *Don't Call Us Dead* (Graywolf Press, 2017), finalist for the 2017 National Book Award, and *[insert] boy* (YesYes Books, 2014), winner of the Kate Tufts Discovery Award and the Lambda Literary Award for Gay Poetry.

Patricia Smith is the author of eight books of poetry, including *Incendiary Art; Shoulda Been Jimi Savannah,* winner of the Lenore Marshall Prize from the Academy of American Poets; *Blood Dazzler,* a National Book Award finalist; and *Gotta Go, Gotta Flow,* a collaboration with award-winning Chicago photographer Michael Abramson. Her work has appeared in *Poetry*, the *Paris Review*, the *Baffler*, the *Washington Post*, the *New York Times*, *Tin House*, and *Best American Poetry*, *Best American Essays*, and *Best American Mystery Stories*. She is a Guggenheim Fellow and 2018 finalist for the Neustadt Prize in Literature. Patricia is a professor at the College of Staten Island and in the MFA program at Sierra Nevada College.

James Thomas Stevens, Aronhió:ta's (Akwesasne Mohawk), attended the Institute of American Indian Arts, Naropa University's Jack Kerouac School of Disembodies Poetics, and Brown University's graduate creative writing program. Stevens is the author of eight books of poetry, including *Combing the Snakes from His Hair*, *Mohawk/Samoa: Transmigrations*, *A Bridge Dead in the Water*, *The Mutual Life*, *Bulle/Chimere*, and *DisOrient*, and has recently finished a new manuscript, "The Golden Book." He is a 2000 Whiting Award recipient and teaches in the undergraduate and graduate Creative Writing Programs at the Institute of American Indian Arts in Santa Fe, and he lives in Cañoncito, New Mexico.

Nomi Stone's second collection of poems, *Kill Class*, is forthcoming from Tupelo Press in 2019. Poems appeared recently or will soon in the *New Republic*; the *New England Review*; *Tin House*; *Bettering American Poetry*, 2017; *The Best American Poetry*, 2016; *Guernica*; and elsewhere. *Kill Class* is based on two years of fieldwork she conducted within war trainings in mock Middle Eastern villages erected by the U.S. military across America.

Paul Tran is poetry editor at the Offing and Chancellor's Graduate Fellow in the Writing Program at Washington University in St. Louis. Their work appears in the *New Yorker*, *Prairie Schooner*, and *RHINO*, which gave them an Editor's Prize. A recipient of fellowships and residencies from Kundiman, VONA, Poets House, Lambda Literary Foundation, Napa Valley Writers Conference, Home School, Vermont Studio Center, the Conversation, Palm Beach Poetry Festival, Miami Writers Institute, and the Fine Arts Work Center in Provincetown, Paul is the first Asian American since 1993 to win the Nuyorican Poets Café Grand Slam.

Randall J. Tyrone's poems have appeared in Electric Literature's *Okey-Panky* and *Oversound Poetry*. He has received a scholarship from Tin House and a fellowship from the Idyllwild Arts Foundation. He has an MFA in poetry from the University of Wyoming. He's very excited for you.

Richard Vargas earned his BA at California State University, Long Beach, where he studied under Gerald Locklin and Richard Lee. He edited and published five issues of the *Tequila Review* from 1978 to 1980 and twelve issues of the *Mas Tequila Review* from 2010 to 2015. Vargas received his MFA from the University of New Mexico in 2010. He was recipient of the 2011 Taos Summer Writers' Conference's Hispanic Writer Award and was on the faculty of the 2012 Tenth National Latino Writers Conference. Currently, he resides in Rockford, Illinois. Published collections include *McLife* (2005), *American Jesus* (2007), and *Guernica, revisited* (2014).

Asiya Wadud writes about borders, limits, and the variegated truth. A member of the Belladonna* Collaborative, she teaches third grade in the daytime and English to new immigrants and refugees in the evening. Her work has been supported by the Lower Manhattan Cultural Council and the New York Public Library, among others. In 2017 Portable Press at Yo-Yo Labs published her chapbook, *we, too, are but the fold*, and her first book, *crosslight for youngbird*, was published by Nightboat Books in 2018. She lives in Brooklyn, New York, where she loves animals.

Stacey Waite is associate professor of English at the University of Nebraska–Lincoln and has published four collections of poems: *Choke, Love Poem to Androgyny, the lake has no saint*, and *Butch Geography*. Waite's articles on the teaching of writing have appeared most recently in *College Composition and Communication* and *Writing on the Edge*. Waite's newest book is *Teaching Queer: Radical Possibilities for Writing and Knowing*, published in 2017 by the University of Pittsburgh Press.

Maya Washington is an award-winning multidisciplinary artist (writer/filmmaker/performer) whose literary work has appeared and is forthcoming in journals and anthologies. Maya holds a BA from USC and an MFA from Hamline University. Her work has garnered fellowships and/or awards from the Jerome Foundation, Minnesota State Arts Board, Minnesota Film and Television, and others. Her recent films, CLEAR, about a woman reconnecting with her teen daughter after a wrongful conviction, and *Through the Banks of the Red Cedar*, about her father, Minnesota Vikings legend Gene Washington, who was a member of the first fully integrated college football team in America, are touring nationally and will be available worldwide soon. Her narrative short film *White Space* (starring ABC Family's *Switched at Birth*'s Ryan Lane) aired on network television and inspired the release of *White Space Poetry Anthology*, a collection of poetry and art from deaf and hearing artists.

Izzy Wasserstein teaches writing and literature at a midwestern university and writes poetry and fiction. She is the author of the poetry collection

This Ecstasy They Call Damnation. Her work has appeared or is forthcoming from *Prairie Schooner, Crab Orchard Review, Lady Churchill's Rosebud Wristlet*, and elsewhere. She shares a home with her spouse and their animal companions. She enjoys slowly running long distances.

Michael Wasson is the author of *This American Ghost* (YesYes Books, 2017). His poems appear in *American Poets, Beloit Poetry Journal, Drunken Boat, Kenyon Review, Poetry Northwest, Narrative, Bettering American Poetry*, and *Best New Poets*. He is *nimíipuu* from the Nez Perce Reservation in Idaho.

Afaa M. Weaver (formerly Michael S. Weaver) is the author of fifteen collections of poetry and several plays and essays. He has received four Pushcart Prizes, the Kingsley Tufts Award, and the Phyllis Wheatley Award. A 1987 graduate of Brown University's creative writing program, Afaa was a 2002 Fulbright appointee and a 2017 Guggenheim fellow. In 2017 he also retired from thirty years of full-time teaching. *Spirit Boxing* (University of Pittsburgh Press, 2017) is his fifteenth book of poems. His new play is titled *GriP*.

Holly M. Wendt is director of creative writing and assistant professor of English at Lebanon Valley College. Their writing has appeared in *Barrelhouse, Memorious, Gulf Stream, Sport Literate*, and elsewhere. A regular contributor to *Baseball Prospectus*'s "Short Relief" feature, Holly is also a recipient of a Robert and Charlotte Baron Fellowship for Creative and Performing Artists from the American Antiquarian Society and a fellowship from the Jentel Foundation. Their scholarship has appeared in the CEA *Critic* and *The Ballad of the Lone Medievalist* (punctum books).

Candace Williams is a black queer nerd living a double life. By day she's a middle school humanities and robotics teacher. By night and subway ride, she's a poet. Her work has appeared or is forthcoming in *Hyperallergic, Bennington Review*, the *Brooklyn Poets Anthology* (Brooklyn Arts Press, 2017), *Bettering American Poetry, 2016* (Bettering Books, 2017), and *Nepantla: An Anthology Dedicated to Queer Poets of Color* (Nightboat Books, 2018), among other places. Candace's first chapbook, *Spells for Black Wizards*, is a winner of the TAR Chapbook Series and was published by the *Atlas Review* in 2018.

L. Lamar Wilson is the author of *Sacrilegion* (Carolina Wren Press, 2013) and coauthor of *Prime: Poetry and Conversation* (Sibling Rivalry Press, 2014), with Darrel Alejandro Holnes, Saeed Jones, Rickey Laurentiis, and Phillip B. Williams. Wilson, a Callaloo and Cave Canem graduate fellow and Affrilachian Poet, teaches on the creative writing faculty at the University of Alabama.

Joaquín Zihuatanejo was awarded the 2017 Anhinga Press–Robert Dana Prize for Poetry. His new collection, *Arsonist*, was published by Anhinga Press in September 2018. His work has been featured in *Prairie Schooner*, *Sonora Review*, *Huizache*, and *Southwestern American Literature*, among other journals and anthologies. Joaquín received his MFA from the Institute of American Indian Arts in Santa Fe, New Mexico. Joaquín has two passions in his life, his wife, Aída, and poetry, always in that order.